W9-BGV-479

An Almost Perfect Moment

Also by Binnie Kirshenbaum

Hester Among the Ruins

Pure Poetry

A Disturbance in One Place

History on a Personal Note

On Mermaid Avenue

An Almost Perfect Moment

Binnie Kirshenbaum

ecco
An Imprint of HarperCollins*Publishers*

For information, address HarperCollins Publishers Inc.,
10 East 53rd Street, New York, NY 10022.

HarperCollins books may be purchased for educational, business, or sales
promotional use. For information please write: Special Markets Department,
HarperCollins Publishers Inc., 10 East 53rd Street, New York, NY 10022.

FIRST EDITION

Designed by Stephanie Huntwork

Library of Congress Cataloging-in-Publication Data
Kirshenbaum, Binnie.
An almost perfect moment: a novel / Binnie Kirshenbaum.—1st ed.
p. cm.
ISBN 0-06-052086-8
1. Brooklyn (New York, N.Y.) —Fiction. 2. Mothers and daughters—Fiction. 3. Teenage pregnancy—Fiction. 4. Jewish families—Fiction. 5. Teenage girls—Fiction. I. Title.
PS3561.I775A78 2004
813'.54—dc21
2003054961

04 05 06 07 08 WB/QW 10 9 8 7 6 5 4 3 2 1

For Richard Howard
and David Alexander, dear friends

Acknowledgments

There are some blessings of which I am sure: Tony, Susan, Louisa, Lutz, and Maureen; Jennifer Lyons is a writer's dream-agent-come-true and a great friend; Katie LaStoria, what would we do without you; much appreciation to Dr. Jon Snyder for his knowledge and patience; Ecco Press is reason to believe and I am indebted to everyone there. Thank you, thank you, thank you especially to Dan Halpern, Carrie Kania, Jill Bernstein, and to Amy Baker and Gheña Glijansky; for Julia Serebrinsky, who is remarkable and wonderful, I sing your praises.

There once was a man who was fixated on, obsessed you could say, with images of the Virgin Mary. He spent his entire life traveling all over the world—to Rome, to Paris, to Mexico City—to study the paintings and carvings and marble statues of the Madonna. When he died, he went to heaven, and there he asked Saint Peter if he could meet the Blessed Virgin. Saint Peter saw no reason to deny this good man's request, and so he brought the man to her. "I have just one question," the man said. "I have studied your face, every rendition of it, for my entire life. Why, in all those countless paintings and carvings and marble statues, do you always look so sad?"

"Well," said Mary, "to tell you the truth, I really wanted a daughter."

Is it permitted to utter a mystery?

—THE GOSPEL OF PHILIP

An
Almost Perfect
Moment

In Brooklyn, in a part of Brooklyn that was the last stop on the LL train and a million miles away from Manhattan, a part of Brooklyn—an enclave, almost—composed of modest homes and two-family houses set on lawns the size of postage stamps, out front the occasional plaster-of-paris saint or a birdbath, a short bus ride away from the new paradise known as the Kings County Mall, a part of Brooklyn where the turbulent sixties never quite touched down, but at this point in time, on the cusp of the great age of disco, when this part of Brooklyn would come into its own, as if during the years before it had been aestivating like a mudfish, lying in wait for the blast, for the glitter, the platform shoes, Gloria Gaynor, for doing the hustle, for its day in the sun, this part of Brooklyn was home to Miriam Kessler and her daughter Valentine, who was fifteen and three-quarter years old, which is to be neither here nor yet there as far as life is concerned.

Therefore, on this Tuesday afternoon, mid-November, it was in a way both figurative and literal that Valentine stood at the threshold between the foyer and the living room, observing Miriam and her three girlfriends—she, Miriam, called them that, despite their middling years, *my girlfriends,* or simply, *The Girls*—who were seated around the card table, attending closely to their game.

Four Bam against Six Crack, the mah-jongg tiles clacking into one another sounded like typewriter keys or fingernails tapping on a tabletop, something like anticipation, as if like Morse code, a message would be revealed, the inside track to the next step on the ladder to womanhood, such as the achievement of the big O or the use of feminine hygiene products, things Valentine had heard tell of but had yet to experience, things for *later, when you're older.*

For Miriam and The Girls, mah-jongg was not recreation, but passion. Nonetheless, and in their Brooklyn parlance, a nasal articulation, they were able to play while carrying on a conversation, which was not so much like juggling two oranges, because, for them, talking was as natural as breathing.

"Am I telling the truth?" Judy Weinstein said. "I'm telling the truth. Could she be a decorator or what?"

"She's right, Miriam. You could be a decorator. Two Dragon. It's a showplace here."

"When I'm right, I'm right. She could be a decorator."

Even if her taste wasn't to your liking, there was no doubt Miriam had an eye for placement and color. The living room, recently redecorated, was stunning, in an Oriental motif. Red plush carpeting picked up the red of the wallpaper that was flocked with velveteen flowers. A pair of cloisonné lamps capped with silk bell-shaped shades sat on black enamel end tables flanking the gold brocade couch. A series of three Chinese watercolors—lily pads and orange carp—framed in ersatz bamboo hung on the far wall. A bonsai tree, the cutest little thing that grew itty-bitty oranges which were supposedly edible, was the coffee-table centerpiece.

"This room takes my breath away. I ask you, does she have the eye for decorating or what?"

"They make good money, those interior decorators."

Waving off foolish talk, Miriam asked, "Are we playing or are we gabbing?" To fix up her own home was one thing. To go out in the world as a professional, *who needs the headache*?

Miriam took one tile—Seven Dot—which was of no help at all, from Sunny Shapiro, while Sunny Shapiro with a face that, in Miriam's words, could stop a clock, applied, on a mouth that was starting to wizen like a raisin, a fresh coat of coral-colored lipstick, the exact shade of coral as the beaded sweater she wore.

Studying her tiles, a losing hand if ever there was one, Miriam Kessler fed a slice of Entenmann's walnut ring into her mouth. Like she was performing a magic trick, Miriam could make a slice of cake, indeed an entire cake, vanish before your very eyes. Miriam swallowed the cake, her pleasure, and then there was no pleasure left until the next piece of cake.

Her grief cloaked in layers of fat, Miriam Kessler was pushing 239 pounds when she last stepped on the bathroom scale back in September or maybe it was August. Mostly she wore dresses of the muumuu variety, but nonetheless, Miriam Kessler was beautifully groomed. Every Thursday, she was at the beauty parlor for her wash and set, forty-five minutes under the dryer, hair teased and sprayed into the bouffant of her youth; the same hairdo she'd had since she was seventeen, only the color had changed from a God-given warm brown to a Lady Clairol deep auburn.

Despite that Miriam never skimped on the heat, rather she kept the thermostat at a steady seventy-two degrees, Edith Zuckerman snuggled with her white mink stole, and so what if it was as old as Methuselah, and from a generation ago, hardly with-it. The white mink stole was the first truly beautiful thing Edith had ever owned and she wore it as if the beauty of it were a talisman. As if nothing bad could ever happen to a woman wearing a white mink stole, never mind that she had the one son with the learning problems and her husband's business having had its share of ups and downs.

Oh-such-glamorous dames, adorned in style which peaked and froze at their high-school proms, The Girls were as dolled up as if on their way to romance or to the last nights of the Copacabana nightclub, as if they refused to let go of the splendor.

But it was Judy Weinstein who seemed to command the lion's share of Valentine's attention. Judy Judy Judy was a vision in a gold lamé jumpsuit. Not the gold lamé as precursor to the Mylar of Studio 54, but lamé, *lahr-may*, they called it, of the fashion flash of the fabulous fifties. And her hair, Judy's hair was bleached to a platinum blond and woven as intricately and high on her head as a queen's crown. Her fingernails, dragon-lady long, were lacquered a frosted white.

Some seven or eight years back, on a Friday morning, it must have been during the summer or some school holiday because Valentine was at home, Miriam had said to her daughter, "Go and ask Judy if she's got a stick of butter I can borrow." Miriam was baking an apricot strudel, the recipe calling for two sticks of butter when Miriam discovered she had but one. Valentine knocked on the Weinsteins' door, and Judy called out, "Come in." It was that way still, this part of Brooklyn, like a small town where there was no need for police locks and Medeco locks and home alarm systems.

Although Judy did sometimes go for the silver lamé and also had in her closet a breathtaking copper lamé sweater set, the gold lamé was her trademark, and when Valentine went through the Weinsteins' living room into the kitchen, behold! There was Judy in a gold lamé hostess gown, her feet shod in gold shoes, pointy with three-inch spiked heels, her face was fully made up, eyeliner whipped into cattails, fuchsia-pink lipstick, enough mascara to trap flies. Diamond earrings dangled from her lobes, which shimmered as if made of pearls instead of mere flesh, while her hands were confidently braiding dough for the Sabbath challah bread. Valentine must've been so overwhelmed by the glory that was Judy Weinstein that she seemed to forget entirely why she was there, what it was her mother had wanted. True, Valentine had set eyes on Mrs. Weinstein pretty much every day, but this might have been the first time she saw light like sunbeams reflecting off the gold and platinum, light radiating like that of the pictures in her book of Bible stories. All Valentine managed to do was gape until Judy phoned Miriam and said, "Valentine is standing in my kitchen with her mouth hanging open. Butter? Sure. I've got butter."

Now Miriam licked the residue of the sugar icing off her fingers and exchanged two of the tiles on her rack for two from the center of the table. So absorbed were they with their game and their talk, not one of these four women had heard Valentine come in the door or noticed that she'd come near to them.

Not until Edith Zuckerman called Five Dot did any of them look up, and only then did they see Valentine. See Valentine and gush. With words detouring through the sinuses and in voices husky from years of smoking Newport mentholated cigarettes, Juicy Fruit gum snapping, they carried on, "Will you look at her? Every day she gets more beautiful."

"What a face. I ask you. Is that a face?"

"She's right. That's some face. Gorgeous. Ab-so-lute-ly gorgeous."

"Honest to Gawd, Miriam, you should put her in the movies with that face. Quint. I've got a cousin who knows somebody big with the studios. I'll give him a call for you because, really, the kid could be a star with that face. I ask you, am I right?"

"She's right. When she's right, she's right."

"I'm telling you, I'm right. She even looks like that actress, Olivia Whatshername."

"Olivia Newton-John? She looks nothing like Olivia Newton-John."

"No. No. Not that Olivia. The other one. From *Romeo and Juliet*. The one who was Juliet in the movie. Olivia Whatshername."

"I don't know who you mean."

"Girls. Girls. Are we gabbing or are we playing?"

"All I'm saying is that the kid is gorgeous. Is she gorgeous or what?"

"The kid is gorgeous."

"Mah-jongg."

All tiles were dumped to the center and flipped facedown to be washed, which is the mah-jongg equivalent to shuffling a deck of cards. Sunny Shapiro was East, the one to go first this round, and when the women looked up again, Valentine was gone. Even though Miriam knew that the plush carpeting, wall-to-wall, muffled the sound of footfalls, it sometimes threw her for a loop the way Valentine moved silently, as if the kid walked on air, the way she appeared and disappeared without warning, as if she were something you imagined instead of a person.

Although Edith Zuckerman would never say so, not even under

torture, because she loved Miriam like a sister, Valentine gave Edith the creeps, the way the kid looked as if she knew everything, as if she had imbibed the wisdom of the ages, as if she knew all your secrets, including the ones you didn't dare admit even to yourself. Yet, at the very same time, she managed to look like a moron, as if the most ordinary things—a Dixie cup, the television set, a doorknob—took her by complete surprise, as if she'd never seen such remarkable things, as if she were a plastic doll with wide eyes painted on and a hollow head.

In this part of Brooklyn, rarely did girls dream big, and Valentine had not, to the best of anyone's recollection, ever articulated desire to be a movie star. Not tempted by fame and fortune, but perhaps by some kind of crazy hope to step outside of the world she knew. When she was thirteen, Valentine wrote a telling essay for school. In response to the question—How Do I See Myself in Ten Years' Time?—she wrote: *A teacher. A kindergarten teacher or maybe first grade. Or maybe I'd like to be floating on my back in a big blue swimming pool warmed by the sun forever and ever. I would like it if there were palm trees around the pool.*

She did resemble Olivia Whatshername.

She also resembled Walt Disney's Snow White.

But Valentine Kessler was the spitting image of the Blessed Virgin Mary as she appeared to Bernadette at Lourdes.

Neither Miriam Kessler nor her girlfriends were at all aware of Valentine's likeness to Mary, Mother of Jesus as she appeared on idols, icons, and Christmas cards even though they had seen this particular rendition of Mary countless times, hanging in the kitchens of many of their neighbors. They saw these holy pictures, but they never really looked at them. Instead, they looked past them and around them and through them because who knew for sure, maybe to really look was to risk God's ire or something worse.

The Girls, Miriam included, were not especially devout; certainly they were far less observant than their own mothers had been, as if each generation had further diluted the formalities of faith. Even Judy, who did prepare a Shabbes meal which included home-baked challah bread, did not keep holy the Sabbath day. Their piety was pretty much limited to temple on the High Holidays, the Hadassah sisterhood, and for the kids there was Jewish Youth Group led by Rabbi Gold, a youngish rabbi from the Havarah movement, which was mostly about commitment to social justice. For those of The Girls who had sons, there were lavish bar mitzvahs such as the one to which Judy Weinstein was referring when she asked, "Did you get your invitation to the Solomon affair? Two Bam. I hear they're having a double-decker Viennese table."

"Three Dragon. Of course I got my invitation. Are you going?"

"Of course I'm going. What about you, Miriam? Are you going?"

"Five Dot. I'm going."

These were the ways they kept the faith, but make no mistake about it. They were Jewish women, and they lived in a bifurcated world: Jewish and not Jewish. For them, each and every person, place, or thing was Jewish or not Jewish. Like this: Doctors were Jewish, politicians were not. New England was for the *goyim*, New York for the Jews. Books were Jewish, guns were worse than *trayf*.

And not just the nouns, but verbs too, as in walking was Jewish, but skydiving was *not on your life*. Far greater than their belief in God, these women believed fervently in *why take chances if you don't have to*. So while Miriam thought nothing of having coffee in Angela Sabatini's kitchen—she had a good heart, that Angela Sabatini even if the fried dough she served with the coffee gave Miriam such indigestion, repeating on her like a defective parrot—Miriam would avert her eyes from the picture of the Virgin Mary or Saint Whoever-It-Was that hung over the kitchen counter.

Valentine, however, had to have been cognizant of her similitude to Mary at least since the previous Holy Family Summer Festival, a weeklong affair held on East Ninety-eighth Street off Flatlands Avenue every August. The Holy Family Summer Festival was closer in kind to an afternoon at Coney Island than to a sectarian fete. Pretty much the whole neighborhood attended, not just the Catholics. There were amusement park rides and games of skill and games of chance where you could win plush toys—poodles or teddy bears in revolting shades of neon blue and hot pink. Rumor had it that there was gambling, real gambling for money, in the church basement, but Valentine and her friends dared not enter there just as they dared not eat a sausage and pepper sandwich, not so much in obedience to dietary laws but rather because who knew what went into those things. They were content to stuff themselves with cannolis and nougat candy that stuck to their teeth, all the while strolling the block on the lookout for cute boys.

In front of the church, the Church of the Holy Family, eponymous with the festival, they stopped and stared at the big statue of the saint or maybe it was the pope, who could tell, and watched the righteous pin dollar bills to the purple satin gown. "Catholics are so weird," Leah Skolnik noted, and the others nodded in assent, the exception being Valentine, who appeared lost in thought.

"Come on," Beth Sandler said. "Let's ride the Ferris wheel." This suggestion was greeted with enthusiasm by all, except Valentine, again the odd duck out, who begged off. "I always barf on those things," she said, which was true. She did.

Free from her friends, at least for a few minutes, Valentine moseyed around the church, not to oogle the statue with money pinned to it, but to peruse the table where the nuns were selling rosary beads and eight-by-ten glossy pictures of Jesus in plastic gold-colored frames and statues of Saint Christopher to fix on car dashboards. Saint Christopher remained a perennial bestseller despite the technicality of having been de-sainted. The nuns also sold votive candles, and night-lights shaped like crucifixes, and prayer cards which had a prayer printed on one side and a picture on the other. The pictures were of Jesus and a lamb, Saint Peter at the Gates of Heaven, the Last Supper, and the one that Valentine bought for fifty cents: Mary, the Blessed Virgin.

Later, at home, Valentine tucked the prayer card inside a book on her shelf, *Jonathan Livingston Seagull,* a book that everybody said was deep. Whatever. Valentine went to the book often, not to read it but to take out the prayer card to gaze upon Mary's face.

~

She was a nice-enough kid, but Valentine Kessler was no angel. Miriam had still to recuperate from the phone call she received three years before from the Macy's security force at the mall telling her that, along with two of her friends, Valentine was in custody for shoplifting. Socks. They'd stuffed socks in their pockets and tried to walk out of the store, pretty as you please.

"Is this going to be in the newspaper?" Miriam asked the store detective. Of Valentine, Miriam asked, "What in God's name is wrong with you?"

No angel, no saint, yet whenever Valentine looked in the mirror, the Blessed Virgin Mary looked back at her.

It had to mean something, didn't it? But what?

While Miriam traded Two Dot for Two Flower, Angela Sabatini, in the house next door, was chopping onions at her kitchen counter and eye to eye with a portrait of the Blessed Virgin as she appeared to Bernadette at Lourdes. She was the prettiest of the Marys. The prettiest, but also the least interesting to look at. Lovely, but lacking a depth of beauty. That Angela Sabatini never noticed how Valentine Kessler was a ringer for this rendition of Mary was likely to be a matter of not allowing herself to notice, to turning a blind eye. After all, this was the Blessed Virgin Mary, Mary, Mother of God.

The Kessler kid was a nice-enough kid, polite and all that, but still Angela Sabatini had a feeling about her. Someday Valentine Kessler would wind up in trouble, the kind of trouble in which only girls wind up. When Valentine was a toddler, she was always darting out of the house naked. In all kinds of weather, even once during a hailstorm, the kid rushed naked from the house and raced around the yard trying to catch hailstones, some of which were the size of eggs. Stark naked, she did that, Miriam right behind her, scooping her up in her arms to bring her inside. At first it was cute kid stuff, showing herself to the world, but then Angela started to think maybe the kid was oversexed or demented or both.

Besides, who would ever think to look for a resemblance between Mary, Mother of God, and the Jewish kid from the house next door?

~

Ten thousand times Miriam had chastised Valentine for her habit of chewing on pencils. "You want to get lead poisoning? Is that it?" Miriam had said, but still, no further along with her homework than when she first sat at her desk, which was made of white particleboard trimmed with pink sweetheart roses and one piece of a matched bedroom set—a dresser, a canopy bed befitting a princess, a bookshelf, and a nightstand—Valentine absentmindedly chewed on the end of the number-two pencil she held in her hand as if it were a lollipop stick.

Ah, it is difficult, nigh impossible, to concentrate, when the heart is burning, and all indications were that Valentine's heart was aflame.

As teenage girls in love are wont to do, Valentine doodled the ubiquitous hearts pierced with arrows, hearts containing the initials of her beloved *JW* entwined with her own. She also wrote *Valentine Kessler loves John Wosileski.*

John Wosileski was Valentine's math teacher. Geometry, and he fell squarely into the category of An Older Man. Nine years older. True, nine years is not a significant age difference when it separates say, thirty-six and forty-five, but when it comes between fifteen and twenty-four, calendar years are more like light-years.

To explain, to rationalize, Valentine's crush on an older man, one could point to her father, if one could've found her father to point to him, that is. With no father of her own, Valentine made a habit of asking the mailman in for lunch, inviting the shoe salesman to her upcoming birthday party. Once, over dinner at a restaurant, little Valentine wrote her name, the last *e* on Valentine written backward, and her address on a paper napkin which she gave to the waiter who'd been *kibitzing* with her. "Can we stay in touch?" she asked. So it's natural to apply a sliver of Saturday psychobabble to the situation and conclude that, in falling for John Wosileski, she was seeking a father figure, that she fell for a man very much like the father who'd left her, but to make such an assumption is to miss by a mile.

Valentine was four years old when her mother told her the truth about her father. "Your father," Miriam said. "Your father is a chippy-chaser," a figure of speech which sent Valentine to look out the window as if chippies were birds, birds like sparrows, and her father had taken off in flight after them; as if all the chippies were little brown birds and her father were a yellow bird.

~

A golden boy. That's the way Miriam Kessler thought of her ex-husband, of Ronald. Her Ronald. The Brooklyn College heartthrob with the big baby-blues and soft brown curls and a physique like Michelangelo chiseled him from marble. All that and dimples too. Ronald. Her one and only love. Her husband of sixteen months. Not a day went by that Miriam didn't think of him, like now, while she lined up Two Flower, Three Flower, and Four Flower, she thought of him and memory brought about desire, a tingling sensation between Miriam's jumbo-sized thighs. *Oh Ronald.*

~

"Your father," Miriam had said to Valentine, "the bastard, was a real looker. Don't fall for a pretty face," she warned her daughter, and Valentine, apparently, heeded her mother's words.

John Wosileski had skin the color of paste. His upturned nose was an unfortunate one, and his eyes were far too small given the circumference of his pie-shaped face. He was stocky of stature, and although, in fact, he was solid, he gave the impression of being chubby and soft-bellied. His beige hair was already thinning. It could be said that he resembled a pig except that he lacked a pig's expressiveness. What he looked like most was a pancake. John Wosileski was no Ronald Kessler. That a girl such as Valentine Kessler should be in love with a man such as John Wosileski seemed to defy all reason; yet we want a reason, we demand a reason so as to make sense of the world. Reason is all we've got to keep us safe from peril. The only way to accept what is given without reason is to trust that God works in mysterious ways.

In the living room, Judy Weinstein, triumphant, called out, "Mahjongg."

Two

Third period of the school day, Valentine took her seat at the second desk from the left of the third of five rows. A metal desk covered with a faux-wood laminate. She opened her notebook and her textbook to the appropriate pages and then, while her classmates clowned around flicking spitballs at Peter Janski's head, making a grab for Richie Weissbart's slide rule, a few girls flirting with Vincent Caputo, Valentine Kessler stared straight ahead, her hands folded neatly on her desk, as if to exclaim a kind of separateness from the others. Also staring straight ahead was Marty Weiner, but he, the biggest pothead in the school, was totally wasted and in another zone entirely.

There were girls at Canarsie High who considered Valentine to be stuck-up. Conceited. Like she was God's gift. *She walks around here like she's God's gift,* they said of her. When Valentine's friends—small in number but devoutly loyal and very pretty as well—would say, "No. Really. She's not conceited at all. Really.

She is so nice," they were not believed. It was near impossible to imagine being so very pretty and not being conceited about it. Moreover, the prettiest girls were never nice. The plain girls and the homely ones knew this for a fact.

Because Valentine was one of the prettiest girls in the school, if not *the* prettiest girl depending on whose opinion was solicited, it baffled everyone who knew her that Valentine did not have a boyfriend. In this world, boyfriends were the center of the universe. Indeed it seemed as if the boys paid her no attention at all, but they did. From afar, the boys at school mooned over Valentine and sometimes, if she walked by when they were in packs, they were inspired to say things like *She can suck on mine any day,* but never loud enough for her to hear and not one of them had confidence enough to approach her, having convinced themselves that she must have a boyfriend, maybe one in college or one who lived in the city, which was what they called Manhattan. Vincent Caputo flirted with her on occasion, but even he dared not attempt to take it further.

Mr. Wosileski—as they called him because this was Brooklyn in the 1970s and not some cockamamie Montessori school in the city where kids were on a first-name basis with their teachers—came into the room, and the class settled down. The way he did every day, for he was a responsible but an uninspired teacher, he said, "I need five volunteers." Five volunteers, one for each homework problem, to go to the blackboard. Six hands shot up like bedsprings. The same six hands that always went up, eager, waving, convulsing almost, as if they were raising their hands to be chosen from the studio audience as contestants for a game show.

In no particular order the Suck-up Six were: Joel Krotchman (need more be said?); Amy Epstein, who later, consumed by radical politics, the aim of which was understood by no one, actually—get this—robbed a bank; Mario Carlucci, a slight and bright boy whom no one messed with because he hinted at family connections, which, in fact, were a fabrication but an indication as to how clever he really was to come up with such a solution for keeping the bullies at bay; Robert Frankel, later infamous for having stabbed his freshman roommate at MIT with a Swiss army knife (the roommate survived, needing only six stitches in his arm, but Robert was expelled); and Peter Janski and Richie Weissbart, the crown princes of Queerdom, *queer* as defined then as *nerd, geek, dork,* or as an adjective for anything unfashionable, such as *That is such a queer shirt, queer jacket, queer pocketbook, queer haircut, ad nauseam,* and entirely unrelated to sexual orientation except for the firm conviction that queers, who invariably wore queer shirts, shoes, etc., would never get to have sex of any sort except with themselves.

Valentine's hands remained folded on her desk. Not inclined to ask questions or to volunteer the answers, Valentine was nonetheless a good student, even if she did dot her *i*'s with little hearts, hearts which she erroneously referred to as her *mascot* as opposed to her *emblem.*

Indeed she was something of a model student, but it must be allowed that the recitation of formulae and dates and vocabulary words is not the same as knowledge. Unbridled curiosity appeared to be neither a vice nor a virtue for her. In that way she was a good student, which says nothing about greater or lesser intelligence in either direction. She did, back in the third grade, along with the rest of her class, take the Wechsler Intelligence Scale for Children, but those records are sealed.

While the solutions to the five geometry problems were going up on the board, Valentine's head bowed as if she were reading or in silent prayer.

~

To the casual beholder, it might have seemed that Valentine Kessler wanted to be invisible, and indeed, given her ways, John Wosileski might not have taken notice of her except that whenever his eyes fell upon her, his heart skipped a beat.

Oh Valentine. She of the oval-shaped face, eyes blue and big, lips drawn in a bow, as if a red ribbon were tied by angels. And her skin. What skin. Despite the hormonal upsets of adolescence that so often result in dermal eruptions, her skin was like peaches and cream. Valentine had long brown hair, parted in the middle and shimmering with incandescence.

Truth be told, when at home alone, at night, when he touched himself—which he did confess to Father Palachuk and for which he had to, the same as always, do a penance of three Hail Marys and two Our Fathers but it was worth it—John Wosileski envisioned Valentine Kessler. Not consciously, but rather, as he neared his climax, in his mind's eye appeared her face, and not even in the throes of ecstasy did he shift focus below the neck. Fixed on her face alone as if viewing her studio portrait, he would groan and shoot his load into the tissue he kept in his other hand expressly for this purpose.

That he masturbated to the image of a beautiful student whose visage nagged at him as if she reminded him of someone, but who it was he couldn't put his finger on, was omitted from his confession. Even to himself, John Wosileski refused to own up to the effect Valentine Kessler had on him. She was a student, a teenager, and it was deviant for a twenty-four-year-old man to be hung up on a fifteen-year-old girl even if she was a heavenly creature, so exquisite he sometimes thought he would perish from the sight of her.

At the close of this particular school day, Beth Sandler was leaning up against her locker tapping her foot impatiently as she waited for Valentine, and waited. Two minutes. Three minutes. The two girls had been walking home from school together since kindergarten, and never once had Valentine, Miss Punctuality herself, kept Beth waiting. Until now. Another girl might've been worried when Valentine failed to appear, but Beth wasn't much of a worrier. Besides, just then Marcia Finkelstein happened by and said, "Hey, you want to go hang out at the mall?" Marcia Finkelstein had frosted hair and was too cool for words.

Teachers were required to stay for forty-five minutes after the last bell rang to give extra help to any student who might want it. But students who would expend the effort to ask for extra help were invariably the ones who didn't need it. And those who did need it didn't care enough to ask, so most teachers used the time to draw up the next day's lesson plan, which was what John Wosileski was about to do. He reached for a pencil, and there, across from him, separated by the width and bulk of his desk stood Valentine Kessler. He hadn't heard her come in. She was just there, like a vision. It took every ounce of his fortitude, all his reserve, not to melt into a puddle.

Like a vision, but no vision ever had an accent like Valentine Kessler's, a thick-as-thieves Brooklynese, as if her larynx were lodged on the roof of her mouth instead of where it belonged, and coming down like a sledgehammer on the consonants, as if *T*'s, *K*'s, *S*'s were rocks to be split apart, R's and W's added where there weren't any, and dropped where they were. It was an accent for which elocution lessons were designed. "Mis-Ta War-sil-eS-Ki," she said.

"Valentine," he said, and he was trembling. "Valentine," he repeated; he yearned to say her name again and again, as if each articulation were indeed a heart-shaped bubble sent off with a kiss.

For the stars to align for this unlikely pair, some great feat was required. Something like slaying a dragon or finding the foot to fit the glass slipper. Like that, but not exactly like that. But something like that. Something beyond the two of them. Something neither of them had yet to dare. So for the time being, they remained where they were; he tucked behind his desk, hidden from the waist down, for which he was grateful lest he get a hard-on, which wasn't entirely out of the question. His elbows were pinned to his sides to keep covered the dark wet circles of perspiration that had spread under his arms. Valentine was positioned on the far side of the desk, as if the desk were a chasm, a wide and fathomless grin in the earth's surface, and the two of them were frozen, no doubt from the terror of possibilities, until Mr. Wosileski pulled himself together well enough to ask, "So, what can I do for you?"

Valentine might have imagined saying such things as *You can awaken me with a kiss, you can shower me with rose petals,* but she did not say anything of the kind. Instead, she shrugged and said, "NuthinG. I just came to say hi."

At a loss as to how to cope, indeed how to survive this moment, a moment he never allowed himself to imagine could happen, forbidding himself such a daydream for fear as to where it would lead, John now feared the end of the moment. To prolong it, he attempted to make light conversation. "So?" he asked. "No cheerleader practice today?" It was a natural assumption, that Valentine was a cheerleader because in his day in high school all the prettiest girls, the girls who would not have given him the correct time had he ever worked up the nerve to ask for it, were cheerleaders.

"I'm not a cheerleader," Valentine said.

"No? So, what then? Marching band?"

"Marching band?" There was indignation in her voice. The high-school marching band was composed of scrawny boys with Adam's apples like erections who played the tuba and the French horn and bucktoothed and cross-eyed girls who beat bass drums and crashed cymbals. "I don't do any after-school activities," Valentine said. "Usually, I go straight home and do my homework. My mother wants me to go away to one of those good colleges with all girls, so I have to keep up my grades."

John vigorously nodded his head; yes, ship Valentine off to a nunnery until it was time for her to marry. Keep her locked behind iron gates, spiked iron gates, a virginal novitiate in a filmy white nightgown.

~

"But why one of those girls' schools?" Edith Zuckerman took a sip of coffee gone cold. "Two Bam. Those schools are for *goyim* and lesbians."

"She's right," Sunny Shapiro said. "Six Dot. My niece went to that Bryn Mawr College, and she told me Protestant lesbians were coming out of the woodwork there."

"I wouldn't be at all surprised if she wound up doing something creative." Judy Weinstein studied her tiles as she spoke. "I could easily see your Valentine as an art teacher or something with children's books. One of the creative fields."

"Well, whatever she does, Four Dragon," Miriam said, "she'll need college first."

Miriam's only real regret in life was that she didn't get to finish college. She would have liked to have had a college diploma. A college diploma in art history, given her flair for decorating. Or maybe psychology because she was interested in people. Other than that, Miriam didn't regret much and definitely not what people would have expected her to regret, namely putting out for Ronald Kessler.

Dreams Miriam once had had for herself were now pinned on Valentine, passed on to her daughter, as if hope were a baton or a pearl necklace.

~

John Wosileski was itching to ask Valentine what did she do on evenings and weekends, once her homework was done. Did she have a boyfriend, and if so, then who was the surely unworthy but abundantly fortunate vulgarian? No teenage boy was good enough for Valentine Kessler. Still, Mr. Wosileski would've bet his bottom dollar that Valentine dated the athletes, those handsome, Adonis-like baboons, simply because she was too young to know better. Maybe he could talk to her about saving herself for a man who would really appreciate her special qualities, although even he was not entirely certain which qualities those were. Opportunity for further inquiry and discussion, however, was denied him.

~

Having run a comb through her hair and having adjusted her panty hose which had begun to sag at the day's end, Joanne Clarke, unable to hold off another minute more, barged in on John

Wosileski and Valentine Kessler and, in the process, shattered something, something as fragile as a flicker of promise.

Miss Clarke taught biology in 215, the room directly across the hall from Mr. Wosileski's, which Miss Clarke considered fortuitous indeed. The proximity of their rooms resulted in a fast, but casual, friendship. Right from the get-go, her sights set on the math teacher, Miss Clarke began working steadily and stealthily to make the congeniality something more.

Back when she was in high school, Joanne Clarke must've had a whopping case of acne. Although the pimples had since dried up, her face bore red scars and pockmarks, the by-product of zits the size of dimes. Not that anyone much looked beyond her complexion, but her features, especially her eyes, were alarmingly without zip. What might have rendered her a "poor thing" was offset by a body that wouldn't quit. Five feet seven inches tall, she was a perfect 36-24-36 and both the thirty-sixes were firm and perfectly round. All that was atop a long and shapely pair of legs. From the neck down, Joanne Clarke was a knockout.

In Miss Clarke's estimation, John Wosileski was husband material. A suitable partner for life, and a mere few months ago, Miss Clarke might very well have snagged her man. A mere few months ago, before Valentine graced his classroom, John Wosileski would've been content, happy even, in his way, to date Joanne Clarke, never minding the bad skin and something of a sour demeanor. They made for a likely couple. A pair of schoolteachers, it happened all the time. Such was the scenario Miss Clarke had in mind—yes, she dared to dream—when John Wosileski joined the faculty. And although thus far there were no signs from his end, no signals of any romantic interest, she had not yet begun to give up.

Indeed, only two days before, she'd brought him a tin of brownies—a gesture that emitted more than a whiff of desperation—loneliness does that to people—which she claimed to have baked herself, but in fact bought them at Nevins Bakery because who had time to make brownies between this job and caring for her senile father. A small fib, *I baked them myself,* and he did eat all four of them before lunchtime. So when Joanne Clarke spied that insipid Valentine Kessler going into John's room, Joanne waited but a minute before popping by herself.

Not that Valentine was competition. Pretty as she was, she was a student, and although she was somehow getting A's in biology, she struck Joanne Clarke as having all the brains of a fern. John might be flattered by her attentions, but nothing could come of it because he was a decent man. And certainly nothing could come of it if he intended to keep his job.

Now Joanne Clarke acted all surprised to find Valentine in John's room. "Oh," she said. "I'm sorry. Am I interrupting extra help?"

At once, Valentine and Mr. Wosileski said, "No" and "Yes," and then reversed themselves, which clarified nothing but looked suspicious, rendering Mr. Wosileski increasingly nervous and tongue-tied. Finally, despite Joanne Clarke looking him right in the eye, he was able to say, "What I mean is, you're not interrupting."

A few days before, there was, in Valentine's biology class, a kind of mass hysteria, the result of a sartorial blunder on Miss Clarke's part. To school that day, over a white blouse, she'd worn a gray wool jumper, snugly fitted, not too tight, just enough to accentuate her curves—so far, so good—that featured two rows of red decorative buttons running vertically from just below the collarbone to the waist, which would've been kind of snappy except for the pair of buttons, red, mind you, sewn exactly dead center on the tips of her luscious breasts. It was like she was wearing her nipples on the outside, and this was just a bit much for tenth graders to take in their stride. A nudge with an elbow, a sly nod of the head, eyebrows raised and wiggled, and giggles suppressed erupted into snorts, and in no time flat the laughter was out of control. Miss Clarke, not only unable to restore order, in fact aggravated the situation by demanding to know, "What is so funny? Someone tell me what is so funny."

Perhaps that's what Valentine was picturing, those button nipples, when her awkward smile manifested itself, prompting Miss Clarke to say, "It would behoove you to wipe that smirk off your face, young lady."

John flinched as if he were the one who'd been snapped at. That he was unable to shield Valentine from the harshness, that he could not demand Miss Clarke apologize, the shame at being rendered ineffectual in his own eyes and perhaps in the eyes of Valentine too, caused him to experience agony.

Behoove you? Who talked like that anyway? *Behoove you*? This was Brooklyn. Not England.

Miss Clarke might have assessed Valentine as a dull-witted girl, but apparently Valentine was quick enough to catch on to the fact that Miss Clarke wanted her gone, and perhaps not just gone from the room but from earth too.

Lifting her books to her chest as if her loose-leaf binder would deflect the poisoned darts Miss Clarke was aiming at her heart, Valentine said, "I've got to be going. See you tomorrow."

Poor, foolish Joanne Clarke. Rather than enhancing her chances with John Wosileski, having rid the room of Valentine Kessler served only to fill him first with resentment and then with despair. Of course he hid his grief from Miss Clarke. He even hid it from himself because steadfast refusal to acknowledge these feelings was all that prevented him from flushing his career down the toilet and ruining his life entirely.

∾

Valentine walked home alone. The clean smell of winter was in the air, although it would be some weeks before the first snowflakes fell.

Three

Over the traditional Sunday-morning meal, a table laden with the bounty of bagels, cream cheese, and lox, Valentine Kessler asked her mother, "Ma, what kind of name is Wosileski?"

Miriam put down her bagel and asked in the rhetorical fashion, "What kind of name is Wosileski? Are you for real?"

"I know it's Polish," Valentine said. "But is it Polish and Catholic? Or Polish and Jewish? You said yourself, the *skis* and the *witzes* can go either way."

Years before, as soon as she'd determined that Valentine was old enough to grasp the concept of *one's own*, Miriam had explained to her daughter, "Names that end with *field, baum, stein, farb,* and *berg* are Jewish. Anything from the Bible, the Hebrew Bible, is Jewish too. You know, like Isaac or Solomon. If the name ends with an *a* or an *o,* they're Italian, but Shapiro is an exception. Don't ask me how that happened because I don't know. Italians are always

Catholics. The American names, the plain ones, Jones, Smith, Anderson, like that, those are your Protestants."

The intent of this instruction, an initiation really, into decoding the clans, was meant to protect Valentine, to keep her safe, not from harm, but from hurt. Miriam had no problem with the *goyim*. They were good neighbors, nice people, but Miriam believed safety was among your own kind. As Miriam told her daughter, the fact of the matter was this: Should you make friends outside, and not that there aren't plenty of lovely boys and girls of other origins, but the truth is that the minute you have an argument, you know what you're going hear?

"I hate you?" Valentine had guessed.

"No. You're going to hear anti-Semitism. Because beneath the surface, they're all a little bit anti-Semitic. They can't help it. You should never have to hear such a thing from your friends and loved ones. And that's just the tip of the iceberg. The problems that come with mixed marriage are too many to list. Trust me on this."

Vast and intricate knowledge and now there was more. "With the Polish ones," Miriam explained, "you can often figure it out by the first name. Jewish girls are never named Theresa or Mary. David is likely to be Jewish," Miriam told her. "John is definitely not Jewish unless it's short for Jonathan. Jonathan can go either way." Then Miriam's antennae went up. "Why are you asking? Who is Wosilwhosits?"

"Wosileski," Valentine said. "Nobody."

"Nobody?"

"Just a teacher at school, Ma. That's all."

The knock at the door saved Valentine from further evasiveness or outright lying. "That's Beth," she said, and she washed down the last bite of bagel with a swig of orange juice, grabbing her coat on the way out.

As they did every Sunday morning after breakfast, Valentine Kessler and Beth Sandler walked along Rockaway Parkway to the Ice Palace. Beth's white ice skates were slung over her shoulder, pale blue pom-poms dangling from the laces. Her skating costume she carried in a vinyl tote bag.

Valentine carried nothing other than her wallet in her jacket pocket plus the minimum of two big secrets she kept from Beth. There is a weight to keeping secrets, not an unbearable weight, but the equivalent of a five-pound sack of Idaho potatoes per secret. Valentine could carry ten pounds of potatoes, but that's not like carrying air.

There's no telling what Beth would have made of Valentine's striking resemblance to the Blessed Virgin, but odds are that had she learned the identity of Valentine's beloved, Beth would have said, "Make me barf. Valentine, that is so gross. You could get any guy at school, and you pick a queer? Plus, he's like a thousand years old or something."

After the nine o'clock mass, where he did not take Holy Communion because, despite Friday night's confession, he was not in a state of grace, John Wosileski went to his parents' apartment for Sunday breakfast. It had been only a matter of months since John had moved from the dreary apartment in the Greenpoint section of Brooklyn to his own dreary apartment in the Canarsie section.

Now he and his father were seated at the table while his mother served them scrambled eggs and kielbasa and sourdough bread. John rested his elbows on the edges of the place mat; the plastic, once yellow, was now brown with age, and he drifted off mentally to picture Sunday mornings at the Kessler house: sunshine spilling through their kitchen window, their table covered with a tablecloth that was clean and white and made from some expensive fabric like silk or satin, a svelte mother who was wearing a real dress and not a housedress from Woolworth's, and maybe even a string of pearls around her neck, and a good-guy kind of dad. John pictured Valentine wearing powder puff pink pajamas and rubbing the sleep from her eyes. He imagined they ate waffles.

~

As Beth and Valentine walked, they discoursed, as they most often did, about sex, about which they had little to no experience. But what teenager doesn't have hot pants? "The first time I do it, I want everything to be white," Valentine said. "In a white room, on white sheets, with white roses in a vase on the nightstand, and I want to be wearing a white nightgown."

"I don't care where I do it," Beth said. "As long as it's not in a car. Or at least not for the first time. After the first time, then a car would be okay, I guess." Beth walked on for two steps farther before she realized that Valentine was no longer at her side. Turning back to get her friend, Beth asked, "What's the matter? Are you okay?"

Valentine put her finger to her lips. "Shhh," she said. "Listen," she whispered.

"Listen to what?" On a Sunday morning, traffic was light. Rockaway Parkway was nearly as quiet as a country road. If it had been spring, they might have heard birds chirping, but it wasn't spring and birds don't chirp when the mercury hovers at the freezing line.

"What? What am I listening to?" Beth said.

Ever so faintly from behind church doors, the Church of the Holy Family, floated the sonorous sounds of organ music and a choir singing, "Ahhhh Vey Maaaaa Reee Ahhhh." Valentine cupped her hand behind her ear to amplify the auditory effect.

"Valentine!" Beth snorted, and stamped her foot like a bull, if it is possible to picture a girl bull with a Dorothy Hamill haircut and a bunny-fur jacket.

"That song," Valentine said. "Don't you hear that? It's sublime." A word which Valentine pronounced as if it were two words or hyphenated: *sub-lime,* like it meant below the fruit.

"Valentine! Come on. Let's go."

But Valentine did not budge, as if she could not budge, as if the "Ave Maria" were a kind of siren's song, the haunting strains wrapped around her, tightening their grip. "You should skate to that song," Valentine said. "We have to find out what song that is, so you can skate to it."

"Whatever it is," Beth said, "it's church music. If I skated to church music, my mother would shit a brick. Now, please. Can we go?"

If the music hadn't ended then, Beth might have gone off alone, gone to skate without Valentine there to watch for the first Sunday in who knew how many years because it sure seemed to Beth that Valentine wasn't going to move until that song was over.

"Honest to Gawd," Beth said to Valentine. "No offense, but sometimes you are so frigging weird."

Joanne Clarke asked the girl behind the counter for six sticky buns. "And let me have a quarter of a pound of those chocolate-chip cookies," she said. Although there was an obvious redundancy to the ploy, John so enjoyed those brownies she baked. Why not bring him some homemade cookies too?

~

The Ice Palace was thusly named in a fit of hyperbole. Nothing about the Ice Palace was palatial. A circle of ice, closer in color to gray than pure white or arctic blue, centered in a concrete warehouse, three rows of bleachers and a concession stand and music—show tunes mostly, orchestral versions of songs from *The Pajama Game* or *Annie Get Your Gun*—played over a loudspeaker that crackled with static. The Ice Palace was a bona fide dump. It was only when Beth skated there that beauty was bestowed upon the drab arena.

Beth Sandler had been a prima ballerina on skates, a hometown champion. It was thought that she would be the Barbra Streisand of the figure-skating world, an exception to the rule of Brooklyn girls with ordinary dreams, and who knows, Beth might very well have gone on to the Olympics and from there to a glamorous career with the IceCapades, but during the state tryouts, the spotlight shining on her from overhead, her sequinned and spangled costume shimmering, Beth stumbled. Her Achilles tendon connecting her calf to her left heel tore in half. The IceCapades were never to be. Competitive skating was now a part of her past, and to her credit, Beth took the misfortune in her stride. "Kay ce-ra ce-ra," Beth said. "It happened. What can you do?" And her energies were thus spent elsewhere, mostly on a boy two years her senior named Joey Rappaport.

Mrs. Sandler, Beth's mother, frequently mentioned, "I swear to Gawd, when Bethie tore her tendon, Valentine cried more than she did."

Still, Beth skated on Sunday mornings, just for the fun of it, and Valentine unfailingly tagged along. She was Beth's devoted fan.

The locker room at the Ice Palace wasn't really a locker room, but rather the toilets, and Beth entered a stall to change into her costume; this particular costume had been designed for a regional competition, a white leotard covered with silver sequins, each sequin sewn on by hand, a white satin flippy little skirt, tights woven with silver thread, a costume which conveyed impressions of snow and ice.

Valentine headed first to the concession stand, where she bought herself the giant-size box of Milk Duds. Valentine could put away the food, but unlike her mother, no matter how much she ate, she never gained an ounce. Her frame was willowy; she was tall, long-waisted, an ectomorph.

The box of Milk Duds tucked under her arm, Valentine waited outside the bathroom for Beth to emerge, from caterpillar to butterfly.

Or from teenager to celestial being. "Oh Beth," Valentine gasped. "You look like a constellation in the sky."

"A constellation? In the sky?" Beth's eyebrows shot upward in time with her inquiry.

"Yeah, like the Little Dipper. You know, all twinkly."

Beth sat on a bench to tighten the laces on her skates and looked up at Valentine, who remained standing. "Valentine, you've seen this costume a thousand times, if you've seen it once."

"I know, and it always gets to me. Right here." She patted the spot between her throat and her heart.

At that, Beth muttered, "Definitely weird," and swept onto the ice.

~

Although Miriam Kessler thought her daughter could've used a little more on top, maybe a B instead of the A cup she barely filled, Miriam was relieved that Valentine did not inherit her heartache with weight; a heartache because it signaled surrender. Indeed Miriam had given up. She had traded a chance at happiness for the midmorning Danish she sank her teeth into, and as she savored the cherry preserves and the cheese and the buttery crust all lolling across her taste buds, she told herself, *I put my life aside to be a mother,* but really Miriam put her life aside because she loved Ronald Kessler with all her heart and soul, with every fiber of her being, and the loss of him was an eternal void. Without Ronald, she might as well eat.

~

From her vantage point, the third and top row of the bleachers, where she sat alone, away from the handful of divorced dads who were looking forward to the close of the weekend visitation, Valentine's eyes beheld Beth Sandler as she did triple toes and figure eights and double salchows and double-lutz combinations to a Muzak rendition of "Funky Stuff." Imagine that. The Ice Palace was modernizing, making an effort to keep up with the times. Soon, within a matter of months, a mirrored ball would descend from the ceiling, and Thursday nights would be advertised as "Hustle On Ice." But now, on a near empty rink, in long, graceful glides, Beth slid effortlessly into a figure eight, which led to a pirouette, spinning like a top on the tips of her blades, faster Beth spun and faster, seeming as if she might spin until she lifted off the ground, all the while Valentine sang softly to herself, *Arrrrre vey Maaaa reee er,* which was far, far away from "Funky Stuff."

Miriam Kessler née Rothstein could scarcely believe it when Ronald Kessler singled her, Miriam, out for a date. She, Miriam, who was certainly pleasant to look at, not gorgeous, but sweet looking, cute, just over five feet tall, and a little bit chunky. Not fat, but plump, with D-cup breasts which looked as if they kept her teetering off balance, as if it took effort not to fall forward under the weight of such a set.

It was that—the D-cup boobs—which caught Ronald Kessler's eye. Ronald was a boob man of the bigger-the-better school, and that girl who was sitting with three other girls at the table across from his in the Boylan Hall cafeteria, she had some pair. Never one to lack confidence, Ronald knew he was smooth with the girls. Walking right up to Miriam, he crouched beside her and whispered in her ear, "I want you," which was a brash and bold thing to say even by today's standards. Then he straightened up and said, "Tomorrow night? A movie? Something to eat?" After all, this was 1959 and girls, nice girls, who attended Brooklyn College, weren't going to put out so easily, not even for Ronald Kessler. Even he, the best-looking boy at Brooklyn College plus the third baseman for the baseball team, had to work for it, put in some serious effort, to get any. These girls never gave it up rashly, even if the desire for it was mutual, or in some cases greater, because Brooklyn College girls were taught nothing if not this: *No one buys the cow when they can get the milk for free.* Had that adage not been drummed into her consciousness to the point of shackling her legs shut, Miriam might have hiked up her skirt right then and there in the Boylan Hall cafeteria, for Miriam was a passionate girl by nature, and Ronald Kessler set her blood to boil.

Having made arrangements for their date, Ronald walked off, and the girls at Miriam's table fell upon her, carrying on as if Miriam had just been crowned Miss Sheepshead Bay.

~

Beth changed back into her street clothes—Levi's, navy-blue Shetland sweater, Stan Smith sneakers, and the bunny jacket, which was also known as a junior fur and the first in a series that would climax with a full-length mink—before going to get Valentine who was still seated in the bleachers and humming away.

"Hey. Earth to Valentine," Beth asked. "Are you ready? Let's go." Yet Beth made no move to walk home. Instead, she sat alongside of Valentine and said, " "Valentine, we need to have a serious talk."

A serious talk from a teenage girl was never going to be good news or any kind of a compliment.

"I have to be honest," Beth said, "because you're my best friend. And it would be wrong of me if I wasn't honest with you. Because that's what best friends are for. Right?"

And serious talks that were honest were the worst kind possible. Beth was bound to tell her something like her breath stank or maybe, like Laura Volkman was told, she had an obnoxious laugh and that she should do something about it.

Valentine crossed her arms in front of her chest. "So?" Her voice went squawklike. "What is it?"

"Now, don't be mad at me," Beth said. "Promise you won't be mad," and then, without waiting for the aforementioned promise, she came out with it. "No offense, but I think maybe you need to see a psychiatrist."

"A psychiatrist? Why?" Valentine asked. "Because I liked that church music? That makes me crazy?"

"It's not just the church music," Beth said, although, in her book, it was a good place to start. "It's that, I don't know, you were always quiet, but now it's like no one is at home in your head. And then when you do talk, you say weird things."

"What weird things?"

"Well, like before when you said I looked like the Little Dipper. That's not a normal thing to say." Ah, normal. Such faith Beth had in *normal.* It was the only way to be. Normal. "You seem weird lately. Everyone says so."

As if she had been a hundred times stung, as if *everyone says so* were a swarm of hornets, the bloodletting of the vicious attack of adolescent girls telling the truth for your own good because you should know all the hateful things being said about you, Valentine's big blue eyes filled with tears. "Fuck you, Beth," Valentine said. "Fuck you."

"Yeah, you wish," Beth retorted because that was the known response to *Fuck you. Fuck you.* Then *Yeah, you wish,* and that should've been the end of it, but instead, as Valentine fled, Beth called after her, "I was just being honest."

Four

When Valentine stopped running, she found herself back at the Church of the Holy Family as the last Mass of the day was breaking. The priest was at the open door, shaking hands with the Catholics as they made their way out. Valentine glimpsed inside to the altar, splendiferous and rococo to the hilt, cherubs and angels carved and painted in gold leaf. The sunlight, coming in from behind stained glass windows, etched sharp lines in the red carpet. *Gloria Tibi, Domine.*

For the duration of their Sunday breakfast together, not one word was spoken. It was that kind of quiet, if it fell on you, it could kill you. John Wosileski's father signaled he was done eating by pushing his plate away.

While his mother washed the dishes and cleaned up the kitchen, her husband drank a Schlitz beer straight from the can—

hair of the dog—and then turned to his son. "So when are you going to give up that pansy job of yours and come work with me?"

"I like what I do," John Wosileski said. "It's a good job."

His father got up, beer in hand, and left the table.

His mother dried the frying pan.

The women, the Catholic women, who had emerged from the church to congregate on the sidewalk, had their heads covered. Not the way the Orthodox Jews covered their heads with hats or *schmattes* or even wigs that you could spot from a mile off. These women wore delicate squares of lace draped over the crowns of their heads. The grown-up women wore mostly black lace, like mantillas from Spain. The young girls all wore white lace like the paper doilies Miriam put between the cake and the plate when she served company. They looked so lovely, these Catholic women, with that lace, it's not impossible that Valentine felt a twinge of envy.

At school, while changing for gym class, the way a toddler reaches for a butterfly, Valentine once reached out to finger the powder-blue enameled medal of Mary that Theresa Falco wore on a fragile silver chain around her neck, and the way Valentine went dumb at the lights at Christmastime—not so much the green and red lights, but the white ones, those little white lights strung on bare trees so that they looked like tiny icicles—it was as if they stole her faculties away. After having sighted a pair of nuns she was moved to ask her mother, "Don't you think it's romantic, the way they give up their lives for God?" to which Miriam said, "Romantic? No. *Meshugge?* Yes."

Given that her name, Valentine, was a saint's name, coupled with the fact she did look exactly like the Mary on the prayer card, it wouldn't have been far-fetched for Valentine to wonder if maybe there'd been some kind of celestial mix-up, maybe she was supposed to be a Catholic.

But to so much as wonder such a thing, if she had so much as wondered such a thing, would be to betray her mother, her grandparents, her ancestors, and all the Jews, and hadn't they been through enough? Valentine had read *The Diary of Anne Frank*. She'd heard plenty about how the Jews suffered, from the very beginning, about the Pharaoh and then the Cossacks and then Auschwitz; Miriam left out nothing. "We were chosen to suffer," Miriam explained. "Don't ask me why. I have no idea. But we were, and so we try to make the best of it. Supposedly, it's a gift from God, to be a Jew." And a gift from God is likely to come with a policy: *No Refunds, No Exchanges.*

~

Joanne Clarke transferred the chocolate-chip cookies from the white bakery bag into a plastic baggie. A nod to the authenticity of the claim of homemade, that plastic baggie.

Crossing from the kitchen to her bedroom, she passed by her father, who was watching television. A golf tournament, maybe. Or *Bowling for Dollars*. Who knew? Who cared? Certainly not her father, who could've been watching little green men land on Flatbush Avenue for all he was aware. And Joanne didn't give an owl's hoot what he watched as long as he was quiet and remembered to get up and go to the bathroom if he had to pee.

Although she was only twenty-six years old, which was still young in most anybody's book, based on her life thus far, Joanne Clarke had concluded that John Wosileski was her last chance at something which resembled happiness. She had a lot riding on cookies.

Valentine found Miriam in the kitchen having a donut with a cup coffee. "Where's Beth?" Miriam asked, because always the girls returned together, to go to Valentine's room to listen to records and to gab about who knows what, boys, most likely.

Valentine shrugged a shrug which implied *I don't want to talk about it* rather than a shrug which said *who knows?* The way some cultures use hand gestures to speak volumes and in some languages inflection conveys meaning as well as nuance, this subset of Brooklynites shrugged. Seated in the chair across from her mother, Valentine picked at the chocolate icing on the remaining donut in the box. Then she asked, "Am I weird?"

"You're beautiful." Miriam reached over and placed her hand on Valentine's. "Quit picking," she said. "Eat the donut or leave it alone. You're the most beautiful girl in the world."

"I didn't ask if I was ugly, Ma. I asked if I was weird."

"Did Beth say you were weird?"

Valentine nodded.

One thing about Miriam, and she was the first to admit it, was that she was incapable of lying. *You want to know the truth, ask me.* Plenty of times, she wished she could lie, but that's just not how she was made. Miriam was as honest as the day is long, except of course, now and then when she lied to herself. "You're special," she said to her daughter. "Special. Very special. Maybe Beth thinks that's weird, to be special. There's something extraordinary about you," which was a bold assertion of faith on Miriam's part because thus far, other than the resemblance to the Blessed Virgin, about which Miriam was blessedly ignorant, there was nothing extraordinary about Valentine. No obvious talents, no rare gifts. Moreover, she seemed as shallow and superficial as the next teenager. Nonetheless, Miriam insisted, "I knew it even before you were born, that you'd be extraordinary."

~

Every woman should know a night like that, like the night when Valentine was conceived. That was the night Miriam decided she would say yes, yes, yes, instead of repeatedly taking Ronald's hand out from her panties and saying no, no, no. A summer night, a full moon, water lapping against the shore, Miriam and Ronald in a rowboat moored to a dock in Sheepshead Bay. That night it would be yes, yes, yes, oh please yes, Miriam wanted to do it all. She wanted to try the different positions; she wanted to put his thing in her mouth; she wanted him to put his mouth down there. She wanted to do all the dirty things she'd heard whispered of in the girls' room, the sexy things she'd read about, the warm and wondrous things she conjured up when she was alone with her hand between her thighs. So there in the rowboat with Ronald Kessler who loved her—didn't he say as much?—his left hand up her shirt, the other tugging at her underpants, her body quivering, her breath short, it was *yes, yes, everything*. And even though they didn't do one-tenth of what Miriam had hoped they would do—who knew that it would be over faster than you could blink—Miriam had been under the mistaken impression that it was something which took at least an hour's time start to finish—it was beautiful. It was the most beautiful night of her life, and no one, not even Ronald Kessler the rat-bastard could take that away from her, how beautiful that night was, how she would remember it always, how she could hold on to it because no matter that now she was big as the *Hindenburg,* so what that no man had touched her in over fifteen, *fifteen,* lonely years, she'd had her night under the stars.

Miriam had missed two periods before breaking the news to Ronald. They were—*oh thank you God for this joy*—in the backseat of Ronald's powder-blue 1958 Chevy. Miriam lifted her bottom off the seat and pulled up her panties and Ronald zipped his khakis, and she took a deep breath, and said, "Ronald, we have to talk about something." Far greater than her fear that he would not marry her was the fear that he would ask, *How do you know it's mine?* Her fear was that he might doubt her love, her devotion. And that he might have found out about the one night when she and her girlfriends went to a party at that Catholic college in the Bronx and Miriam got so drunk—who knew that the punch was mostly vodka—so she didn't remember a thing, only that she came home without her bra, this is what frightened her. "I'm pregnant with our child," she said, and she saw that Ronald's face, illuminated by the streetlight, was blank. Miriam held her breath, and then Ronald grinned. "Really? I hit a home run? Really? Wow." Ronald equated this with his other athletic accomplishments, as if he'd placed first in a competition of darts.

They married in the rabbi's office at Temple Beth Israel, and for a wedding gift, Ronald's parents bought them the house.

It was very generous of Ronald's parents to buy the young couple a house, but it was no hardship. Ronald's father did well, very well, in wholesale foundation garments. He was the Baron of Brassieres, and although business fell off dramatically in the late sixties when those nutty women burned their bras and let their bazooms bounce and flop to kingdom come, he'd already amassed a small fortune, so it wasn't the end of the world. But back when Ronald and Miriam married, Sy Kessler was still raking it in, and it was his pleasure to support the young couple while Ronald finished his education because his Ronald was going to be a dentist or a CPA. A somebody. And indeed Ronald did continue his education. He continued to study economics, he continued as third baseman for the Brooklyn College baseball team, and he continued to *schtup* a variety of big-breasted girls while Miriam quit school to take care of her husband, *her husband,* her Ronald, to cook for him, to keep the house clean, to rub his back, to take his thing in her mouth, to prepare for the baby's arrival, and to grow fatter by the hour.

Who knew that Ronald Kessler wasn't happy? And whoever said happiness has anything to do with anything anyway? The pursuit of happiness is not guaranteed for couples with the responsibilities that come with marriage and a baby.

So, what kind of man abandons a wife and baby daughter? What kind of self-centered skunk would pick the morning of February 14, Valentine's Day *and* their daughter's first birthday, to pack his bags while his young wife was out buying extra cone-shaped paper hats and another box of devil's food cupcakes just in case she ran low at the party? What kind of man would leave a note on the kitchen table that read *I deserve to be happy* for his young wife to find when she got home, bags in one arm, baby in the other? What kind of man would break his young fat wife's heart into so many pieces?

After Miriam had found and read Ronald's note *I deserve to be happy,* she pressed it to her cheek, and she wept. She wept her *kishkas* out, and after that, she wept more.

Being married to Ronald was like having heaven on earth, and then God opened the trapdoor and Miriam fell from grace.

Even Ronald's own mother, *his mother,* would come to spit at the mention of her son's name, *like Sy's father, Willy, may he rest in peace, a criminal.* Such was the disgrace Ronald brought upon them. The *goyim* do things like that. Not Jewish men. Jewish men were good husbands. Good fathers. Family men. Didn't Miriam learn so, a golden rule, at her mother's knee? And wouldn't she, despite the glaring evidence to the contrary, tell Valentine the very same thing? The way Miriam explained it, there was one lemon in the apple orchard and she picked it. What she would never tell anyone, but what was ever so true, was that, given the opportunity to live her life over, she'd pick the lemon again, and again, and again. The lemon that was yellow like the sun.

In the kitchen shrouded in the deep purple of the November night, Miriam and Valentine sat at the table and ate dinner: bananas and sour cream sprinkled with sugar. The sour cream was rich enough, thick enough, to fill some need, but only temporarily.

Just as Miriam put out the dessert, a honey cake with almonds, the phone rang. It was Beth calling.

"Hold on," Valentine said. "I'll take it in my room," and she took the stairs two at a time.

Teenagers. One minute they're wallowing in the pit of human suffering; the next minute they're walking on air.

Valentine picked up the extension and called down, "Ma. Could you hang it up?"

The girls waited for the click which ensured their telephonic privacy, and then Beth said, "I'm sorry. I didn't mean to hurt your feelings, but promise me something." Thus, having extracted the promise that Valentine would make a concerted effort to act more normal, Beth was willing to forget the entire incident because she was dying to talk about Joey Rappaport. In fact, it was that desperation to talk about her beloved Joey Rappaport which prompted Beth to call Valentine in the first place. Marcia Finkelstein wasn't at home and Leah Skolnik was in the middle of dinner and couldn't talk. Valentine got the call by default.

Any chance that Valentine might have talked about Mr. Wosileski the way Beth talked about Joey had to have been obliterated by the promise to try to act more normal. Just the fact that she was in love with someone she called *Mr.* Wosileski precluded normal, and never mind all the times Beth had said to her, "Is Mr. Wosileski the biggest queer you ever saw or what? The man is so not normal." But what girl doesn't want to coo about her beloved's dreamy coefficient, even though in this case she'd be hard-pressed to find it.

"I definitely want to *do it* with Joey," Beth told Valentine, *it* being the big *it,* "but I'm going to wait until Hanukkah." For Hanukkah, Beth was expecting Joey to give her a gold heart-shaped locket with a diamond chip in the center, which was the precursor to the preengagement ring, which, unlike the engagement-engagement ring was not a diamond, but a pearl or an opal or an amethyst maybe. The gold heart-shaped locket meant you weren't anywhere near ready to be talking marriage, but it was some kind of commitment. "I mean," Beth said, "Joey is so adorable and I am so in love with him. It's really tempting to *do it* now, but you know how it is. No one buys the cow if they can get the milk for free."

Despite the sexual revolution, the folkways in this part of

Brooklyn really hadn't changed much at all in the years since Miriam and her friends refrained from putting out for that very same reason. In fact, the only change really was the price of the cow, which now cost a gold locket instead of a wedding band.

"He's definitely going to get you the locket for Hanukkah," Valentine assured Beth.

"Really? You think so?" Beth asked, although how could Valentine be sure of such a thing?

"I don't think so. I know so." Valentine told Beth exactly what Beth wanted to hear, and then it would seem she ventured to dip her toe in the waters of public opinion by asking, "Do you think teachers know about the gold lockets with the diamond chips? I mean, do you think they have that same rule?"

"Teachers?" Beth said. "How would I know? Besides, who cares?" Then Beth launched into some story about the cuteness of Joey washing his car.

Valentine put down the phone. Beth could babble on for another twenty minutes without taking a breath. At the window, Valentine looked out into the winter's night. Her reflection in the glass was vague, indefinite; a visual parallel to the way that church music was audible but elusive.

Down the hall, in the bedroom Miriam once shared, albeit briefly, with Ronald, Miriam snapped off the light. In the darkness, her hand, the right one, traversed her belly, not too fast but directly, as if being guided by the spirits. She opened her legs wide enough to accommodate this hand because everyone, even Miriam, has needs. Her fingers stroked gently at first as she imagined, as she always imagined, that it was Ronald caressing her. Lost in the pleasure of the memory and the act of pleasure, stoking the flame that would neither be entirely gratified nor consumed, but eternal, she was only dimly aware of her daughter's voice, and maybe it wasn't even Valentine singing, but a choir of angels rejoicing as Miriam groaned to the faint sonants of *Arrrre Vey Ma-ree-erhh.*

Five

Literally overnight the weather turned from cold to a freezing and exhilarating cold. Children, on their way to school, exhaled so as to see their breath. Teenage boys zipped up their parkas. Under their pea jackets and midi-coats and bunny furs, teenage girls sported the latest in sweaters, novelty sweaters with a puff to the sleeve and patterns of kittens or apples knitted into the weave.

As if he'd had a mild headache for the last few years, and now it was gone, John Wosileski felt okay, maybe even good. Having something to look forward to does that, brings light. John Wosileski walked to work with a slight bounce to his otherwise *shlubby* step.

Joanne Clarke ducked into Nevins Bakery, selected four cupcakes with vanilla icing, and asked the woman behind the counter to put them in the tin Joanne had brought from home instead of a bakery box.

~

During homeroom, the fifteen minutes at the start of each school day when attendance was taken, when announcements were made concerning choir practice or class elections, when information was given concerning schedule changes, Mrs. Kornblatt passed out a flyer announcing the formation of a ski club.

Valentine Kessler looked down at the flyer, at the words SKI CLUB printed in large, bold letters. What use would she have for a ski club? For all her loveliness Valentine was a spaz. This was a girl who could not throw a ball so that it would sail past her feet. Unable to master riding a bicycle, she never got beyond wobbling for perhaps half a block before falling sideways into the hedges. In gym class, she was the one left standing when teams were chosen; then the team that got stuck with her would groan audibly. Not once in her life had Valentine volunteered to partake in an activity which required coordination. But as she was halfway into the act of crumpling up the Ski Club flyer, her eye landed on the fine print at the bottom of the paper. *Faculty Advisers: Mr. Ornstein and Mr. Wosileski.*

~

Skiing, a rich man's sport, was beyond John Wosileski's means until Mark Ornstein, a history teacher, had left a note in all the faculty mailboxes asking for someone to assist him in the formation of a school ski club. *If we can get 25 kids signed up for a ski trip, all our expenses will be paid. i.e. WE SKI FREE!* To sign up twenty-five students, to arrange for a bus, to endure three hours in a bus with twenty-five students, to purchase the lift tickets, to rent skis and bindings and poles for those without equipment was an atrocious job, but oh so worth the effort. Thirty-five dollars, the price for a day on the slopes, was, for a school teacher in those days, a hefty chunk of change.

And yes, the thought did cross John Wosileski's mind—*Leave it to a Jew to come up with a way to ski for free*—but he didn't think it in a mean way, the way his father would have. Rather, he was impressed with how clever they are, the Jews. With the note flapping in hand, John raced to the third floor, to Mark Ornstein's room, hoping, hoping he wasn't too late, hoping some other teacher hadn't gotten there before him, and he burst through the door and said, "Yes. Please. Me."

John Wosileski was a skier, and a good one, which could be considered out of character. That he should be skilled at a sport and that there was something about which he was passionate seemed antithetical to his otherwise passive and bloblike demeanor.

When he was eleven years old, John was sent from Brooklyn to Plattsburgh, New York, to stay with relatives—Uncle Joe and Aunt Marie and their three sons who were much older than John, teenagers already—because his mother was sick and needed an operation for something that no one would mention by name except to call it female troubles. On his first Saturday in Plattsburgh, very early in the morning, so early that really it was still night, his cousin Thomas woke him up and asked, "You want to come skiing with me and my father?"

John Wosileski knew nothing of skiing, but that his cousin Thomas, John's idol, had extended the invitation was reason enough to say yes.

"Dress warm," Thomas said, "in layers. We'll meet you downstairs."

In the kitchen, Aunt Marie insisted they have a hot breakfast. Farina, which John had never had before and didn't much like either. Nonetheless, he ate it all because Aunt Marie had said, "No one's going nowhere until those bowls are empty."

The drive was short, and when they arrived, John's feet were fit into boots that were bound onto skis. Uncle Joe gave him a few pointers. "Knees bent, like this. Poles here. Yeah, like that. You're a natural," Uncle Joe said. "Ready?" he asked, and John was set free. He let go. Let go and down the slope and *whoosh,* he let go of all that was bleak and dour and sad. Let go of his unhappy parents and their dreary apartment with the yellow ruffled curtain at the kitchen window that faced an air shaft, the only attempt at gaiety, yellow which was fading to a dingy off-white the same color as his underpants. Let go of the stink of kielbasa and cabbage and beer that permeated the walls and the ceiling and even his pillow smelled from it. Let go of the tension between his mother and father, tension as thick as his father's neck. Who knew there could be such absolution? Who knew there could be snow crisp and clean, free of black soot, free of yellow dog piss; white snow as it was meant to be, and fir trees, evergreens, and *whoosh* down a mountain trail and his cheeks were red like candy apples and his nose ran and even falling was like being sprung from a trap, the way he could get up and go *whoosh* again in an instant.

John skied as if the trail and towrope were perpetual, with no beginning and no end. Refusing to stop even for lunch, and on the drive home, his uncle behind the wheel and Thomas in the passenger seat and John alone in the back staring out the window, he prayed to God for his mother to die. If his mother died in the hospital, then maybe he could stay here in Plattsburgh, live in the house with Uncle Joe and Aunt Marie and his cousins, especially Thomas, and he could go skiing every day. *Please, please, please, God. Let her die. Please.* Then, realizing what he was asking, the horribleness of it, worse than a mortal sin, a one-way ticket to hell for sure, John took it back and instead asked if God could keep his mother in the hospital until the spring thaw.

Two weeks later, John Wosileski was back in Brooklyn and whatever female troubles his mother had appeared to be over. Everything was exactly the same as it had been before except maybe now his mother looked even more pinched, more haggard, and also now John had a dream for himself. His dream was to someday, somehow, find a way to live in Plattsburgh, New York.

When it was time to go to college—something his mother had wanted for her son but his father considered a waste of four years when the boy could be out earning a decent wage—John went to the State University of New York at—ta-da!—Plattsburgh—Ski Whiteface! Instead of living in a dormitory with other students, he stayed with Uncle Joe and Aunt Marie, his three cousins now grown and living away from home. A student loan covered the tuition, and his part-time job as a clerk at a convenience store at night afforded him a pair of secondhand skis and lift tickets. During the winter he got to ski on weekends. During the winter, on weekends, he could be happy and it was wondrous until the end of his junior year, when Aunt Marie and Uncle Joe told him that they were selling the house and moving to Arizona because they were getting too old for the harsh Plattsburgh winters.

John returned to Brooklyn, finished his last year of school at

Brooklyn College, and because he had no idea what he was going to do after graduation, he went to see the career counselor, who suggested he fulfill the required number of education credits so he could teach high school math. "They always need math teachers," she said. "Math and science can always get a job." If nothing else, the job provided him with the relief of his own apartment. Although his own place was not a cheerful one, it was not oppressive; no longer would he have to bear witness, every morning, to the circles under his mother's eyes, or be confronted with her collarbone, jutting out from the top of her ratty bathrobe, vulnerable like a wishbone to be snapped but without the hope attached. He was free from his father's temper and his misery and his fat face. What went so terribly wrong for these two people? John often wondered, *Were they ever once in love?* Or like so many, did they come together only because the timing was right and the fear of being alone was too great, too much?

~

Valentine Kessler folded the Ski Club flyer in half and in half again before tucking it away in her purse. She spent the remainder of the homeroom period, which was but a matter of two minutes more, making an addition to her Hanukkah Wish List.

~

Between the first and second periods, the woeful Joanne Clarke popped into Mr. Wosileski's room. She did this at least once a day, stopping by on some pretense or another: Does he have an extra piece of chalk? What time is the faculty meeting on Friday? Would he like a homemade cupcake? She baked them herself. Yet, for all her efforts, Joanne Clarke was no further along on the road to romance with John Wosileski. He didn't want a cupcake.

"Thirty-five dollars and you have to sign the permission slip." Valentine placed the paper beside her mother's plate and pointed to the dotted line. "Here. You have to sign here."

It was not the money which caused Miriam to hesitate signing the permission slip for a one-day ski trip to Hunter Mountain. For all the hardships in her life, the lack of money, thank God, was not one of them. True, she was no Mrs. Rockefeller, but she was comfortable. She owned the house outright. And when, the year after Ronald left, her parents, may they rest in peace, died in a car accident, a head-on collision with a truck whose driver had fallen asleep on Interstate 95, Miriam, their only child, inherited their savings account, their insurance policy, and the condominium in Florida, which she sold. Also there was a settlement with the trucking company, but that money was tucked away for Valentine's college education. On top which, Ronald's parents were very generous. Each and every time they came to visit, which was often because Valentine was their joy, Sy Kessler would press an envelope upon Miriam, an envelope containing cash. "Please," Miriam would say. "I don't need it. We're fine." Nonetheless, after her in-laws left, Miriam would find the envelope in the silverware drawer or in the coffee canister. Plus, there was Ronald's check, which he did send regularly. It wasn't much, but it was something. Miriam kept this particular source of income from Valentine because, as Miriam had told The Girls, "I don't want to get her hopes up that maybe he cares about her." Although he never missed one payment of child support and alimony, Ronald Kessler made no attempt ever to see or to speak to Valentine. He lived somewhere up in Canada, way north of Brooklyn.

No, the expense of the ski trip was not the cause for Miriam's hesitation. It was simply the oddity of it, the sudden desire springing from nowhere on Valentine's part to engage in an athletic activity. Out of doors. In the cold.

"Does this have to do with a boy?" Miriam wasn't born yesterday.

"No. I just want to go because, you know, all the kids are going." Was Valentine Kessler becoming something of a prevaricator?

Although she feared, more than she feared most anything for her daughter, that Valentine would get married and have a baby before she got a chance to finish college and have a life of her own, Miriam was a modern person, up on things like psychology. She knew perfectly well that if she harped on her fear, if she forbade Valentine to go out with boys, all she would be doing was pushing her daughter into maternity dresses before she was twenty. Valentine was a good girl and Miriam had no reason not to trust her, and besides—let's be real here—the times had changed. They had birth control now. And Miriam was no hypocrite. When she'd sat Valentine down for the "facts of life" talk, she advised only, "Save yourself for someone you love." She wasn't going to feed her daughter the bit about the cow and the milk. Not only was it nonsensical in this day and age to suggest she save herself for marriage, if Miriam had saved herself for marriage, she would've lost out on those, albeit few, most spectacular nights of her life.

But even under ideal circumstances, even if Mr. Wosileski had been closer to her own age and Jewish, it's not likely that Valentine would have confided in her mother about her love for him.

Never before did Valentine speak to Miriam of any boy in particular. Even the subject of boys in general, she brushed off as if somehow she thought she was protecting her mother's feelings, as if Valentine were a *have* and Miriam a *have not.* When Miriam spelled out the facts of life—his thingie goes into your thingie—it probably never occurred to Valentine that Miriam was a woman who knew passion. No one much thinks of mothers in this position: sprawled naked, bosom heaving, mouth open, knees apart, legs flailing, hips rollicking, and loving it. And who in this world would have looked at Miriam Kessler and thought, *Now there's a hot tamale?*

Miriam signed the consent form and wrote a check for thirty-five dollars. "You skiing." Miriam shook her head. "I must be out of my mind to let you do this. What if you break your legs?"

"Ma, I'll be fine. I swear to you. I won't get hurt," Valentine promised, and Miriam said, "From your mouth to God's ear."

Valentine took the check and the permission slip and kissed her mother on the cheek. As she headed to her bedroom, Miriam called her back. "Your Hanukkah Wish List," Miriam said. "Do you have it?"

Sitting on his couch, an orange-and-navy-blue plaid, stained and worn and purchased at the Salvation Army for seven dollars, John Wosileski drank an after-dinner beer. The television was on, but he wasn't watching it. He was thinking about the ski trip, not just the skiing part, but the possibility that this venture might result in a friendship between himself and Mark Ornstein. "My friend Mark," he said out loud. "My buddy Mark. I think I have plans with my chum Mark that night." Then he fantasized plans to meet

Mark at the diner for a hamburger and who should be there but Valentine Kessler, and John fantasized saying, *Valentine, fancy meeting you here. Me? I'm meeting my buddy Mark. Mr. Ornstein.* "My buddy Mark."

John had a hard time making friends. People didn't actively dislike him. At least not since he was in high school. They disliked him then. Plenty. But after that, no one was overtly nasty to him, nor was he treated cruelly. Still, even after three months at Canarsie High, he had yet to be invited out with any of the groups who went for "Thank God It's Friday" drinks. No one ever asked him to go to a movie or a ball game. The only person who had shown any interest in him was Joanne Clarke, and well, isn't that all too often the way? To have zero interest in the one person who has interest in you.

~

Joanne Clarke looked in on her father. Even asleep, he looked befuddled. Joanne wondered which was worse: to be stuck with her father as he spiraled toward a kind of infancy? Or to live alone, to have no one, no one at all. She wasn't there yet, but she was near to giving up on John Wosileski. Three months without so much as a nibble on the line. Resignation was on the horizon like the first ribbon of light heralding the dawn.

Joanne Clarke took off her terrycloth robe, under which she wore a flannel nightgown, red with little yellow flowers. She got into bed and closed her eyes, but sleep did not come to save her.

~

It just happened that they, The Girls—having taken a break from their morning routines, which were centered around vacuum cleaners and dust cloths, spotless their houses were—found themselves at Judy Weinstein's house having an impromptu midmorning coffee at her kitchen table, which was wrought iron painted white and covered with a glass top. They, The Girls, were that way sometimes, spontaneous. Miriam didn't know how Judy lived with that glass tabletop, with every fingerprint and smudge glaring, you've got to spend half your life spraying the Windex and wiping, with a table like that one.

Judy served an apple cake that was out of this world.

Miriam Kessler stirred the half-and-half in her coffee, which frankly was not up to the standards of the cake. "I asked her to write up her list. What she wants for Hanukkah this year."

"Did she ask for those baggy dungarees?" Judy Weinstein wanted to commiserate. "What do they call them? Carpenter's pants? Like the workmen wear. My Marcy wants three pairs of those. Two in blue and one in off-white. I said to her, 'What do you want those for? They're not the least bit flattering. What about the Jordache jeans? Or the Gloria Vanderbilt?'"

"That's what my Ellen wants. The Gloria Vanderbilt," Edith Zuckerman said.

"At least the Gloria Vanderbilt show off the figure. My Marcy has a cute shape. What does she want to hide it for?"

Valentine did not put carpenter's pants on her wish list, and not Jordache jeans or Gloria Vanderbilt's either. She did not put down anything that was rational to Miriam. Last year, her Hanukkah Wish List was rational. Last year she wanted what all the other girls her age wanted: Huk-A-Poo blouses, a Bobbie Brooks blazer, a gold S-chain bracelet, the Princess telephone. From Grandma and Grandpa Kessler, she got a new stereo. This year, Valentine's Wish List read, in its entirety: (1) a white silk shawl (2) a blue silk shawl (a very specific shade of blue that didn't even have a name, but Valentine had glued an itty-bitty snippet of something this shade of blue to the piece of loose-leaf paper), and (3) a pink ski jacket.

In light of the ski trip, the pink ski jacket at least was a rational request, but the rest of the list, or rather the lack of a list, that wasn't normal. Three measly things she asked for? What teenage girl can't name three thousand things she wants? Plus there were eight nights of Hanukkah.

"That's it?" Edith Zuckerman asked. "That's all she wants? A ski jacket and two *babushkas*? She's going through a phase?"

Miriam hoped that's all it was, a phase. A phase comfortably explained away all aberrant behavior. Kids go through phases. Like when the Moskowitz girl quit eating, and when the Gloskin boy got mixed up with drugs, and when their own Sunny Shapiro's son insisted on wearing eyeglasses that he didn't need, and when the Samuals twins joined up with that cult and dressed exclusively in orange—phases, all. *This too shall pass.*

"The skiing is a phase. They're all skiing now." Sunny Shapiro lit up a cigarette. "It's the fad. My David, he went skiing last weekend. They're knee-deep in snow already up there at Cornell." Sunny Shapiro never passed up an opportunity to let drop *my David* and *Cornell* in one breath.

"Valentine isn't going to ski," Judy Weinstein said knowingly. Each of The Girls had their own memories of Valentine: Valentine catapulting off a swing; Valentine bowling a zero, a *zero,* twenty gutter balls at Ellen Zuckerman's bowling party; Valentine catching a softball right between her eyes. The fact that she never even once got seriously hurt or so much as needed stitches had to have been the result of God watching over her. "Trust me on this," Judy Weinstein said. "She's going to spend the day sitting in the lodge. That's what I did the one time I went skiing."

"You went skiing?" Miriam was skeptical. "When?"

"Years ago. Before I married. I was dating a boy who wanted to try it. So we went. He skied, and I sat in the lodge where I struck up a conversation with another girl who ended up fixing me up with her brother. Believe me, Miriam. She's going to spend the day sitting in the lodge, drinking hot cocoa."

"Maybe I should get her the whole outfit. Not just the jacket." Miriam asked The Girls for their opinion on that.

"Why not?" Edith Zuckerman said.

"Get her one of those knit sets, you know, the sweater, hat, scarf, gloves all in the same pattern." Judy Weinstein knew fashion. "They're adorable, those sets."

Edith Zuckerman wrapped her mink tighter around her shoulders and asked, "But tell me, Miriam. Why does she want these shawls? Is it the style now?"

"I don't know. I suppose so." Miriam helped herself to another slice of apple cake; The Girls didn't stand on ceremony with one another. "They must be the style. Why else would she want them? Maybe the gypsy look is in again."

"That was a cute look, the gypsy thing. Not for us. But for the young girls, it was cute as could be."

Miriam didn't really believe the gypsy look was in again. She'd seen no evidence that it was. Frankly, it disconcerted her that Valentine wanted such things. What good could come of two shawls that weren't even the fashion? Valentine must've wanted the two shawls to express herself, her individuality, which wasn't a terrible thing provided it didn't go too far. Miriam would have to keep an eye out for that, for *too far* because while individuality wasn't the worst thing—creative people were often individualistic—to be an out-and-out nut was another story altogether.

Despite that she didn't have all good feelings about this, Miriam wouldn't dream of denying Valentine, so she chalked up the Wish List to *dementia praecox*, which is Latin for *Teenagers; don't even try to make sense of them.* "My biggest problem right now," Miriam said, "is where am I going to find silk shawls? The last thing I want to do is *schlep* into the city for them."

The last time Miriam *schlepped* into Manhattan was almost ten years ago. She and her girlfriends went to see a show, *Man of La Mancha,* on Broadway, a Sunday matinee, which, they concurred, was fan-tas-tic. After they went to dinner at Mama Leone's, a famous and fancy place back then and often the actors went there for dinner too.

"Kleinman's," Judy said. "You know, the big bridal shop in Bay Ridge. They'll hem two squares of white silk. There's no shortage of white silk at a bridal shop. Then they'll dye one of them the color you want. Every day they're dyeing shoes to match the bridesmaids' gowns in colors like you wouldn't believe. They do gorgeous work."

Fueled with a sense of purpose, a mission, the four women, right then and there, left their coffee and apple cake, and got into Judy Weinstein's emerald-green El Dorado, to journey to Bay Ridge. Miriam sat in the backseat, where she watched out the window to see if anyone on the street was wearing a silk shawl, because who knew? Maybe it was a style.

On the way to the faculty dining room, John Wosileski met up with Mark Ornstein. John quickened his pace, just a little, so that he could fall into step alongside the other teacher, and then, just as he'd rehearsed it, he said, "Hey, Mark, you want to grab a beer after work, and you know, talk over the ski trip."

Mark Ornstein's eyes darted, almost wildly, as if he were scouting for an emergency exit in a burning building, or looking for someone, someone not John Wosileski, but rather someone who would rescue him from John Wosileski. "Ah gee," he said. "I can't. Sorry." No excuse was offered. No *I've got a dentist appointment.* No *I have to drive my mother to the chiropractor.* No *I've got exams to grade.* Not even *I have other plans.* Nor did it escape John Wosileski's attention that there was no *Perhaps some other time* either.

Lest Mark Ornstein be judged harshly, before it is said, *Oh, how could he be so heartless? Couldn't he just have a beer with the poor guy?*—a truth, an ugly truth but a truth all the same, must be revealed: Everybody does it. Everybody shuns life's losers, the weak, the unattractive, the poor, the dispossessed, the friendless, and not because we want to be cruel, but because we can't bear the responsibility of them; they need more than we can give; we will fail them. No matter what we do, we will fail them.

In the faculty dining room Mark Ornstein joined a group of hail fellows. John Wosileski took a seat at a table that was empty until Joanne Clarke came by. She set her tray down across from his and said, "Well, fancy meeting you here."

John Wosileski, someone you would think would be empathetic, closed his eyes to Joanne Clarke's suffering.

~

Talking with pins in his mouth, Mr. Kleinman told The Girls he'd be with them shortly. He was in the middle of a fitting. Miriam, Edith, Sunny, and Judy basked in the radiance emanating from the bride-to-be as she stood perfectly still while Mr. Kleinman tucked and pinned the white taffeta along her waist. "It's true," Edith said. "All brides are beautiful." Edith made mention of this because, stripped of the white gown, this one would have been anything but beautiful with that schnozzola and a half, what a nose on her.

The Girls moseyed around the shop, oohing and ahhing at the gowns and veils and tiaras. Miriam fell in love with a tulle-and-lace gown, but Judy returned to the first one they'd looked at, an ecru satin bridal gown, artificial seed pearls sewn at the bodice and cuffs, and said, "I still say this one for Valentine, when her day comes. Seriously, Miriam. Picture your Valentine in this. Can you imagine how gorgeous?"

Miriam often fantasized about Valentine's wedding day. What mother doesn't, and especially with an only daughter and also because Miriam didn't get to have a real wedding of her own. When the time came, Miriam intended to make Valentine a celebration elaborate enough for both of them: first an engagement party at a catering hall; then a bridal shower at the house; the wedding itself she'd like to have at one of those Long Island mansions you can rent for special occasions; Valentine's gown would take your breath away—the heaviest silk and an eight-foot train. She'd carry a bouquet of pastel roses and baby's breath, the bridesmaids in peach-colored chiffon and the maid of honor in yellow the same as the flower girl.

Miriam had yet to breathe a word of these plans to anyone, not even to The Girls, and definitely not to Valentine. For the time being, it was Miriam's own to decide if the candy coating on the

Jordan almonds should be all white or the same pastel colors as the bridal bouquet, and to picture, God willing, Ronald's father walking Valentine down the aisle, and when they reach the *khupah,* the organist will play "Sunrise, Sunset" from *Fiddler on the Roof,* and there won't be a dry eye in the house. At that juncture in her musings, Miriam began to hum and then to sing softly, "Is that the lit-tle girl I car-ried, is that the lit-tle boy at play, I don't re-member growing older, when did they?" Judy Weinstein and Edith Zuckerman and Sunny Shapiro joined in with the chorus—"Sun-rise, sun-set—" and in a heartbeat the four of them were bawling like babies.

That's how Mr. Kleinman found them, standing in a row in front of the mannequin in the white satin gown, tears rolling down their faces and singing, like an a cappella girl group from the fifties, "Sun-rise, sun-set."

"So tell me, ladies," he said. "Tell me, how can I make your dreams come true?"

Six

The sun set and Valentine lit the candles to commemorate the second night of Hanukkah. The glow from the flames framed her face, the yellow light fluttering and then growing strong as it had done more than two thousand years before when the faithful trusted that God would provide oil for eight days of light. Neither Valentine nor her mother nor her grandparents recited the blessing—*Blessed are You, Adonai our God, Ruler of the Universe, who performed miracles for our ancestors in ancient times and in our days*—because who knew from that anymore? Tradition may have outlasted its original function to keep the faith, but then it got other functions such as keeping up with the Christians.

Valentine was too old to play *dreidl*, but she wasn't too old to get Hanukkah *gelt* along with her gifts. Grandpa Kessler slipped her a fifty-dollar bill and told her, "You buy yourself something pretty, sweetheart."

Valentine kissed her grandfather on his cheek, a small gesture of affection which set his heart to flood.

Grandma Kessler gave her one and only grandchild—her granddaughter, the light of her life with a face like you wouldn't believe, so beautiful and sweet as honey—a small black velvet box. "Wear them in good health," she said.

Valentine opened the box to reveal a pair of diamond earrings. "Oh," she gasped, and the diamonds winked.

Miriam leaned over her daughter's shoulder and her eyes bugged at the size of the stones. "Rose," she admonished her mother-in-law. "She's a kid. When you said diamond earrings, I thought you were talking chips. These are like the Rocks of Gibraltar. What does a kid want from diamonds like that?"

"So she'll have them for later. When she's older." Rose Kessler wasn't going to buy her only grandchild little *pitseleh* nothings.

While her mother and grandmother were having it out, Valentine put the earrings on and went to the mirror. Ice-blue light flickered and danced from the diamonds to her eyes and back again, light even more ethereal than that from the candles. Ever since anyone could remember, Valentine had an open affection for things that glittered and shone. The earrings were no exception. "Ma, look," she gasped. "Look how beautiful."

Valentine's face, so radiant, coupled with the fact that her daughter's reaction to the diamonds was a normal one, as opposed to something mental like eschewing material goods, this caused Miriam to melt. "You're crazy," she said to Rose, "but they do look gorgeous on her. Thank you."

The previous night, the first night of Hanukkah, Miriam gave Valentine the pink ski jacket, which fit her like a glove. On this night, the second night, Miriam handed her the box from Kleinman's Bridal Shop, wrapped in blue paper and tied with white ribbon. Even though the two shawls exactly fit Valentine's expressed desire—they were geniuses over there at Kleinman's, they got the shade of blue neither more nor less, but flawlessly precise—diamond earrings were a tough act to follow. Valentine opened the box, and then looked at her mother with tears in her eyes, which Miriam could not decipher. Tears of gratitude? Tears from disappointment? "That is what you wanted? No?" Miriam asked.

"Yes. Thank you, Ma," Valentine said.

"Try them on," Miriam urged. "The blue goes nicely with the sweater you're wearing."

But Valentine wouldn't try them on. She wouldn't so much as lift the shawls from the box; rather she left them folded just so between layers of tissue paper. "They're perfect," she said. "I don't want to mess them up."

Later that night Valentine would put the fifty-dollar bill between the pages of *Jonathan Livingston Seagull,* where there was, along with her prayer card of the Blessed Virgin, the hundred-dollar bill that Grandpa Kessler gave her for her last birthday, along with some twenties, and the two ten-dollar bills she'd earned baby-sitting for the Silverberg kids, which she swore she'd never do again under penalty of death. They were maniacs, those children. Plus Mrs. Silverberg left Hydrox cookies for a snack. Hydrox. A poor imitation of an Oreo. Clearly, Valentine was hoarding the money, but for what? What did she want that Miriam wouldn't buy for her?

The box from Kleinman's she slid under her bed, where it stayed, with the two pristine shawls inside, for some time to come.

Once the gifts were opened, wrapping paper in the garbage can, ribbon put away to be used again, Miriam said, "Dinner's ready," and the four of them sat around the table for brisket and string beans and potato latkes with applesauce. Miriam surveyed her family, such as it was, and while the ache for Ronald involuntarily pulsated, the wound never healed, nonetheless Miriam felt grateful for what she did have, and as she chewed a piece of brisket that was, frankly, a little bit stringy, she thought to herself more than to any deity, *Please God,* God in many ways being nothing more than a figure of speech, *watch over Valentine and don't let her do anything stupid.* But as Miriam's mother, may she rest in peace, was fond of saying, "If wishes were horses, beggars would ride," and if God had ever heeded Miriam Kessler's prayers, Ronald would have strolled through the door as casually and happily as he walked out all those years ago. But all old stories are driven by desire, and it was an old story already, Miriam's wish for Ronald to come back to her.

After Sy and Rose went home, after the dishes were washed and put away, Miriam swept the kitchen floor. Somehow the Kessler house seemed darker than usual. True, it was late December and after eleven at night and the kitchen light, overhead, cast a white halo, a halo which, rather than heralding the arrival of an angel, radiated a kind of desolation. Miriam felt the weight of sadness come over her. A sensation which was no stranger to her, although no one else, not The Girls, not Valentine, knew that daily, even if only for a few minutes, Miriam experienced profound grief. She sat herself down on one of the kitchen chairs, her arms wrapped around the broom, and she stayed that way until the feeling passed.

Upstairs, the mood was different.

In her bedroom, Valentine sat cross-legged on her bed, her Princess phone in hand, listening to Beth Sandler in ecstasy. The kind of ecstasy that emanates from a gold heart-shaped locket with a diamond chip in the center. "So, now that we've made this step toward preengagement," Beth said, "tomorrow night his parents are going out. We're going to do it."

"Are you nervous?" Valentine asked.

"Yeah," Beth admitted. "Kind of."

Two years or so before, at Beth Sandler's house, Beth and Valentine, behind the closed door of Beth's bedroom, had an exhaustive talk about *it,* about *doing it,* or more specifically, *how it is done.* Aware that their knowledge of *it* was garnered in bits and pieces and from sources not always reliable, they worried about, when the time came, *doing it* right because their mothers had taught them there was a right way and a wrong way for doing all things under the sun. Just then, Mrs. Sandler happened to come into Beth's room with a tray of tuna-fish sandwiches and two glasses of juice because it was time for lunch. "Ma," Beth asked, "how do you know if you're *doing it* right? You know, after you're married and on your honeymoon, how do you know what to do?" Beth added the bits about *married* and *honeymoon* to avoid the cow-and-the-free-milk speech. "Girls," Mrs. Sandler said, "the dogs know how to do it, the cats know how to do it, when the time comes, you'll know how to do it too."

And now here they were, on the cusp of Beth's loss of her maidenhood, and Beth was overcome with a rush of generosity toward Valentine, the kind of love that is often the antecedent to permanent separation, like the heat of one final fling. "I still don't get it," she said. "How come you don't have a boyfriend? You're the prettiest girl at school. Everybody says so. No one gets why you don't have a boyfriend. It's like a mystery. There must be a thousand guys who are dying to go out with you. All you would have to do is snap your fingers. You could get anyone."

"But I don't want just anyone," Valentine said, and Beth thought that was a stuck-up thing to say. What? Did Valentine think Beth was compromising with Joey Rappaport? Hardly. Joey was adorable, plus he was so smart. He scored almost perfect on his SATs and was in the National Honor Society, which was very competitive intellectually. If Valentine Kessler thought she could do better than Joey Rappaport, she had another thing coming.

~

In his two-room apartment over a dry-cleaning establishment on East Ninety-sixth Street, John Wosileski, having, hours before, finished with his dinner—a Swanson's Hungry Man meal, double portion of meat and potatoes and no vegetables—returned to the kitchen for a snack. Actually, John didn't have a kitchen. He had a kitchen area that ran along the rear wall of the living room. There he opened a bag of pretzels and a beer, which he drank straight from the can. The television was on, but only for whatever warmth the blue light provided and for the comfort of a voice not his own. John was neither watching nor listening to the TV. If he had been watching the television, he would have gotten up to fiddle with the reception, as there was something like the opposite of a shadow, something like when a photograph is overexposed, something like a halo over Mary Tyler Moore's head.

~

Or maybe it wasn't something like a halo over Mary Tyler Moore's head; maybe it was indeed a halo. It wouldn't have been the first time such a thing—Mary bathed in light—had appeared on television. To Zeitun, the very place where Mary and Joseph and Jesus had come when they fled King Herod, Mary—not Mary the actress but Mary the Blessed Virgin—returned some one thousand nine hundred and sixty-eight years later. The figure of Mary in a halo of light was filmed and shown on Egyptian television, which resulted in the otherwise unaccountable healing of untold numbers of open sores, shrinking of tumors, and twenty-twenty vision for the blind.

~

And if John Wosileski had been paying attention to the television, he would have heard that it was telling of another miracle, the miracle of light on this second night of Hanukkah; he would have heard the anchorman on the ten o'clock news—*wishing all our Jewish friends*—but John Wosileski was caught up in his own thoughts; John Wosileski was examining his life, which is always a dicey proposition. *What is to become of me?* he wondered, and all he could come up with was more of the same. That at age fifty-four nothing would be different for him than it was now at twenty-four: He would still be teaching geometry at Canarsie High; he would come home every day by four, check homework or grade exams, put a Hungry-Man dinner in the oven, touch himself, go to sleep. Nothing worth noting would ever happen for him.

Even if Valentine Kessler weren't legally off-limits, he could never win the heart of such a creature. Things like that happened only in the movies, and John Wosileski knew all too well that his life bore no resemblence to a romantic comedy. His life was bleak; almost entirely devoid of pleasure. The loneliness would never go away, but in time it would mutate into something worse than loneliness: the surrender to it. Worse yet bearable. And so on this night, on this second night of Hanukkah, sitting alone in the dark but for the blue light of the television, and drinking his third Pabst Blue Ribbon, which was not unlike piss water, John Wosileski, friendless and unloved, cried, which was something he had not done, cried, since the night of his high school prom; a night he spent alone, alone in his bedroom with the door closed crying while in the kitchen his father drank whiskey and his mother washed the dishes and mopped the floor and then cleaned out the refrigerator. Anything to avoid going to her son because what could she possibly have said to him? She had no words of comfort to give.

Crying, in and of itself, is sad, and it is particularly sad to cry alone. However, crying can be cathartic. And indeed, after he was all cried out, John Wosileski emerged from this bout of anguish with a new resolve. Or something close to resolve. Maybe it was resignation. Either way, he would take the initiative, the plunge. He would ask Joanne Clarke out on a date. To dinner. Maybe a movie. Why not? She liked him. And she was a good woman. Good enough. He couldn't quite picture himself falling in love with Joanne Clarke. She had a mean streak, whereas John, a romantic at heart, dreamed of sweetness, but he was rapidly warming to the idea of a date. The thought of them holding hands sped like electricity to the thought of fondling those pretty breasts of hers. And sex! Real sex with a live woman! He did imagine he could grow to like Joanne. He imagined that they could be compatible, and he even imagined that maybe someday they could get married and that marriage to someone you didn't love was probably preferable to being alone. In short, that night he imagined the very same things about Joanne Clarke as she had been imagining about John Wosileski all along.

Determination took hold, and he opened the Canarsie High School Faculty Directory.

~

Joanne was as startled by the ring of the phone as if she'd been in deep slumber instead of cutting her toenails. No matter what time of day or night it happened, the ring of the phone would have startled her because no one ever called.

Apologizing for phoning at such a late hour, John Wosileski said, "I hope I didn't wake you."

"No. No, not at all," Joanne said. "I just got in. I was out with . . ." Here she paused, deliberating, *Which would have greater effect?* Out with a friend, thus implying a date? Or with friends, plural, thus letting him think she had friends? The former could maybe get a little jealousy going, everybody wants what someone else has got, but it also came with the risk of turning him away. "With friends." Joanne opted to play it safe. "What can I do for you?" she asked him.

"I was wondering if you'd like to go out? Saturday? For dinner?"

"Mmmmm, Saturday. Let me check my calendar." Joanne put down the phone, and ruffled the pages of *The Reader's Digest* on her nightstand. Is it embarrassing to witness Joanne Clarke as she pretended to have social engagements? Or is it just plain sad? "As it turns out," she said, "I am free on Saturday."

"I was thinking we could go to Beefsteak Charlie's," he said. Beefsteak Charlie's boasted an All-You-Can-Eat Shrimp and Salad Bar.

After solidifying plans with John, Joanne Clarke went to her father's room. "Dad," she said, softly but hoping to wake him all the same, because she had to tell somebody. "Dad."

His eyes opened and Joanne's father smiled at her in recognition, which was yet another reason for her to be happy.

"Dad," she said. "Guess what? I've got a date for Saturday night. With a nice man. Another teacher."

Mr. Clarke's smile twisted into something else and he let go with a hair-raising shriek worthy of Edvard Munch.

Nine days came between the end of Hanukkah and Christmas, and like the way a seesaw goes, as the holiday anticipation for the Catholic and Protestant families soared high, the Jews plunked down. Their holidays were over, and the snowmen, the Santa Clauses, the angels, the trees, the lights, the colored balls, the tinsel, all of it was a big party to which they weren't invited. Aiming for stoicism, they acted like they couldn't have cared less. They tried to go about their lives, business as usual, but still, you couldn't ignore it completely. Not when your next-door neighbors, the Sabatinis, had Christmas carols coming from a loudspeaker hooked up to a Santa in a sleigh with the eight reindeer on the roof of their house.

"Honestly, Miriam. I don't know how you stand it," Sunny Shapiro said. "It would drive me up a wall. Five Bam."

Miriam exchanged three tiles. "They're good people and good neighbors. Once a year, I can put up with it."

"Last night," Edith Zuckerman said, seemingly apropos of nothing, "I dreamed we were at a tournament and all my tiles were blank. I kept picking tiles and there was nothing on them. Then I looked down and saw I was naked except I was wearing elf shoes. Pung." Edith had a hand of three Four Dots.

Nor could they escape from the Christmas specials on television, The Charlie Brown one and *Miracle on 34th Street* and that movie with Jimmy Stewart which was shown practically nonstop.

And how everyone said, "Merry Christmas," as if it were a universal greeting.

It's a depressing time for Jews, no matter what they might say to the contrary.

~

Of the Jewish contingent of Canarsie, only Beth Sandler and Joey Rappaport seemed genuinely unaffected by the Christmas tidings and joy. That's because they were fucking like bunnies, which was one of the reasons Beth hadn't called Valentine for days. When she wasn't thusly engaged, she preferred talking with her other friends. So now, when she did call, Valentine said, "Beth? Beth who? I don't know anyone named Beth."

"Come on, Valentine. Give me a break here. I'm sorry I haven't called you. Really I am."

And so all was forgiven, and once all was forgiven, Beth filled Valentine in on all she'd been up to, sparing no details. "You would not believe how good it feels."

"Like what? Compare it to something." Valentine stretched out on her bed, as if to prepare herself for the sensuality of the analogy.

Beth thought for a moment and then said, "It's really not like anything else, but it's a little bit like, you know, when you have to pee *sooooo* bad, like you're holding it for hours, and then finally you can. It kind of feels good like that."

"It feels like peeing?" Valentine's voice registered disillusionment. "Peeing isn't so great."

"Trust me on this one," Beth said. "You've got to do it. It's better than peeing."

As if she were madly in love, which she wasn't exactly, Joanne Clarke entertained a light-headed, silly mood which prompted her to stop into Woolworth's on her way home from the beauty parlor, where she'd gotten herself a fresh haircut. Really just a trim, a shaping. There, at Woolworth's, she bought a Christmas tree. Neither fir nor spruce, but spurious. A fake. An impostor. A polystyrene put-up job that wasn't even as tall as her legs. But it was a Christmas tree nonetheless, Adirondack green, and it came fixed on a stand. Joanne Clarke hadn't had a Christmas tree since her mother died, which was a long time ago. To decorate her tree, she bought one box of little gold-colored balls, one box of candy canes, and a package of tinsel.

As she exited Woolworth's, Joanne Clarke did not take notice of the obese woman and her pretty daughter entering through the adjacent door, which was a blessing because the sight of Valentine Kessler might very well have diminished her moment of holiday cheer.

Miriam Kessler went directly to the party-goods section in search of those little paper umbrellas used to garnish tropical drinks. Miriam wanted them to decorate a pineapple cake.

Valentine wandered off in some other direction in search of who knows what. Now that Valentine was no longer a child, her wanderings no longer caused Miriam the consternation they once did, when, whether it would be in Macy's or Stern's or in the A&P, it didn't matter, Miriam would suddenly find her hand holding empty space, air, instead of little Valentine's hand. Miriam's heart would jolt and she'd go racing up and down the aisles until, inevitably, she found her child either in the toy department or jewelry or fine furnishings or frozen foods. That, or else over the public-address system she would hear, "Would Valentine's mother please come to the manager's office." There, Valentine would be waiting for Miriam, her mother who would be short of breath and nauseous from worry, but Valentine would be as tranquil as the Buddha, licking the lollipop lost children are invariably given.

Now Miriam was confident that, when the time came, she and Valentine would find each other, and sure enough Miriam spotted her daughter in one of the several aisles devoted to Christmas. She was fingering a miniature fir tree. Not a real tree. Not like Miriam's little bonsai. This tree was made from wire and silver bristles like a garland. It was less than a foot high, in a foil-covered pot. From its branches hung little silver balls.

~

John Wosileski's apartment was devoid of Christmas spirit, but at his parents' apartment there was a plastic wreath on the door and another one on the coffee table. Seven Christmas cards, all from far-flung relatives, were displayed on a shelf. One card was particularly beautiful. It depicted the Nativity scene and the snow was real crystal flakes, like glitter but white. The Wosileskis no longer put up a tree. Mrs. Wosileski said it was because John wasn't a little boy anymore, so why go through all the trouble and expense, but really it was because of that one Christmas Eve ten years ago already, when his father, drunk and angry, kicked the tree over and stomped the glass balls to bits. The plastic wreaths were all that survived that year. Everything else broke for keeps.

An Almost Perfect Moment

After the groceries were put away, Joanne Clarke undid the knot in the rope around her father's ankle. The other end of the rope was tied to his bedpost. Before anyone gets aghast at the idea that she kept her father on a leash, understand that she had no choice. If she didn't, he would leave the apartment and roam the streets of Brooklyn clad only in a bathrobe for warmth. Twice already the police brought him home that way, and Joanne simply could not afford a full-time sitter for him. Besides, he didn't seem to mind.

"Come here," she said, holding out her hand for her father to take. "I have a surprise for us." She led him to the living room, to the artificial tree. "Do you know what that is?" she asked him.

"A puppy," he said.

"No. It's a Christmas tree. We're going to decorate it. Won't that be fun?"

"I don't know." He scratched his genitals.

"Well, it will be fun. Here. Let me show you." Joanne opened the package of tinsel and pulled out a few strands, letting them fall onto the branches of the fake tree. "Like that," she said. "Do you think you can do that?"

Joanne busied herself with the gold balls, placing them just so, not too close together, not too far apart, and all the while she sang "Winter Wonderland" and allowed herself to hope that maybe next Christmas would be entirely different, maybe, just maybe, by next Christmas she might even be married and she and John would have a real tree. When the last ball was hung, and Joanne went for the candy canes, she caught sight of her father stuffing a handful of tinsel into his mouth. Before he could swallow, she grabbed him, squeezing his cheeks hard between her fingers with one hand to force him to open wide. With her other hand, she reached in and pulled out the tinsel, which was wet with saliva. "Did you have to ruin this too?" she snapped at her father.

Her father began to cry, but for the life of him, he couldn't remember why he was crying.

~

On the morning of the last day of school before the Christmas vacation, which would later come to be called Winter Recess, John Wosileski entered his classroom to find, on his desk, a little silver Christmas tree in a pot. He looked around to see if there was a card to tell him who'd left it there, but he couldn't find one. With no evidence to the contrary, he assumed it was from Joanne Clarke. This assumption did not intoxicate him, but it wasn't entirely dissatisfying either. Even though he didn't much care for the thing—who really wants a tinfoil tree in a pot—no one before, other than his mother, had ever given him a Christmas gift, and she always gave him things like flannel shirts and underwear. John started to walk to the door, to cross the hall, to thank Joanne for the gift, when he was brought up short by the sight of Valentine Kessler just outside his door. He had no idea how long she'd been there looking in, but when their eyes met, she turned and took off like a little deer bounding through the forest. John went back to his desk, reminding himself that he'd have to thank Joanne later.

~

Valentine made a beeline for the girls' room, the ubiquitous puke-green bathroom on the 2nd floor, barging in on Beth Sandler, Leah Skolnik, and Marcia Finkelstein, all of whom went deadly quiet when they saw Valentine. This sudden halt of what had been an animated conversation could very well have been an indication that Valentine was the subject of said animated conversation except then Marcia Finkelstein said, "Not in front of the virgin." The three of them giggled and toyed with their gold heart-shaped lockets with diamond chips in the center.

~

Between the fifth and sixth period of that last school day before Christmas vacation, which might as well be a vacation day for all the work that gets done, John Wosileski and Joanne Clarke met up in the hall. "Thank you," he said to her, and she said, "For what?"

"For the tree," he said, and missing a few beats, she said, "Oh, don't thank me. It was nothing."

~

Christmas Eve found: John Wosileski at St. Stanislaw's, sitting in a pew beside his mother; Beth Sandler and Joey Rappaport boinking in the backseat of Joey's Ford Torino; Joanne Clarke and her father watching *It's a Wonderful Life* on television; Miriam Kessler in the kitchen picking at the remains of the chicken they had for dinner; and Valentine Kessler in her bedroom, at the window, her gaze fixed on the sky as "Joy to the World" burst forth from the loudspeaker on the Sabatinis' roof.

Seven

Decidedly peeved about having to work the day after Christmas—*It's one of our busiest weeks of the year,* her supervisor had said, *no one gets off*—Lucille Fiacco was deep into the latest issue of *Glamour* magazine—a benefit to the job of a librarian, Lucille got first crack at all the finest magazines—when she was interrupted. "Excuse me," said a teenage girl.

A pretty girl, but if she did a little something more with herself, she'd be a knockout. Mascara for sure and some eye shadow, blue. Not baby blue, but maybe like a midnight blue with a little glitter to it. And definitely a more flattering hairstyle, something with layers and wings. This was a hobby of Lucille Fiacco's, mental makeovers. On the bus or in a doctor's waiting room, Lucille would select a plain woman and give her a mental makeover. There was many a day when Lucille thought it had been a mistake to become a librarian; that her real calling was cosmetology. Well, just because she was a librarian didn't mean she had to look like one. Her hair was dyed blond and frosted silver at the tips. Her lipstick was a Christian Dior—*thank you very much*—called Passion Fruit.

"Yes?" Lucille asked the teenage girl. "Can I help you?"

"Do you know about the music? Over there?" Valentine pointed to the section of the library which consisted of a listening booth and four bins of LPs. "I'm looking for a song, but I don't know the name of it."

"Do you know who the recording artist is?"

Valentine shook her head.

Lucille had little patience with these people who came to the library asking for books whose titles they couldn't recall or the article they simply had to read only they didn't know what magazine it was in. What? Did these people think she was a miracle worker?

"But I can sing a little bit of it," Valentine offered and Lucille thought to herself, *Oh great. Now we're playing Name That Tune.*

Leaning forward, in a less than mellifluous voice but on key, Valentine sang softly so that no one but the librarian could hear, "*Arrre Vey Maaaareeee er.*"

"The '*Ave Maria.*' Of course I know it." The librarian, Lucille Fiacco, had been going to Sunday mass since day one of her life. She was listening to the "Ave Maria" while still in her mother's womb.

"Do you have it here?" Valentine asked.

"Try the liturgical section." What Lucille, she too of Brooklyn, did with the word *liturgical* was a vocalized wonder, the way it came out in fits and snorts, like the warm-up on a trumpet.

The liturgical section comprised six LPs which included Handel's *Messiah,* Mozart's *Requiem,* and Dean Martin's *Favorite Christmas Carols,* so it didn't take long for Valentine to find the "Ave Maria" as performed by the Vienna Boys Choir. She settled herself into the listening booth, where she adjusted the headset and leaned back into the chair.

~

Watching the clock does nothing to encourage the passing of time, so instead Joanne Clarke went to her closet to pick out what she would wear for what would now be her third date with John Wosileski. Tonight they were going to the movies. Not to the Canarsie Theater because there they risked running into students. Although she agreed with John entirely that such a meeting might be awkward, part of her wanted to chance it. If they ran into a group of students, maybe after the movie they'd all go for a pizza or ice cream, and then when school started up again, she and John would be popular teachers like Mark Ornstein or Bethany Sullivan, teachers who sat embosomed by students, popular students too, at school basketball games. Joanne imagined that to be one of the popular teachers would compensate for having been a colossally unpopular teenager. She thought it was possible that she and John could be included in an "in crowd," and better late than never. It was a thought, but not a realistic one. Let's be honest here: If Joanne Clarke and John Wosileski had been spotted together at the movie theater by students, they would have been the target for spitballs and hooting and mirth.

~

"So where's Valentine today?" Judy Weinstein passed two tiles—a Three Dragon and a Five Flower—to Miriam.

Miriam returned the two tiles to the wall, *clickity clack*, and said, "At the library, do you believe? I don't know whether to be pleased as punch or worried sick." In fact, Miriam was at neither end of that spectrum. While she wasn't unconcerned over Valentine's recent foray into solitude, her daughter was not a drug addict and her grades at school were good. So really, what could be so wrong? A falling-out with her friends? A phase of trying to find herself? *Whatever it is,* Miriam had decided, *it's not the end of the world.*

Edith Zuckerman's hands moved as quick as the eye, exchanging one tile from her rack with one from the wall, as she asked, "What is she doing there, at the library?"

"They all go to the library now," Sunny Shapiro said. "My David, in from Cornell for five minutes and he's at the library. The one in the city, mind you. He's doing some big report."

~

Sunny Shapiro was mistaken, as was Lucille Fiacco's supervisor. They didn't all go to the library, and far from one of the busiest days of the year, this day after Christmas was proving to be the slowest in Lucille Fiacco's memory. Besides the pretty girl in the listening booth, Lucille had assisted only two people thus far, which was well into the afternoon: Mr. Brickman, who came in every damn day without fail to read the newspaper because, even though Lucille happened to know for a fact—her sister's husband was the old man's accountant—that Mr. Brickman was sitting on a mountain of money, he was too cheap to spring for the *Daily News.* The other man who asked for help was lost and wanted only directions to Atlantic Avenue.

Having finished with *Glamour,* Lucille paced the floor. If there'd been bars on the window, she would have rattled them, that's the kind of stir-crazy she was going. The kind of stir-crazy that prompted her to say, "Oh, what the hell," and the kind of stir-crazy that led her to the listening booth.

Most likely it was because she was wearing earphones, the pretty girl did not respond to Lucille Fiacco's rap on the door, nor did she look up until Lucille tapped her on the shoulder. Then the girl slid the headset down around her neck, wearing it like a futuristic collar, as if science fiction took up the medieval punishment of the yoke.

Lucille perched on the edge of a table, facing the girl. It was then that Lucille noticed the diamond earrings the girl wore. Holy Mother of God, what Lucille Fiacco wouldn't have given for a pair of earrings like that. "What are you listening to?" she asked.

" 'Are Vay Maria,' " the girl said.

" '*Ave* Maria.' " Lucille corrected the girl's pronunciation, but you'd be hard-pressed to have caught the distinction between the two deliveries. "So that's it? You've been listening to the same song for over two hours?"

"It's so beautiful," the girl said. "I heard it for the first time maybe a month ago, and I can't get it out of my head."

"I take it you're not Catholic," Lucille said. "There's no offense in that. It's just that if you were Catholic, the 'Ave Maria' would be coming out your ears."

"Jewish," the girl said, and Lucille Fiacco nodded knowingly. She would've guessed that. Jewish. If only because of the earrings. Those Jewish girls have jewelry to die for. "What's your name?" Lucille asked.

"Valentine."

"Valentine? Like the saint?" Lucille leaned forward, closer to the girl, and although there was no one to hear them, she nonetheless whispered, "Have you ever read *Lives of the Saints*? It is so hot."

Twelve years of parochial school with the nuns taught Lucille Fiacco to sneak cigarettes in the ally behind the rectory, to drink vodka because it doesn't smell, to roll up the waistband of her plaid skirt, the uniform of St. Joseph's School in Bensonhurst, until it was at the midpoint between her crotch and her knee. She made out with boys named Vinnie and Paulie and Sal. She was what was known in her neck of Brooklyn as *fast*.

It was at the College of Mt. Saint Vincent where Lucille Fiacco's intellectual horizons expanded. There, among other sizzling theological works, she read and reread *Lives of the Saints*. For the hot parts.

"Hot?" Valentine asked.

You want teenagers to read? Give them books with hot parts.

"I swear to you," Lucille confided in this girl, "I'd read a chapter or two of that and have impure thoughts for a week after."

"Really?" Valentine arched her back, as if in preparation for an impure thought of her own. "Do you have that book here? Can I take it out."

"It's in biographies. Two weeks, but you can always renew if you want to keep it longer. And the best part is, you don't even have to hide it because everybody just thinks it's a holy book. Unless you've read it, you don't know that there's smut on every page." Lucille eased off the table. With her feet on the ground, she said, "I better get back to my desk." She took two steps in that direction and then turned to Valentine, about to offer a friendly suggestion—eye shadow—but when she looked at the girl again, Lucille decided she was wrong about that. Maybe it was the diamond earrings adding that extra spark, but the kid didn't need any eye shadow.

~

Joanne Clarke did not have in her possession underwear that could be classified as lingerie, but with careful deliberation she chose her most recently purchased bra, a Playtex Cross-Your-Heart, and a fresh pair of panty hose to wear beneath her beige wool slacks and the brown V-neck sweater, because *maybe*—it would be their third date—*it* could happen.

It had happened three times before. All three times during her senior year of college. The first was with a groundskeeper at the school, in the shed where he kept his tools, and maybe that sort of thing was Lady Chatterley's idea of a time to remember, but for Joanne Clarke it brought about nothing but a brief moment of pain and a shame that would never leave her. Next was a boy her own age, a blind date where clearly each party was disappointed at the sight of the other. Then he asked her, "So what do you want to do?"

Joanne said, "I don't know. I guess just go someplace and talk." *Someplace* meant maybe a diner to talk over a cup of coffee or even to a bar; she would've had a glass of beer, but he drove to a motel off the Long Island Expressway. Joanne didn't know how to tell him that this wasn't what she meant by *someplace,* that by *talk* she really meant *talk*. He rented the room for all of two hours, and they had time coming when he checked out. He never called her again, but she wasn't expecting that he would.

Last was her Bio-Chem II professor. Professor Chase. A nice man, but already near retirement age. His wife had died the year before, he told Joanne. He was lonely without her. Did Joanne know what it was like to be lonely? Yes, yes, she did. And so they sought solace with each other right there in the lab, and Joanne thought maybe she might even be a little bit in love with him. She imagined having a husband so many years her senior. She imagined being a faculty wife, the other faculty wives clucking over her, mother hens tending to their new chick. She knew in time that she would be a young widow, but she could always say, *I wouldn't have traded our days together for anything in the world.*

Many wisdoms are gleaned in girls' bathrooms, vital information is shared, hard lessons are learned, and it was in the girls' bathroom, the one down the hall from the chemistry labs, that Joanne Clarke overheard Melissa Greenberg say to Karen Elliot, "I can't believe it. That disgusting Professor Chase made a pass at me."

"Did he give you the story about the dead wife? About how lonely he is?"

"Yes!" Melissa Greenberg's pitch was high enough to shatter glass. "How did you know?"

"He tries that on everyone. Meanwhile, his wife works over in the admissions office."

Joanne Clarke remained locked in the stall in the bathroom until night fell.

Now Joanne refused to think about such things. This, this night was different. After behaving like a perfect gentleman, concluding each of their previous evenings together with a brief kiss, but on the lips, John Wosileski obviously both liked and respected her. Therefore, if things were to go in *that* direction, she might very well say yes.

John Wosileski was thinking about sex too. It was possible that tonight he could get lucky, and he felt a slight pressure in his groin at the prospect of a live woman. Because, he knew, Joanne Clarke lived with her father, if anything did happen, it would happen here, at John's place, and so in preparation, should the event come to pass, he brushed off the bits of debris and crumbs from the sheets, and he picked his dirty socks up from the floor.

~

Valentine Kessler came in through the back door and raced up the stairs to her bedroom, where she hid a book under her bed. No matter what the librarian said about not having to hide it, the librarian wasn't Jewish.

Then, easy as you please, Valentine joined her mother in the kitchen, where Miriam asked, "What was that about? The charge upstairs?"

"I had to go to the bathroom," Valentine said, which Miriam knew to be a lie. The upstairs bathroom had plumbing that reverberated throughout the house. When that toilet was flushed, the Sabatinis could hear it next door.

Later that evening, Valentine curled up on the couch with a bag of Cheez Doodles watching *Get Christie Love,* the adventures of a sassy undercover girl cop, on the television. In real life, Teresa Graves, the actress who played Christie Love, died under suspicious circumstances in a fire, but that was to happen far off in the future, in the next millennium.

With Valentine thusly engrossed, Miriam took the opportunity to snoop. You can't expect teenagers to consistently be honest, and what mother isn't nosy? It is a rare mother who doesn't snoop every now and then, and Miriam Kessler was no exception to the rule. The last time Valentine tried to sneak something past Miriam, it was one of those tube tops, a strip of elasticized cotton covered with sequins designed to barely conceal the boobs. "Over my dead body will you go out of the house with this on," Miriam had said, and Valentine had cried and sniveled about how all the girls were wearing them, but Miriam wasn't interested in what the other girls were wearing. So what was it this time? A micromini? Bikini underpants?

After finding nothing new in the closet or the chest of drawers, Miriam got down on the floor, no mean feat for her, and reached under the bed, where, alongside the box from Kleinman's, she found a book. On the spine was the white label displaying the Dewey decimal. A library book. *Well,* Miriam reasoned, *a library book, it's not pornography.* But still. *Saints? What could she want from saints?* Then Miriam opened the book to the table of contents, and she had to laugh. *Saint Valentine,* and Miriam was satisfied. Here was nothing more than a display of adolescent self-absorption. *Valentine.*

~

Valentine. Like the offspring of most young Jewish couples, now second- and even third-generation American, Ronald and Miriam Kessler's baby would be named in memory of a deceased loved one, but not exactly. You couldn't saddle an American kid with a moniker from the old country. So you compromised. A daughter named for *Bubbe* Hodle got called Holly or Honey. *Tante* Lippe would get remembered as Larry or Lisa. Children named for *Zeyde* Moshe were called Michael and Marla, and because it never occurred to Ronald or Miriam or anyone on either side of the families that Willy was spelled with a *W* and not a *V* as it was pronounced, *Villy,* the young couple—in memory of Ronald's *zeyde,* may he rest in peace, who had died the year before but, thank God, didn't suffer much—bandied about names such as Veronica, Vera, Vance, Valerie, and Victor.

Perhaps knowing that he would soon enough dishonor the family name, Ronald opted, on this occasion, to honor the patrimony. Besides, Ronald Kessler had adored this grandfather of his, *Zeyde* Willy, a small-time bookie.

According to Dr. Isaacson, Baby Vera or Vance was due to be born during the third week of January. By the end of the second week of February, with Miriam the size of Cleveland and about to rip her hair from her head, Dr. Isaacson induced labor. On February 14, Miriam and Ronald Kessler became the proud parents of a beautiful baby girl, and in an unimaginative gesture, but one of loving enthusiasm, they scrapped Vera and named her—what else?—Valentine.

That Valentine's Day was a Catholic feast day and not only a holiday by Hallmark was not of concern to the Kesslers. All that mattered to them was that their precious little girl was as sweet as the candy that came in a heart-shaped box covered with pink satin.

~

Sharing a large buttered popcorn, but each with their own Coke, in the fifth row from the back not quite dead center, Joanne Clarke and John Wosileski sat side by side, their eyes fixed on the screen, watching *Silent Movie*, which was supposedly a comedy.

Curiously enough, outside of the confines of school, John rarely found Joanne annoying. But what he didn't factor into the equation was Valentine. When there existed the possibility of feasting his gaze upon Valentine, Joanne was an irritation. Take away all but the most remote chance of that and Joanne Clarke wasn't so bad. Of course he didn't couch it in such terms, but at least some of John's pleasure with Joanne's company originated from the same place as his burgeoning desire to have sex with her; the place where absence is located, which is to say Joanne Clarke, as a person unique unto herself, was somewhat irrelevant.

His eyes were on the screen, but his focus was on strategy: how to get from point A, the movies, to point B, his bed. *Do you want to come in for a beer?* Too bad he had nothing to show her. No etchings. No tropical fish. Nothing in the latest stereo equipment. In fact, there was no stereo of any sort. *You want to watch television for a while?*

Joanne Clarke pressed her leg against his.

~

The vast majority of the people who came to the library required nothing more of Lucille Fiacco than to stamp the due date on whatever mystery novel or romance they were taking out that week. That, or to ask where the toilet was. For this she got a master's degree in library science?

But every day this week, that Valentine kid sought her out to ask advice, as if she were the oracle at Delphi, like she knew the answer to every frigging question on the planet, *Do you think a red sweater would look better with these pants?*, and to untangle the mysteries of the world, *If you don't actually blow on it, why do they call it a blow job?* Lucille's conversations with Valentine served to remind her that she was a highly knowledgeable person as well as a very attractive and stylish one and if she didn't have a date for New Year's Eve it was because those Bensonhurst *goombahs* were too thickheaded to recognize her qualities. Lucille Fiacco told herself that she really needed to start associating with a finer caliber of persons.

~

That Valentine did not have a date for New Year's Eve was one thing, but her claim that she wasn't invited to a party, that was a matter for concern. She'd always had friends. She'd always been invited to parties. "*No one* is having a party?" Miriam asked her for the third time.

"No one that I know of," Valentine said.

Nor did it escape Miriam's attention that not once all week, the entire Christmas vacation, did the phone ring for Valentine. As nonchalantly as it is possible for a mother who is prying, Miriam asked, "So what's Beth been up to?"

"I don't know," Valentine said. "Off with her boyfriend, I guess."

Miriam then offered their house if Valentine wanted to invite some friends over for a little get-together.

"No thanks," Valentine said. "Really, Ma. I don't want to do anything. It's not a big deal."

Miriam wasn't sure how to react to her daughter's display of emotional maturity. Yes, emotional maturity was one way of looking at it, if you happened to be the sort of person who found the silver lining in every cloud. If Miriam, at fifteen, hadn't had plans for New Year's Eve, she would have cried for a week. But this display of emotional maturity could just as easily be yet another whorl in a pattern of aberration. Would a normal teenager be so blasé about staying home alone on New Year's Eve?

~

For the first time in either of their lives, John Wosileski and Joanne Clarke did not spend New Year's Eve in cruel isolation. At John's apartment they met for an aperitif of Asti Spumante, which was like champagne but nowhere near as expensive. John Wosileski was agog to discover that people actually drank something as costly as the bottle of Moët he'd looked at. John didn't have anything like champagne glasses, or wineglasses either, but he, in fact, did have a pair of brandy snifters which had been left in the apartment by the previous tenant, who'd forgotten to pack up the contents of the far left kitchen area cabinet. There John had found the two snifters, an unopened box of Minute rice, and a can of mushroom gravy. He was proud of the snifters. He thought they were sophisticated. He filled each of them nearly to the brim with sparkling wine and passed one to Joanne.

She took a few sips and he took a few sips and then they kissed, which isn't anything to dwell on. Later they would go to a Chinese restaurant on Mott Street in the city.

Miriam Kessler was going to a party at Edith Zuckerman's house around the corner. It was a tradition, Edith's party. Every year, for as long as anyone could remember, Edith and Stan made a New Year's Eve party, and every year, Miriam went. This night she squeezed into a slimming black dress and she put on her good pearls and patent-leather pumps bought only weeks before but already they were too narrow for the plumpness of her feet.

From her window Valentine, already in her pajamas, watched Miriam as she made her way down the street, walking as if her feet hurt. As soon as her mother was beyond her line of vision, Valentine reached around and under her bed for *Lives of the Saints.* With a package of Oreo cookies by her side, she opened the book to the chapter about Perpetua stripped naked and thrown to a mad bull. Valentine read while she licked the vanilla icing from the chocolate wafers.

~

In Edith Zuckerman's living room, Miriam parked herself in a chair near the buffet table, and thought to herself that Edith could be a professional caterer. Such a spread—miniature quiche lorraines, four kinds of meatballs in chafing dishes to keep them hot, olives which Edith stuffed herself with cream cheese and pimiento, macaroni salad, smoked salmon on bite-sized triangles of toast—Edith outdid herself. Well, knock wood, her husband, he'd had a good year.

~

As is customary in Chinese restaurants, John and Joanne ordered dishes to share: scallion pancakes, dumplings, shrimp with lobster sauce, and moo shu pork. A feast.

They, along with everyone else at Ho Fat's, wore cone-shaped paper hats on their heads. Noisemakers were set on the table alongside the silverware, and even though it was well before midnight, it was as if the room were quivering in anticipation of the hour, that brief moment of time when happiness is obligatory. Joanne Clarke was considering her own happiness, how her future seemed like a red balloon filled with helium, bright and light, and as long as you hold on tight, you can keep it from floating away. John Wosileski was also contemplating happiness. He wondered if this was indeed what he was feeling, and if so, was it as good as it got? Was this it?

~

At twenty minutes before midnight, Miriam helped herself to a few more of the olives and then, without anyone noticing, she got her coat from the bedroom and slipped out the back door. The air was cold. Sharp. Miriam could see her breath, and a fine layer of frost dusted the sidewalk and the bare branches of the trees.

Once home, after hanging up her coat in the hall closet and taking off her shoes—her feet were killing her in those shoes—Miriam went upstairs and looked in on Valentine, who was asleep.

Miriam considered waking her daughter so that together they could welcome in the new year. She considered it, but did not because in the final analysis, Miriam could not face the pretense of joy.

For Valentine's sake, and her own too, Miriam made it a point to reek of indifference as if it were a perfume mist. *A good sport, tough as nails, a brick, a trooper* are words The Girls used in reference to Miriam, in reference to *the lousy hand she was dealt in life and yet, she enjoys the game nonetheless. You got to admire her.* Only when she was alone could Miriam indulge in the truth.

Alone with herself, Miriam could admit that she feared rejection more than she feared being fat, and that she feared the unknown more than she feared being lonely.

On the cusp of the new year, standing alone in the dark hallway between her daughter's bedroom and her own, Miriam could admit that she lived off romantic recollections that probably weren't even accurate.

The clock struck midnight, and the revelers at Ho Fat's erupted into a public exclamation of merriment and sentimentality. A party of ten seated around a circular table sang "Auld Lang Syne." John Wosileski and Joanne Clarke, each leaning in to the other, kissed; a kiss long enough and deep enough that John Wosileski's eyes closed, and he did not open them until the vision of Valentine Kessler faded away.

~

The truth was: What could a new year promise Miriam? If anything was different, in this year after year after year, it was that by now, over time, she had given up on herself entirely, as if hope for herself were birdseed that had sifted out through a hole in her pocket.

All hope was now pinned on Valentine. Miriam meant well. No one could dare say otherwise, but to pin her hopes on her daughter was to deny Valentine hopes of her own. It was to be unaware there was a possibility, however small, that perhaps Valentine did not want a college diploma from a good school, a respectable career she could return to after the children are grown, a husband who loves her, who worships the ground she walks on, a *mensch*. Those were Miriam's dreams and was it too much to ask for? Ordinary dreams. No special privileges. Just a little happiness.

Miriam was blissfully unaware of what was to transpire in this new year. If she had known, well, then and there you might as well have given her a knife and let her cut her heart out.

Eight

It was that darkest of hours, no sign of the dawn that would come within a matter of minutes, when the thirty or so students gathered on the sidewalk in front of Canarsie High School before getting on the bus that would transport them to Hunter Mountain, which was early into the Catskill Mountains. Despite the boast of the longest chairlift in the Catskills (over one mile long!)—and big whoop to that because long is not high, the Catskills are hardly the Alps—Hunter isn't much of a mountain. To ski Hunter is not an ultimate experience, but it was the ski area nearest to Brooklyn, and even then it was three hours to get there. The few students who'd had skiing experience—Sheila Rosen in particular, with the thicket of lift tickets stapled to the zipper on her jacket—they, the experts, huddled together and compared notes on other mountains, better mountains, mountains of significant proportions, but most of the students of the Canarsie High School Ski Club had never skied before. The inferiority of this slope was irrelevant to them.

~

As these things often are, the rental shack was built to resemble a Swiss chalet, and those without their own gear waited to be fitted for rented boots and bindings, for skis and poles. Despite having no equipment of her own, Valentine Kessler—head to toe in pink—did not queue up for boots and skis. Instead, she made straight for the lodge, which wasn't a lodge in the traditional sense. No overnight accommodations were offered, but it was a pavilion with high ceilings. One wall, made entirely of glass, offered a view of the mountain. Chairs and tables were placed around a fireplace made of stone set into the far wall. With her back to the mountain view, Valentine sat as if she were posed for a portrait: *Girl in Pink by the Fire;* a vision to still any man's heart. She ordered a hot chocolate. Valentine gave no indication that she had any intentions whatever of hitting the slopes. She could've been sitting in a lodge in the Negev desert for all advantage she took from the area.

While the other first-timers were flopping along the bunny trail, Valentine idly flipped through the most recent issue of *Seventeen,* the one magazine to which she subscribed and read religiously.

~

This day at Hunter Mountain was a gift, and John Wosileski was having fun. That might not sound like much, having fun, but it was something wondrous.

~

By noontime, a half-dozen members of the Canarsie High School Ski Club, girls all, having concluded that this was not the sport for them, *too cold, too wet, harder than it looks, bore-ing, that frigging sucked,* joined Valentine in the warmth of the lodge. They took turns looking at Valentine's *Seventeen* magazine. They ate frankfurters and french fries and donuts. Cathy DiChiaro suggested to Valentine that she highlight her hair. "Just a few blond streaks. That would look so gorgeous on you."

"Really?" Valentine was showing herself to be as fluffy-minded as the best of them. "You think so?" she asked, and the others were wild with enthusiasm for the idea.

Each slice of pineapple on the top of the upside-down cake was shaded with its own individual paper umbrella. Normally, when baking, Miriam, like all The Girls, stuck to her mother's and grandmothers' recipes, which meant strudels and poppy-seed cakes and marble loaves. They didn't have pineapples in Poland, so who knew from a pineapple cake? Miriam got the recipe from *Woman's Day* magazine. Miriam had baked the pineapple upside-down cake in Sunny Shapiro's honor, and The Girls clapped their hands at the sight of it, except for Sunny, who was too choked up to clap. Sunny Shapiro and her husband Mel were going on a second honeymoon. To Hawaii. The kids were going to stay with Sunny's parents in Flatbush. Miriam was happy for her friend, really she was. Look, she baked a cake and the pineapple upside-down was no child's play, but while tears of joy made their way along the crevices of Sunny's raisin face the way rainwater travels a brook, Miriam turned to the window, to the cold gray afternoon, and cried on the inside, just a little bit, for herself, for the second honeymoon she would never have. *Oh Ronald.*

John Wosileski zigged and zagged and whooshed down Hunter East to reach the end only to begin again. Shortly after midday, he boarded the Hunter West chairlift for the run known, in some circles, as Daredevil Dan, Hunter Mountain's most perilous trail. His stomach grumbled, but John disregarded the call to lunch, as if he could ski for days with no more sustenance than the clean cold mountain air. Poised at the summit, he took a few deep breaths and surveyed the view. The sun, high in the sky, cast a golden glint on the snow and broke through the thicket of fir trees on either side of him. John pushed off, and as he cut a clean path between the trees, he thought he saw a pair of birds, one yellow and the other the colors of a peach, perched on an upper branch of a blue spruce, but that would've been impossible. No doubt it was the glare from the sun on the snow and the ice and his own sweet delight teasing the eye, and leaning forward to pick up speed, he left great clouds of powdery snow in his wake.

~

At the day's end, when the sun was red and paused between the trees, Mr. Ornstein came to collect the girls, and if Valentine was terribly disappointed that Mr. Wosileski never did show up to the lodge for lunch or a hot chocolate, she gave no indication of it. "Everybody up and out," Mr. Ornstein said. "Single file into the bus. No pushing. No shoving."

Although Valentine exited the Lodge as part of a group, once in the parking lot she drifted off, away from the others. On this darker side of the mountain, the snow appeared indigo and violet, the way it sometimes does in oil paintings when the artist goes through a phase and does everything in shades of blue. Valentine craned her neck, her eyes roving the line of her classmates waiting to board the bus. Then, quick as a wink, Valentine took a place in the chain, right behind Mr. Wosileski.

~

John Wosileski took the first-row window seat on the right side of the bus, and when Valentine Kessler settled herself into the seat beside him, his heart bolted with a thud like a racehorse out of the starting gate and kept on racing. Valentine Kessler. She smiled at him, and John Wosileski felt queasy and thrilled.

Not yet having depleted their energy supply, rather invigorated by the activity of the day, as if adolescent energy thrived on itself, ingesting itself to grow larger and stronger, some kind of mutant creature, the busload of teenagers shouted and slapped at one another's heads, teasing, joking. No one paid the least bit of attention to the two people who sat quietly in the first row of the right side of the bus.

Words were forming on the tip of John Wosileski's tongue like a blister, and the words burned there until John blurted out, "I once saw a frozen waterfall. Frozen solid," he said. "In midflow." This, having seen a frozen waterfall while taking what he thought might be a shortcut through a wooded area from his aunt and uncle's house to the convenience store, was something that he had never before told another living soul. What he didn't say was how the sight of it, the surprise of coming upon such a thing, made his heart expand with a kind of grief, and how it seemed to him that he was seeing something no living person was supposed to see. Nor did he mention that he mentioned it now only because, she, Valentine, as she sat there, frozen too in a way, was also a thing of unspeakable beauty.

"Really?" Valentine said. "A frozen waterfall. That's weird."

Although Valentine pronounced *weird* without the *r*, as *weid*, there was no mistaking it for another word. Such a response—that's weird—caused John to dearly wish he could rewind time, just a minute, and take back his words. Not so much because he regretted sharing a secret with Valentine, but because he didn't want her to think anything connected with him was weird. He so very much wanted her to like him.

It took another bout of silence for John to rev up his nerve again to ask, "So, did you have fun today?"

"No, not really."

Did every exchange with this girl have to lead to regret? Couldn't she go easy on him just once? But Valentine was like her mother in that way; more often than not, she told the truth.

"You didn't enjoy skiing?" he asked.

In the seats behind them, Max Schumer and Paul Taglio played Monkey in the Middle with Lisa Hochstater's hat. Valentine looked back at the shenanigans and then she said, "I didn't enjoy it or not enjoy it. I didn't do it."

"You didn't ski? You came all the way here and you didn't ski? Why not?"

Valentine scrunched up her nose, her perfect nose, one that had, on three separate occasions, caused strange women, women she didn't know from a hole in the wall, to stop her, twice on the street and once at the mall, to ask her, "Do you mind my asking? Who did your nose?" And even with that nose—a nose that could have been sculpted by the world's leading plastic surgeon—all scrunched up, Valentine Kessler's face was angelic. "I'm not very good at sports," she said. "And I don't like being out of doors in cold weather."

So why in the world, then, did she get herself up before dawn, shell out thirty-five dollars, and endure a long bus ride if she had no intention of skiing? Why, indeed? What else could it be other than some boy, a crush on some boy, yes, that had to be it, and John shifted in his seat to see who it was across the aisle, who it was that Valentine wanted to be near, and there was Vincent Caputo. It made sense, but still, it was horrible.

Vincent Caputo was well aware of Valentine Kessler in the seat across the aisle. How could you not be aware of it when a doll like Valentine Kessler was in close proximity? And tempting as it was to take advantage of the nearness of her, he had a another fish on the fire. You can't be wasting time on small hope when a certainty is at hand; the certainty in the person of Alison George, who the following year would have her nose done, seated on his other side. Vincent was banking on Alison to give him a hand job during the trip home. To this end, he took off his ski jacket and placed it over his lap. Shifting in his seat, Vincent turned his back on Valentine. Poor Valentine stuck in the seat next to that queer teacher.

Twilight descended into a night sky, and the interior of the bus went dark except for the faint beams of light, eerie yellow and particles of dust free-floating, from the small bulbs overhead. Exhaustion too won out, and everyone settled down. Some of students even fell asleep, while others whispered softly with their seatmates. Vincent Caputo's voice rustled like curtains, barely audible, and smooth as silk. "Come on. No one will see. Please, Alison. For me."

Alison, a slut in her own right, didn't need much convincing. Under the cover of his jacket, she stroked Vincent, and he was feeling *so good, yeah, oh baby like that, yeah,* until he glanced around and there was Valentine Kessler smiling at him, the sweetest frigging smile he ever saw, a smile that made Vincent think of someone who talks to birds, and Vincent Caputo lost his erection.

"What happened?" Alison asked. "What's wrong?"

"Nothing," Vincent said. "Nothing's wrong. Forget it. Just leave me alone, okay?"

~

John Wosileski fixed his gaze into the heartache of that overhead light, that insignificant yellow beam under which the dust particles seemed to defy gravity, and Valentine closed her eyes. Leaning ever so slightly toward him, she let go with a deep sigh, a sigh as if, after having wandered for ages, she'd found her way home. Then her head came to rest on his shoulder.

Who can control where your head lolls while you sleep? But was she sleeping? Or only pretending to be in a downy slumber? Was she indeed wide-awake? Did she not lose so much as a blink of the pleasure afforded by the simple act of one person leaning into another?

As for John Wosileski, he went stiff. Stiff as a board. Stiff as a rod. Stiff as a pole. All of it. Stiff with fear. Stiff with the pang and stiff with the tingle and stiff with an erection that towered with desire and throbbed and threatened to explode Vesuvian-style. John wished he'd had the foresight to put his jacket over his lap instead of putting it in the overhead rack, where now he couldn't get at it without disturbing the sleeping beauty, and what would happen if Valentine woke and saw the bulge in his pants, ski pants made of material that stretched and moved when you did? So John Wosileski sat perfectly still until passion, as it so often does, turned to pain.

Miriam lowered the flame under the soup, a thick vegetable soup—practically a stew, you could eat it with a fork—and let it simmer. In the oven she had a nice chicken and two Idaho potatoes warming. She looked up at the clock on the wall. Valentine would be home any minute, and Miriam was glad of that. For reasons unknown or maybe it was because Sunny Shapiro's husband adored her to such a degree as to take her on a second honeymoon, whatever it was, Miriam was feeling very emotional. Not for one second did Miriam begrudge her friend the happiness. For herself, Miriam was a little down in the dumps. But hungry as she was, she would wait for Valentine to have dinner.

The bus pulled up in front of Canarsie High School, and Valentine woke or feigned waking up, did a lithe little stretch, and John Wosileski covered his lap with his hands. Reaching to the overhead rack for her jacket, she said, "Hey, Mr. Wosileski. I'll see you around sometime, okay?" Behind the others, she stepped off the bus, leaving John Wosileski alone with his agony and his hard-on and the sweet scent of Valentine, which had filled his nostrils as if he'd been in a rose garden instead of on a bus.

Before she would eat, Valentine insisted on changing her clothes. "I'm too hot in this." With her tongue hanging out, she tugged at the neck of the sweater as if it were choking her. Ah, the drama of youth.

"Make it fast," Miriam said. "You don't want the chicken to dry out."

In the privacy of her bedroom, Valentine undressed, neatly folding the pink ski jacket, layering a piece of tissue paper between it and the pink sweater. Another sheet of paper went over the pink ski pants. The pink cap and mittens she wrapped as if they were a gift, and the way a bride puts away her wedding dress and veil, something that will never be worn again but must be kept pristine, Valentine put her ski outfit into a drawer she'd emptied as if for that purpose, as if it were a keepsake box.

Nine

During the week which began with the Purification of the Blessed Virgin Mary on the second day of February, the wind bit and the remnants of the last snow looked more like charcoal briquettes, fist-sized and sooty black, and everybody was good and goddamn sick of winter. Spirits were generally low, but Valentine's Day would be a reprieve, the bright spot in an otherwise bleak month.

Valentine's Day was a highly respected holiday in this part of Brooklyn. To make the most of it, the shops along the avenue were festooned with paper cutouts of red hearts and metallic gold Cupids. Children were eyeing greedily the boxes of candy displayed at Woolworth's; teenage girls were pressing their noses to the window of Harry's House of Gold and Other Fine Jewelry, and they clustered together to read aloud the Valentine's Day cards at the stationery shop. And on this Valentine's Day coming, Valentine Kessler would turn sixteen. Sweet Sixteen was a milestone, a very big deal. The commemorative party was to be a memorable event of the sort that produces a photo album, and a scrapbook, and a bouquet made from the ribbons and bows from the plentiful gifts.

∾

Joanne Clarke found herself browsing at a jewelry store—not at Harry's, which was too close to the school and therefore risky because suppose someone, another teacher or, worse yet, a student, saw her, so she went to Kretchfeld's Jewel Box—just to look. It was highly unlikely that John would give her a diamond, an engagement ring, for Valentine's Day, but it wasn't impossible. They'd been dating for nearly two full months. Much of their free time was spent together, weekends and dinners during the week, and not that it was anybody's business but yes, they been doing *it* regularly. To get engaged after seven weeks would be something to tell their children. *We just knew we were right for each other.*

∾

John Wosileski had been thinking along the lines of flowers or a box of chocolates. One or the other until a week or so before the big day itself. Over dinner that she cooked for him—a steak, very fancy, and mashed potatoes which came from flakes in a box but he liked them—at his place—they always went to his place because of her father, who, John had gathered, was sick or maybe crippled and never went out—Joanne swallowed a piece of the steak and then she blushed, which did not become her. "Are you okay?" John feared that perhaps the meat had lodged in her windpipe. She was that kind of red.

"I'm fine," she said, and then in an offhand manner, she made mention, "I heard that Paul Martinelli is buying Katie O'Brien an engagement ring. For Valentine's Day." Paul Martinelli and Katie O'Brien were also teachers at Canarsie High School—chemistry and Spanish respectively. That Paul and Katie were an item was common knowledge around school, but not so about John and Joanne. Joanne kept it secret because what if it didn't work out? Then she would be publicly humiliated. John told no one because he lacked the desire to utter the beloved's name that usually accompanies romance. He wasn't bubbling over, effusive, giddy from the lightness of love. They were dating. That was it. Besides, whom would he have told?

He didn't have friends. He didn't have much of a family. He was alone, and he would always be alone if he didn't do something radical to alter his destiny. So why not marry Joanne Clarke? He could have done worse. She was nice to him. She baked him brownies and cookies and she did have that knockout body. He liked having sex with her. Not that he had much to compare it to. Two other girls in college, and one wasn't really a girl but a local woman, in her twenties, and he had to pay her money. So why not marry Joanne Clarke? With both their salaries combined, they could live comfortably. Maybe even get themselves a little house of their own. And someday they could have a family. He could be a father with children who loved him. In that instant, he decided he would do it. He would get Joanne Clarke an engagement ring for Valentine's Day, and the idea made him smile and he felt warm and kind of fluttery, in a good way.

In this part of Brooklyn, at this time, some of the girls had Sweet Sixteen parties to rival their brothers' bar mitzvahs. Catered affairs in rented halls; roast-beef dinners and dance bands.

That wasn't what Miriam had been proposing. "But a party of some sort," she said.

"Really, Ma. I don't want to make a big deal of it."

"But it is a big deal," Miriam argued. "It's a very special birthday." Miriam was devastated. She had ideas, plans, themes. She never dreamed that Valentine would not want a Sweet Sixteen party. With the thought of making the party a luau, she had Sunny Shapiro bring back three dozen paper leis from Hawaii. "But it should be a day to look back on."

"It will be," Valentine promised her mother. "I just don't want a party."

What was up with this kid? First she wanted almost nothing for Hanukkah. Now she didn't want a Sweet Sixteen party. Moreover, it had not escaped Miriam's attention that, as of late, Valentine no longer used the telephone. Up until a few months ago, you'd have thought that the phone was a fifth extremity, that the kid had two legs, two arms, and a phone. Now, when the phone rang, ten times out of ten it was for Miriam. "What's going on with you and Beth?" Miriam opted for an Ockam's-razor type of explanation; the least complicated reasoning for Valentine's solitude and who could fault a mother for grabbing hold for dear life of the easy, the simple, the obvious when dealing with a teenager daughter? "What happened between you two?"

"Nothing happened. She's got a boyfriend, and she's with him most of the time."

Miriam reached over and smoothed her daughter's hair, a gesture of reassurance, of promise, and Valentine said, "There is something I want for my birthday. I want highlights. You know, some streaks of blond in my hair. Maybe I could have that done for my gift."

"You have beautiful hair," Miriam said. "I don't know why you'd want to do anything to it, but if that's what you want, then that's what you want. I'll make an appointment for you with the girl I go to." Despite that Miriam spoke the truth in regard to the issue of Valentine's hair, she was nonetheless pleased by the request. Vanity was normal and Valentine's desire to put blond streaks in her hair was evidence that fundamentally all was right with the world.

Between the preparations for Valentine's Day and the big day itself came Ash Wednesday. That day at school, the Catholic kids wore the smudge of ash on their foreheads as if they were marked for something as magnificent as martyrdom. "It's kind of beautiful, isn't it?" Valentine asked Beth. They were on the lunch line, cafeteria trays sliding along the rail. "What?" Beth reached for a cup of chocolate pudding. "The *schmutz* on their faces? They look dirty."

"But it's symbolic or something." Valentine took two brownies.

"Symbolic of what?" Beth asked, and Valentine said, "How should I know? I just think it looks kind of hot. That's all."

"Hot." Beth shook her head, and concluded that her days as Valentine's friend were numbered.

Miriam was hosting the game that afternoon, and no sooner did they get set up, before any of them even had a chance to assess the tiles they'd drawn, than Judy Weinstein touched on a raw nerve. "Isn't Valentine having her Sweet Sixteen? What are you doing about the party?" she asked Miriam.

"Did she like the idea of the luau because I've got all kinds of suggestions for that." Sunny Shapiro was now the authority on all things tropical.

"Valentine doesn't want a party," Miriam said.

"My sister's kid just turned sixteen, my niece Lisa. She didn't want a party either." Edith Zuckerman cuddled with her mink as if the notion of not wanting a party were chilling. "She's going through that homely stage, the kid. So boys are a sensitive issue right now. No boys. No party," Edith explained. "Instead, she invited three of her girlfriends for a day in the city. My sister got them tickets for a show, a matinee. They had lunch in a nice restaurant. They spent an hour in Bloomingdale's. They had a ball. Maybe Valentine would want something like that."

"Maybe," Miriam said, but she was not optimistic. "Two Dragon." Lest The Girls think there was something wrong with her daughter, Miriam let them know, "She wants to have blond streaks done in her hair. So that will be part of her present."

"Sounds like there's a boy on the horizon." Judy Weinstein took three tiles from the center. "Could be she has a date?"

"Five Bam," said Edith Zuckerman.

~

At the end of the school day, much to her chagrin, Beth Sandler found Valentine waiting by her locker. Beth didn't hate Valentine or anything so extreme as that. It's just that Beth was ultraorthodox when it came to normal, as if only the conventional could be trusted. And also by now she was pretty much best friends with Marcia Finkelstein. But it wouldn't kill Beth to walk home with Valentine, and so she did, and as long as they were walking home together, they had to talk about something and a preengagement ring was first and foremost and mostly the only thing on Beth's mind. Was Joey Rappaport going to give her a preengagement ring as a token of his love on this Valentine's Day? It had slipped from Beth's mind entirely that Valentine's Day would also be Valentine's sixteenth birthday. "So what do you think?" she asked Valentine. "An opal? Or maybe a garnet?"

"Don't get your hopes up. You're not going to get a ring," Valentine said.

"What makes you so sure?" Beth asked.

"You just got the locket for Hanukkah. You're rushing things."

"Well, maybe you're just jealous," Beth said, to which Valentine said, "Yeah, maybe I am."

Beth was flabbergasted by this admission. No one knows what to do with the truth. It ends up being embarrassing, so it's best to ignore it. "You're probably right," Beth said. "About the ring. It's too soon to get preengaged. Maybe he'll get me an S-chain bracelet." With that settled, the girls turned the corner and stood on the sidewalk in front of the Kessler house. "You want to come in for a while?" Valentine asked. "My mother bought a cheesecake yesterday. From Junior's."

Because Joey Rappaport was working at his father's real estate office that afternoon and Marcia Finkelstein had to visit her grandmother in the hospital, Beth didn't have anything better to do. Besides, who could say no to a slice of cheesecake from Junior's?

No one could say no to a slice of cheesecake from Junior's. By the time Valentine and Beth got to it, the cheesecake was no more. Miriam and The Girls had devoured it down to the last morsel. "I'm sorry," Miriam said. "We couldn't resist. There's a Pepperidge Farm cake in the fridge. Five Flower. Angel food. You know, chocolate *chawk-lit,* with the white icing."

Valentine cut two hefty slices of cake and poured two glasses of

Diet Pepsi. Except for the clinks and tinks of forks against plates and glasses set down after drinking, Beth and Valentine ate and drank beneath the suffocating, dank blanket of silence, all the while Beth wishing she were hanging out with Joey now or Marcia Finkelstein or even to be at home with her mother would be better than this.

~

John Wosileski hurried along the few blocks to the Church of the Holy Family, which was not his family parish. There he knelt before the priest and received the ashes, not so much in the spirit in which they were intended—*thou art dust and unto dust shalt thou return*—but rather as if they were a public penance. For Lent, he vowed he would give up all thoughts of Valentine Kessler and he would refrain from self-pleasure. He vowed to give up both as if they were unrelated.

~

Upon leaving the Kesslers' house, Beth Sandler had to face reality as she saw it: Valentine was simply no longer normal. But really, who could live up to Beth's rigid standard of what normal should be? The year before she'd cast out Randi Rubin from her crowd for wearing two different-colored socks. One red sock and one black sock. "It wasn't an accident. Like she got dressed in the dark and didn't see what she was doing. She did it on purpose. I'm sorry. That is too weird." Beth justified that banishment, and this one too. *Ashes? Hot? Not normal.*

~

Alone in her bedroom Valentine opened the window all the way, the rush of cold air giving her goose bumps, and lit the cigarette that earlier in the day she'd bummed from Alison George. "Since when do you smoke?" Alison had asked.

"I just want to try it," Valentine explained, and when Alison handed her a book of matches too, Valentine said, "Later. I'm going to try it later," and she slipped the cigarette into her coat pocket.

Leaning out the window so that her bedroom wouldn't smell from the smoke, Valentine took a few puffs of the cigarette, just enough to produce a quarter of an inch of ash, which she tapped into a saucer. After extinguishing the cigarette and flushing the remains of it down the toilet, she stood before her mirror and wiped a smudge of ash onto her forehead. Valentine Kessler was not the first Jewish girl, nor would she ever be the last, to put a thumbprint of soot on her forehead on Ash Wednesday. This seemingly blasphemous act is usually nothing more than curiosity coupled with the vague eroticism of sackcloth and ashes; an eroticism which seemed to have affected Valentine. Her nipples hardened and from there she engaged in an interlude of touching herself, the climax to which, as it had thus far all along, remained elusive.

She washed her hands and her face before going downstairs, so that the ash on her forehead was yet one more thing her mother did not see.

~

On his way home from church, John Wosileski boldly entered Harry's House of Gold and Other Fine Jewelry, which Harry was keeping open until nine every night during the week before Valentine's Day, which was his busiest week of the year. John stood at the showcase counter while Harry, to best contrast the diamond's sparkle, placed a ring on a black velvet pad. "Will you look at that,"

Harry said. "Like a star in the night sky." If truth be told, Harry's stones were flawed but so what because no one in this part of Brooklyn was buying a top quality rock anyway. Even this one he was showing, a quarter of a carat with more imperfections than man himself, would be out of this *schlemiel's* price range.

So it was no surprise to Harry when John peeked at the white sticker fixed to the band and said, "That's a little steep. Do you have one that isn't so expensive."

"Of course," Harry said, and he brought out a tray of rings, the whole lot of them didn't total a carat. Chips and dust these were. Crap. "These are all quite reasonably priced," Harry said, and to show just how reasonably priced they were, he held out the sticker, price side up.

~

Not so many blocks away, Joanne Clarke stood at the kitchen counter dipping fish filets into a batter of egg and bread crumbs. On the stove, the oil in the skillet was beginning to sizzle, and in the living room, pitch dark but for the blue light of the television, her father, dozing in his armchair, began to snore. Joanne wondered how much more of this life she could take, and she prayed to God, not really so much to God Himself because Joanne Clarke quit believing in God when her mother died an agonizing and putrid death from breast cancer when Joanne was twelve, but more of a *pro forma* plea to the fates to push John Wosileski to ask for her hand in marriage, to save her from being an old maid, a bitter spinster schoolteacher caring for a senile father, who sooner or later would have to be put in a home anyway.

~

Under the partial darkness of dusk, the streetlights came on as John Wosileski walked home from Harry's House of Gold and Other Fine Jewelry. The diamond ring, in a red velveteen box, was clutched in his hand, which was snuggled in his ski jacket pocket. Maybe it was the twilight, sorrowful and lovely at once, which was responsible for his melancholy, the vague sense of despair. This should have been a time for joy in John Wosileski's otherwise predominantly desolate life. He was going to propose marriage to Joanne Clarke, a good woman who will make a fine wife and don't forget, her figure was nothing to sneeze at either. Soon he would no longer come home to an empty apartment, drafty and dark, to turn on the television simply to feel less alone. And he thought of this as he stepped inside his drab abode, snapped on the light, not an overhead light, but a lamp on an end table. The sixty-watt bulb cast a faint yellow candescence which was hardly enough to brighten the room.

Miriam Kessler was cleaning up after the her mah-jongg game. She carried the dishes to the kitchen sink, emptied the ashtray—telltale coral colored lipstick on nearly all the butts, Sunny Shapiro was smoking like a chimney—and she was folding up the card table when Valentine snuck up behind her mother, practically giving her a heart attack. "Ma," Valentine asked, "where's the phone book?"

"The White Pages? Or the Yellow?"

"White," Valentine said.

"Hall closet," Miriam told her. "Second shelf on the left side."

At the kitchen table, Valentine flipped open the telephone book, running her finger down the columns. Miriam, standing at the sink, turned on the faucet and took a sponge to a cake plate.

Having copied out an address and phone number, Valentine folded the piece of loose-leaf paper into fours and then eights before tucking it into the zippered compartment in her pocketbook.

The cake plate was one from Miriam's set of good dishes. Royal Dalton china, which was a wedding gift from her parents. Miriam soaped the plate and worked the sponge in concentric circles and even when it was very, very clean she continued washing it as if the motion were involuntary when the plate slipped from her grasp and broke on the floor.

Miriam bent down to pick up the pieces, and grunted from the effort, which prompted Valentine to rush over. "I got it, Ma. I got it." While Miriam went to get the broom, Valentine picked up the larger shards and dropped them in the trash. Turning back, she was face-to-face with her mother, who had the broom in one hand, the dustpan in the other, and two fat tears, having left wet streaks on her cheeks the way snails leave a trail of sludge, now hung in the balance before she wiped them away.

"Hey, Ma. Come on. It's only a plate."

Only a plate. But a plate which was part of the set which Miriam had planned to pass along, intact, to Valentine on her wedding day. But that's one of the problems with plans: the unforeseen making a mess of it all.

In this year, as it happened, Valentine's Day fell on a Saturday, which was a boon for the restaurant business. You'd think each and every couple in all of Brooklyn would be dining out that night, the way reservations were required, even at Dominick's Pizzeria. Big Dom was advertising a price-fixed extra-large heart-shaped pie with two soft drinks of your choice for $7.95. Not that Beth Sandler was the sort of girl to be content with pizza on Valentine's Day, heart-shaped or not. Forget that. Joey Rappaport had reservations for Chez Toulouse, which was a French restaurant. Romantic. And expensive.

For Valentine's Day John Wosileski was going to take Joanne Clarke to Ho Fat's on Mott Street in the city; a return engagement to the place where they celebrated New Year's Eve, which was a demonstrably romantic-type gesture on his part. Ho Fat's was destined now to become *their* place.

They'd take the train to the city—the LL to Fourteenth Street and transfer for the D to Grand Street—to Chinatown, and once at Ho Fat's, he'd say, "Happy Valentine's Day," as if this, dinner at *their* place, were his gift to her. Wonton soup, egg rolls, scallion pancakes, moo shu pork, and then when the bill came weighted down beneath a pair of fortune cookies, he'd reach into his pocket as if to pay, but instead of his wallet, he'd take out the velveteen box and place it on the plate alongside her other fortune.

That was his plan.

And it was a good plan, and he was satisfied with all of it except for the melancholy that came over him at seemingly random intervals, which he chalked up to a case of the jitters.

~

All Joanne Clarke knew of John's plans was that they were going to meet on Valentine's Day at six-thirty, at the token booth at the Glenwood Road subway, and that they would be going out for dinner. Somewhere special.

That morning, Valentine's Day, Joanne Clarke was at the King's County Mall when the doors opened. She had her heart set on buying herself a red dress because this was the first Valentine's Day ever that she had herself a honey who was taking her out for a Valentine's Day dinner. She wanted to wear something to suit the occasion.

After she tried on several dresses, all of which looked cheap in her opinion, the saleswoman brought her one more. A soft red, more like a dark pink, sleeveless gabardine knit. It was a nice dress. Very nice, but how much? Joanne snuck a peek at the price tag. Although it was more than she'd intended to spend, she nonetheless tried it on, and wouldn't you know, it was like it was made for her. She stepped out of the dressing room for the saleswoman's take, which was, "Stunning. Absolutely stunning. Like it was made for you."

And for the first time in her life, Joanne Clarke asked herself, *Why the hell not?* Why not treat herself to something special? And so she did, and as long as she had done one nice thing for herself, why not do another? And another? The idea of such frivolity made her giddy.

Such frivolity came in the form of new shoes—black patent leather, square-toed, and that fashionable chunky heel—to go with the new red dress, and then—all caution to the wind—Joanne found herself seated on a stool at the Estée Lauder counter in Macy's, where a Puerto Rican woman applied makeup to her face. "This"—the woman held up a tube of something—"this is like the miracle. This will smooth out the skin tone like you wouldn't believe. Now close your eyes," she instructed, not as precursor to a surprise—but to apply a glittery mauve eye shadow.

~

Reclining in the bathtub, Valentine held her nose and slid back and under the water, emerging seconds later with her hair wet for washing. With her left hand, she squeezed a dollop of Clairol Herbal Essence into the open palm of her right hand, where she looked it at for a while, maybe a full minute, as if she were expecting to discover a revelation in the green globule of shampoo. Then she washed her newly highlighted hair.

~

Miriam was over at the Weinsteins'; Judy's husband, Artie, worked on Saturdays. Artie had a dry-cleaning establishment and Saturday was the busiest day of his week. On Saturdays, he never got home before seven. He worked like a dog, that Artie, and a nicer guy you could never meet and so what if he was hirsute like a monkey.

To those who would judge them for playing mah-jongg on the Sabbath, those who would condemn The Girls for not keeping the day holy, The Girls said, "Piffle." What? They shouldn't have some pleasure after all the cleaning and the cooking and the baking and the shopping and the *schlepping*? What? With everything going on in the world, God was going to be offended at this? Nah. Old-fashioned nonsense, that.

They were modern women, The Girls.

Judy, a dish in a gold lamé pants suit, put out a plate of apricot ruggeleh that of course she baked from scratch and a store bought coffee crumb cake because who had time to bake twice in a day? And The Girls got down to business. Sunny Shapiro lit up a Newport cigarette. Miriam bit into a ruggelah and groaned from the exquisiteness of it. "Oh, Judy. This is dee-lish-ous. Really, you could sell these. Really. Sunny, try the ruggelah and tell me she couldn't sell these."

Sunny put her cigarette in the ashtray and popped a ruggelah into her mouth. Her eyes rolled to the heavens as she chewed. After she swallowed she said, "Miriam's right, Judy. You could sell these."

Edith passed three tiles to Judy, who passed two tiles—Four Crak and Three Bam—to Miriam, who called, "Pung."

Sunny lit another cigarette.

"For crying out loud, Sunny," Edith said. "You got one going in the ashtray."

Sunny snuffed out the first cigarette and asked Miriam, "So what did you wind up getting her for the Sweet Sixteen?"

"An Add-A-Pearl necklace," Miriam told them. "With sixteen starter pearls. From Harry's."

In unison, the girls nodded their approval. "You get good value at Harry's," Sunny said.

"And I got her a couple of blouses," Miriam said, as if a couple of blouses were nothing. "Huk-A-Poo and Wayne Rogers. The saleswoman said the kids all go for the Wayne Rogers now."

"It's true. They're all wearing them. They're cute, those blouses." As the fashion maven of the group, Judy gave her imprimatur to the polyester blouses, fitted to the form and in an array of not-so-subdued prints.

"And she got her hair highlighted. Blond streaks. It looks adorable. Still," Miriam said, "I would have liked to make her a party," and then Edith said, "Mah-jongg."

~

Home from the mall, Joanne Clarke took her purchases from the bags and spread them out on her bed, as if creating a layout for a fashion magazine. This was exhilarating, to shop for new things for the big date. Joanne wondered how many big dates it would take before the sting of all the nights alone would be relieved. Well, there weren't going to be any more sorry times. John Wosileski was definitely coming around and in a significant way too. She could envision them engaged within a year's time, married, and a baby soon thereafter. A baby. Joanne never liked babies. Their red faces and the way they shrieked and wailed and pooped in their pants disgusted her. Babies had that smell about them, that fetid smell she had come to know so well. Her father smelled that way often enough. But with her own baby, it would be different. She'd heard plenty of women say so, that when it's your own baby, the poop smells like perfume.

Her reverie was interrupted by her father's cry coming from the living room. "Joanne," he called to her. "Joanne."

Her teeth set on edge, she counted to ten to keep her temper in check before she went to him. "What is it, Dad?" and then she saw what it was. He'd wet himself. Again. The large wet spot spread across his pajama bottom. She kept him in pajamas around the clock now. What was the point of dressing him? It's not like he was going anywhere.

Soon, she thought to herself, *soon I'll be done with this.* No one could expect a newly married woman with a baby to continue to care for a senile old man, and she led her father to the bathroom to clean him up.

~

Valentine emerged from the bathroom, squeaky clean and smelling of Jean Naté Lemon-Scented After-Bath Splash. She put on her one pair of lace underpants, white, and her newest blue jeans. Although brassieres were the garment on which the family fortune was made, Valentine was not in possession of a pretty bra, an incongruity common enough to have become a cliché in the guise of cobblers' children going barefoot. Maybe that, not being in possession of an especially pretty bra, was why she didn't put on a bra at all. Or maybe it was the irony of the fact that she didn't really need one. It's not like she had much to rein in or strap up. Valentine, in her blue jeans and bare-breasted, the luster of her skin, the coy sexuality hinted at, the innocence she radiated, conjured up angelic sensuality that could have been reviled as kiddie porn. Next,

Valentine put on a blouse, one of the new Huk-A-Poos Miriam had bought for her, a floral print, little lilies of the valley against a midnight-blue background and one hundred percent polyester of the sort that was like Styrofoam to the touch.

In the kitchen, Valentine wrote her mother a note on the pad which hung on the wall next to the phone for that very purpose. *Dear Ma, I'm with a friend. I don't know what time I'll be back, so eat without me. Love, Valentine.*

With an address written down and the paper folded and nestled in the zippered compartment in her pocketbook, Valentine left home.

~

Miriam won big at that afternoon's game, largely because not once, but twice, Judy discarded the one tile Miriam needed to complete her hand, which, according to the mah-jongg bylaws, meant Judy had to pay double. True, they played for nickels, so we're not talking a fortune here, but to have such luck twice in one afternoon put Miriam in a jovial mood; a jovial mood which was enhanced when she discovered her daughter's note. *With a friend. With a friend,* that was good because it pained Miriam to think that her daughter was alone for her Sweet Sixteen. *With a friend* brought about an alleviation, a load off Miriam's mind, and so Miriam opened the refrigerator and surveyed the bounty.

~

John Wosileski was fixing himself a bromide. Indigestion. Not indigestion as he had known it before, not bile backing up on him or burning, but rather he felt as if he'd swallowed a golf ball; heavy for its size, weighing on him. Having stirred the Brioschi in a glass of water, he waited for the fizz to settle. The bubble and tickle of drinks sparkling, be it Asti Spumante, ginger ale, or the Fizzies of his childhood caused him, not to sneeze but to want to sneeze, which was yet another desire unfulfilled. Holding his nose because the taste was terrible, he drank the Brioschi down in one long swallow and put the glass, coated with chalky residue, in the sink. From there, he was headed to the bedroom, where he intended to pick up his dirty laundry from the floor, when he was detoured by a knock at his door.

Wearing jeans and an old SUNY Plattsburgh T-shirt, frayed at the neck, and his moccasins over socks with a hole at the big toe of his right foot, John lumbered across the living room wondering who could it be? A neighbor needing to borrow something or perhaps to ask if he smelled anything funny? (He did, but it was nothing new; the chemical odor from Weinstein's Dry Cleaning in 24 Hours was always present.) Or maybe it was Joanne Clarke with some sort of a surprise? Or maybe it was a Jehovah's Witness or the Mormons coming to talk to him about God.

~

Despite acknowledging the poor odds of getting a preengagement opal or garnet ring this Valentine's Day, Beth Sandler couldn't help but think that *maybe, just maybe, you never know, you can't give up hope. Just because Valentine Kessler said it wasn't going to happen? Who died and made her God?*

~

To find Valentine Kessler at his door sent John Wosileski into a tailspin. *I must be hallucinating*, he thought, as if she could not be flesh and blood, but particles of light, as if he were to put his hand out, it would go right through her.

"Hi," said Valentine. "Can I come in?"

John could produce no words, but after what was only a few seconds, albeit seconds in very slow motion, a garbled noise shot forth from him as if he'd brought up a hairball.

Apparently Valentine—if that was Valentine and not the result of a psychoactive mushroom winding up in the can of Campbell's vegetable soup he'd had for lunch or else wishful thinking run amok—she read the retching sound to be an answer in the affirmative. She stepped around him and she entered his apartment, which really was something of a shithole. An armchair, his most recent purchase and the color of liverwurst, was stationed directly across from a television with a wire hanger filling in for one missing rabbit's ear of the antenna. A poster of Jean-Claude Killy was tacked to the wall.

Because of the intent way she scanned the surroundings, John feared she might take it upon herself to tour the place. "Excuse me for a minute," he said before dashing into the bedroom, where he gathered his dirty laundry as if his underwear were rosebuds. He shoved the bundle under his pillow and just in the nick of time. Or maybe not. Who knew for how long she'd been standing there behind him?

Valentine Kessler's gaze was concentrated on John Wosileski's twin bed; that is to say, a single, a bed for one. Unmade, dingy sheets, a lumpy pillow, a blanket which had once been a banquet for moths and discolored too, stained with God knows what, and all it represented—loneliness and worse, the resignation to loneliness. What kind of single guy in his twenties doesn't buy a bed big enough for two, big enough to, at the very least, anticipate the possibility of a little action? Also, it was enough to cause your skin to itch.

But it wasn't as sad as all that, was it? John was on the cusp of triumph over loneliness, his resignation having yielded just enough to give him a chance at something else, and you really don't have to be in love with a person to have a life together; sometimes a life together is good enough.

Now John Wosileski wondered, how was he going to get Valentine Kessler out of his apartment, and especially out of his bedroom? Moreover, did he want to get Valentine Kessler out of his apartment, and especially his bedroom? Valentine Kessler in *his* bedroom! Talk about your pie in the sky, but this was also, in a Brooklyn colloquialism, pissing on the third rail. John Wosileski, dream as he did, was also a realist. If Valentine was discovered here, he'd be out of a job before the next heartbeat. Or worse, this could be some kind of prank, a practical joke at his expense. It was impossible for him to think that Valentine would deliberately do something cruel, but the others could. It wasn't so long ago that John Wosileski was a teenager himself and the butt of many practical jokes. One in particular which still stung when he thought of it, and he couldn't help but think of it now: Donna Monforte, the prettiest girl in school, left him a note. Often John had received notes at school, loose-leaf paper folded four times over and then wedged in the grating of his locker for him to find at the end of the day. Mostly they were crude drawing of pigs with the words *Oink! Oink!* scrawled across the page. Other notes read: *I'm going to kick your fat ass,* and variations on that theme. One time, the two subjects merged into a rather well-done sketch of a boot kicking a pig high in the air as if it were a football, although the play on pig and pigskin was not known to the artist, thereby rendering the sketch less clever than one might think. But this other note, the one from Donna Monforte, John Wosileski had never before received anything of its kind. *Dear John,* she wrote in red ink, *I really like you. Do you really like me? If you do like me then meet me on Saturday at the Greenpoint Movie House at 2:00 P.M.* Need the rest of this tale of woe and humiliation be detailed? Nine years later and still John burned from the shame of it, from standing there in front of the Greenpoint Movie House gripping, in sweaty hands, the box of Russell Stover candies he'd bought for her, while Donna Monforte and her horde of cohorts—how many were there? five? six? well over a thousand? all of Brooklyn?—surrounded him, laughing themselves sick, at the Oinker falling for it, as if dishy Donna Monforte could ever really like *him. Dream on, Oinker.*

From the bedroom window, John peered out onto the street to see if there was a pack of kids standing around howling, laughing all over themselves, rollicking at the prospect of a joke as much as at the joke itself. But the street was deserted save for one man carrying away his dry cleaning, a freshly pressed powder-blue suit with Bozo-sized lapels slung over his back. Late in the afternoon, on the afternoon of a holiday, most everyone was done with their errands, and now they were getting ready for the big night.

~

With her father cleaned up, Joanne Clarke set about preparing herself for the evening ahead. With one foot in the bathroom sink, she balanced herself on the other foot like a stork or an egret—some odd-looking bird most often depicted standing on one leg, the other leg retracted, folded up like a music stand—Joanne shaved that leg, nicking herself twice, once on the shin and once on the knee. After pressing bits of toilet paper to the cuts, which bled profusely, she switched sides and shaved the other leg, taking greater care to avoid cutting herself. She shaved her armpits, and then, with tweezers, plucked a few stray hairs from between her brows.

Not in possession of anything as luxurious as Calgon bath salts or bubblebath, Joanne Clarke made do adding a capful of shampoo—Alberto VO5—into the tub as it filled, producing not a fun-filled wellspring of sweet-smelling froth, but a layer of white soapy bubbles, kind of like soap scum. First testing the water with her big toe and finding the temperature to her liking, Joanne stepped into the tub, taking her washcloth with her. She scrubbed herself clean. All over. Everywhere. Especially there.

Wrapped in a terrycloth bathrobe which was, after years of wearing and washing, bald in patches and not at all fluffy, rather closer in texture to burlap, Joanne put a few curlers in her hair to give it some body. Next, she would do her nails.

~

"Can I use your bathroom?" Valentine Kessler asked John Wosileski.

"Yes, of course." John pointed to the bathroom door, which was on the far left side of the bedroom. "There," he said, and he thought he should take this opportunity to step back into the living room, out of the bedroom—the *bed*room and all that it implied—and nearer to getting her the hell out of his apartment. Plus, from this vantage point he would hear her tinkle, but it was as if he were riveted to the floor. He did not, could not, budge. Although loath to admit it, he wanted, desperately he wanted, to hear her tinkle and he wondered how he would confess this one to Father Palachuk.

On those occasions when Joanne Clarke got up from his bed, the top sheet wrapped around her like a toga, to use the bathroom, she always ran the faucet while she tinkled, to drown out the sound, but for naught. Even though on those occasions he tried not to listen, John Wosileski could hear the two distinct flows of water. Now, however, he heard nothing. Was it possible that even her tinkle was like gossamer?

Eleven

All that remained for Joanne Clarke to do was slip on her dress, step into her shoes, and apply the new makeup. We're talking twenty minutes of preparation tops, and here it was only a few minutes after five. Oh yeah, and make dinner for her father. She'd make him a sandwich and so wouldn't have to worry about him with the utensils.

Without bothering to put on her robe—what difference would it make now if her father saw her in her bra and panty hose, the man was so far out in gaga-ville—Joanne went to the kitchen and opened the refrigerator to see what was there when an egg tumbled out and onto the floor, breaking the shell into ten pieces. "Goddammit," Joanne said out loud. "Who the . . ." Her words trailed off. Who else but her father would've left an egg on the edge of the shelf?

She reached for the paper towels, but then changed her mind. Let it be. She'd clean it up tomorrow rather than risk mussing herself now mopping up the glop of an egg.

Eggs, cottage cheese, half or almost half of a Sara Lee marble loaf, a Hebrew National salami, two liters of Diet Pepsi, English muffins, a jar of kosher dill pickles, an apple, Miriam considered the contents of her refrigerator. If Valentine wasn't coming home for dinner, who could be bothered to make a big meal? Miriam would have a *nosh* instead. Maybe fry up the salami with some eggs.

The fact that it was Valentine's Day, the other part of Valentine's Day that wasn't her daughter's birthday, was not lost on Miriam. She tried to think of it the way she thought of Christmas. You can't ignore it, the reminders are everywhere in your face, but you have to accept that it's not for you. In this regard, her heart weighed as heavy as the rest of her. How does a woman, a woman who still has needs, go on with life, all the while knowing that there will never be a lid to her pot? *Every pot has a lid,* her mother, may she rest in peace, used to tell her. There are men who go for fatties. Miriam had read about them somewhere. She wondered how she might go about meeting such a man. Maybe there were clubs she could join or maybe matchmakers made the introduction. Miriam imagined such a man, a man who went for fatties, as being extremely thin. A string bean. And bald. With glasses. A low level accountant and a pervert, an assumption which discouraged further consideration of the subject.

Valentine emerged from the bathroom, and she walked to where John stood, which was exactly where she'd left him. One of her smooth and slender hands reached out and took one of his hands, and John's heart and stomach both flipped like a pair of Mexican jumping beans, which don't, in fact, jump but rather tumble head over heels. And then Valentine said, "Kiss me. Please." Please. It was that, the *please,* which eased away any residue of restraint.

And they kissed and he groaned and she led his hands to the buttons of her blouse. One by one the buttons opened and John Wosileski's heart stopped. Or at least it felt as if his heart stopped, and that was okay. If he were to die right then and there, it would have been worth it, to have seen heavenly beauty and to die for it was a square deal.

But God is good. God is so good that He let John Wosileski live, to live and to further feast his eyes upon further splendiferousness.

As simply a point of information, John Wosileski had a handsome manhood. Thick, with a pink hue to the flesh, and nicely proportioned, with no peculiarities like a crick or a mole with hair growing from it. His erection hid the fact that he wasn't circumcised. John did not know that his manhood was good-looking. He'd never showered with the guys after gym class, and Valentine had no basis for comparison. Consequently, his one handsome feature went unappreciated.

Apparently Mrs. Sandler, Beth's mother, knew of what she spoke when she'd told the girls that instinct would prevail. Valentine spread her legs apart as if about to make an angel in the snow, if one could imagine that unappetizing bed as anything crisp and freshly driven. She then brought up her knees and her hips arched to meet his.

John Wosileski had no idea he could get as hard as all that, as hard as wood, and it seemed as if you flicked it, it would ping like crystal or hum like a piano wire.

Hard as he was, he should have slipped right inside her, but nothing bigger than a slender tampon or her index finger, which were more or less the same size, had ever been in there. John guided himself to where the opening ought to have been, but there was no give. He pushed, but she did not open. John worried, what if he was at the wrong door? But no, he was where he was supposed to be. He could sense the sweetness, as if from between her legs a moist whisper coaxed him, *come in, come in,* and John was nearly out of his mind with want and need. He trembled and pushed again, the tip of him neared against her pink flesh, and John's world exploded. A flash of light and he emitted a noise, a grunt or a sob, and then he felt as if he were melting, quick and thick and warm like wax beneath a flame.

Having already flushed once, he then flushed again, but this second time was from the shame, the humiliation, the desolation of the premature ejaculation.

He rolled off her, and at her side, he said, "I'm sorry." His throat was tight as if it wouldn't take much to get him to cry. And no wonder. Given the circumstances, who wouldn't have cried, or better yet, killed himself?

"Something went wrong," Valentine said. Said or asked. A question or a statement of fact, John couldn't tell.

"Not exactly wrong," he said. He tried to put this in the best light possible. "It happens sometimes."

"I never heard of it," Valentine said.

"It was because you're so beautiful," he dared to tell her, he had to tell her. "I dreamed of this, of you, but I never thought it would happen. I got too excited."

"So I'm still a virgin." Again, it was impossible to determine if the statement was interrogatory or declarative.

"Well, yes," he conceded. "But we can do it again in twenty

minutes. An hour at most. We'll have something to eat. We can talk for a while. I'll order up a pizza. Do you like pizza?"

But Valentine was rising from the bed, like Venus from the clamshell. "No," she said. That was all she said. No. No to pizza, no to talking, no to trying it again. No to all of it. No.

~

While she was unable to achieve quite the same effect that the saleswoman at the Estée Lauder counter got, Joanne Clarke was nonetheless pleased. The miracle in the tube did mask the red of the pockmarks, and the lipstick, a soft pink, was a becoming color for her. Joanne Clarke smiled, really smiled, at her reflection in the mirror.

Her father was in his armchair, the television tuned to *The Flintstones*. Joanne had fed him a sedative with his sandwich, so he would fall asleep within minutes in front of the TV and sleep through the night. He would not get up to go to the bathroom, but would piss on himself, and she'd have to clean him in the morning. So be it. She wasn't going to aggravate herself with that now. Not when Fred Flintstone was going "yaba-daba-do," and her father was happy and she was happy.

"Dad," she said as she took her coat from the rack. "Dad. I'm going out now."

Only then did he look at her, and his eyes went wide, as if she were a gift-wrapped package. "Oh Theresa," he said, "you look beautiful."

Who the hell was Theresa?

~

Valentine dressed quickly before John could stop her. Not that John would have dared to try stopping her. His head was in his hands as if he were a broken man, broken like an egg.

~

Despite walking at a snail's pace in her attempt to be a few minutes late, Joanne Clarke arrived early at the subway station, the point of rendezvous. John was not yet at the token booth, and because the stench of urine there was overpowering, Joanne opted to wait on the street at the entrance to the station, where, yes it was cold, but at least you could breathe without gagging. Under the glow of a streetlight, Joanne checked her watch again. It was six twenty-four. With any luck, John would be early too.

~

If Valentine had gone directly from John's apartment to home, surely her mother would have asked questions: *Why are you back so early? Where did you go? What happened?* And what could Valentine have said? *I went to my teacher's* schmutzy *apartment to have sex with him and it didn't happen the way I imagined it would?* Wisely, Valentine went to Enzio's Pizzeria and ordered two slices plain and a Diet Pepsi.

~

As if the winter night air wasn't cold enough, the wind was picking up. Joanne made an attempt to hold her hair in place, but it was futile; her carefully coiffed do was turning into a rat's nest. Six twenty-nine and Joanne's eyes maintained the search for John up and down the avenue. Passersby hunched over and held their coats tight at their necks to keep the cold from slicing through as they hurried to wherever they were headed: home to the family, to the store for a quart of milk, to a bar to meet a friend for a drink, or to a romantic Valentine's Day dinner.

At six thirty-three, Joanne was beginning to get, not worried, but irritated. It was highly inconsiderate of John to keep her waiting on a darkened street corner in the freezing cold. *I'll give him five minutes more,* she thought, *and then I'm leaving,* but any residue of ultimatum, along with the irritation, vanished, *poof,* in the instant she spotted him halfway down the block. She brightened, stood up straight, and patted at her hair, hoping it wasn't as much of a fright as all that.

In the dark and in the flurry of passengers filing out from the station, Joanne realized that John didn't see her, so she waved her hand high in the air, and called out, "Yoo-hoo. John. Over here."

John, at a distance, was revealed close up to be an elderly Chinese man. Joanne's disappointment was disproportionate to the circumstance. John was a little bit late, that was all. No big deal. Maybe she would even tell him how, from a distance, she mistook the elderly Chinese man for him, her date. She would tell him if she could manage to say it in a lighthearted way.

Joanne opened her pocketbook, and from her change purse, she took out a dime. A tricky maneuver because she was wearing gloves, and then she crossed the street to the phone booth on the opposite corner.

~

The ringing of the phone was not enough to snap John out of his blank despondency. Although Valentine had been gone for well over an hour—gone, Valentine, gone, gone forever—John stayed where he was on the edge of the bed, naked, his head in his hands. Oh, he heard the phone ringing, but he lacked the will to answer it.

~

Joanne let the phone ring four, five, six times before hanging up, satisfied that John must be on his way. Well, it was highly inconsiderate of him to be late, but he probably couldn't help it. No matter. From his apartment to the appointed corner was a ten-minute walk, tops. So even if he left just a minute before Joanne called, she'd have to wait nine more minutes at most. Such was her reasoning.

~

The clock on the wall at Enzio's Pizzeria was mounted onto a cutout of a hen silhouetted in gold tone, and it read eleven minutes past seven. Enzio was starting to give Valentine the fish eye because she'd been taking up that table now since what, five, six o'clock. Not that anyone was lining up in wait for it, but Enzio didn't like the kids loitering in his pizzeria.

At seven-thirty on the dot, Valentine got up and started for home.

~

It was seven-thirty on the dot, and Joanne Clarke was still waiting at the entrance to the Glenwood Road subway when her nose began to twitch. Her chin quivered, and that was that. Her new makeup was not waterproof, and it went all streaky and striated, and brushing away her tears, she only made matters worse.

~

At ten minutes to ten o'clock on the night of her sixteenth birthday, Valentine Kessler was in bed along with a package of cookies and a book. Licking the vanilla frosting from an Oreo opened like a jar, Valentine read from *Lives of the Saints* about Cecilia placed naked in a scalding bath, and about Agatha burned with red-hot irons, torn with sharp hooks, laid naked on live coals, and about Eulalia, whose breasts were burned "in a most horrific manner," and then about Irene, who was sent naked into the streets to be shamed and then burned alive. Valentine read herself into a state, and when she let the book fall in order to put her hands between her thighs as if to calm herself down there, just the opposite happened. The groan, the spasm, the release left no room for interpretation. The trumpets had sounded and Valentine Kessler, on the close of her sixteenth birthday, was, by all indications, visited by the angels. *Oh hallelujah.*

Twelve

Calling in sick that Monday was an option, but when John Wosileski reached for the telephone on the nightstand beside his bed, the bed of the scene of his shame, he went limp in defeat. The man lacked the gumption to tell so much as a little lie which wasn't even really a lie at all. He did feel sick, but not with any ailment he could name. Much the way a condemned man comes to his last meal knowing it's going to taste like cardboard no matter that it's a T-bone steak, listlessly John Wosileski picked up a shirt from the floor, and without sniffing at the underarm areas as he usually did before putting on a less than fresh shirt, he began to dress.

Despite having cried and cried for some thirty-six hours, give or take, Joanne Clarke was no closer to a catharsis. Rather, each tear was like the prick of a pin, and as is the way in evolution, nature was providing for her in the shape of an impenetrable shell calcifying around her heart.

Joanne Clarke did not lack the gumption to tell a lie. What? She should own up to having been hurt and humiliated to some sniggering secretary? Of course not. The flu would do just fine as an excuse. She would call in sick with the flu. That was her intent, but as she went for the phone, the sound of her father whimpering from the next room sent her from the rock to the hard place. Which was worse? To go to work and face that music? Or to stay at home with her father? She had no idea what prompted her father's crying, only that he did so more and more frequently. Rather than evoking sympathy or even pity, his crying got on her nerves. She wanted to smack him across the face to shut him up. Instead, in her darkened bedroom, by the faint glow of a bedside lamp which was really more of a night-light, she lifted her nightgown up and over her head.

From her closet, where the red dress was now crumpled into a ball and stuffed behind the row of her three pairs of shoes, she took out a brown pants suit—pull-on trousers and a tunic top—made from a fabric which was similar to that of a synthetic sponge.

~

Forget pulling the wool over Miriam Kessler's eyes when it came to illness, neither feigning it nor denying it. Although it never once entered her narrow lexicon of pipe dreams, Miriam would have made a first-rate physician. But not even in the 1970s did many girls in Brooklyn consider becoming doctors, never mind in Miriam's day. To marry a doctor, to that a girl could aspire. To be a doctor? Whoever heard of such a thing? And nursing was not a nice profession for Jewish girls. Emptying bedpans and changing sheets? You call that a profession? That's not a profession. Teaching, now that's a profession.

Miriam might've been ignorant as to the whereabouts of Valentine's heart and soul, but she was like a specialist when it came to appraising ailments of the digestive and respiratory tracts. Never could Valentine claim a stomach ache or nausea or a sore throat or a cough where none existed.

One morning the summer before, when all the kids were going to Coney Island for the day, Miriam took one look at Valentine and said, "You're not going anywhere except to bed."

"Ma," Valentine argued. "I feel fine." Valentine did three jumping jacks as if that were proof of good health.

"Well, maybe you do feel fine," Miriam said. "But you're sick as a dog. Bed. Now."

The last time Valentine asked to stay home from school—she said she had severe menstrual cramps—just happened to be the same day as the big dodgeball game in gym class and Valentine had reason to fear both the ball coming at her as well as her teammates' ire at her incompetence. Miriam looked her in the eye and said, "You think you can fool your mother? Maybe you can fool other people, but not your mother." And indeed Valentine did fool other people, in particular, Miss Dench, one of the gym teachers, who didn't question Valentine's claim to severe menstrual cramps and genially excused her from the game. Or maybe she did suspect that Valentine was faking it but was just as happy to let that delicate little puff sit it out on the sidelines.

Any attempt to deceive Miriam would be an exercise in futility, so when Valentine, after getting dressed and on her way down the stairs, announced, "I'm not hungry," maybe she really was sick, because Valentine always had an appetite. An appetite which, sure enough, go figure, returned to her once she got to the kitchen and found that Miriam had made buttermilk pancakes.

~

Beth Sandler could not wait to get to school that day, itching to show off her new S-chain bracelet, her Valentine's Day gift from Joey Rappaport. Instead of taking time for breakfast, she grabbed a chocolate-covered donut and headed out the door.

~

At the kitchen sink, Miriam, with a Brillo pad, scrubbed the skillet she used to make the pancakes. The dishwasher, however much a blessing, was not equipped to scrape off batter baked into aluminum. For that, you needed steel wool and plenty of elbow grease. As she scrubbed, Miriam chastised herself, her own foolishness, for making buttermilk pancakes on a Monday morning. But they were Valentine's favorite, and Miriam wanted to do something nice for her daughter. Lucky for Miriam, she was scheduled for a manicure tomorrow because this steel wool was sanding away her nail polish at the tips. Finally the damn thing was clean, spotless, because Miriam was nothing if not meticulous. She was rinsing it under the faucet when, from the kitchen window, she thought she saw two birds, pinkish-yellow birds or maybe orange, flit from the armrest of a lawn chair to the post of the chain-link fence. Miriam's heart broke for the poor little things, canaries maybe, no doubt escaped from a cage and out an open window. Now they might freeze to death, out there in the middle of winter. She wondered if she could coax them into the house, but although she didn't notice them flying away, they were now nowhere to be seen. It occurred to Miriam that she had imagined the birds or that maybe it wasn't a pair of birds but some kind of trick with the light.

~

As if he'd literally lost his spine, John Wosileski was slumped over his desk, and instead of teaching, he assigned the class six problems from the textbook. "Do the problems on page one twenty-four," he said, and then he said nothing else.

"Mr. Wosileski?" Joel Krotchman asked, tentatively, softly, as if he thought perhaps Mr. Wosileski had a migraine headache or a death in the family. "Are we going to be graded on these?"

"What? No, no. You're not going to be graded. Just do them."

Learning they weren't going to be graded gave license to the majority of the class, that is, everyone but the Suck-up Six and Valentine Kessler, to carry on as if they were in the lunchroom rather than the classroom. The Suck-up Six had, no surprise, turned to page 124 and were diligently doing the assignment. Valentine was looking at Mr. Wosileski. He was looking out the window, the very same window that might well have been the egress for Valentine's love for him. And, as we all know, when love flies out the window, clarity of vision fills the vacuum. The spell is broken. As suddenly and surely as Titania recognized Bottom as an ass, did Valentine see Mr. Wosileski as a pasty-faced math teacher?

~

Across the hall, in Room 215, Miss Clarke's class was in a similar state of disorder. Not that Joanne Clarke willingly abdicated authority the way John Wosileski did. She was a stern, no-

nonsense schoolteacher, and while perhaps the students respected her or perhaps they did not, they did fear her. Until now.

It's a gift of the young: the ability to sense weakness, vulnerability, to sense it and to exploit it. Perhaps not consciously aware of it, but they knew, viscerally her students knew, that the Joanne Clarke who now stood before them desperately trying to get their attention, to get them to follow her pointer as it coursed the diagram of the circulatory system, this Joanne Clarke was not the same Joanne Clarke who dismissed them on Friday with more homework than they thought was fair.

Instead of dutifully taking notes, Linda Haber examined her hair for split ends, Hank Alpert doodled sketches of humongously breasted women, Terri Calabrese and Alison George were passing notes back *(gorgeous)* and forth *(conceited)* about Vincent Caputo. Scotty Rosen, because he forgot to do it the night before, took the opportunity to do his history homework, which would be collected next period. And so it went.

Blame it on the stars or maybe there was something in the water, but during the fifth period, in Mrs. Marmor's room, an incident was under way, and all because Cathleen Curran didn't look up in the dictionary, and then write down, the definition of the ten vocabulary words Mrs. Marmor had assigned for homework. Of course, Mrs. Marmor was not entirely without blame. She had to have known that Cathleen didn't do her homework. Cathleen never did her homework, but still Mrs. Marmor called on her. Cathleen stood up, as Mrs. Marmor required students do when defining vocabulary words, as if five-dollar words demanded such respect.

"Niggardly," Mrs. Marmor said. In retrospect, *niggardly* was not a wise choice of a vocabulary word, but the times were different then, and it was a word which, for reasons unknown, appeared often on the standardized tests for which Mrs. Marmor was trying to prepare her class.

Cathleen remained mute, except for the sounds she made swallowing hard.

"Niggardly," Mrs. Marmor repeated. "The definition, please."

Cathleen cleared her throat. "Niggardly," she said. "Niggardly. Of or having to do with the black persuasion."

Every head in the room, including Mrs. Marmor's, swiveled to look at Beverly Johnson, who was the only black student in the class and thereby exempt from any kind of ridicule because that would've been prejudiced. The entire class curled up and died of embarrassment.

When the bell rang, when they gathered their books to move on to the next class, Amy Epstein said to Valentine Kessler, "Don't you feel *soooo* bad for Beverly."

"A little bit," Valentine said, "but I feel worse for Cathleen Curran. Beverly Johnson, she'll get over Cathleen's stupidity, but Cathleen Curran, she's going to be stupid for life."

Such an assessment struck Amy Epstein as profound, which was weird, seeing as how it came from Valentine Kessler, whom Amy had heretofore considered to be no more than an inch deep.

~

At the end of this day, Valentine Kessler walked home from school alone. Some twenty paces behind her, also walking home from school, was Beth Sandler and her clique, which was led by Beth's new best friend in the world: Marcia Finkelstein.

To have remained best friends or even friends at all with Valentine Kessler would have had grave consequences for Beth Sandler. Practically overnight, in a matter of days, Valentine had become a full-fledged queer. It was most unusual, such a fall from grace. Before this, no one at Canarsie High had ever heard tell of such a plunge in popularity, but rules were rules: To be friends with a queer rendered you a queer by association.

Okay. It's possible that Valentine wasn't quite the queer Beth was making her out to be; maybe *queer* was nothing more than Beth's excuse to change best friends. After all, Marcia Finkelstein was the coolest girl at school, no contest. It was an honor to be chosen as her friend because everybody worshiped the ground Marcia walked on. Whatever. The last threads of friendship with Valentine, Beth pulled them out by the roots. Worship demands sacrifice, and also the giving of gifts.

And so as if she were the little drummer boy, Beth offered Marcia and company a gift in the form of a *rum-pa-pa-pum,* music to their ears. "You know that song that the Catholics sing in church?" Beth sang in a mock-operatic voice, "Arrre-vey Ma-ree-er." Just that and no more of it because she didn't know any more of it, but that was enough to make her point. "She gets like hypnotized by it. Really, she goes into some kind of trance. It's so queer, you wouldn't believe it."

Always there is strength in numbers and perhaps nowhere else is social Darwinism as brutal as in a pack of teenage girls. On that afternoon on that street in the Canarsie section of Brooklyn, five teenage girls sang "Arrre-vey Ma-ree-er," with the sole intent of tormenting a sixth.

Although Valentine was neither a child nor a drunk, the two groups renowned for being under God's special watch, it could have been that He was watching over her that afternoon.

As if she were oblivious to the girls behind her, she never once looked back to the source of the song. The question remains open as to whom she thought was singing, or if she'd heard the singing at all. It could have been a miracle, the opposite trick of the lame walking or the blind seeing, that for a brief but significant period of time, Valentine went deaf as a post. Or to appease the skeptics, the agnostics, the flat-out nonbelievers, you could say it was not a little miracle but rather a law of physics, that the sound waves, caught by the wind, were bent back on themselves, and thus never reached her. Still, even if that was the case, you could wonder, just the way you could wonder about the parting of the Red Sea, that yes, it could be rationally explained by the tides and tectonic shifts, but was it merely coincidence that it happened to shift just as Moses and his people got there? Albeit on a small scale, the wind picking up on that afternoon was that kind of coincidence, the kind that had God's fingerprints all over it. Whatever the explanation, Valentine seemed impervious to the hurt of Beth's betrayal.

So where was the fun in it when they failed to elicit a reaction from Valentine? Beth and company quit with the song and instead Beth solicited admiration anew for her S-chain bracelet.

~

In Edith Zuckerman's living room, The Girls were deep into it. Maj-jongg tiles *clikity-clacked,* Judy Weinstein striving for the coveted win of Two Dragons with a Pearl, Sunny Shapiro's cigarette smoke curling overhead, Miriam keeping an eagle eye on Edith's discard while savoring the buttery pound cake as it dissolved in her mouth, and yet no one missed a beat in the conversation, which at this moment was centered around another neighbor, Elaine Winston, whose frugality was legendary and often a bone of contention.

"I could not believe it," Judy said. "Literally, her hand was open. Waiting for her change. Seven cents. Four Flower. I'm sorry, you go for lunch with a person, you split the check down the middle, but there she was with her hand out, telling me hers came to seven cents less than mine."

"So what did you do?" Sunny asked. "Two Crak."

"I gave her a dime and told her to keep the change."

"She can't help it," Miriam said. "It's a sickness, to be cheap like that. She once told me that she was very poor while growing up." Miriam passed one tile, a Four Bam, to Judy. "That some nights her mother went without dinner to feed the children. So now she worries about not having."

"But they're rolling in it," Sunny said. "Do you have any idea how much her husband makes? Sixteen fortunes."

"It wouldn't matter if he made seventeen fortunes." Miriam reached for the cream to add to her coffee. "The poverty left a mark on her. That doesn't go away."

"Miriam's right," Edith said. "When she's right, she's right."

Reluctantly, Sunny agreed and then added, "You're very perceptive, Miriam. You always were. You see right through people. You could be a psychiatrist, the way you're perceptive."

It was true. Miriam was a very perceptive person. It was like a second sight, the way she could see through people. Except for her daughter. Most every mother has blind spots where her children are concerned, and Miriam was no exception. Teenagers, they're like alien creatures from another planet. On top of which, Valentine was never an easy person to know. Frankly, Miriam was just as glad that she could not read Valentine as if the kid were an open book. It was her philosophy that there were some things a mother was better off not knowing, and she was confident that if there were any serious problems, those she would see.

"Mah-jongg," Edith Zuckerman called, and the tiles were washed for the next round.

~

On the kitchen table, Valentine found a note from her mother: *I'm at Edith's. Fresh fruit is in the refrigerator. I'll be back around 4. I love you. Mom.*

Valentine took a pear and went to her room, where she opened her desk drawer and got out her diary. A pink vinyl book with gold trim and a lock with a small key that Valentine never bothered with. Placing the diary on her desk, she opened it to the first page, January 1 of that year, and using her index finger as a pointer, she scanned each entry. Coming upon any mention of John Wosileski, she tore out that page. She tore out the page, then tore the page in half, then in half again, and again until she'd torn it to bits. And so it went. All pages where John Wosileski's name or initials appeared were excised and shredded.

Then she ate the pear.

The core of the pear and the stem attached to it, she wrapped in a tissue, which she left on the desk while she went through the drawers, one by one, systematically examining each scrap of paper. All doodlings of telltale hearts, of initials joined by an ampersand and a *4 Ever* written in an especially florid script, were consigned to her garbage can.

By the time her mother got home from her mah-jongg game, a little before five, Valentine had successfully purged any remnant of John Wosileski from her environment and assumedly from her heart.

~

Miriam Kessler was about to make a meat loaf when Angela Sabatini knocked on the door. Holding out a jar of her homemade tomato sauce, which Angela called *gravy*, Angela said, "I made too much. It doesn't keep. The freezer gives it an aftertaste. I thought maybe you could use it."

"You're a doll," Miriam told her neighbor. "I was about to make a meat loaf. So I'll make spaghetti with meatballs instead. You want to come in? I'll put up some coffee."

"Ah, I can't. I got the stove on," Angela said, but before she left, she passed on words of wisdom: Don't cook the pasta for more than five minutes. I don't care what they say on the box. You don't want it too soft. You want *al dente*.

There were things that Angela Sabatini knew. Spaghetti was one of them.

~

John Wosileski took the Swanson's Hungry-Man meal from the oven and placed it on the kitchen counter. The television was on. The news? A game show? A rerun of *I Love Lucy*? Who cared? Standing there at the stretch of counter between the sink and the stove, John sliced off a piece of the Salisbury steak—really just a hamburger without the bun—and popped it into his mouth. He bit down on the meat and his teeth hit ice; the center of the patty was frozen. All he had to do then was put it back in the oven for another ten minutes, but it didn't seem worth the effort. He ate it as it was, his teeth crunching the ice particles. The mashed potatoes were frozen at their center too.

Joanne Clarke fed her father an American-cheese sandwich on rye bread along with two bananas because bananas are binding, and his bowel movement had been a little loose. For herself, although she could've dined on misery alone, she made tuna-fish salad, which she ate but did not taste.

Valentine devoured a mountain of spaghetti and a pyramid of meatballs and then she licked her plate clean of sauce, for which Miriam admonished her. "Young ladies don't lick their plates," Miriam said. "You're going to do that when some boy takes you out to dinner?"

Valentine rolled her eyes heavenward in that exaggerated way of teenagers everywhere, and such a gesture, such a typically teenage gesture, comforted Miriam, comfort that spread like warmth; warmth that morphed into love, a mother's love for her only daughter.

Thirteen

On the afternoon of the first night of Passover, while at the library, always a site for wonder, Valentine Kessler stumbled upon an astounding discovery. Not an astounding discovery new to the world, but astounding and new to her. Valentine brought the book *The Grand-Ducal Medici Court,* a hefty tome of pictures of art, to Lucille Fiacco's desk and asked, "What is the story with this?" Valentine had the book open to a print of *The Circumcision* by Franceso Mazzola.

Lucille Fiacco wasn't familiar with that particular artist. All she knew was that she was staring at a picture of the pale light of the moon reflecting the halo over the head of baby Jesus with his weenie exposed. Exposed and about to go under the knife. Twelve years with the nuns did not prepare Lucille Fiacco for this picture. Both weenies in general and the circumcision of Jesus in particular were not areas the nuns would've touched with a ten-foot pole. But, Lucille Fiacco reminded herself, she held a master's degree in library science. She was an educated and enlightened person, and so she told Valentine, "So? It's a picture of baby Jesus getting circumcised."

"Catholics get circumcised?" Valentine asked.

"Jesus wasn't a Catholic," Lucille explained, although admittedly, it was not an easy thing for her to say. "He was Jewish."

The whole business of Jesus being born a Jew was a hot potato for the Catholics and for the Jews alike. The Jews simply didn't know what to make of it. Moreover, to bring the subject up was inviting trouble of some sort. Best to leave it alone, and for the Catholics, it was preferable to remain ignorant than to get mired in the conundrum of worshiping a Jewish man, of calling to His Jewish mother in your times of need. Better for all concerned to think of the Common Era as a time bubble, at least as far as religion was concerned, some years separate and adrift from the continuum of history. Better to think that for the fifty years before the birth of Christ and the fifty years after, nobody was anything, religiously speaking, which was why it is perfectly plausible that Valentine would have had no idea that the Holy Family and her own family had that in common.

"Back then, everybody was Jewish," Lucille Fiacco said. "There was no choice," which wasn't exactly accurate, but so what?

"And Mary?" Valentine asked.

"Jewish," Lucille said. "Joseph too. I just told you. Everybody was Jewish."

"Mary was Jewish?"

"Yes. Mary was Jewish."

"The Blessed Virgin Mary was Jewish?"

"Yes," Lucille snapped. "Yes, the frigging Blessed Virgin Mary was Jewish. Are you satisfied?"

Mary, Mother of God, the Blessed Virgin, was Jewish!

At Beth Sandler's house, with the family seated around the Seder table, seated before plates that were used only for Passover and one plate piled high with matzoth that Mrs. Sandler bought not at the supermarket but in some basement in Crown Heights where it was blessed especially for this night and tasted like sawdust, Beth Sandler's aunt Sylvia asked her niece, "How is that pretty friend of yours doing? You know, the one with a face like an angel."

"We're not friends anymore. She's gone over the deep end," Beth said.

"Drugs?" Aunt Sylvia's voice went throaty with the inquiry, as if the thought were choking her up. "I don't know what's with you kids and the drugs."

"Not drugs," Beth said. "She's just weird. You know, not normal. She's off in her own world half the time."

"She's in a cult? You stay away from her if she's in a cult. They brainwash you, those cults. I read all about them. Five minutes with them and they've got you like a zombie."

"She's not in a cult, Aunt Sylvia." This conversation was cut short when Beth's grandfather stood at the head of table and in a haunting voice that sounded like a reverberation of the ages, as if a voice could be the ripples made by a stone skipping across the water, candlelight casting his face in flickering shadows, he intoned the first blessing of many that night.

A pot roast, a baked chicken, three kinds of potatoes, asparagus, and kasha, and so what if it wasn't a traditional Seder and maybe a little closer in kind to Thanksgiving than to the Passover dinner? Would anyone really care that Miriam didn't bother with all the *mishegoss* with the egg and the nuts and honey and the bitter herbs? The whole bit about slavery and Moses, we're talking over what, five thousand years ago, who even knew if that story was true? It was the spirit of the thing that mattered. A Seder was nice as a family get-together.

Valentine set the table with the good china. One plate for herself, one for her mother, one each for her grandparents, and a fifth setting for the prophet Elijah, should he decide to show up.

One look at that fifth plate and forget the prophet. The reminder of Ronald made for a pall hanging over the Seder as surely as a black cloth is draped over the mirror while sitting *shivah*, and Miriam felt a chill as if death were nearby. She chided herself for being a sentimental fool. *It's that empty place setting, getting to me.* But to remove the fifth plate, to put it away in the cabinet, would reveal more to her family than Miriam was willing to let on. So it stayed and so she would live with it.

John Wosileski stood at the bathroom sink washing his socks with Ivory soap, which wasn't the soap for the job. A lonely act, washing socks in a sink.

Excepting the occasions when he had skied, none of John's days had even been lit with what could be considered giddy fervor, but ever since the incident with Valentine Kessler, it seemed to him that the sad parts of his life had traveled the short but painfully sharp course from the dumps to despair. Also, it seemed to him that the sad parts of his life were the sum total of his existence.

He suspected, and rightly so, that Joanne Clarke would have forgiven him had he bothered to invent some excuse for standing her up—a family emergency, a subway broken down, trapped in a stalled elevator—and they could've gone on together, married and all that, had a life like other people get to have—a house, some kids, a car. Before Valentine, he had hope for himself that way. And even though experience had taught him that to have hope is to open the door for hurt, even hurt was preferable to how he felt now. Now he felt nothing. Nothing at all. He did not ask for Joanne Clarke's forgiveness. How could he? To be with Joanne Clarke after Valentine would be an abomination.

~

Miriam brought one more bowl, this one filled with roasted potatoes, the small red ones, to the table, and Rose said, "You outdid yourself here, Miriam."

And yet something similar to guilt gnawed at Miriam for not—you'll pardon the expression—going whole hog, making the Seder the way it is written, the way it is supposed to be done. And frankly, Valentine didn't help matters any when she surveyed the bounty which Miriam had slaved over all day and then had plenty to say about it. "Where is the salt water?" Valentine asked. "Where are the greens? This wine isn't kosher, Ma. Why didn't you get kosher wine?" What was with this kid? Now she was going to go through a religious phase? *God help me with that one,* Miriam thought. "Valentine," Miriam admonished her daughter. "Stop it. Will you stop it, please."

"*Bubeleh,*" her grandmother said gently, for Valentine was the apple of Rose Kessler's eye, she cherished her gorgeous granddaughter more than life itself. "Your mother made a beautiful meal here. Enjoy."

As Miriam reached for the mashed potatoes—mashed with sour cream and chives and exquisite—Valentine nearly had a seizure. "Ma! Don't!" The kid was carrying on like a regular Sarah Bernhardt of the *shtetl*. "We didn't the say prayers," she said as if life depended on prayer, as if prayer got you someplace.

There was not a Haggadah on the table, nor one in the house for that matter, but Valentine insisted they say a blessing over the matzoth and that they ask the Four Questions. Rather, as the youngest member of the family, it was she who would ask the Four Questions, which is really only one question, which boils down to: *Why is this night different from all other nights?* Four times it is asked, each time with a variation.

The aroma of the potatoes was driving Miriam wild with desire; her mouth watered with want, but just because God had failed her, this was no reason for Miriam not to humor Valentine's sudden, and surely superficial, piety. Moreover, Miriam was an adherent of the principle of *it could be worse*. As Valentine recited from memory what she must have picked up at Youth Group or from the street—*Why on this night do we eat only matzoth? Why on this night do we eat bitter herbs? Why on this night do we recline instead of sit?*—Miriam had to admit, it was sweet and harmless enough. It was not like, God forbid, the kid came home dressed in a sheet and chanting *Hare Krishna*.

Moreover, her grandfather was tickled pink by his granddaughter's attempt to retain the solemnity of the observance, and so what if Valentine got the fourth question dead wrong. In lieu of the one about the dipping of vegetables, she asked, "Why on this night do we drink kosher wine?" and still, across the table, Sy Kessler was *kvelling*. The older Sy got, the more he regretted abandoning the ways of his father and forefathers before him. For Sy, now it was too late. An old man is set in his ways, ways which included a Friday-night poker game and the occasional ham-and-cheese sandwich, but to see his granddaughter, his cherished granddaughter, picking up the ball he'd dropped, caused pleasure to fill up inside him, the kind of pleasure you could burst from.

~

Joanne Clarke opened a can of Chef Boyardee cheese ravioli and dumped it into a pot. Turning the flame up high, she gave it ten minutes, which might have been five minutes too long, and without bothering to transfer the ravioli into a bowl, she set the pot, along with a spoon, on the place mat in front of her father, who was wearing nothing but his bathrobe. He peered into the pot and then recoiled, backing up as far away from the table as his chair would allow. "What is that?" he asked.

"It's ravioli," Joanne said.

"What's it for?"

"It's for dinner. It's for you to eat."

Her father shook his head vigorously from side to side. "I'm not eating that. I'm not." Then he started to cry. Snot bubbled at his nostrils.

"Then don't," Joanne said, and she picked up the pot by the handle and dumped the piping-hot ravioli on her father's lap.

Never ever before had she done such a thing. No matter how much he'd tried her patience, no matter how she, all alone, had to care for him as if he were a baby, no matter how sometimes she wished he'd hurry up and die, never before had she hurt him. And apparently he was hurt. He was screaming, and not only because she'd frightened him. The ravioli, cheese in particular having a high heat capacity, scalded his thighs and his privates.

She should've been ashamed of herself for having done such a terrible thing, but she wasn't. She should've felt positively awful, but she didn't. She should've been filled with remorse, but instead she was filled with nothing but resentment. Bitterness had taken hold of her as if it were resolve.

When she could no longer stand one minute more of his screaming and crying, she called 911 and said to the operator, "I need an ambulance. My father burned himself. I don't know how it happened, but somehow he managed to dump scalding-hot ravioli on his lap. It looks pretty bad."

~

Soon after her in-laws went home and Valentine went to her room, Miriam went for just one more macaroon. In the box she found a chocolate one stuck to a thick envelope. She popped the macaroon into her mouth and opened the envelope to find a wad of one-hundred-dollar bills. Miriam counted them. Fifty. Fifty one-hundred-dollar bills. It was nothing new that Sy Kessler should leave her money in an envelope. No matter how often Miriam admonished him for it, Sy was always leaving her money in an envelope. Miriam knew why he did it. To try to somehow make it up to her for what his son had done. And both Miriam and Sy Kessler knew perfectly well that no amount of money could soothe the constant ache of a broken heart, and no amount of money could have bought Valentine a father. Still, it made Sy feel better to give it, and who was Miriam to deprive him? But it was usually fifty dollars that he left, sometimes one hundred. But five thousand dollars?

Miriam had to sit down. Not because five thousand dollars was a lot of money to find in a box of macaroons. Miriam sat because she understood that Sy was dying.

~

On this same first night of Passover, it should be noted, it was now nearly nine weeks since Valentine last went to the closet where she kept the tampons. Ever since she first started menstruating when she was twelve, you could set your watch by Valentine's periods. But it was due on March 2 and here it was the first week of April and still nothing.

If Valentine were aware that her period was late, she gave no indication of it. She did not dart to the bathroom every three minutes to check for spots, there was no audible praying to God to *please, please make it come. I'll never complain about cramps ever again, I swear* the way some of her ex-friends checked for spots and prayed. Girls who were *doing it* without taking precautions had good reason to mark their calendars with Xs, to count days, to shit green if they were late. Even though they should have been sensible and gone to Planned Parenthood to get themselves on the Pill, teenagers can be imprudent. Sometimes the boys did use rubbers, but mostly not, and sometimes they promised they'd pull out before they came, but you can be sure that never happened. Instead they'd mumble, "Sorry," as if they'd spilled a drink as opposed to their seed. It was those girls, those who were sexually active without taking precautions, who kept strict tabs on when their periods were due, those who lived on tenterhooks until, with that first drop of blood, came release. Still they rarely wised up. Again and again, they played Russian roulette with their futures, and again and again they held their breath and checked their panties and said their prayers. But

Valentine was not a part of this crowd. Plus, who would think twice about something as inconsequential as her last period when her grandfather, her beloved grandfather, was dying? Who, smack in the middle of such grief, would've paid attention to her monthly comings and goings, to life?

A cold and wet April was followed by a cold and wet May, but the showers brought flowers, and by the end of the month, lilacs and posies and forsythia bloomed and the sun was big and yellow like a daffodil in the sky. Spring fever hit Canarsie High School in epidemic proportions. Young love abounded and hormones were ricocheting off the walls. Boys and girls took all and any opportunity—the few minutes allotted between classes, before and after lunch—to nuzzle in the hallways, and as Mr. Fischel the principal put it, "For Christ's sake, it's like a petting zoo around here."

And what these kids wore to school made Mr. Fischel yearn for the good old days when at least there was a dress code. When students came to school clothed decently and modestly instead of wearing provocative skimpies. Now the boys sat in history and English class as if dressed for a basketball game, and the girls, *Jesus H. Christ,* who could believe their parents let them out like that; shorts so short you could see practically everything and tube tops, and halter tops which showed more than everything.

~

Although she was as style conscious as the next girl, Valentine was not wearing short shorts because that Friday morning when she put on her white cutoffs, she found she could not zip them up. The same thing happened when she put on the blue ones; nor could she button her dungaree skirt. Not one thing from last spring season fit her. Valentine felt around her hips and turned in the mirror to check out her butt. These things, metabolism and obesity, are often genetic, and certainly it was possible that Valentine had embarked on the road to rotundity.

The only thing in Valentine's closet that fit her was a demure dress which had been a gift from her grandmother. It was exactly the sort of dress a grandmother would buy, and later, after Rose had gone home, Valentine had said to her mother, "Ma, I can't wear this. It's queer."

"So don't wear it." Miriam was with-it enough to know what the kids did and did not wear and that the consequences of wearing the wrong thing could be dire. "Hang it in your closet, and one night when your grandmother is coming over, you'll put it on and make her happy."

Now, in the kitchen, Miriam poured Valentine a glass of orange juice and asked, "That's the dress Grandma Rose bought you? You know, it's cute and she always buys quality, but it's not very becoming on you." Miriam, so kill her for it, was characteristically honest.

Valentine shrugged and said, "Nothing else fits me. I've gained weight."

"I thought so," Miriam said. "A few pounds maybe. So we'll go to the mall tomorrow and get you some new things."

"I don't know, Ma. I think maybe I should go on a diet."

But Miriam disagreed. "It suits you. You were too thin before. You were looking drawn. This is just right."

Valentine ate four waffles smothered in maple syrup, and still hungry, she rummaged through the pantry for potato chips.

"Potato chips?" Miriam noted. "For breakfast? Who eats potato chips for breakfast?"

~

For breakfast, John Wosileski ate potato chips because that was all he had in the cupboards. Potato chips, and a can of Dinty Moore stew. There were two Swanson Hungry-Man dinners in the freezer, and fours cans of beer in the refrigerator. It did occur to him that potato chips for breakfast was kind of disgusting, but he couldn't say that he cared. Try as he did, John couldn't manage to care about much of anything. No, wait. That—try as he did—isn't accurate. He didn't try to care. To make an effort indicates that you at least want to be among the living.

Wiping his fingers on his khaki trousers, potato-chip grease leaving telltale stains, John Wosileski left his dispiriting little apartment, and he was halfway to work when he too was afflicted by spring fever. Not the way the students were touched by the season of rebirth; he did not long to toss a Frisbee, and although he might have liked to kiss a woman, the fever was not concentrated in that area. For John Wosileski, spring fever revealed itself with a keen desire to walk, to walk along Rockaway Parkway, past Avenues J and K without turning to enter Canarsie High School. He was overtaken with something like a gust of wind propelling him onward, a gust of wind he imagined to be like the wind of childhood cartoons, where the wind was personified and had a face with big, puffy cheeks, the same wind he imagined whenever Father Palachuk made reference to the Holy Ghost. And because this wind was inside of him as opposed to an external force, John Wosileski might very well have been filled with the Spirit, the Spirit telling him to blow off work, not just that day but forever, to walk from Canarsie to East Flatbush to Crown Heights and across the Williamsburg Bridge to Manhattan and from there to the Bronx and from the Bronx to Yonkers following the Post Road all the way to Albany and from there to Plattsburgh. He considered how he could get an apartment in Plattsburgh and a job as a math teacher. Didn't the career counselor tell him that math teachers were always in demand? Why should Plattsburgh be different in that way from Brooklyn? He could teach math and buy himself a used car and every weekend all winter long he could ski and live as near to a happy life as John Wosileski would ever know.

~

Before leaving for work, Joanne Clarke gathered up the brochures she'd been perusing; brochures for nursing homes, private nursing homes, spanking-clean places with good medical care and the latest in occupational therapy and recreation—checkers, bingo, and ballroom dancing—for the infirm aged "because you want nothing but the best for your mother or father."

Not that those prices, I don't. Joanne Clarke dumped the glossy brochures in the trash basket.

~

By no one's account was Beth Sandler an enthusiastic student, but oh, on that morning she could not wait to get to school. Bounding out of the house with a bunnylike bounce to her step, Beth hurried to get there early; early enough to make out for ten minutes, ten glorious minutes, with Joey Rappaport before the bell rang. Beth Sandler was wildly in love with Joey Rappaport and she thought, on this beautiful spring morning, that she would explode from it. Indeed, love burst from her heart and spread all inside her like strawberry jam. She was, as the expression went, creaming in her jeans.

~

John Wosileski got as far as Flatlands Avenue, all of three or four blocks toward his dreamed-of destination, before turning back. Any semblance of determination deserted him, the gust of wind died to a standstill when he remembered that he had no money other than the seven dollars in his wallet and the $56.42 in his checking account, which was not enough to buy a used car, never mind first and last month's rent plus a security deposit on a new apartment. And he'd never get another teaching job if he walked out on this one before the year's end.

Another man, in the face of this reality, might have retained sufficient spunk at least to plan for a move, to start saving, to work an extra job on weekends, to start looking for a job in the Plattsburgh area. Another man could have made such a move before the start of the new school year, just weeks really before the ski season began. But John Wosileski was not such a man. Inertia stopped him in his tracks. The thought of rallying exhausted him. Laziness, in the guise of fatalism, won out as he determined that there were no choices for him anyway, that his fate was sealed, and a woeful fate it was. His hope vanished in the same way it happens when you forget what you were going to say. The particulars vaporize, leaving behind nothing but a vague sense of frustration. Many lives are ruined by that, by laziness.

~

Mr. Fischel walked through the hallways, his eyes taking in far more than he preferred seeing. Legs, thighs, shoulders, bobbling breasts, cleavage galore. It was sickening. At least there was one student, the principal took note, who, in his estimation, was attired for school as opposed to a day at the beach. It was that pretty girl, the one who seemed a little dopey, who distinguished herself by wearing a daisy-print dress, which, although stopping several inches short of her knees, at least allowed her to bend over without showing her underpants. Some of these girls bent over would reveal the whole panties. Mr. Fischel supposed he ought to be grateful that they at least wore panties. God, he hated this job.

~

Valentine's assessment that the dress from her grandmother was a queer dress was confirmed when, after homeroom, on her way to art class, she passed by those who had cast her out as irrevocably as Eve from the garden, and Marcia Finkelstein said, "Nice dress, Valentine," whereupon Beth Sandler and the others giggled their pretty selves silly.

~

The game was at Edith Zuckerman's house, not because it was her turn, but because Edith had gotten a new couch, and she wanted to show it off. A white sectional couch. "White?" Miriam questioned the wisdom of that. "Edith, white is going to show every mark and stain. What were you thinking? White."

"I got the plastic slipcovers," Edith said. "I'll keep them on except for when I'm entertaining."

Miriam made a face. Plastic slipcovers, which weren't really plastic but vinyl, were horrible. Never mind even how they stuck to your skin, they looked so cheap. You could have a million-dollar couch; if you cover it with those plastic slipcovers, it'll look like you bought it at Levine's, that cheesy discount furniture showroom on Flatbush Avenue, the one where he tried to pass off imitation Capodimonte as the real thing.

The day would come when Miriam would be relieved that Edith's couch was protected with plastic slipcovers; not quite as relieved as Edith would be, but relieved nonetheless because a ruined couch is the sort of thing that could come between friends.

That day, however, was months in the future, a future that none of them could have predicted, not in their wildest dreams, so while Sunny Shapiro spread her hands over the tiles, washing them, Miriam said what she was thinking. "Slipcovers or not," Miriam said, "I still think you should've gone with a print. A nice floral."

"I know you have an eye"—Judy Weinstein deferred to Miriam this much—"but I think the white is stunning. So she'll keep the slipcovers on when there's no one here to see. When she's got people to impress, she'll take them off."

It was a good thing all the way around that Edith never thought of The Girls or their husbands or children as anyone to impress. The Girls and theirs were extended family.

"Did I tell you"—Miriam discarded one tile—"that Rose is going to Israel?"

Sunny Shapiro took a tile from the wall and made a face. Sunny always gave her hand away with those faces she made. "Rose is going to Israel? For a vacation?"

"My mother-in-law went last year," Judy said. "With the Temple Seniors. She's still talking about it."

"Rose has a sister there. In Tel Aviv. They haven't seen each other in twenty years. Sy, may he rest in peace, had a mortal fear of flying. So she's going for a visit." Miriam reached for a cookie. "For a month. It was a spontaneous decision, but it's been a dream of hers for as long as I can remember."

"That's so beautiful. I'm choked up just thinking about it." Sunny wiped at her eye. "What a joy for her."

"Girls," Edith said, "are we gabbing or are we playing?"

Valentine took her gym suit—a hideous outfit if ever there was one, part jumpsuit, part bloomers, and in hospital green—from the locker, and like the other girls getting ready for the volleyball game, she was in a state of undress when Miss Marks, the other gym teacher, the one the girls liked as opposed to Miss Dench whom they all hated, save for the tennis team, came through the locker room blowing her whistle. "Ladies! Ladies!" she called out. "Let's get a move on it. On the count of—" Miss Marks stopped short, distracted by the sight of Valentine Kessler standing there in her bikini underpants and bra.

From time to time the rumor floated that Miss Marks was a lesbian, and that she, just like Miss Dench, came through the locker room with the express purpose of checking out the half-naked nubile girls, but this was only a rumor, invariably revived by some mean-spirited girl. While all the girls professed a kind of horror over the possibility, no one ever reported such a thing to either Mr. Fischel the principal or to her parents. The truth of the matter was that whether or not Miss Marks was a lesbian, she came through the locker room with her whistle only because she knew, from experience, that if she did not hurry them along, these girls would dawdle away the forty-minute period and never get on the volleyball court.

Rest assured that there was nothing untoward about Miss Marks stopping short at the sight of Valentine in her underwear. Rather, it was genuine concern which caused her to say, "Valentine, get dressed and meet me in my office." Then she blew her whistle and ordered everyone onto the court. As the girls filed out of the locker room, Miss Marks selected Terry Ambrose and Mindy Silverman to be team captains and Beverly Johnson would referee. "I'll be with you as soon as I can," she said. "I don't want any trouble out there."

It did not go unnoticed by the other girls that Valentine Kessler was not among them, which was a good thing because she really stank at volleyball and no one wanted her as a teammate. The gratitude experienced by both teams did not, however, diminish their curiosity and they asked one another what was going on. Why was Valentine in Miss Marks's office? *Is she in some kind of trouble?*

~

While her class hacked up earthworms in a vain attempt to observe the digestive track, Joanne Clarke put pen to paper and with her signature committed her father to a nursing home. Not to one of the ones advertised in the glossy brochures, but to a state nursing home, which was something of a snake pit. She told herself that she didn't want to do this, but that she had to, it was for his own good, and perhaps it was for his own good, and while it was true that, at some point in the future, she really would not have been able to care for him, now, at least some of the time, he found his way to the bathroom. Yes, she did have to prepare food for him, but he could feed himself, and he was happy enough in front of the television set, especially when cartoons were on. She did not *have* to do this; she *wanted* to do this. Yes, it would've been nicer all the way around if she'd been able to afford a decent nursing home, a clean and well-staffed place as opposed to the state-subsidized hell-hole to which she was consigning him for the rest of his days. But she couldn't afford it and any money he had saved, which wasn't much to begin with, was pretty much gone.

She licked the glue on the envelope and then sealed it shut. The stamp was already affixed. She would drop it in the mailbox on her way home.

To alleviate any residual guilt generated by this less than filial devotion, she rationalized her decision by asking herself a rhetorical question: Where was he when she was a lonely fifteen-, sixteen-, seventeen-year-old girl with a face like a pizza pie and crying herself to sleep every night? On the other side of her bedroom door, in the living room, with the television turned up loud to drown out the sounds of her weeping, that's where he was. But Joanne Clarke was mistaken to think that her father was indifferent to her suffering. He kept the television volume up high because it hurt him to hear his daughter cry like that, and worse, he simply didn't know what to do about it. He was useless, but he cared. If Joanne Clarke were to know that, to know that her suffering caused him heartache too, would she still have gone ahead and signed those papers? Probably yes. Yes, she would have done exactly the same thing regardless, because, no matter how or when she got that way, Joanne Clarke had become a cold woman.

~

Miss Marks was one of the nicer teachers, but gym was definitely Valentine's worst subject, and it was with a slightly green pallor that she entered the office. "You wanted to see me?" Valentine said.

"Yes." Miss Marks smiled and pulled a chair up close to her own. "Come. Sit down."

At the warm reception, Valentine's expression changed to one of surprise and delight, as if butterflies had flown up from her stomach and fluttered out of her mouth, like in a surrealist painting.

Miss Marks leaned in toward Valentine. "Valentine," she said, "I need to ask you something personal, okay?"

Valentine nodded. "Sure," she said.

"When was your last menstrual cycle?" Miss Marks did not beat around the bush. "Do you remember?"

Valentine's brow furrowed deeply, as if in abetment to recollection, as if her brain were constipated, but no matter how she bore down, she could not recall. "I really don't know," she concluded. "I guess it's been a while."

Her reason for concern now realized, Miss Marks took Valentine's hand into her own. She formulated, in her mind, just how she would phrase this before speaking. "Valentine, I'm not judging you here. I'm talking to you as a friend. You can trust me, okay? Is there any chance that you might be pregnant?"

Now remember, as a gym teacher, Miss Marks had heard it all. Every lie imaginable; teenage girls were a font of mendacity. Consequently, Miss Marks had a finely tuned sense of perception when it came to prevarication. As she put it, "I've got a built-in bullshit detector."

Miss Marks would've bet the farm that Valentine Kessler was four months along, but when Valentine said to her, "I'm still a virgin," Miss Marks saw no evidence of fibbing, none of the telltale signs of a tall tale. Could it be that Valentine was indeed telling the absolute truth? Had it been any other girl, any girl not Valentine Kessler, Miss Marks would have let it go at that. But this gym teacher was a wise woman, and the thought did cross her mind—*With this kid, it's possible that she did it but doesn't know she did it. With this kid, it's very possible that someone took advantage of her; she's not stupid but she is an innocent*—because Miss Marks knew a knocked-up teenager when she saw one, and she saw at least one every year.

As these were days when a person could still be a good Samaritan without fear of being sued for it, days when teachers could be confidants to students, days when they were expected to be *in loco parentis*, Miss Marks did not hesitate to step into it. "Valentine," Miss Marks said. "After school today, I want you to come with me to see a doctor friend of mine. I'd like her to take a look at you. Will you do that? For me?"

"If you really want me to," Valentine said, "but I am a virgin, Miss Marks. Really. I am."

"I believe you," the gym teacher said. "But humor me, okay?"

Valentine sat in the passenger seat, and Miss Marks drove in the direction of Mill Basin. At a stop sign, Miss Marks saw the oddest thing—a pair of birds, not sparrows of which there were zillions, but a pair of yellow and orange and pinkish birds, sort of like canaries, perched on top of a telephone pole. She turned to Valentine and said, "Look. Look on top of that telephone pole."

Valentine looked, but said she didn't see anything, and when Miss Marks looked again, she didn't see anything either. "Oh, they must've flown off. Canaries. They probably escaped from a cage and flew out an open window."

"Chippy-chasers," Valentine said.

~

Although he'd still be with her for another couple of weeks, at least, Joanne Clarke started to pack up her father's things. *Why wait until the last minute?* was her rationale for filling a suitcase with pajamas, a bathrobe, slippers, socks, underwear, and a new toothbrush.

As far as his personal effects went—his books on fly-fishing (why he had those was a mystery to Joanne; as far as she knew he never went fishing, but he must have had thirty books at least on the subject and all of them clearly read), his sergeant stripes from the army (too old for combat in the Second World War, he nonetheless enlisted and was made a clerk at Fort Dix), some crappy old fountain pen he was attached to for reasons beyond his daughter, a brass plaque commemorating twenty years of service with the Metropolitan Life Insurance Company—all this she would throw in the trash. It's not like he'd know the difference.

His watch she would keep because it was gold.

~

Dr. Stern, who was a woman, gave Valentine a paper cup and told her to pee in it. Then she was to put on a green hospital gown, open in the front. This was Valentine's first visit to a gynecologist, and while she'd heard tell of the ordeal, you really do have to experience the stirrups firsthand to appreciate the wretchedness, and the cold speculum forcing you open is not unlike the torture of the Iron Maiden. "I know." Dr. Stern patted Valentine, to comfort her. "It's a little uncomfortable."

"A little uncomfortable?" Valentine spoke rhetorically. "You're kidding me, right?"

Moments later, the doctor snapped off her surgical gloves. "All done," she said, and she dropped the gloves in the trash. "See, that wasn't so bad, was it?"

"A regular day at the beach," Valentine said, and then Dr. Stern was at her breasts. Feeling her up!

"Are your breasts tender?" Dr. Stern asked, while fondling them still. "Do they hurt at all?"

"Yes, they hurt," Valentine said. "Of course they hurt when you're pinching at them like that."

"Sorry." The doctor apologized, which didn't stop her from pinching the other one before saying, "Okay. When you finish dressing, meet me in my office. It's the second door on the left. We'll talk then." Dr. Stern shut the door on her way out, leaving Valentine alone, about as alone as a teenage girl could be.

~

Sometimes the very worst pain is that with no discernible fault. John Wosileski sat catercorner from his mother at her kitchen table, covered with a pinkish oilcloth, knowing that although there was once a point of origin for this anguish he was suffering, its whereabouts were lost because the anguish had spread like a cancer.

"John." His mother reached out for his hand, but he pulled it away, as if what held him together was of such a delicate balance that the slightest breath of contact would cause him to collapse like a game of pickup sticks. "John," she said again, softly, so that her husband in the next room drinking a beer from the can and looking at the *Daily News* wouldn't hear. "John," she asked, "are you happy?"

Under the pretense of rubbing his eyes as if he were tired, John covered half his face with his hands and said, "Sure, Ma. I'm happy." As Miriam Kessler could've told him, *Truth can walk around naked; lies must be clothed.*

It struck John as extremely peculiar that his mother should ask such a question. Never before had she made any such inquiry. He wondered if maybe she was dying. While each of the Wosileskis had experienced their rare moments of happiness, John thought that they might have been better off had they not; that the moments of happiness served only to accentuate the despair. Had John never skied Whiteface and Mount Snow, had he never known those excruciatingly beautiful seconds with Valentine Kessler, had Mrs. Wosileski, twenty-four years ago, not walked down the aisle as a grateful bride and hopeful mother-to-be, had Mr. Wosileski not, those same twenty-four years ago minus a few months, known a surge of pride and love, yes, love, at the sight of his newborn son, had he not twice—twice!—bowled a perfect game, then the Wosileskis might not have understood that they were unhappy now. With nothing to compare it to, a dreary life would've been a flatline, which is something like a contented one. But they did know rapture and so the loss of it, the fleetingness of it, rendered the sadness that much more acute.

Mrs. Wosileski reached into the pocket of her housecoat—a cotton smock which seemed to John to be new, the print of oranges and cherries was vivid, almost shockingly so—and she pulled out what John first thought was a bankbook or a passport; it was a little booklet of some sort and she kept it hidden beneath her hand. Beckoning her son to come in closer, she revealed to him what she had. Plaid Stamps. Trading stamps given out by the A&P, the number of them determined by how much you spent on groceries. Pasted into these booklets, they were redeemed for valuable merchandise. Six and a half books of Plaid Stamps got you a steam iron, or a whopping eighty-seven books got you a set of luggage, or you could exchange two books for a punch bowl. A mere one and one quarter books was the price to pay for a kitchen clock mounted on a hen silhouetted in gold tone.

There was a report of a miracle not entirely unrelated to the redemption and joy of Plaid Stamps, yours for the taking at the A&P. At a supermarket in a suburb in California, the Virgin Mary appeared in a ball of light and, in a voice gentle and melodious, instructed a young housewife to erect a seventy-five-foot-tall cross in the parking lot. Had she known she was going to meet the Blessed Mother, this housewife, Nicole Dempsy, would have worn something other than cutoffs and a halter top, but she thought she was just going to pick up a half gallon of milk and a quart of orange juice. The Virgin appeared to Nicole Dempsy on thirty-two more occasions, each time with further specifications regarding the cross. It was to be made of redwood. It was to be edged with small white lights. It was to be based in the parking lot, in row D, spot fourteen. Although the supermarket manager consistently refused to so much as consider the Blessed Virgin's request, he did devote two rows of supermarket shelves in aisle four to the sale of religious items, such as framed photographs of Jesus, books of illustrated Bible stories for children, and snow domes featuring the Nativity scene because row D, spot fourteen had become a shrine and thousands flocked to the parking spot of miracles, where, it was claimed, silver rosary beads turned gold, rosebushes bloomed from concrete, the deaf could hear the angels singing, a ninety-six-year-old man got an erection for the first time in fifteen years to the day, and another young housewife heard her name called over a loudspeaker, announcing that she was the winner of the Supermarket Sweepstakes—all the groceries she could load in a cart in a mad ten-minute scramble for bounty.

~

"I've got hundreds of them, of these books, all filled." Mrs. Wosileski trembled with the thrill of it. "He doesn't know about them." She cocked her head in the direction of the living room, indicating *he* as her husband. Hardly for the first time, Mrs. Wosileski wished a stroke on her husband, a stroke that would leave him paralyzed and without the power of speech, but this wish was between her and God, never ever uttered aloud.

John asked his mother where the stamps came from because, as far as he knew, she'd never shopped at an A&P. His father forbade it, demanding she shop the old-world way at the local markets where there was kielbasa and pierogi and fresh bread and none of that packaged garbage. "When the old lady upstairs died. Mrs. Sygietynska. You remember her? With the humpback? Father Palachuk asked me to clean out her apartment. She had no family. And I found these. Two shoeboxes full. I brought them to the father, and he said I could keep them. Two boxes full of them, John." She spoke as if the shoeboxes were filled with real gold. "We can get some nice things. Me and you. To make us happy."

Mrs. Wosileski, John's mother, contrary to all experience,

believed in miracles, and she had already picked out a Dacron polyester kitchen curtain with matching valance (two books) and a framed picture of the head of Christ (one book) and an electric organ (twenty-two and a half books). John tried to smile back at his mother, but he couldn't because forget curtains and punch bowls, it would take more than that to make them happy. If John did believe that God might have answered his prayers, he would have, at that moment, surely put in a request, but he didn't bother. John Wosileski had somehow gotten the idea that those who are not supremely blessed, people such as himself, get an allotment of one miracle, and John had used his up already. *Oh Valentine*, which he likened to Jesus healing the lame guy only to have the former cripple walk off a cliff.

~

"How is that possible?" Miss Marks asked Dr. Stern. "I just can't believe it."

Dr. Stern sat at her desk across from Miss Marks. "It's a first for me, you can be sure. I mean, I've read of it, and I knew it was theoretically possible, but it's also theoretically possible to walk on water, and I don't imagine I'm going see anyone do that anytime soon. Frankly, I rarely even see a hymen these days. Usually it's long gone just from riding a bicycle or gymnastics or something like that."

Just then, Valentine Kessler, who neither rode a bicycle nor was capable of mastering the parallel bars, having gotten dressed, opened the office door. She was backlit by a shaft of sunlight, and Dr. Stern had to shield her eyes to make out who it was standing at the threshold. "Valentine," Dr. Stern said. "Come in. Sit down. We need to talk."

Fifteen

Valentine took the chair beside Miss Marks, and Dr. Stern asked her, “Valentine, do you have a steady boyfriend?”

“No,” she said. “I don’t have a boyfriend. Not steady or otherwise.” Valentine was not making Dr. Stern’s job any easier here.

Dr. Stern took a deep breath to fortify herself against the hysteria that dollars-to-donuts would ensue upon breaking the news to a sixteen-year-old virgin that, against all odds, she was nearly four months pregnant. It was at times like this that Dr. Stern wished she’d listened to her mother and gone to law school. “Medicine will eat you alive or it will turn your heart into a pebble,” her mother had said. “It’s no job for a woman.” Not yet pebble-hearted, Dr. Stern concluded that it was kindest in the end to be swift. “Valentine,” she said, “you’re pregnant,” and she moved the box of Kleenex so that tissues were handy to the girl.

Miss Marks put her arm around Valentine, but Valentine took

the news better than the teacher and the doctor had anticipated. Whatever her distress, it was absent blood and thunder. She reached for a tissue and blew her nose, which honked, and then she smiled; a smile that was positively serene, as if her world were now bathed in white light, illuminating all of which, heretofore, had bewildered her. As if there were shape to what had been formless, order to the chaos, rhyme to the reason, God's plan revealed. *Arrrre Vey Maaaaa-reeee-er.*

Or the other possibility: She was in a kind of shock, denial, unable to face the fact, she simply refused to comprehend what was said. Perhaps Valentine had retreated behind some bubble that only looked like bliss.

Well, whatever it was, Valentine was going to have to snap out of it, because decisions had to be made and they had to be made fast because already Valentine had entered her second trimester. Having been a powerful advocate for legal and therefore safe abortion, Dr. Stern said a quick and silent prayer of thanks to the Supreme Court for its wisdom in regard to *Roe* v. *Wade* and then said to Valentine, "We're going to have to schedule the abortion for as soon as possible."

"Abortion?" Valentine shook her pretty head. "No. I can't do that."

Miss Marks and Dr. Stern both tried to reason with the girl, *Think of your future. You're throwing your life away. You're so young. What about college? This is going to kill your mother,* to no avail.

The doctor and the teacher, two women who had marched and demonstrated and signed petitions to help girls like Valentine, they were getting nowhere with her.

Miss Marks tried another route. "And what about the boy, the father of this baby? Is he ready for this?"—to which Valentine responded, "There is no boy."

"There is no boy? There has be a boy, Valentine," Dr. Stern said.

Valentine shook her head. "There is no boy," she repeated. It was certainly possible that she was telling the truth as she knew it. It was possible that all memory of the seedy encounter had been eradicated, that a reclamation of innocence had taken root. It was possible because anything is possible.

"Come on, Valentine." Miss Marks stood up. "I'll drive you home."

~

Home from her game, Miriam was three dollars poorer—Edith Zuckerman had cleaned up—but none the wiser when she called up the stairs for Valentine. "Valentine," she called, but got no response. "Valentine?" she called again, louder. "Are you here? Valentine?"

Miriam looked at the watch on her wrist. Just after five on a glorious Friday afternoon in springtime, where could she be? Out? Out with friends perhaps for the first time since her sixteenth birthday, and whatever happened that night, Miriam had a hunch it wasn't what Valentine had wished for. Not when she came home early and went straight to bed. What had happened that Valentine should suddenly become a loner? This was a question that Miriam still refused to address, and now, it seemed, she wouldn't have to. Not when she was convinced that Valentine was out, with friends.

Mothers have an limitless capacity to delude themselves where their children are concerned.

Maybe for dinner a nice chicken cutlet, dipped in flour and egg, then fried in butter, that sounded good to Miriam, with a salad and rice. She got out the necessary ingredients and was whisking the eggs in the bowl when Valentine came home and into the kitchen, kissing her mother on the cheek. Then she, Valentine, took Miriam by the arm and led her to the table. "Sit down, Ma. I've got to tell you something."

It was then that Miriam saw Valentine's face, flushed, her cheeks pink as carnations, and she wasn't wearing a drop of makeup. And her eyes, there was something about Valentine's eyes, as if her eyes had taken on the properties of cut glass, like blue topaz, as if they gave off beams of radiance sweeping like searchlights across the darkness.

"Ma," Valentine said, "I'm going to have a baby," and before Valentine could say another word, Miriam let go with a piercing lament, a howling, an ululation, the sound of the inconsolable.

Years later, when this story had become something of an urban legend, it was said that Miriam's cry echoed throughout Canarsie, from one house to the next, like the call to prayer. This, of course, was hyperbolic, to say the least. No one but Valentine heard Miriam's wail; God's ears must have been plugged up with wax.

John Wosileski did not want to break the news to his mother, but better she should hear it from him than from a stranger. "Ma, listen to me, okay. These are worthless." He slapped the book of Plaid Stamps against the edge of the table.

His mother reached over and snatched the book back, holding it to her bosom, such as she had one, all skin and bone, she was. "No, you're wrong," she said. "You can trade them in for beautiful things, John."

"Not anymore, Ma. They stopped that a couple of years ago. It was in all the newspapers. They gave it up." The A&P no longer issued Plaid Stamps. The redemption centers had closed up shop. There would be no beautiful things for Mrs. Wosileski, and now she understood this. What a simpleton she was to imagine otherwise, and having pushed herself up from the table, she turned her back on her son and asked, "You'll stay for fish?"

Despite Vatican II and the concessions made to the modern age by the Second Ecumenical Council of the Roman Catholic Church, the Wosileskis continued to have fish for Friday dinner. Partly this was out of habit and partly because Mrs. Wosileski couldn't quite believe that all of a sudden out of nowhere God had changed His mind. No matter that the pope said it was now okay to have meat on Fridays, the Wosileskis had fish. No. God never changed His mind. Mrs. Wosileski knew that because she was the living proof.

~

Once before, Valentine had witnessed her mother in such a state, but because she was only a year old, she couldn't have remembered how Miriam had collapsed when Ronald left her. But even if Valentine had remembered, that was a long time ago. Miriam was a younger woman then and a good sixty-seven pounds lighter. Now she was heaving and gasping and snorting for breath and it looked as if Miriam were going to give out and expire like a punctured beach ball.

Having no experience with emergencies, Valentine did the sensible thing. She ran from her house to the Sabatinis' house, where she beat her fists against their door.

One look at Valentine Kessler and Angela Sabatini didn't so much as take the time to ask what was wrong. She raced across the lawn, Valentine at her heels, and in the Kesslers' kitchen she found

Miriam on the floor, seemingly passed out in a dead faint or well and truly dead itself. Angela Sabatini—bless her—kept cool, as if she were a professional in crisis management. After checking for a pulse and—thank you, God—finding one, she called for an ambulance and then made a cold compress with ice and a dish towel, which she held to Miriam's forehead while Valentine went outside and stood on the front step like a beacon.

The wail of the ambulance siren was a call to the neighbors to evacuate their houses. Up from their dinner tables, away from the evening news, homework abandoned, every man, woman, and child on the block swarmed onto the street, where they congregated in front of the Kesslers' house. *What happened? What happened?* They asked one another over and over *what happened?* but no one had any answers. Having left a corned beef simmering on the stove, Judy Weinstein broke through the crowd and rushed up the walkway to Valentine, grabbing the girl by her shoulders. "Your mother? Is your mother okay?" Then, not waiting for an answer, Judy entered the Kessler house to find the two medics crouched on either side of Miriam, supporting her as she sat on the floor with her head lowered between her legs. Angela Sabatini was making a pot of coffee. "What happened?" Judy asked, and one of medics said, "A distress reduced the blood flow to the brain causing aggravated syncope."

"She fainted," his partner clarified.

"A distress?" Judy asked. "What distress? Is she going to be okay?"

The first medic, the officious one, who clearly fancied himself some kind of Dr. Kildare, said, "Impact can cause contusions of the brain."

Judy looked to the second medic, the one who wasn't a *schmuck*. He shifted Miriam's weight nearer to his shoulder to relieve an ache in his arm and said, "The only danger with fainting is if you hit your head in the fall, but this one, she went down like a pillow. She's fine."

"I'm fine." Miriam spoke in a clear voice, as if nothing had happened. "Let me up. I'm fine," and the two men helped Miriam to her feet, and then into a chair at the kitchen table. Angela Sabatini poured everyone, except for Miriam, a cup of coffee. For Miriam she poured a little sherry from a bottle she found in the cabinet, which smelled like medicine and not anything good like *grappa.*

Before they left, the medics took Miriam's blood pressure and listened to her heart, pronounced her fit as a fiddle, and told her to take it easy. Outside, they found Valentine standing just as before. "Your mother is fine. She fainted, is all. You got nothing to be afraid of," the second medic said. The other one, the blowhard, made his way through the throng of neighbors waiting. "Coming through," he said. "Medical personnel coming through." His partner followed, assuring everyone that Miriam was not dead, or even a little bit sick. "She fainted," he told them. "That's all. She fainted."

Fainting wasn't very interesting, and it was dinnertime, so the crowd broke apart. Everyone went back inside their houses. Everyone, that is, except for Angela Sabatini and Judy Weinstein, who had forsaken her own Shabbes dinner, having called home to tell her daughter to light the candles in her stead, which was perfectly acceptable, religiously speaking, because it was the Jewish way to choose life over law. Miriam needed her now, and Judy Weinstein embraced her friend.

Miriam cried on Judy's shoulder, the gold lamé chafing against her cheek.

The hum of uneasiness was felt more than heard. John Wosileski watched his mother move her food around on her plate, but she brought none of it to her mouth. His father, on the other hand, was shoveling it in, assuring a reserve of energy for later. They, his brethern at the Polish American Club, were counting on him, their star. To have bowled two perfect games made Pete Wosileski a legend. On this night, his team was up against the Italians of Bay Ridge. Mr. Wosileski had tried to interest John in the sport, but John never took to the dank-smelling lanes, to the floors sticky with spilled beer, to the boisterous men slapping one another on the back. Bowling was not his game, although he might have made more of an effort to like it if he'd known that his father had once hoped they'd join the father-son league. But it wasn't his father's way to ask, and the best John could do now was to feign interest. "So, you think your team will win tonight?"

"I don't know," his father said. "Those wops are good." Then Mr. Wosileski thumped his fist against the center of his chest and belched. His wife got up to clear away his plate while he went to put on his bowling shirt.

~

The conversation at Phyllis Marks's dinner table was animated. Neither Danny, her fiancé of four years five months and holding (so she wasn't a lesbian, after all), nor the two friends they had over for Chinese takeout, could believe it. "The poor fucking kid," Danny said. "What shitty luck."

"Knocked up without any of the fun." Hal talked with egg roll in his mouth. Hal Wortsberg was Danny's fellow real-estate salesman at DelMore Properties, and because he was unattached, Phyllis had insisted that she and Danny fix him up with one of Phyllis's single girlfriends, of which there were many. So Danny invited Hal and Phyllis invited Tina for what was supposed to be a home-cooked meal (the idea being to show Hal what he was missing), but after such a day, Phyllis couldn't manage anything more than ordering in.

When the food arrived, Tina followed Phyllis into the kitchen to help her carry out drinks and plates and utensils, and as Phyllis reached into the cabinet for glasses, Tina said, "I thought you said he *owned* the real-estate company. I didn't know he just worked there."

At the same time, in the living room, Hal was telling Danny, "She's flat as a ironing board. I like them big." Hal cupped his hands in front of his chest. "Like melons."

While Danny didn't give a damn if Tina and Hal clicked or not, Phyllis had been hoping they would fall for each other because if they were to get married, that might light a fire under Danny. As Mrs. Marks, Phyllis's mother, was fond of saying over and over again, "It's not natural to have such a long engagement. I think he's playing you. He should, you'll pardon the expression, shit or get off the pot." But now, on the heels of this experience with Valentine, it wasn't that Phyllis didn't care if Hal liked Tina and *vice versa.* Rather, she understood that she had no say, no place, in the determination of the fates of others, and that included Danny. For Phyllis Marks, the question remained open only as to whether she had any say in her own fate or not.

∾

Before going home, Angela Sabatini paused on the front step alongside Valentine. Mrs. Sabatini touched the girl lightly on the arm. "Valentine," she said, "I've been married for fourteen years and four months. My Joey is fourteen years old on the nose." She made a face which said, *What are you gonna do?* "It might seem like the end of the world, but it's not." Angela Sabatini derived no satisfaction from the realization of her prediction that *that Kessler kid is going to wind up in trouble with a capital T* had come to pass. She would not indulge in the pleasure of *I told you so. Didn't I say that would happen? Haven't I been saying so for years?* "It'll work out," Angela Sabatini said, and when Valentine turned so that she was looking directly at Mrs. Sabatini, Angela experienced something like déjà vu or whatever it's called when someone affects you for no reason at all. Angela Sabatini was haunted by a recognition of love for this girl. Her heart burned with love, she was awash in love as if love were water and she were bobbing like a rubber ball in a tub, but the very strangest part of loving her was that she did not want to comfort Valentine; rather, she wanted Valentine to offer *her* comfort, as if it would be something significant if this teenager would hold Angela Sabatini's hand or kiss her brow.

At a loss, Angela Sabatini said to Valentine, "Now go inside. Your mother needs you."

In Joanne Clarke's kitchen, pandemonium reigned. For no reason at all, or no reason that Joanne could ascertain, her father, fresh from defecating on the linoleum at the foot of the refrigerator, went wild-eyed as if something like fury had erupted inside of him. He proceeded to smash dishes on the floor, to fling pots and pans against the wall like a man possessed by a demon or by hatred. Joanne barricaded herself in her bedroom, where she called for emergency services.

The police arrived along with the paramedics to find her father, wearing only his pajama top, hurling fruit, apples mostly, although he did fling a pear and two bananas, at the stove.

"He's senile," she said. "He doesn't know what he's doing," she explained to the policemen. One paramedic held her father down, one shot him up with Haldol, and then they strapped him, naked from the waist down, onto a gurney to take him to the hospital.

While her father was being loaded into the back of the ambulance, like a crate onto a truck, Joanne came racing out the door from her building and along the path to where the ambulance was parked. "Wait," she called out. "Wait a minute." When she got to paramedics, she handed one of them her father's suitcase, the suitcase she'd packed weeks before and had waiting. "You might as well take this," she said. "He's not coming back."

Joanne watched as the ambulance pulled away until it was no longer in her line of vision, and the wail of the siren was a distant hum in her memory. She turned to go back inside, back inside to the mess that would have to get cleaned up, but then changed her mind. She stayed where she was, on the sidewalk, long after the streetlamps lit.

It was dark and Valentine was still outside on the front step. From there, she looked up as if she were searching for stars, but the thing about living in Brooklyn, you almost never see stars in the sky.

The way Adam begat Seth and Seth begat Enos and Enos begat Cainan and Cainan begat Mahalaleel and Mahalaleel begat Jared and Jared begat Methuselah and Methuselah begat Lamech and Lamech begat Noah and Noah beat Shem, Ham, and Japheth, and the next thing you know there are a billion people in China, this was how the word spread. Come midmorning Monday, there wasn't one person at Canarsie High who hadn't heard the big news: Valentine Kessler—get this—was pregnant.

The students celebrated that on this day the dulling sameness was enlivened by scandal. A delectable piece of gossip is the elixir of life, and all of them—students and faculty alike—were drunk on it. What a lark! Oh, the rumor about her being a virgin did float, but like dust motes, insubstantial and without foundation, it was brushed aside. No one really believed such a story, and speculation as to who the father might be was irresistible. A *college boy? Someone from the city? Do you think maybe she was raped? I heard it was some-*

body famous? Somebody famous? Where would she meet a celebrity? Hey, has anyone seen Vincent Caputo today?

~

Joanne Clarke was humming, literally humming, audibly humming *Oh what a beautiful morning, oh what a beautiful day,* while she wrote on the blackboard in capital letters: THE REPRODUCTIVE SYSTEM, underlining it twice. The reproductive system was, as far as Joanne Clarke was concerned, the most worrisome installment of the biology curriculum. She'd saved it for the end in the hopes that they wouldn't have time for it. Not that detailing the excretory system for high-school students was a bowl of cherries, but it was the reproductive system that contained the parts most noxious. It wasn't that Miss Clarke was so much of a prude. Rather she feared association; that to stand before her class and articulate words such as *mons pubis* and *labia majora* and *vaginal orifice* would be to draw attention to her own *mons pubis, labia majora,* and vaginal orifice, which led to the fear that since she was the center of attention, her own sexual parts would be deemed lacking.

Now it was the dawn of a new era. The reproductive system was her friend, having done Joanne a favor, offering her this choice opportunity to indulge the mean and petty parts of her nature. Irrational though it may have been, she believed that girls like Valentine Kessler—or rather the kind of girl she assumed Valentine to be—pretty girls, confident girls, popular girls, snotty stuck-up bitches—somehow got Joanne Clarke's share of happiness. As if there were a quantifiable amount of it, and that there simply was none left when she got to the front of the line because they got there first. Furthering this misconception, she expected to somehow profit from Valentine's reversal of fortune, as if happiness could be handed over like canned goods.

~

Miriam Kessler was on the phone with Dr. Stern, on the receiving end of this loony story about her daughter being a pregnant virgin. "How could that be?" she asked. "Whoever heard of such a thing?"

"Granted," the doctor said, "it's rare. And this is the first time I've encountered it personally, but it does happen." Dr. Stern explained to Miriam how it happened that while the penis did not penetrate the vagina, the ejaculate got close enough. Making a mad dash for the pool, some sperm then swam like Mark Spitz, that handsome Jewish boy who won seven gold medals in aquatic sports at the 1972 Olympics. Against all odds, one sperm in a moment of triumph and jubilation, crossed the finish line. "All it takes is one," Dr. Stern said.

"Yeah, tell me about it." Miriam knew all too well how it takes but one slippery sperm to make a baby. What she heretofore didn't know was the lengths to which this sperm would go to get there. "The women in my family," Miriam said, "we're very fertile."

~

As with all generalities, there is always an exception. John Wosileski, for example, was not the least bit titillated by the news of Valentine Kessler's condition. Nor did he take satisfaction in thinking he was right all along, that there was a boyfriend in the picture, that he'd had a snowball's chance in a furnace at ever winning her affections. Why she had come to him on that February afternoon was, and would forever be, a mystery. All that remained for him of that day was the irrevocable shame of it, and, of course, the despair which followed.

~

Another person not exactly overjoyed with the day's tidings was Mr. Fischel. As the principal of Canarsie High School, he now had to deal with this girl. Mr. Fischel hated dealing with students; he despised the little shits. And no doubt this girl was going to blubber and cry and he was going to have to pretend that he gave a fuck about what happened to her. Two years and a few weeks more of this pimple-ridden gulag and he'd be eligible for his pension. Goodbye, Canarsie High. *Adios. Au revoir*, and a Bronx cheer to all that. Well, at least now he had Mrs. Landau to help him with this mess. She could comfort the girl. Isn't that what guidance counselors were for? What the hell else did they do?

~

Mrs. Landau, the overworked and underappreciated guidance counselor, was at her desk acquainting herself with Valentine Kessler's records. She carefully read over files that followed Valentine from kindergarten—*well behaved, enjoys the company of other children but sometimes drifts off from play to stare out the window; physical coordination below average; very good at finger painting*—to this point: a transcript of all A's and B's. All Mrs. Landau could think was, *What a shame,* a nice kid who never caused a minute's trouble and here she is *in trouble* in the lousiest sense. A seemingly bright future cut off at the knees.

Closing the folder, Mrs. Landau tucked it under her arm and walked down the hall to the principal's office, where he gestured for her to sit on a green Naugahyde chair, which Mrs. Landau admitted did look like genuine leather.

Mr. Fischel flicked the switch to the public-address system, and for the entire school to hear, he said, "Valentine Kessler, please report to the principal's office." And just in case he hadn't been clear, he repeated the message. "Valentine Kessler, please report to the principal's office immediately."

Mrs. Landau frowned. *Really, couldn't someone simply have collected the girl from her class rather than call further attention to her in front of the entire school?*

And, make no mistake about it: attention was called. In each and every classroom, looks were exchanged. Elbows jutted out, making contact with rib cages at the next desk over. Giggles erupted. Teachers demanded everyone settle down. "All right. All right. Enough of that. Back to work," they said, practically in unison.

In the midst of this seismic ripple, Valentine Kessler stood up from her desk and gathered her books. To the puzzlement and to the defeated expectations of her classmates and particularly dissatisfying to Miss Clarke, whose class she happened to be in then, Valentine did not look near to tears. Her gaze did not reflect her reduced circumstances. Rather she appeared almost haughty, as if she were being summoned to the principal's office to receive an award of honor as opposed to the mark of disgrace.

The calm that Valentine exuded also rattled the principal and the guidance counselor. Both of them had expected, indeed had braced themselves for, sniveling and sobbing and recriminations, but here she was as calm as if the Buddha had returned in the guise of a slim, very pretty girl instead of a fat bald man. It appeared as if Valentine had achieved *the peace that passeth all understanding.*

Even when asked about the boy who played some part in her predicament, Valentine did nothing but shake her head. Well, if she didn't want to say who put the bun in the oven, that was her business. The school's business was simply to get her the hell out of there, out of sight, and to make arrangements for her to be educated at home. In these enlightened times, Valentine would keep up with her schoolwork from the comfort and privacy of her mother's house. Gone was the era when pregnant teens were shipped off to homes for unwed mothers, which, rumor had it, were as warm and cozy as a Dickensian orphanage. Tutors would come to Valentine three times a week, work would be dropped off, and picked up when done, and if she chose to, she could, at any point, take the high-school equivalency exam. What she could not do was attend classes or show her pregnant self anywhere on school property.

"I hope that you understand that you are not being punished," Mrs. Landau explained. Her heart went out to this girl.

"It's just that you can't be here," Mr. Fischel chimed in. "It's disruptive to the others." While there wasn't one communist hair on Mr Fischel's head, he nonetheless adhered to the Marxist doctrine of sacrificing the individual for the common good.

Valentine seemed to grasp the reality of this situation because the only question she asked was, "Can I go home now?"

"Yes, certainly," Mr. Fischel said. "But your mother is going to have to come get you, and she'll have to sign some papers. We'll need her written consent before we can release you."

~

Unbeknownst to Miriam, the telephone was ringing. She didn't hear it because she was in the bathroom, running the water for her tub. Miriam took baths as opposed to showers in order to preserve her hairdo, to keep it dry and intact. The kids, with their stick-straight hair, they could take showers. After slipping off her house-coat and gingerly pulling her nightgown up over her head—careful of the hair—Miriam caught sight of her naked self in the full-length mirror on the back of the door. Given the parameters of the bath-room, this glimpse was not easily avoided, but usually Miriam turned away from her reflection before it registered. On this morn-ing, however, she faced it, and Miriam's body unclothed was not a pretty sight, but it was an honest sight. Miriam zeroed in on her breasts; these same breasts that were like a central axis, attracting Ronald Kessler the way liquid is pulled in spirally. Well, no. Not these same breasts. The breasts that Ronald frolicked with were full, and although the laws of gravity dictated that the sheer heft of them precluded acclivity, they were firm. Now they were soft and pendulous and hung down to her waist. And the rest of her was no prize package either. Skin the texture of cottage cheese, large curd, and so much of it.

Miriam turned off the faucet, and easing her bulk into the tub, in a demonstration of Archimedes' principle, water equal to her weight was displaced. Some of the displaced water sloshed over the rim and onto the floor. Miriam stretched her legs out in front of her and leaned back, her head resting on the lip of the tub as if it were a pillow. Miriam was a firm believer in the therapeutic prop-erties of a bath, but no sooner did she close her eyes than did the phone ring again. This time she heard it. As a mother, there was no way she could not answer a ringing telephone. Suppose, God for-bid, something had happened to Valentine, something worse than what had already happened to her, and Miriam didn't answer the call. So dripping wet and holding a towel over her private parts—she'd had enough of her own nudity for one day—Miriam picked up the extension phone in her bedroom.

"Mrs. Kessler? This is Paul Fischel, the principal at Canarsie High School."

"What? What happened? Is Valentine hurt?"

"She's fine. Everything is fine. She's sitting right here. But I do need you to come in. We've worked out an arrangement, given her circumstances, pending your approval. I'd like to go over it with you." Mr. Fischel navigated carefully, lest there be a lawsuit here of some kind. It wasn't unheard of, parents suing the schools over all kinds of screwy issues: the big stupid kid is ineligible for football because he's failing every subject and the parents go to court, the psycho kid is expelled for pulling a knife on a teacher and the parents call their lawyer, budget cuts result in the elimination of art class and the artsy-fartsy parents claim their kids are being denied their civil rights to express themselves. It wasn't so paranoid that Mr. Fishel should be worrying about covering his ass when dealing with a delicate issue such as this one.

"I'll be there within the hour," Miriam told him, and when Mr. Fishel hung up, he told Valentine to go wait in the nurse's office, as if being pregnant were the same as being sick. "We'll send for you when your mother gets here."

~

Sunny Shapiro and Edith Zuckerman both prided themselves on their unerring punctuality. You could set your watch by those two, which was why, coming from opposite ends of East Ninety-fourth Street, they converged at Judy Weinstein's doorway on the dot of noon.

Sunny rapped on the door to alert Judy of their arrival, and the two women stepped inside just as Judy emerged from the kitchen, the telephone at her ear and her index finger signaling for quiet at her mouth. Then to whoever was on the phone, she said, "So you'll call if you need anything. Promise me that."

As if there were some reward—a badge of goodness perhaps—for proximity to misery, Judy took on a proprietary tone when she told her other girlfriends, "That was Miriam. She can't make it." This was disheartening news in and of itself because without the fourth, there'd be no game. Without the game, their togetherness lacked structure, as if trying to hang your hat not on a rack, but on Jell-O, resulting in a disconnected moment, but Judy rallied and saved the day. "Come," she said. "We'll sit in the kitchen and talk."

Judy set out cups and saucers and cake plates, which were bone china with gold edging. The flatware was gold toned. Sunny never understood why Judy used such elegant service for every day, but that was Judy Weinstein for you; a woman who could not bear life without beauty.

While waiting for the coffee to percolate, Judy explained why Miriam wouldn't be joining them. "The principal from the school called her. She has to go over there. They're making arrangements for Valentine."

"Arrangements?" Edith asked. "What kind of arrangements?"

"For her to finish up school at home. Really, it's better this way. It's no good for the kid to be in school in her situation."

"Did Miriam get anywhere finding out who the father is?" Edith asked.

"No," Judy said. "Valentine continues to insist there was no one. And Miriam never saw her with a boy. But I say, forget that.

The boy could only complicate matters, and things are bad enough."

"When I think of what poor Miriam must be going through." Sunny's hand went to her heart.

"She has no luck, that one." Edith stroked her white mink—never mind that it was practically summer already—as if the stole were a rabbit's foot to wish upon. "I never saw anything like it. The way she has no luck. Everything she touches turns to *dreck*."

"Life is not fair," Judy said, as if such a pronouncement were a bold and new theory. "Miriam is such a good person. That she should have no luck, I ask you, is that right?"

Sunny sliced off a piece of apple strudel. "You made this?" she asked Judy. "Or you bought it?"

"I made it. This morning."

"I thought so. You can't buy a strudel with a crust this light."

Judy Weinstein took in the compliment—she had a knack with a crust, it was true—but who could think about strudel when Miriam's world was falling apart, and, mind you, not for the first time. Judy worried that Miriam might've reached her limit in how much disappointment a person could take before she went to pieces. "Miriam needs us now," she said. "More than ever. We have to be there for her. Things can't get much worse for her than they already are." Because these were words to tempt fate, words which Judy should not have uttered out loud, Edith Zuckerman picked up the saltshaker and tossed salt over her shoulder. This was something her mother did against any incursion against *that Power which erring men call Chance,* and as far as Edith was concerned, it couldn't hurt.

Before the afternoon was over, although the strudel was long gone even without Miriam there—it was that delicious—Judy

Weinstein, Sunny Shapiro, and Edith Zuckerman made a pact. They would stick by Miriam like glue; they would do whatever they could to help see her through this; they would be, in essence, three pairs of helping hands, a trio of fairy godmothers, a triumvirate of *lares familiares,* the Intercessor, the Consoler, the Paraclete. Such care they had for Miriam, such concern, such love for their friend, they plumb forgot about Valentine. It was as if this downturn of events had nothing to do with her at all.

Mrs. Rosenthal sat in the hard-back chair across from Mr. Fischel, who sat in one of the plush Naugahyde ones. She had a yellow pad in one hand, her pencil in the other, poised to take dictation. Mr. Fishel cleared his throat, as he always did before giving dictation. A vociferous clearing of the throat as if he were gargling. This little tic of his drove Mrs. Rosenthal bananas, but you'd never know it. Her face gave away nothing because the benefits and the hours to this job, you couldn't do better. In shorthand, she wrote as he dictated:

> *Dear Mr./Mrs./Miss, fill in the appropriate name, Please be advised that due to a medical condition, Valentine Kessler will no longer be attending your class. However, her mother, Mrs. Miriam Kessler, has requested that Valentine complete her education at home. As mandated by state law, we are required to assist in that endeavor. Therefore, on each Monday morning you must from here on in through the remainder of the school year bring to Mrs. Landau's office (Room 102) your week's lesson plans, all homework assignments, and a copy of all tests and quizzes. These will be retrieved from the Kessler household, and the completed work shall*

be returned to you weekly for grading. The board of education will be sending tutors for home study and to proctor exams. You can rest assured there will be no irregularities. As Valentine Kessler will not be returning to this school, ever, this will be the procedure until she receives her diploma, unless she elects otherwise. For the next year, a new batch of teachers will be selected for this duty. If you have any questions blah, blah, blah, Ed Fishel, principal, blah, blah, blah.

Mrs. Rosenthal made copies for each of Valentine's teachers, which she would hand-deliver to the appointed classrooms. In reference to how Mr. Fischel and the board of education were treating this girl as if she were a criminal or worse, and the father of this child, he gets off free and clear, Mrs. Rosenthal thought, *This stinks.*

~

Miriam signed the papers in triplicate. Signed, sealed, and done with, and once they were off school property, she suggested to Valentine that they not go straight home. "Let's go to Rossi's and have a cannoli," she offered. Miriam didn't know if she could face the house just then, just the two of them there alone. When Valentine was a little girl, Miriam would take her to Rossi's Bakery after shopping, a treat for being good. The Italians did that nice, the way they put a few tables in the bakery, so you could sit and have a pastry and a cup of coffee or a lemonade like you were in some café in Greenwich Village or Paris even instead of Canarsie. Valentine, who seemed to be in no hurry to get home either, readily agreed.

Leaning in close to her daughter, which wasn't difficult because the tables were the size of breakfast trays, Miriam said, "Valentine, we need to talk about something. Dr. Stern says it's late but not impossibly late to, you know, end the pregnancy. Have you thought long and hard about that? Because this is going to change your entire life, Valentine. All your plans for the future."

Dipping her finger into the shell of the cannoli, Valentine extracted a dollop of cream, which she popped in her mouth. With some other teenage girl, a dollop of cream poised on her fingertip sliding into an open mouth might have seemed obscene, but it really was, despite her condition, near impossible for Valentine to appear anything other than the personification of innocence. "I think maybe God made other plans for my future," Valentine said, and Miriam, assuming Valentine was referring to nothing but the stroke of lousy luck, smiled and said, "It would seem so. But it doesn't have to be. Dr. Stern said if we make arrangements right away, like today, it's still possible to have, you know, an . . ." Miriam mouthed the word which she could not bring herself to say.

"No," Valentine said. "No. I can't do that."

Miriam, no feminist to be sure, did however believe that girls should have a choice. She remembered the stories from her youth, stories of girls and coat hangers and back alleys. That was wrong, that a girl should have no choice, but Miriam wouldn't insist on an abortion for her daughter if Valentine didn't want one, especially at this late date.

Moreover, she was of the same opinion as The Girls in regard to Valentine's refusal to name the boy. What good could come of identifying him? What? They could get married? Just so he could leave her high and dry? Whoever he was, he was out of the picture now and good riddance to him. Miriam found she was coping with this situation far better than she would've predicted. There was a reserve of strength she didn't, heretofore, realize she had, and Miriam experienced a surge of empowerment. The hell with this boy, whoever he was. After the baby was born, Valentine could return to school, not to Canarsie High, where she'd surely be ostracized, but she could go to some other school. A private school was not beyond their means. Miriam would take care of the baby, and then Valentine could go to college. Maybe not away to one of the fancy schools Miriam had hoped her daughter would attend, but still, there were plenty of universities in greater New York City. This didn't have to be the end of the world.

Near the end of the lunch hour, at a window table in the cafeteria, Marty Weiner sat as still as a pillar of salt. Marty Weiner, who had smoked so much dope before digging into a hot open-face turkey sandwich, assumed he must be hallucinating those two pink-and-yellow birds perched on the nearest branch of a spruce tree. A pair of pink-and-yellow birds staring right at him, like they had something to say. *Too fucking weird.*

Trees are renowned as favored places for spiritual visitations. In Denver, Colorado, there was a report of Mary's likeness on the trunk of a willow tree. A pine tree in Colman, New Hampshire, revealed the Virgin's image on a flat portion where the branches seemed to have been cut away. In Halifax, Nova Scotia, the Blessed Mother's visage was formed in the age rings of an elm. In the empty spaces between the bushy branches of a thirty-foot-high black locust tree in Hartford, Connecticut, the Virgin Mary appeared, arms spread and a crown on her head, as well as in the bark of an oak tree in Watsonville, California. Admittedly, some of the faithful who made the pilgrimage to Watsonville thought the image was that of a quail or a bell. The point being: You either see or you don't, but even the most cynical can understand how the desire to see, the need to see, can produce the vision, whether it be in the clouds, on a freshly painted wall, or in the near branch of a spruce tree, or on the burned part of a potato chip.

Miss Clarke clapped her hands sharply for attention. "Okay, everybody. Let's settle down," she said, for the fifth time in as many periods that day. "We are going to begin our study of the reproductive system. Who can tell me what the aim of the reproductive system is?" This would seem to be a question geared for the stupidest of the stupid, but Miss Clarke was not one to ever overestimate her students' intelligence. "The aim of the reproductive system is . . . ?" She repeated the question and someone from the back of the room, one of the boys, quipped, "Ask Valentine."

"That's enough of that," Miss Clarke said, and she bit back the tail end of a smile.

Although it was only a part of a smile that got through, it did not go unnoticed by Beth Sandler. Despite the fact that Beth and Valentine were no longer friends and had not been friends for ages now, and despite the fact that they would never be friends again, a decade of best friendship cannot be erased without leaving a trace of affection behind. Beth bristled at the teacher's obvious delight in Valentine's misfortune, and then it dawned on Beth that all day long, up until just this very minute, she too had been in love with the news, cross pollinating the scoop as if she were a little butterfly of the gossipmonger species, flitting from person to person, deep breath, big grin, and, *Brace yourself. I've got such news. You will not believe it.* And then the laughter and the speculation, and now Beth's indignation at the teacher morphed in shame of self. For the first time in her life, Beth Sandler was ashamed of herself. Oh, there were other times when she should have been ashamed of herself, but she wasn't. Now she was. Big-time shame.

At the start of the last period of the day, John Wosileski's world took yet another hit. Never again was he going to feast his eyes upon Valentine Kessler's visage. That was the upshot of the memo which Mrs. Rosenthal brought to him.

Given what had happened between them and given his absolute certainty that she would never be his, you'd think he'd be glad that she was now to be forever out of his sight. Out of sight leads to out of mind, but it was precisely that, that there would come a day when he would no longer be able to remember her face, no longer able to conjure her image in his mind's eye, which pained him most. She would be lost to him entirely. Even the memory of her would leave him, that crumb that he'd had, that crumb of recollection, was at least something.

Until this too, her presence, was taken from him, John hadn't been aware that her mere attendance in his classroom was a faint ray of sunshine, and now that light was extinguished, snuffed out like an ember. And so from this, John Wosileski was forced to learn yet another of life's hard lessons: Sorrow is a bottomless pit.

Taking attendance as if each name on the roll were a weight to be carried, John told the class to open their books and do problems one through eight on page 162.

"Are these going to be graded?" asked Michelle Ratner.

"Yes." One other thing Mr. Wosileski had finally figured out was that if it wasn't going to be graded, they wouldn't do the assignment. "It's going to count as a quiz," he said, thus ensuring that they would work quietly and not go wild. There was a collective groan throughout the class, but the students got down to work.

What John had yet to learn was to ignore, completely and totally ignore, that smidgen of hope which occasionally rose up from the pit. He should have ignored it, he should have known from experience that to have faith in redemption had gotten him nowhere, but then again, the sorrow would not have been as profound if faith had not been in the picture.

~

As a biology teacher, Joanne Clarke was all too aware of life-forms that clung to toilet seats, especially in warm weather, and even in the women's faculty bathroom and not one shared with students, but the pressure on her bladder was tremendous. No way would she be able to hold it in until she got home.

Lining the seat with squares of toilet tissue, but nonetheless taking care to squat as opposed to actually sitting down because you can't be too careful, Joanne Clarke peed profusely. Thus relieved, she flushed and then went to wash her hands with hot water and soap.

It was there, at the bathroom sink, while washing her hands with the vigor of a surgeon, that Joanne Clarke looked up and into the mirror. She closed her eyes for a moment, as if that would clear the slate, and then she looked again. Oh no! This couldn't be! But it was. The return of her cystic pustular acne in the guise of four mammoth pimples. Two on her chin, one on the left side of her nose, and the one dead center on her forehead was like a beacon glowing red.

~

At the end of the school day, Beth turned down invitations to go for pizza with Marcia Finkelstein, to go hang out at the park with Leah Skolnik to watch the boys shoot hoops, to go with Joey Rappaport to *do it* at his house, where no one, he assured her, was home. It was the very last thing Beth Sandler wanted to do that afternoon. It wasn't because she feared that pregnancy might be going around like a bad cold. She'd gotten herself on the Pill, but the truth was that *doing it* with Joey was nowhere near as dreamy as she'd proclaimed it to be. In fact, it left her wanting, but wanting in ways she could neither pinpoint nor articulate. Sex with teenage boys will do that, leave a girl wanting, not more, but wanting something. "I don't feel so good," she told Joey, and she went off alone, although she wasn't sure where she would go. All she knew was that she wanted to be by herself. Desire for solitude was a new inclination for Beth, and she worried that this craving might be the onset of her growth as a person.

~

Having treated themselves to, and subsequently having finished a second cannoli each, Miriam Kessler and her daughter Valentine headed for home. Together, side by side, they walked. Although she might not have said so in so many words, Miriam was warming considerably to the idea of a baby in the house. Really, who can resist the idea of a baby, no matter what the circumstances? *We'll be fine. It'll all work out for the best in the end,* Miriam thought, and she searched for a way to let Valentine know how much she, Miriam, loved her. To express that kind of love, words would fall short. A dramatic action is needed to express big love, the way children open their arms as far as they can go and say, *Do you love me this much?* and the mother says, *Much more than that.*

Seventeen

Miriam tapped her teeth with the eraser end of her pencil as if that would get her creative juices flowing, to come up with designs for the baby's room. They, she and Valentine, were going to turn The Guest Room into The Nursery. As was befitting a guest room, those walls were white, the shag carpet was slate gray. A double bed, the gilded headboard against the far wall, was covered with a blue-on-blue brocade spread. Framed and hung over the bed was a seascape done in oil paint which Miriam got a deal on at the art gallery in the mall. On the night table, a vase was filled with blue silk flowers which you really had to touch to know they weren't real. As Judy Weinstein had said, "It's like a room in a four-star hotel, like a Hilton. So elegant," but *elegant* wasn't the tone you wanted for a baby's room.

This, decorating the baby's room, was supposed to be a mother/daughter project, a project for them to do together, but Valentine was lacking opinions on how to do up The Nursery, as she was lacking opinions on damn near everything these days. Whatever Miriam suggested, whether it was pale yellow carpet for The Nursery or liver for dinner or what to watch on television, Valentine invariably said, "Whatever you want, Ma, is okay by me." It was as if she had no desires or needs or wishes of her own, and frankly, this humble subjugation was getting on Miriam's nerves. Now, when Miriam asked, "What do you think about having a rainbow going across one wall?" and Valentine said, "Whatever you want, Ma, is okay by me," Miriam lost it. "What do *you* want? *What* do you want, Valentine?" she shouted at her daughter. "You act like nothing matters. But I got news for you. Things matter, Valentine. It matters whether we paint a rainbow in the baby's room or Old MacDonald's Farm."

Yes, she'd lost her temper, which was not something that happened often, but Miriam was sane enough to know that it wasn't the question of the theme of the baby's room which triggered her outburst. It was Valentine, and how she seemed so removed from her own life, how she acted like her life was happening to some other girl. Miriam was desperate for a way to connect with her daughter, and desperation caused her to shout, "You're not special, Valentine. You're acting like you're somebody special when you're just one more Brooklyn girl who got knocked up. I don't even know you anymore." This was both true and not true. True, Valentine was yet another girl from Brooklyn who got knocked up, but she got knocked up in a most unusual way and that did render her special.

It didn't take so much as a half of a second before Miriam regretted her words, words spoken in the heat of the moment and she didn't mean any of them, but before she could apologize, Valentine asked, "Did you ever, Ma? Did you ever know who I am? Because to love isn't the same as to know."

Miriam was taken aback by her daughter's words because Valentine was not wrong. To love is not the same as to know. Miriam lived for Valentine, but to live *for* her was to live *through* her, and that precluded any ability to fathom her.

~

John Wosileski was desperate for a way to communicate his feelings to Valentine. The sands of the hourglass were running low. With but days of school remaining, this final exam would be the last opportunity to send Valentine a note along with the problems of angles, planes, and the circumference of circles.

On a separate sheet of paper, he wrote *Dear Valentine.*

Ask yourself this: What good could come of it, of his writing to her? None. No good at all. It's not as if a note from him was going to change anything. He knew that. She wasn't going to suddenly decide that she loved him, or even liked him, for that matter. Yet John Wosileski, and hardly for the first time either, allowed a smitch of hope to rise up, and that's all it takes, a smitch of hope, which has the configuration and properties of a virus. *Dear Valentine, The thought that I will never see you again makes me want to die.* He read that over, crossed it out, and tried again. *Dear Valentine, I was very sorry to hear that you will not be returning to school.*

To put his feelings down on paper was proving to be a confounding enterprise. For starters, he wasn't even sure what those feelings were. It seemed to him that his feelings for Valentine were like apparitions, a presence sensed, hovering ghostlike. All he knew was he wanted her to exist, to be. That's what he wanted to tell her; that her very existence mattered to him, made a difference, the way it makes a difference if the sun rises or not.

John Wosileski reached for a fresh piece of paper.

When the lemon cake had cooled, Judy Weinstein covered it with Saran Wrap and brought it over to the Kesslers' house. At the sight of it, Miriam's salivary glands activated, but still, Miriam said, "Judy. Enough. We're not sitting *shivah* here. No one died."

"God forbid," Judy said. "We just want to help out, is all." The Girls had kept their pledge. Each day one of them, in rotation, brought a cake or a side dish or a pot of soup to Miriam, like an offering. "We want to show you that we love you."

"I know you do." Miriam set the cake on the table. "Sit."

While Miriam spooned coffee into the pot's filter, Judy picked up the yellow pad and read over Miriam's notes regarding the decor of the nursery, and she put in her two cents, "The rainbow. Definitely."

"That's the direction I was leaning toward," Miriam said. "The rainbow on the wall, and for the ceiling, I was thinking sky blue with a big yellow sun in one corner and puffy white clouds dispersed throughout."

"Adorable." Judy clapped her hands. "Absolutely adorable. And very with-it. You know, modern. The farm is a little old-fashioned."

Miriam got out cups and cake plates, and Judy asked, "Which did Valentine prefer?"

Miriam made a face. "Who knows what Valentine prefers. Nine times out of ten, she's walking around here with this loopy little smile on her face and agreeing to everything I say. She's like a happy zombie. It's driving me nuts."

Judy reached over and put her hand over her friend's hand. "Miriam," she said. "You forget when you were pregnant? Remember feeling all blissful? It's the hormones."

~

The dermatologist stepped back and guessed, "It could be hormonal. Are you going through any changes in your life? Any stress?"

Joanne Clarke shook her head. "Not that I'm aware of," she said.

The doctor reached for his prescription pad and scribbled on it. "Stay away from oily foods," he advised, "and keep your face clean. Wash frequently, once an hour." Such advice would prove to be in error; it would soon be demonstrated to the satisfaction of an authority no less than *The New England Journal of Medicine* that potato chips and fried chicken had no bearing on the complexion whatsoever, but this—that greasy food and chocolate too caused acne—was still the prevailing wisdom of the day. Also, frequent washing, in fact, stimulated more oil production, but who knew? The doctor tore the top page off the prescription pad and handed it to Joanne Clarke. "Apply this topically at bedtime," he instructed.

She looked down at it. Benzoyl peroxide. The very same ointment she used when she was a teenager, applied topically every night at bedtime along with the prayer *Dear God, please make this work,* the prayer that went unanswered for seven long and hateful years.

Outside, she crumpled the prescription into a ball and littered the street with it. The early evening air was still, not even a hint of a breeze, and so the crumpled prescription stayed put where it had landed, the same as if it were weighted with stones.

~

Miriam was sitting on the toilet when Valentine rapped on the bathroom door. "Ma," Valentine said.

"A little privacy would be nice." Miriam didn't ask for too much, did she? But no matter whether it was too much to ask for or not, she wasn't going to get it.

From the other side, the door between them, Valentine said to her mother. "Ma, I'm sorry. For what I said before, you know, about how you don't know me. I didn't mean it."

"There's no need to apologize," Miriam said.

"I'm not perfect," Valentine allowed.

"Yes, you are," her mother told her. "As far as I'm concerned, you're perfect." Maybe Valentine wasn't perfect, maybe she was, but Miriam was not one to shirk from her own shortcomings, and she wasn't going to lie to herself: Valentine had hit the nail on the head. Miriam loved her daughter more than life itself, but she didn't know the kid from Adam. "Now," Miriam said, "could I please get a little privacy."

Joanne Clarke could not face going home to her apartment where it was all too likely that she would catch sight of herself, her image, in the mirror. And not only did she dread seeing the zits, but she feared seeing something else in her reflection, something like her soul or her future revealed, neither of which would be any more lovely than her complexion.

So she took advantage of the weather, and she headed to Canarsie Park. It was a balmy evening, and the sun was nearing the horizon. Joanne sat on a park bench, and fishing her cardigan sweater from her book bag, she draped it over her shoulders.

The little children had all gone home for dinner and baths and soon to bed. The swings and the seesaws and the roundabout were stilled and deserted, as if the children had never been there at all, or not for many years.

Some older boys, they looked to be college age, were shooting hoops on the basketball court, laughing it up, slapping palms. Friends. Buddies. Pals. They were. And Joanne Clarke had to ask herself how was it that she had no friends. None at all. Not one. She'd placed the blame for that, for having no friends, at her father's feet. Caring for him had taken up all her free time. Even before he went senile, she had to cook him dinner and keep the house. So she didn't have time to cultivate friendships. She didn't have time to go to the movies with the gang. She wasn't free to hang out in the diner with a group of girls. She had to take care of her father. That's what she'd told herself, but it wasn't the case. One night when she was in high school, sitting down to dinner, meat loaf and baked potatoes—the things one remembers—Joanne was shaking ketchup onto her plate when her father said to her, "Joanne, why don't you go out with some friends? When I was your age, I was out with my friends all the time. You shouldn't be spending every night with your old man. Go out and have some fun."

She did have one friend once. Sort of. A girl at college. One of the few other girls majoring in biology. Back then, Joanne had ideas about becoming a doctor. No doubt this idea was connected to the death of her mother, but her solid B average, while respectable, was nowhere near good enough to get her into medical school. Instead, her solid B average offered her the opportunity to become a lab technician or high-school biology teacher. That she chose the latter, because the pay was better and the benefits more generous, was an example of common sense not always being the wisest choice because for Joanne Clarke teaching was hardly a vocation. This girl from college, Debra—also known as De Bra because she had enormous breasts which weren't at all sexy but were rather horrible, and college boys were still immature enough to think that sort of thing, De Bra, to be funny as all get-out—had for a while been Joanne Clarke's friend. Well, not really her friend. More of an acquaintance. Debra had dandruff which flaked not only onto her shoulders, but onto her eyeglasses, rendering them cruddy. Joanne and Debra had lunch together a few times following their eleven A.M. anatomy-and-physiology class.

During one of these lunches, the last of them as it turned out, Debra asked if Joanne wanted to go to the aquarium at Coney Island that coming weekend. There was a special exhibit on mollusks that Debra especially wanted to see.

"Sounds good," Joanne said, her spirits soaring. A date! Well, not a *date* date, but this was the first time since puberty that she had plans with a friend for a Saturday afternoon, and that was reason enough to smile.

Inside, the aquarium was dark. Only the tanks were lit. Side by side the two young women stood looking at the hammerheads. They could see the teeth as the sharks swam toward the glass. Rows and rows of terrifying teeth. Joanne was so engrossed with the sharks that she was unaware of Debra's hand, so close to her own, that their hands were touching. Barely. But still touching.

The mollusk room was deserted. Apparently on that day, no one, save for Debra, was interested in the exhibit on mollusks. For reasons beyond Joanne, Debra was agog. Near to tears. "Look," she gasped again and again. "Aren't they beautiful?"

Joanne deemed neither the clams nor the mussels nor the oysters nor the whelks nor the sea snails slithering up the glass right in their faces to be the least bit beautiful. She thought they looked like big globs of snot or, worse, girl parts, from down there. Looking at them was kind of embarrassing the way she was embarrassed, when curiosity got the best of her and she'd looked at herself that time in the bathroom, a mirror positioned between her open legs. To see that was embarrassing enough when she was alone. To see it with someone standing by her side was embarrassing and creepy. Joanne much preferred being frightened by the sharks and she was about to suggest that they go back and look at them again when Debra kissed her. On the mouth! A wet one! With her tongue! When Debra broke away, she gazed at Joanne with love in her eyes, and in return, Joanne spit in her face. Real spit. Right in her face.

Now Joanne might've felt bad about that except that Debra had gone on to medical school. Now De Bra was well on her way to being a big-cheese doctor, while Joanne, a schoolteacher with a cardigan sweater draped over her shoulders, sat alone in Canarsie Park until the sun was but a sliver of orange at the end of the sky.

On her way home, Joanne passed by the Chinese take-out place where the smell of pork fried rice enticed her sufficiently to step back with the idea of getting dinner to go. A well-deserved treat, but as she went for the door, she saw, standing at the counter, John Wosileski waiting for his dinner to go.

There was no good reason to avoid John. It was not as if something ugly had gone on between them. Yes, he had crushed her like a bug when he stood her up, but that was months ago, and why not let bygones be bygones, they could at least be pleasant with each other; it was silly, childish really, to carry on as she had been, giving him the cold shoulder, and here was a perfect opportunity to patch things up, to walk on over there and say something like *Fancy meeting you here,* and then they would at least be on speaking terms and who knows, maybe they could even go to a movie together sometime, and maybe that could lead to something, maybe they could pick up where they left off, maybe a life together wasn't impossible, you never know.

You never know and no one will ever know because Joanne Clarke suffered from that venial, but most deadly, of sins: pride.

I don't need him, she told herself. *I don't need anybody.*

~

I need to know that you are in the world. Seeing you every day made me feel like everything would be okay. Or at least not awful forever. As long as I saw your face, I had hope. I didn't have hope that you would ever love me, but I had hope that not everything in this world is sad. Does that make any sense to you? Probably not. It doesn't really make sense to me either. But seeing you was like skiing and now all the snow has melted.

She'd read this letter a dozen times at least, and pacing from her kitchen to her dining room and back again, Gert Landau still didn't know what to make of it.

Hours ago Mrs. Landau had called it quits for the day. She'd put in time above and beyond the call of duty. When she rose up from her seat and reached for her linen jacket on the coat rack, the folder with Valentine's final exams, set on the edge of her desk, had—no surprise given the precariousness of its position—slipped to the floor. The papers slid out and fanned around the folder, and the way a magician can get one card to jump from the deck, one paper had gotten away from the others. Mrs. Landau crossed the room to get it, and bending down, she retrieved the letter that John Wosileski had written to Valentine Kessler.

Mrs. Landau read the letter over once. Then she sat back down at her desk and read it again more carefully. Then she read it a third time. And a fourth, after which she put it in her briefcase and went home where, with a cup of tea, she read the letter again. And again, and despite the rereading of the aforementioned letter a dozen times at least, the same question remained: What should she do about it? Also the other question: A handful of school days to go and this had to happen? A handful of school days left and a bomb had to land in her lap?

There was no one with whom she could discuss this dilemma. Her friends were all colleagues. To discuss it with any of them was tantamount to making a decision, to blowing the whistle, a choice she wasn't sure was the best one.

The only thing to do now, Mrs. Landau concluded, was to sleep on it. The morning would cast a new light.

~

Miriam got into bed, but sleep did not come easily to her. She stared at the ceiling, and trying to fathom the mysteries of the universe, she spoke out loud. "Why?" she said, but to whom was she speaking? "Why?"

~

Also in bed, awake and staring up at the ceiling, was Valentine. What, if anything, she was trying to fathom will remain a mystery, but her expression conveyed weightlessness, as if a breeze, had there been one, would have carried her off like a fallen leaf.

Along with end-of-term forms to fill out, grade sheets, and umpteen memos, John Wosileski found a handwritten note in his faculty mailbox. *Dear John,* it read, *Please come see me (Room 102) at your earliest convenience. Yours, Gert Landau.*

Having no idea why Mrs. Landau, the guidance counselor, wanted to see him, prompted in John a general sense of foreboding that lasted until his lunch hour when he rapped lightly on the frosted glass pane of the door of Room 102.

From the other side, Mrs. Landau called out, "Come in." She was seated at her desk, which was covered with folders in stacks piled in varying heights. Mrs. Landau's glasses were perched at the edge of her nose. "John." She smiled cordially. "Sit down, would you?"

While John pulled up a chair, Mrs. Landau cleared away some of the folders, placing them on the floor so that there was a clean space on her desk between herself and the math teacher. On that space, she placed his letter to Valentine. "Do you want to tell me anything about this?" she asked.

It felt to John as if every drop of blood in his circulatory system rushed to his face. Several drops of urine did escape from his bladder, and John's hands went to his lap to cover the spot.

"This is between us," Mrs. Landau said. "No one else knows about this."

"Thank you." He managed to get out *thank you,* a whisper, but he said it without falling to pieces, which was an accomplishment.

"Well, don't thank me just yet," she said. "I'd like to keep it that way, between us, but there are no guarantees on that. You have some explaining to do. I have to ask you, John. Are you the father of that girl's baby?"

"No," he said, truthfully, the truth as he knew it, what he believed to be true.

"So what's this about?" Mrs. Landau leaned back in her chair, prepared to listen, but nothing was forthcoming, and Mrs. Landau, who really was trying to give John every opportunity, said, "You're going to have to do better than that."

One of John's hands covered the other, as if he were consoling himself. "She's just so sweet," he said. "I miss seeing her face. When she was in class, I, I felt . . ." John swallowed hard, which did nothing to alleviate the lump in his throat. "Like someone cared about me." Snot began to bubble at his left nostril. "Like I wasn't completely alone."

Mrs. Landau knew what it was like to be alone in the world. She'd lost her husband four years ago to a heart attack in the prime of his life. Rachel, her daughter, was in New Guinea, in the Peace Corps, volunteering in a health clinic. Mrs. Landau filled with pride as she always did whenever she thought of her daughter dispensing medicine to those in dire need, but couldn't she have found people in dire need closer to home? Although Gert Landau did know what it was like to be alone, she didn't know what it was like to feel alone the way John Wosileski did. Mrs. Landau got up from her desk and put her arms around the sorry young man, held him in the way she'd not held anyone for a long time, not since her daughter was a girl. Touch, the warmth of human contact, acted like a hammer on an egg, and John Wosileski broke.

Gert Landau held John Wosileski to her bosom until his blubbering subsided, until a hiccup signaled the end. Satisfied that this letter was a one-shot deal, that he had not snuck other letters in with Valentine's homework, nor would he ever again do anything so foolish, and satisfied that there was no hanky-panky going on between John Wosileski and Valentine Kessler or any other student, in fact satisfied that there was nothing going on between John Wosileski and any person whatsoever, Mrs. Landau handed him a tissue and said, "I'll tell you what we're going to do, John."

~

In the girls' bathroom on the third floor of Canarsie High School, a group of three pretty girls clustered around Beth Sandler, consoling her, their glee in the high drama camouflaged in staunch loyalty. "No offense, Beth. But you could do better than him anyway. You're too good for him. That's the truth."

"She's right, Beth. When she's right, she's right. You're too good for him."

Torn and vacillating equally between genuine heartbreak and

the genuine jubilation at being the center of attention, Beth had to make an effort to keep the tears flowing. As miserable as she was that Joey Rappaport had dumped her, out of the frigging blue he dumped her, she never saw it coming, this attention from the girls was more delicious than Joey had ever been.

~

It was lucky for John Wosileski that Mrs. Landau was a compassionate woman, and it was lucky for him that this situation arose these many years before issues of sexual harassment and child molestation took center stage in the theater of social ills. If this had happened in, say, 1995, no matter what sort of person Mrs. Landau had been, John Wosileski would've been crucified. Rather than getting him fired from his job and then fed to the tabloids, Mrs. Landau picked up the letter from her desk and she tore it in half. John winced, as if some tender part of him were being slashed, but that was to be ungrateful. When the letter was torn to scraps, Mrs. Landau let go, and the bits of paper fluttered like doves in the air on the way into the trash can.

~

Beth's summer plans and her plans for the future in general were ruined. Graduation parties, afternoons at Brighton Beach with Joey, her Joey, evenings hanging out with everyone and then slipping away somewhere so that she and Joey could *do it*, Joey winning her a fuchsia-colored teddy bear at the Holy Family Summer Festival, and the heart-wrenching, highly emotive, near-to-tragic farewell as Joey left for college followed by the highs and lows of the long-distance relationship which was supposed to produce a preengagement ring before he went away, the real-deal engagement ring his senior year, and the wedding ring the minute he finished law school. Ruined. All ruined.

What Beth had not factored into her life's calculation was that the distance between Canarsie and New Haven was measured not in miles but in worlds.

"No offense, Beth, but ever since he got into Yale, he's been walking around like he's God's gift."

"We had such big plans for the summer," Beth sobbed, and then sobbed harder, not from pain but from the humiliation when she realized it was *she* who had the big plans. Joey had never said boo about the summer, their summer. Plans for summer fun and summer love melted like ice cream under the summer sun.

"Really, Beth. Don't cry. We'll have a great time. Us girls. You'll see. I promise you. It'll be the best summer ever. Fuck him and the horse he rode in on."

~

Some of the teachers from Canarsie High School would teach summer school. They considered themselves fortunate to be asked to do so because the pay was good, but as far as Joanne Clarke was concerned, there was no amount of money that could tempt her to spend her summer trying to teach the losers, the discipline problems, the imbeciles who failed their exams, which were geared to the lowest common denominator to begin with. *No, thank you,* she would have said, had she been asked. She wasn't asked because preference was given to those with seniority or some other favored few. Other teachers, the younger ones such as herself, took any old job they could get, minimum-wage jobs, just to make a few extra bucks. Joanne considered such work to be beneath her. A college graduate with a master's degree in science education could hardly spend two months bagging groceries for chump change and still retain her dignity. Suppose one of her students saw her at the A&P wearing a red smock with her name embroidered over the breast pocket ringing up canned goods at the register? You know those little shits would point and snicker and tell the whole world and no one would ever respect her again. That's assuming they respected her in the first place, which wasn't a given. They, her students, knew not to cross her, but that was not the same as respecting her.

Invitations to an afternoon swim, a day at the beach, a weekend at a country house, a backyard barbecue would not be forthcoming.

Joanne experienced a pang of longing for her father, if only because caring for him filled the days. Now, on this first day of summer vacation, without him to tend to, she had nothing to do; literally nothing. She stood there in her living room, which she had already cleaned, and was struck by the emptiness as forcefully as if emptiness had heft. The summer, the prospect of July and August, stretched out like the desert. Hot and endless and without mercy. And you can be sure the humidity did nothing to improve her situation with the acne.

For want of anything better to do, Joanne went to her bedroom to lie down.

~

The bedrooms in the Kessler house had air conditioners, but you couldn't spend your life in the bedroom. The heat affected Miriam terribly, and although she was determined that Valentine eat three nutrient-rich meals a day, it was getting to be too much for her to stand over a hot stove.

Valentine's offer to do the cooking was rejected. "You'll faint," Miriam said, "with this heat and the oven and in your condition. You know what I'm going to do? The butcher over on Flatlands has one of those chicken rotisseries. A roasted chicken. How bad could it be? I'll pick up one of those chickens and I'll make a salad and some Minute rice. For a minute, I can stand at the stove."

At the end of his first day on the new job—a summer job which paid minimum wage, which was better than nothing and so he tried hard to be grateful for it—John Wosileski had to wonder if he was ever going to get used to the stench. "Hey, be grateful," his father had said. "I had to pull strings to get you in there." *There* being Stanislawski's Butcher Shop, where John was hired to clean up in the back, a revolting job at any time of the year but particularly so in the summer months, what with the blood and guts and bone and gristle and flies and that smell of rotting meat. Not that Stan Stanislawski ever in his entire career sold bad meat.

John took a hot shower and lathered himself all over with Irish Spring soap, with the hope that it would eradicate the smell of death, but that, the smell of death, once inhaled, is not so easily washed away.

Because it was still hot outside and would remain so even after the sun went down, and his apartment wasn't air-conditioned, John was wearing only his underpants, which were the color of a squirrel by now, when he opened the freezer to see what he had on hand for dinner. He reached for a frozen dinner, and looked to see which kind it was. At the sight of the picture of the Salisbury steak, along with mashed potatoes and green beans, on the box of the frozen dinner, John's stomach turned over. John made himself Kraft macaroni and cheese, which he ate while sitting in front of the television. During the summer months, all that was on television was reruns.

John didn't really mind reruns, though. *Life is kind of like a rerun,* John thought.

Then John picked up a pad and pencil and calculated: forty hours per week times the minimum wage of $2.10 per hour comes to $84 a week times eight weeks equals $672 before taxes. Exactly the same number he'd come up with the day before and the day before that. Six hundred and seventy-two dollars and no cents.

Six hundred and seventy-two dollars and no cents before taxes wasn't the sort of money that could change a person's life any. But really, no amount of money was going to change John Wosileski's life in any way that mattered. Then, for lack of anything better to do, he slipped a hand inside his underpants, but desire wasn't located there. Mostly to see if he could work up an appetite, he fiddled with himself, but when he got no response, he gave it up in short order.

~

Having rapped twice on Valentine's door, Miriam got no response, which is license for a mother to enter. Valentine was asleep in her bed on top of the covers and fully dressed.

Miriam walked to the foot of the bed, where she took off Valentine's shoes. Who can sleep comfortably with shoes on and never mind what sleeping in shoes can do to the circulation and a girl with child needed all the circulation she could get. Then Miriam sat herself down on the edge of Valentine's bed and watched over her daughter. It occurred to Miriam how often she'd done this, watched Valentine sleep, how she did so without thinking, the way ritual evolves into a part of being. From the day Valentine was born, Miriam stood over her as she slept. And on this occasion, she did so for a long while, long enough so that the night came and moonlight came through the window. Watching her daughter who would soon be a mother too, Miriam, as she always did whenever she looked at Valentine, filled with love and then more love came, a flood of love, and Miriam began to fear it, so overwhelming the love was.

~

Crammed into a booth at Junior's, home of the famous Junior's cheesecake, six teenage boys were making lascivious comments about the four teenage girls in the booth across the aisle. Although they could not hear what the boys were saying, the girls were very well aware of being the center of the universe, at least as far as these boys were concerned.

Leah Skolnik leaned over to Beth Sandler and said, "That cute one with the Yankees cap on, he is definitely giving you the eye."

Beth looked up. He was kind of cute, the one in the Yankees cap. Nonetheless, Beth said, "I'm not interested."

"Beth," her friends squealed in exasperation. "Quit being a martyr here."

"Don't start with me," Beth warned. "I'm not over Joey. I still love him. I'm not ready to be seeing other guys."

Brooklyn was not a place for false optimism, and Leah Skolnik, in particular, was a daughter of the soil. "You got to face it, Beth," Leah said. "It's over. You got to wake up and smell the caw-fee."

~

Joanne Clarke woke with a start. Disoriented, she reached for the clock on her night table. It was almost ten-fifteen, but morning or night? It took a moment for her to connect the dots, to ascertain that it was dark outside, therefore it was ten-fifteen at night, barring the improbability of a full solar eclipse or the world having ended.

She tried to remember when did she get into bed; certainly it was well before dinnertime. She hadn't had dinner, but she wasn't hungry.

~

John Wosileski stared at the television, although, if he was asked, for the life of him he wouldn't have been able to tell you what show he was watching.

~

Miriam Kessler bit into a cold chicken leg, and when she'd eaten all the meat from it, she sucked on the bone.

~

Right there in the booth in Junior's, right in front of her friends and the cute guys in the booth across the aisle, Beth Sandler started to cry and couldn't stop crying.

~

Only Valentine, so it seemed, was spared.

Summer days somehow operate on a different equation for time than the other seasons. They move languidly, lacking definition; they meld together, so that effort is required to keep track as to whether today is Wednesday or Friday. When Miriam Kessler thought about the days passing, about keeping track of them, she did not picture drawing big, red Xs with a Magic Marker on a calendar on the wall. Rather, as if the calendar were a bingo card and, instead of plastic chips, time was marked with pebbles and stones.

Miriam did need to keep track of the week. There were appointments with the beautician, appointments with the obstetrician, Fridays were for heavy cleaning, and on this Tuesday the game was to be played at Edith Zuckerman's house, and so under the noonday sun Miriam and Valentine walked there; Miriam *schvitzing* profusely, and a thin line of perspiration broke out on Valentine's upper lip.

"Do you believe this humidity? It's the humidity, not the heat."

Miriam took a tissue from her purse and mopped at her face and around her neck.

Edith was standing at the door to let them in when her attention was directed beyond them. "Hey, look at that." Edith pointed into the branches of a white birch tree.

"What?" Miriam said. "I don't see anything."

"Oh. They're gone now. But there were two birds, pinkish-yellow ones, beautiful," Edith said. "Do you believe it?"

"I believe it," Miriam said. "Would you believe I saw them once before. In the winter, and I was worried about them. Canaries. They must have flown out a window." Miriam took this as a good omen, that the canaries survived, maybe flourished even. An omen that let Miriam feel lucky as she took her seat at the table.

Valentine sat off to the side of the game, on the couch. At this stage of things, Miriam preferred that Valentine not be left alone any more than necessary. Suppose there was some prenatal complication requiring emergency medical attention and Miriam wasn't there? Then what? Better Valentine should come with her and sit and read a magazine or just stare out the window, which was something Valentine could do for hours on end.

~

On the morning of the twenty-second of July, Pete Wosileski, John Wosileski's father, was loading crates from the warehouse onto a truck, the man was an ox, and then the next thing you know, *bam!* He was lying on the ground with his skull broken.

While at work in the butcher shop, John got word that his father was dead, killed by a loose stone that fell five stories from an abandoned building, as if hurled from the heavens, to hit him square on the head. This was the high point of John Wosileski's summer, in so far as it broke the monotony.

The butcher, Stan Stanislawski, gave John a week off from his job, and he promised to provide smoked meats for the gathering after the wake, which would be attended by John and his mother and, of course, Father Palachuk, and perhaps a few of Pete's bowling buddies, but that would be it. "Tell your mother not to worry about food. I'll send over a ham," Stan said. Maybe some of John's fellow teachers would've attended the wake, had they known. But with school not in session, who would've spread the word? The former Plattsburgh relatives were his mother's family, and they were too far-flung to make the trip regardless, and they never liked Pete either. But they would send flowers, carnations mostly, and mass cards.

John Wosileski took off his bloodied apron and went to the bathroom to wash up before going to his mother. He looked in the mirror and said, "My father died." He said, "My father died, my father is dead," several times over not because he didn't believe it was true, but because he had a need to say it out loud, as it, *my father is dead,* is a turning point in a man's life. So to speak, John was now the man of the house. Because his father died on a Thursday and therefore was likely to be in a state of mortal sin, John prayed for his eternal soul, which was in purgatory at best, assuming all went according to what they'd been taught.

Mrs. Wosileski did not pray for her husband's soul; she was content to keep him where he was.

Going to his mother, John found her in the middle of preparing lunch, as if nothing at all had happened. Oh, he did not expect to find her weeping, a distraught and grieving widow. Rather, he watched for signs of lifting spirits, for a lightness in her step, a flicker of life in her eyes. He assumed that she would be cheered by his father's death. But thus far no pleasure was revealed. It was as if oppression had permeated her being, the way the smell from the Polish sausages had permeated their apartment. Also, Mrs. Wosileski had been denied the satisfaction of seeing her husband suffer.

~

Mothers are born to suffer and children are born to torture them. At least that's the impression you'd get from listening to The Girls. "I'm sick," Judy Weinstein said. "Physically ill. He's doing this to torture me. I know it. Three Dragon. California. Who goes to college in California? He was all set, going to Brandeis. And even that, Boston, is far away. But now it's UCLA or nowhere. California. I never heard of such a thing."

Edith Zuckerman exchanged one tile and asked, "Does he know what this is doing to you?"

Sunny Shapiro called, "Mah-jongg," and then added, "Of course he knows. That's why he's doing it."

"The boys are worse than the girls," Edith said. "Be thankful, Miriam, that you have just the daughter." Then, remembering that being Valentine's mother was no great shakes, she said, "Ah. Boys. Girls. It doesn't matter. Either way, they're the death of us."

The tiles were dumped into the center, and after turning them facedown, Sunny, with hands spread, moved them about, to wash them for the next round. Miriam got up from the table to help herself to a smidgen of marble cake, which frankly wasn't the best she'd ever tasted but it was edible, while Edith said to Judy, "They make us bleed, these kids. And tell me, what can we do? Not a damn thing except love them."

Children making their mothers bleed sounds like stigmata. Stigmata for all women, not just the saints and martyrs, unless you're of the school that believes all women, by virtue of being women, are saints and martyrs.

"Hello," he said, pleasantly enough, but clearly addressing a stranger. He didn't recognize her. Her own father and he hadn't a clue as to who she was.

"Dad, it's me," she said. "Joanne."

"Joanne?" He cocked his head as if he were trying to place the name. In fact, he was trying to place the name.

"Your daughter." Joanne tried to help him out, but it did no good.

The nurse, an extra-large black woman, came into the room wheeling a cart, and Mr. Clarke brightened at the sight of her. "You know, some days are better than other days," she said to Joanne. She had an accent, one of those lilting ones from the Caribbean, and a gold tooth, a gold incisor. "Today, he's so-so." To Joanne's father the nurse said, "How you be today, Mr. Clarke?"

"Good," he said. "I'm good. How are you?"

"I'm fine, thank you," the nurse said, and then she asked him, "Do you know who I am?"

"Yes," he said. "You're Vivienne."

"That's very good. And you're ready for your dinner now, Mr. Clarke?" Dinner, in the nursing home, was served at five in the afternoon. A bedtime snack—usually a cookie—was handed out at seven-thirty, and lights were out by eight.

And yet, Joanne was feeling far sorrier for herself than she was for her father. He didn't know enough to feel sorry for himself; it didn't shame him any to be on a toddler's schedule, and it didn't cause him grief to have forgotten that he had a daughter. He didn't miss her any more than he missed staying up for *The Tonight Show* with Johnny Carson, but Joanne felt she'd been discarded like an old shoe, dropped in favor of oblivion, and the pain of that, albeit irrational, smarted nonetheless.

If nothing else at all, nurses are breathtakingly efficient, and this nurse set up a tray in a jiffy. Then she said to Joanne, "Why don't you feed him? He makes a big, big mess of it when he tries to do it himself." She uncovered the dish, and Joanne saw steam rise from the ravioli on the plate. "Go ahead. He likes to be fed. It'll be fine." The nurse misinterpreted Joanne's expression. Not exactly misinterpreted, but she took it to mean that Joanne was nervous, unsure about feeding her father while a professional looked on as opposed to what it was: furtiveness sprung from a seed of guilt.

Joanne sat beside her father and prepared to feed him his dinner. She shook out the napkin and tucked one corner of it into his pajama top, the remainder acting as a bib. The silverware was exactly the same as that used in the Canarsie High School cafeteria. Joanne stabbed a ravioli, the bite-sized kind, and she brought the fork near to her father's mouth.

Mr. Clarke's eyes opened wide and a little cry escaped from him as if he were waking from a nightmare. Which maybe he was, waking from a nightmare. Who could tell what was going on in his mind or what was left of it. With his hand clamped over his mouth, he recoiled from his daughter. Joanne dropped the fork. It, along with the speared ravioli, clattered against the floor.

Forks on the left, Valentine set the table, and Miriam went to the refrigerator for two slices of cheese.

"No cheese for me," Valentine said.

"What is this about?" Miriam asked, and not for the first time either. "We're not religious people, Valentine. But if you want to be a religious person, there's a whole lot more to it than abstaining from cheese on your burger. I'm sure that Mrs. Weinstein would be happy to go over all the rules with you." Miriam was a great believer in the powers of reverse psychology.

"It makes me nauseous, that's all," Valentine contended. It is true that pregnant women have all kinds of bugaboos going with food combinations, but usually it's that they make everyone else nauseous with their sardines and sour cream or the way they'll eat butter; just butter, no bread, no nothing. Just munching away on a stick of butter like it's a carrot.

Miriam set the burgers on plates alongside healthy portions of french fried potatoes and a kosher dill pickle for each of them. Lest Miriam be accused of hypocrisy—that she insists on a kosher pickle while disparaging Valentine's bit of *kasrut*—kosher dills were the pickle of choice for the same reason she bought kosher frankfurters. The taste, the flavor, the overall quality of the product. A choice between an all-beef Hebrew National frank or an Oscar Mayer wiener which is nothing but bologna, that was no match.

Sitting across from her daughter, Miriam poured ketchup on her cheeseburger while Valentine closed her eyes and thanked God for hamburgers and trees. Miriam wondered when, and if, her daughter was going to get back to normal. Then she wondered what that was for Valentine. Was Valentine ever normal? Miriam couldn't recall.

~

"Miss Clarke." The fat nurse with the gold tooth and the accent caught Joanne on her way out. "Come sit a minute with me." She led Joanne into a small conference room, where she offered her a cup of tea. "There's nothing like a nice cup of tea to soothe the soul."

"No, thank you," Joanne said, although she would have liked a cup of tea. She was always doing that, refusing something she wanted, driven not by shyness but spite, which was ridiculous. Who was she fixing, but herself? *Don't cut off your nose to spite your face,* she remembered her mother telling her, but she never listened.

"I been working here more than twenty years now, Miss Clarke, and I see many sad things."

"Yes," Joanne said, "I'm sure you do."

"It's very hard on the children when the parents get like this." She passed a hand over her head, indicating the going of the mind. "I can see you are a good daughter, Miss Clarke. But I see too, you are all alone. There is no man. No children. This is not a good thing."

Joanne felt her blood rush to her face, which grew hot and throbbed like a toothache. She groped for a response, something along the lines of *Mind your own damn business, you fat cow,* but the sound of the pulsating in her head drowned out all words, and when her mind quieted, the nurse was already talking again. "A puppy or a kitten. A living thing to love. We all need the love, Miss Clarke. I tell you the truth."

How dare she? How dare this woman, this woman who empties

bedpans for a living, poke her nose into Joanne Clarke's life? How dare she, this woman who gives sponge baths to demented old men, dispense advice to a teacher? The nerve of some people.

"Are we finished here?" Joanne spoke tersely.

On a hot summer day, such as this one was, the Kings County Mall was an oasis. Cool air, an escalator gliding effortlessly, a fresh water fountain, plenty of foliage, walls of glass, shopping to die for, and a Baskin-Robbins ice-cream stand all under one roof. What more could you ask for in life?

With Valentine in tow, Miriam entered Tiny Tots, an emporium for all of a baby's needs. Miriam got out her list: crib, bassinet, changing table, bottles, diapers, a mobile, a rattle, a few outfits in white and yellow, colors which were gender neutral, as opposed to pink and blue. Pink or blue outfits would have to wait until after the baby was born because you can't put a girl in blue or worse, a boy baby in pink; that's the sort of thing which could scar a child for life.

While Miriam and the salesman discussed the safety features of the various cribs, Valentine wandered off down the aisle, coming to a full stop alongside a white cradle. Valentine knelt down and set the cradle into motion. "Ma," she called for Miriam. "Ma, come here."

Excusing herself from the salesman, Miriam followed Valentine's voice until she found her daughter, her head moving like a metronome, keeping time with the rocking of the cradle. "Ma, could we get this instead of a crib?"

"It's not very practical," Miriam pointed out. "You can only use it for the first few months or so, and then you're going to have to use a crib regardless."

"Please, Ma." Valentine looked up at her mother, her blue eyes begging wide. "Please," she implored.

Because heretofore, in regard to the baby, Valentine had expressed exactly zero number of preferences whatsoever, Miriam didn't want to refuse her the one request. Moreover, Miriam couldn't put her finger on any good reason to oppose the cradle. In her grandmother's day, they feared keeping the baby so near to the ground because of rats, but a rat in Miriam Kessler's house? Bite your tongue.

Despite her misgivings, whatever they were, Miriam relented. "Okay, okay, but we have to get a crib too."

And when the bough breaks . . .

~

On this last day of the week of his father's death, John was having lunch with his mother. A dutiful son because to eat by yourself is to dine on grief. There is no avoiding loneliness at mealtime. Not even watching television or reading the newspaper can alleviate the excruciating isolation of breaking bread alone. So even though it was for her sake, it was kind of nice, having lunch with his mother, even though you could never describe her as a good companion.

Mrs. Wosileski dished out pork chops with applesauce and roasted potatoes. Three chops for him and one for her. For herself, she took only a forkful of potatoes. *She eats like a bird,* he thought, although, in fact, that simile was inaccurate. Proportionately speaking, birds are big eaters. *She looks like a bird too. Like a sparrow caught in a downpour.* That simile was accurate. Mrs. Wosileski looked as if she were perpetually shivering. "Ma," John said. "You really don't have to make a big meal like this. Especially in this heat."

Although he would eat it to please his mother, ever since working at the butcher shop, John had lost his taste for meat.

"Your father insisted on a hot lunch."

John's father never took a sandwich to work with him or grabbed a burger with the guys. Every day at twelve-thirty, he came home for lunch, which was every bit of a meal as dinner was, and watch out if the lunch wasn't ready the minute he walked in the door. If a meal—lunch, dinner, and even breakfast—were not to John's father's liking, or if the beer he drank with dinner wasn't sufficiently cold, John's mother was made to suffer. Yet, as little sense as it made to John, it seemed that now with each day passing, his mother grew sadder and sadder.

Often, in the past, Mrs. Wosileski had imagined her husband's death, and how it would be after he was gone, but the trouble with fantasies is that they are not bound by the practicalities of how things are. For example, Mrs. Wosileski imagined that being sprung from the tyranny of her husband would somehow include also being sprung from their sad apartment, from the darkness of the Greenpoint area of Brooklyn, from Brooklyn altogether. Her husband's death, she thought, would have relieved her of the burden of herself. Mrs. Wosileski had spun elaborate fantasies about living in a little house in the country where she could grow vegetables and flowers, where every day the sun would shine, where she would be the sort of woman who wore a straw hat and kept cats. What John took to be his mother mourning his father was really her coming to grips with the fact that the reality of any situation was bound to be a disappointment.

At the Baskin-Robbins where they stood on line to get themselves each a double-scoop cone of Rocky Road, Marcia Finkelstein elbowed Beth Sandler and said, "Quick. Look. Over there. By the Florsheim. Do you see who I see?"

Beth craned her neck and she too spotted the biology teacher, who was looking at the window display of shoes, sensible shoes. "Ew," Beth said. "I hated her. Didn't you hate her? And that skin on her. Gross."

"Let's follow her." Marcia pulled Beth from the line. "Let's see what queer stuff she buys."

"But what about our ice cream? Two scoops of Rocky Road," Beth reminded her friend.

"Later," Marcia said, and eight paces behind Joanne Clarke, they paused when she paused again, this time at Pet World.

~

While John had a second cup of coffee, his mother sorted the laundry. Whites in one pile, darks in another. When she was done sorting, she said to him, "I'll be back in a couple of hours," and she carried the two baskets down five flights of stairs and three blocks to the Laundromat, which had to be like a sauna bath on a day like this, with all those dryers going at once.

It was then that John had an epiphany of sorts, a thought which was pure of heart. His original intent, in regard to the extra money earned and saved this summer, was to blow it on skiing. Now skiing seemed irrelevant to him. Perhaps ski season was simply too far off in the future to contemplate for real. Can a person rightly imagine crisp white snow while suffocating in a Brooklyn apartment in July? Or perhaps, although he never would have considered it himself, it was possible that Valentine took from him the one pure joy he knew. But whatever the reason, forsaking the slopes did not seem like much of a sacrifice. Not in the face of goodness. He would use the money to buy his mother a washing machine and dryer. A washing machine and dryer all in one unit and have it installed in the kitchen. It was the least he could do for her, for this woman who gave him life, this mother of his, whom, try as he might, he just could not manage to love.

~

As she watched a pile of puppies cavort in the pet-store window, Joanne Clarke's heart tugged at her sleeve. A longing for something to love. *A puppy or a kitten.* If only that nosy nurse hadn't suggested as much; Joanne hated to prove her right. *A puppy or a kitten.* Well, a puppy was out of the question. Dogs require time and effort, otherwise they'll poop all over the floor, and Joanne was done cleaning up the excrement of others. And kittens, cats, scratch the furniture, and also Joanne wasn't entirely unaware of the association between a single woman with a cat and the resignation to the fact that there never will be a man in her life. But she could get some other type of pet. Fish, maybe. A tank with brightly colored gravel and an oxygen pump in the guise of a little plastic deep-sea diver. Tropical fish in startling shades of blue darting out from behind plastic foliage to greet her when she came home from work might bring some warmth to her life. Or an iguana. As long as she would get neither a puppy nor a kitten, then Joanne was able to separate the nurse's solicitous, and, in Joanne's book, patronizing suggestion from her current decision. Entirely unrelated. An iguana was nothing like a puppy.

Birds were nothing like puppies and kittens either. A wholly other species of being. Joanne stood before a large cage bustling with parakeets. Blues ones and green ones hopping and chirping and fussing about. Joanne remembered hearing that parakeets can learn to talk, although not as eloquently as their grander relation, the parrot.

That could be something to have, a talking bird, a bird that returned your greeting, a bird that could express affection in English, a bird that could ask for a cracker *ad infinitum*; it could be something with enormous potential to get on her nerves.

Joanne was set to give up on the birds, to return to the idea of fish, when a flutter of commotion erupted in the parakeet cage. Squawking and wings flapping, and as if playing a game of musical chairs, they all shifted position, hopping from one perch to another. When the dust settled, Joanne noticed what she had not noticed before: a pair of canaries in the cage. Or at least she thought they were canaries. Yellow and pinkish orange, and one of them looked right at her while the other trilled a lovely little song. Joanne was smitten. She wanted those birds. To have and to hold for her very own.

Locating an employee, a young man with jug ears who was taking note of the curves of the behinds of two teenage girls who had abruptly turned their backs to him, Joanne Clarke interrupted his appreciation to ask, "The pair of canaries, how much are they?"

"Canaries?" he said. "We don't carry canaries. Just parakeets."

"You are mistaken," Joanne said. "There are two canaries in with the parakeets."

"Maybe you saw yellow parakeets. They come in yellow."

"Why don't you come look for yourself," Joanne said, and so he did.

"Well"—he shook his head—"I'll be damned. You're right. Those are canaries."

"I know they're canaries. What I want to know from you is how much do they cost?"

The jug-earred man scratched his head. He wasn't sure what they cost because Pet World didn't carry canaries.

"How about this?" Joanne suggested. "How about you sell me those two yellow parakeets, the funny-looking ones?"

And so a deal was struck. Along with the two funny-looking yellow parakeets, Joanne chose a cage, a cover for the cage, a box of birdseed, and a little plastic ball with a bell inside.

She named the birds: The Captain and Tennille, which she thought to be the opposite of what an old-maid schoolteacher would do. Naming her birds for the singing sensation with the hit record "Love Will Keep Us Together," she'd show *them* how with-it she could be, except for the fact that there were no *them* to show.

~

Whatever fun this was supposed to be was long over, and Beth Sandler asked Marcia Finkelstein for the third time in half as many minutes, "Can we please go now? She's buying birds. Big frigging deal." Their former biology teacher was standing on line behind a woman who was buying a case of Puppy Chow and a book titled *Your Shih Tzu and You.*

"Okay," Marcia acquiesced, finally. "Let's go to Macy's. I want to try on blue jeans."

"What about our ice cream?" Beth had yet to give up on two scoops of Rocky Road.

"Forget the ice cream. I want to get new jeans. Sassoon's."

Beth looked back at Miss Clarke and her birdcage and she was struck with a lonely feeling. As much as Beth hated to admit it, sometimes she missed Valentine. Marcia Finkelstein was so bossy. Valentine was so agreeable.

"No offense, Beth," Marcia felt compelled to add. "But you don't need any ice cream."

Beth also missed Valentine because sometimes Marcia Finkelstein could be such a frigging bitch.

∾

John Wosileski wound his way through the home-appliance section of Sears, past refrigerators and dishwashers and convection ovens until he got to the washing machines. There he looked at the prices.

A salesman was by his side in no time flat, singing the praises of a Kenmore washer-dryer unit. "A solid machine," the salesman said. This one wasn't the top of the line, but it was *a solid machine that will last practically a lifetime*. The top of the line would have been extravagant. Even the salesman agreed. "That's for your big families," he said. "People who do three, four loads a week." The machine came in white, copper, and avocado green. "If you take the green," the salesman said, "I can shave a few bucks off the price."

Avocado green it was, and the salesman worked out payment on the installment plan because this was in a time before every Tom, Dick, and Harry had a credit card.

It was not true altruism—giving anonymously and of course without any reward, including lunch or the pleasure of giving—but it was near to what Maimonides prescribed, and buying his mother a washer-dryer made John Wosileski feel good about himself, which was something.

Perhaps it was the light in her apartment, but when Joanne got them home, The Captain and Tennille—the canaries—no longer looked peach-colored. Rather, they were just yellow. Plain yellow canaries. Well, no matter. They were her babies. "Aren't you my babies?" she cooed at the birds, although, if truth be told, her heart wasn't in it. They were nowhere near as pretty as she'd thought them to be in the store. Then she wondered if her parents had thought the same thing about her.

Miriam was handy with a screwdriver. Of course she had to be, all those years without a man in the house. Alone, she assembled the crib, and had stepped back to admire the job well done when Valentine called from the living room, "Ma! Where are you?"

"Here," Miriam called back. "In the baby's room." *The baby's room*, Miriam repeated to herself, as if she depended on litany to believe, *We're having a baby, and this is the baby's room.* The walls and ceiling were painted like the sky, not like the real sky which was capable of turning gray or even black. This was a happy sky with a big yellow sun and a few fluffy white clouds and, just as Miriam had imagined it, a rainbow across one wall.

Valentine joined her mother. Of the crib, she said, "It looks good," but she sat beside the cradle. "When the baby gets delivered," she said, *when the baby gets delivered* as if the baby were a package to be delivered by the United Parcel Service, "it has to sleep here, in this." Valentine rocked the cradle, as if she were a child rocking her Betsy Wetsy doll.

"Valentine," Miriam admonished her, "a baby is not a toy. It's a baby. Do you understand? Your whole life is going to change."

"Guess what, Ma? It already has," Valentine said, and she let go of the cradle, which continued to rock on its own force of momentum.

Summer, with its way of lazing along, as if it were going to go on forever and ever, suddenly, like a tornado, gathers speed and races toward its end. Autumn was wafting in with the late August breeze, and John was of two minds. He was decidedly glad that this was his last day at the butcher shop, but whether or not he was glad that the first day of school was just around the corner was up for debate. The same sensation was experienced on Sunday nights, the end of the weekend, albeit in a lesser degree, by students and faculty alike. That a new school year was about to commence, that the days of summer remaining could be counted on less than two hands, made for a balance, equal parts of anticipation and dread. Certainly John preferred teaching to cleaning up the blood and guts in the butcher shop, but there was hollowness to the prospect of September too. A feeling that left him as empty as if his insides were tossed in the Dumpster along with those of the pigs and the chickens.

~

Valentine and her mother sat in the waiting room of the obstetrician's office. Experience had taught them that they would be waiting for an hour minimum. What experience would never teach them was this: You might just as well come late. But to suggest such a thing to Miriam? Bite your tongue. Never. Far better to sit and twiddle your thumbs for an hour than risk offending the esteemed Dr. Hammlisch, who was doing you a favor by seeing you in the first place, the man was so busy and important, and only because he was Edith Zuckerman's sister-in-law's cousin did he take Valentine on as a patient to begin with.

Having finished with her magazine, Valentine went and got a pamphlet off the wire rack that stood in the corner, displaying six different pamphlets on subjects such as birth control, menopause, the stages of gestation, and prenatal nutrition. The one Valentine took was on breast-feeding. Printed on pale pink paper, it featured a sketch of a mother with an infant at her breast, only the breast wasn't much visible. It was nothing like the pictures of the Mother and Child that were in the art books at the library. In those books, the Mother's breast was almost always visible and the Child didn't always look so much like an infant but often like a miniature adult person.

Valentine's breasts were getting bigger and bigger, and, as she'd complained to Miriam, they hurt. "You think it's all fun and games being a woman?" Miriam had said. "Believe me, when you're a woman, everything hurts. And when you're a mother, it hurts twice as much."

~

Beth Sandler was hurt beyond belief. To see Joey Rappaport was painful enough, but to see him with another girl, and such a girl, such a *shiksa*—who knew where he found her, certainly not in Canarsie—was like a knife in Beth's heart. On the inside, she was bleeding profusely, but she wasn't about to cry in front of Joey or in front of the girl, whose legs were so long that Beth felt like a dwarf, a chubby dwarf, standing beside her.

Also, Beth had the sneaking suspicion that Marcia Finkelstein had done this on purpose, and what kind of best friend rubs your nose in your agony? Well, maybe it wasn't really Marcia's doing. Maybe it was only a coincidence that while walking the boardwalk, two steps beyond Hirsch's Knishes, Marcia was genuinely seized with the need for a cherry knish; she might have perished if made to go knishless. Maybe that really was why Marcia pulled Beth back the two steps and—*Oh my Gawd! What a surprise!*—who should be on line directly ahead of them but Joey Rappaport with a girl, blond and leggy and wearing not a dot of makeup, a golden girl.

Introductions were made all around, and in the awkward moment that followed, the shiksa said, "Joey tells me that I must try a nish."

"Ka-nish," Beth corrected her, and instantly regretted having done so. *KEH-nish* sounded so Brooklyn. This girl spoke as if she were from Maine or Rhode Island or someplace like that. Someplace sophisticated. Someplace that was nowhere near Brooklyn. Maybe even the city.

"Ka-NISH." The girl tried to get it right, but as to be expected, she failed miserably and elegantly.

"So where did you two meet?" Marcia Finkelstein asked the golden girl. That Marica's tone was a gleeful one did not escape Beth Sandler's notice.

When they got to the front of the line, Marcia Finkelstein suddenly no longer wanted a knish after all.

If school weren't starting in a few days, Beth Sandler might've told Marcia Finkelstein to go fuck herself. But school was starting in a few days and Beth needed Marcia. Canarsie High School was no place to go it alone.

~

With only days remaining to work on her tan, Judy Weinstein was stretched out on a chaise longue. The two weeks in the Borscht Belt, at the Nevele Hotel and Country Club, had slipped away as if time were as greased up as Judy was with Bain de Soleil tanning oil.

When the sun shifted, Judy checked her watch and got up. She stepped into her gold-tone wedgie sandals and over her gold lamé swimsuit, she slipped on the matching beach jacket. It was three in the afternoon, peak tanning time was over, and she was scheduled to round out the fourth in a game of mah-jongg.

By setting up the table poolside, these women could keep one eye on their children as they swam and frolicked and cannonballed off the diving boards, and called out, "Ma! Ma! Look! Look at me! Watch!"

The woman with the horse face—Judy didn't catch her name—waved to her kid—a butterball wearing red swimming trunks that slipped down to reveal an inch of the crack in his ass. "I'm watching. I'm watching," she said, and then turned away as Judy watched the kid belly flop off the high board. Judy winced sympathetically. That had to hurt.

~

Having taken note of the pamphlet that Valentine had selected, the pamphlet she was now reading, Miriam tugged it from her daughter's hands. "You don't need that," Miriam said. "Start on the bottle first thing. The other"—meaning the breast—"isn't sanitary. On top of which, you're trapped with the feeding schedule. Trust me. That's not for you."

Just as it was in the weeks before the summer, come September Valentine's school work would be sent to the Kessler house as if Valentine were taking a correspondence course, like the "Draw Winky" art school. But not for long. Miriam, in her infinite wisdom, had already made arrangements for Valentine to attend a new school in January; a private school in Brooklyn Heights. She wanted Valentine to resume as much of a normal life as was possible given the circumstances. That's what Miriam had planned.

What Valentine had planned, who knew?

According to plan, Mrs. Wosileski went to do the grocery shopping and no sooner was she out the door than the washer-dryer arrived. In no time flat, the two men wearing overalls and carrying toolboxes got it installed and ready for its maiden load. When they left, John cleaned up the debris and stuck a red bow he'd bought at Woolworth's on the dryer's porthole.

Shortly after four, Mrs. Wosileski came home carrying sacks of groceries, which she placed on the kitchen table and then looked to where her son was standing; standing there beside an avocado-colored washer-dryer with a disheveled red bow on the porthole, and he was beaming. Mrs. Wosileski took one look at that red bow and tears filled her eyes. Clearly she was overwhelmed by her son's gesture, but overwhelmed how?

What John did not know, and how could he have, really, was that going to the Laundromat was Mrs. Wosileski's one reliable pleasure. It was there she could sit with the other women in the neighborhood and gripe and gossip and laugh a little; the Laundromat was an urban version of the quilting bee, a chore that had to be done but also a way for women to come together, almost like a party, a hootenanny for oppressed women city-wide. It was only then, while doing the wash, while waiting for the clothes to dry, while folding towels and sheets and pairing socks, the once-a-week task, once a week for two hours, that Mrs. Wosileski felt like a person, fully alive. Other than church, the Landromat was the full extent of her living it up. And now her well-intentioned son took even that from her.

~

Claiming sunstroke for herself—*really dizzy; I think it's sunstroke*—Beth Sandler begged off from the remainder of the day at the beach. She gathered together her things, her towel, her rubber flip-flops, her Coppertone lotion and Marcia Finkelstein asked, "What about tonight? Are you coming to the party?"

Leah Skolnik's parents were away at Grossinger's, and Leah was taking advantage of their absence. "Not a party," she'd told Beth and Marcia. "Just a few people coming over. I can't have a real party. My parents would kill me." But word had spread that her parents were away, and Leah could call it what she would, it was going to be a blowout.

Beth brushed sand off her arms and said, "I don't know. Maybe I'll be there. If I feel better."

But she wasn't going to feel better, and she knew as much. She was feeling perfectly miserable, and worst of all, there was no one for Beth to talk to about Joey and the *shiksa* and why Marcia Finkelstein took pleasure in Beth's pain. *Oh Valentine, did you have to get so frigging weird?* Such was Beth Sandler's refrain, and the answer to that question? It depends. It depends on whether or not you believe in free will or if you fall into the predetermination camp. It depends on whether or not you believe that God did indeed have a divine plan for Valentine Kessler. Or do you believe that such a belief in God is no different from such a belief in the Tooth Fairy and that once you're no longer a gullible child, such a belief is cockeyed in and of itself.

~

"Look at her." Sunny Shapiro nudged Edith Zuckerman and nodded in the direction of where Valentine sat in a gold brocade armchair, fixated on the television soap opera *All My Children*. "She's the picture of serenity."

Indeed, Valentine wore a slight smile and one of Miriam's tent-like dresses because she could no longer fit into her own clothes.

"Still waters run deep," Edith said, and then she said, "Miriam, what brand of coffee is this? It's delicious."

With Judy Weinstein vacationing in the Borscht Belt, The Girls were decidedly incomplete. Still, they came together to drink coffee, to have a little *nosh*, to enjoy the companionship of their friends because no person was an island.

Yet, no matter the pleasure, still they suffered from mah-jongg withdrawal. Edith's hands periodically twitched circles as if washing the tiles, Sunny smoked one cigarette after another, and Miriam did what she did whenever she didn't have something else to do—she ate. "So yesterday"—Miriam swallowed the last bite of an apple turnover—"I got a call from Rose. She's extending her stay."

"Again?" Edith asked. This was the second time now that Rose delayed leaving Israel to come home.

"Now she says she wants to be there for six months more. She's on a kibbutz. My mother-in-law. Do you believe it? On a kibbutz."

"Rose is picking peaches? That's what Elaine Meyer's kid did when she spent a summer on a kibbutz. All day long, she picked peaches. The kid was positively miserable. I can't see Rose picking peaches."

"She's not picking peaches. She's sixty-two years old. You think she's going to climb trees at that age? She's going to work in the nursery school. With the little ones. She's in seventh heaven. So she says. The only thing that was stopping her was Valentine, but I told her, 'Rose,' I said, 'don't revolve your life around Valentine. She's a teenager. She's going to go to college soon.' "

"It's true," Sunny said. "Once they go to college, they're lost to you. Since my David went to Cornell, he might as well be a stranger for all the time he spends with me."

"I gather you haven't told Rose yet." Edith said. "About Valentine."

"No. I'm ashamed to admit, I don't know how to break it to her. So for now, let her be happy. Ignorance is bliss, is it not?"

"And everything else?" Edith tapped a fingernail lacquered fire-engine red, against the side of her head, sign language for inquiry into Valentine's state of mind.

"Who can tell? Something is going on." Miriam spoke in a stage whisper, loud enough for The Girls to hear, but out of Valentine's audile range, especially with the television going. Valentine was quiet, maybe too quiet. Polite, maybe too polite. Agreeable, maybe too agreeable. "But whenever I ask her how she's holding up, she tells me everything is fine. I don't want to nag or push or interfere. For now, I try to let her be."

In that day and age, in the day and age when your parents were your parents and not your friends, a day and age when families didn't *share* or *open up* and there were no television commercials dictating *talk to your children,* Miriam's course of inaction was the accepted one.

"That's wise of you." Edith reached for Miriam's hand and squeezed it in her own.

"She's got enough pressure on her." Sunny snuffed out a cigarette. "She has no idea what to expect. Be patient with her. Love her. That's all you can do."

"You're right," Miriam said. "When you're right, you're right. As much as I want to help, I have to let her alone. She needs to sort things out for herself." Such was the path Miriam took, and it seemed like the right one at the time.

Twenty-one

As the gourds and pumpkins that would soon decorate porch steps and shop windows grew big, so did Valentine Kessler's belly. She was huge. "You'd think she's carrying triplets, with the size of her," Miriam said.

Edith Zuckerman—having exchanged a Four Dragon for a Seven Bam, which clearly pleased her—said, "It means she's having a boy. When you carry big like that, it's a boy."

"You're talking an old wives' tale." Sunny tapped the ash from her cigarette. "I carried big like that. Remember? With the two of mine. I thought I was going to give birth to elephants. Instead I had a boy and a girl, both normal sized."

Judy Weinstein called mah-jongg, Edith Zuckerman said, "Dammit," and while the tiles were being washed, Judy asked Miriam, "Where is she anyway?"

"Out in the backyard. Getting some sun."

As she passed by him in the hall without so much as a nod of acknowledgment, Joanne Clarke noted, with a certain satisfaction, that, coming through the far window, a ray of sunlight like a pointer illuminated the bald spot on the back of John Wosileski's head. In no time at all, she surmised, he'd have nothing but a fringe around the sides, like some monk. Joanne was not attracted to bald men. She liked a thick head of hair, with curls, soft curls, on a man. *The next man I get involved with is going to have gorgeous hair,* she decided.

As he passed by her in the hall as if they were two strangers as opposed to two people who had once been intimate, John Wosileski was slightly skeeved out at the sight of Joanne Clarke's skin in the unforgiving direct sunlight. *More like boils than pimples,* he thought. He pondered the fact that he'd put his lips to that skin, and although he knew for sure that he had done so, when he tried to bring the image to mind, he could no longer picture it.

Memory is tricky. If there is no one or nothing to remind you of an event in your life, it can be like it never happened. And in that way, Valentine Kessler should have been erased from John Wosileski's memory banks. For most everyone else at Canarsie High School, it was as if Valentine had never graced those halls. Only the guidance counselor was there to remind John of Valentine, not so much of the mess he'd so nearly made of his life—bless Mrs. Landau, as good as her word; never again was the subject of the letter so much as alluded to—but rather her presence kept fresh in him the feelings of love and disgrace commingled. Still, he and the guidance counselor rarely crossed paths. He should have been able to forget Valentine. But as if her image had been burned indelibly into his flesh, she was with him always.

~

Valentine was in the backyard, but she wasn't getting much sun. Having severed several small branches from the tree—not the simplest task for a very pregnant teenager—she gathered together foliage from hedges and bushes and made a mess of a half-assed roof for the *sukkah,* the temporary shelter that observant Jews build in celebration of Sukkoth, which is the Jewish version of Thanksgiving. Valentine's *sukkah* was not built to specifications, although that she constructed the walls from the industrial-size Hefty plastic garbage bags Miriam kept under the kitchen sink for spring cleaning was not, in and of itself, an irregularity. Technically, the walls can be of any materials provided they can withstand the wind, which these walls could not.

~

After dinner, and already dark out, night coming sooner and sooner, the kids were upstairs doing their homework, and her husband was in the living room with the newspaper, Angela Sabatini was in the kitchen washing the dinner dishes. Although she had a dishwasher, Angela didn't trust it; no machine could get the dishes as clean as Angela could, and frankly, for pots and pans, the dishwasher was useless. For that, you really had to scrub with steel wool and scalding water, which was why Angela wore rubber gloves.

After the dishes were washed and dried and put away, and just before turning out the light, Angela Sabatini kissed the tips of her index and middle fingers, which she then pressed to the mouth of the picture of the Blessed Virgin that hung in her kitchen.

That night, the wind dismantled Valentine's *sukkah* and blew the plastic garbage bags into the Sabatinis' yard, which spared Miriam the knowledge of the *sukkah*'s existence, however brief. Had Miriam been aware that Valentine was not out sunning herself that afternoon, but building a hut from garbage bags and tree branches, what would she have done about it? Chalked it up to a phase, and this too shall pass? Justified it as a manifestation of Valentine's fear of her future, and be glad she found some comfort? Who can say? Valentine was all that Miriam had in the world. When all that you have in the world is one person, you don't want to rock her boat too hard. Besides, what could Miriam have done? How does a person alter the course of events?

"Beth," her mother called to her. "Quit dawdling. You're going to be late." But Beth Sandler was in no hurry to get to school, where her star had fallen precipitously and who knew if it stopped there. Things could get worse yet. How did one short year bring about so much transformation and none of it good?

In the practice known as scapegoating, Beth blamed Valentine—*It's all that frigging Valentine Kessler's fault*—for the loss of Joey Rappaport's love, and for Marcia Finkelstein dumping her as a best friend. "I think Valentine tainted you or something," Marcia had said. "Because now you're weird too."

"I am not," Beth protested urgently. "I am not weird. I am totally, completely normal."

"I'm sorry to inform you," Marcia said, "but you're not totally, completely normal at all. You cry every time someone looks at you funny, and no offense, but you're gaining weight. Also that Dorothy Hamill haircut of yours is not a good look for you."

No wonder Beth was in no hurry to get to school. *It's all that frigging Valentine Kessler's fault.* She held Valentine responsible for all of her woes, including the accident which prevented Beth Sandler from becoming an ice-skating champion, from perhaps someday having a haircut named in her honor, which would've been more than enough to make Marcia Finkelstein and Joey Rappaport sorry as shit that they dumped her.

~

Along the way to putting up a pot of coffee, Angela Sabatini glanced out her kitchen window and out loud said, "What the hell is that?" On closer inspection, *that* turned out to be garbage bags, maybe ten or a dozen black Hefty garbage bags caught in her shrubbery and on her forsythia bushes and wrapped around the base of the birdbath. In her nightgown and barefoot, Angela darted out the back door and, on tiptoe because the ground was cold, she collected the black plastic bags, all the while baffled as to how they got there. A mystery.

~

On her way to the beauty parlor, Miriam Kessler dropped Valentine off at the library, where she sat alone at one of the tables looking at pictures in art books. A handful of senior citizens wandered the stacks.

Lucille Fiacco kept an eye peeled on Valentine. For one thing, although not due for another month, the kid looked ready to pop.

The librarian didn't want to be far away from the girl in case she was needed. But that wasn't the whole of it. Lucille watched the girl because she couldn't seem to stop herself from watching her. Lucille found herself drawn to Valentine. *Jeez, I hope I'm not turning lezzie or something,* she thought. *Nah, that's not it.* Lucille liked men. That much she knew.

Getting up from her desk, she went to the table where Valentine was intent on a picture of scribbles or something. "My nephew who is six draws better than that." Lucille hoisted herself up and sat her bottom alongside the book. Her legs dangled. Although Valentine's pregnancy was hidden beneath the table, Lucille gave a jut of her chin in that direction and drawing out the word as if there were a story to it, she asked, "Sooooo?"

Valentine looked at her blankly, something at which Valentine excelled, looking blank.

"So, what are you hoping for? A boy or a girl?" Lucille's question was one often asked of pregnant women, but maybe not so often of pregnant girls.

"That's not up to me," Valentine said.

"Well, yeah. Sure. But you know, if you were able to pick."

"But I'm not able to pick."

"I know that." A twinge of irritation shot through Lucille, like a raw nerve hit. "I know you don't get to pick. You don't have to be so literal about it. I'm just saying if you could pick, which would it be?" But this time, Lucille didn't wait for an answer. Instead she went all airy, like she was sitting on a cloud instead of a Formica table, and she said, "I'd want a girl. A little baby girl. Ah, wouldn't that be something? Dressing a little baby girl. Those outfits for baby girls are so cute. I mean, if I had a boy"—Lucille sobered somewhat—"I'd love him with all my heart, but it wouldn't be the same as having a girl. Of course I have to get married first." She stopped short; she was not so far gone that she didn't realize her faux pas. "Sorry," she said. "No offense. It's just that, coming from a Catholic family, I'd get disowned or worse. So I'd have to be married. I haven't met the right guy, you know. Here, at the library, there's no one except old geezers and weirdos. At night, my girlfriends and me go out to discotheques. I meet lots of guys at the discotheques. Oh, I meet plenty of guys. But losers, all of them. Losers and liars. Bullshit artists from the word *go*. Have you been to a disco yet? You really have to. So you know, I'll dance all night with someone and he'll buy me drinks and then after, sometimes we, you know, and then he says he'll call, but he never does. What's with these guys, promising to call? Maybe I shouldn't, you know. To be honest with you, I'm getting a little worried about the whole thing because I'm twenty-eight years old."

All the while Lucille disburdened herself, Valentine neither uttered a word nor moved a muscle; as if she were carved from ice or marble or a block of Cheddar cheese like the rendering of Moses at Gerald Wolff's bar mitzvah.

"All right," Lucille said, as if compelled to own up to the truth. "I'm thirty. Going on thirty-one. What's going to happen to me if I don't get married and have babies? I can't be a librarian for my whole life."

"Why not?" Thus spoke Valentine.

"Why not? I'll dry up like a prune. That's not a life. I'm telling you, I'm asking you, I'm begging you . . ." And at that, Lucille got ahold of herself because she was losing it there, pouring her guts out to some kid who you know didn't have two nickels' worth of good sense otherwise she wouldn't be knocked up in the first place. Lucille slid from the table and said, "I've got to get back to my desk," where, in fact, she had nothing much to keep herself busy when Valentine said, "Don't worry. You'll get married. Soon. You will."

"From your mouth," Lucille said, "to God's ears."

Three times in one day Joanne Clarke had the misfortune to set eyes upon John Wosileski. Twice in the hall and once in the teachers' lounge. Then, during fifth period, somebody, that Noodleman kid, she suspected, farted and it was pandemonium; the way the kids carried on, you'd think it was cyanide. And now, at the nursing home, her father grabbed her and tried to put his tongue in her mouth. "Come on, baby," he said, "you know you want it," a flash of desire which flared and then extinguished itself in a flood of tears.

"Why are you crying?" Joanne Clarke's patience was exhausted. "Tell me why you are crying." Desire found and then lost again is enough to make any man cry, but that didn't occur to Joanne. But even if it had occurred to her, there was nothing to be done about it.

At home, she plopped herself down on the couch. "That's it," she said to The Captain and Tennille. Although Joanne never came out and said so—never mind to whom she would say so—it was kind of okay having the birds around. Like now. Talking to the birds gave her voice. Talking to birds might be considered eccentric, but talking to yourself was considered pathetic. "I'm not going there ever again," Joanne told the canaries. "What's the point? The man is completely out of his mind. He has no idea who I am. He has no idea who anybody is. Tell me, what is the point of going back?"

Of course the birds did not respond, but still, Joanne had the feeling that they were looking at her with beaks pursed in disapproval, with *for shame* in their black beadlike eyes. To get out from under, Joanne Clarke went to the kitchen and set about making herself something to eat.

Standing out on her front step, Miriam marveled at how dark the early night was, and quiet. So quiet that she could hear the dry leaves rustle as the wind swept them along the street. All of it—the night, the chill, the autumn wind—coaxed her memory, back to Halloweens of years before and Thanksgivings past and to one night in particular when she was six months pregnant with Valentine and stood on this very step on a night very much like this one waiting in vain for Ronald to come home for dinner; waiting and waiting, but instead of being hurt or angry, the waiting actualized into anticipation, anticipation that went hand in hand with desire. Oh, how she wanted him that night, her Ronald, how all of her erogenous spots wept for his touch.

Oh-such-desire now recalled put Miriam in something like a fugue state, and standing there, all these years later, on her front step, in the dark and quiet of an autumn night, Miriam Kessler unbuttoned her blouse and held it open wide as if offering herself to the moon. Then, just as fast and just as sure as if she'd heard a snap of the fingers, she came out of it. Looking down at herself practically half naked out in public, Miriam pulled her blouse closed and dashed into the house.

Twenty-two

Shortly before the game was due to break up for The Girls to get home in time to prepare dinner, while sitting on Edith Zuckerman's still new white couch, Valentine Kessler's water broke. *Thank God for the plastic slipcovers* was all anybody could think.

And in that instant, the dynamic in the room changed radically, but calmly, rationally. The Girls were old hands at things like water breaking and babies coming. There was no slapstick hysteria that would later make for a funny story. Rather, as if they were synchronized swimmers in a water ballet, Judy Weinstein and Miriam each took hold of Valentine, Judy on her left, Miriam on her right, and they helped her into Judy's car, her emerald-green El Dorado, which was parked in the Zuckermans' driveway because Judy didn't care to walk no matter how short the distance. Miriam slid into the backseat next to Valentine and Judy drove, while Edith called the doctor and the hospital to notify them that Valentine was on the way. Meanwhile Sunny dashed over to the Kessler house to get Valentine's suitcase, where Edith Zuckerman, driving her slate-blue Nova, picked her up.

Smooth as satin, without a hitch, Valentine was checked into the maternity ward. A modern state-of-the-art maternity ward, with plenty of doctors and anesthesia and sterile conditions. In this time and place, natural childbirth was for women who didn't shave their underarms.

In the fourth-floor corridor, Judy, Edith, and Sunny took turns at the pay phone on the wall alongside the soda machine. Each of these women called home to tell her husband and her children, "I'm at the hospital with Miriam. Valentine is having the baby. You're on your own for dinner. Order up a pizza or Chinese."

In Room 411, Miriam was at her daughter's bedside, holding her hand. Valentine's knees were bent and wide apart. Dr. Hammlisch poked his head up there like an old-fashioned photographer draped under the black cloth looking through the lens of the camera.

"Is everything okay?" Miriam asked, to which the doctor said, "Pretty as a picture."

~

John Wosileski sat at his mother's kitchen table while she stood over the stove keeping an eye on the potato cakes in the frying pan. Mrs. Wosileski was wearing a housedress. On her feet were terrycloth scuffs. John tried to picture his mother in real clothes, a dress and hose and leather shoes. He knew that she had such things. He'd seen her in them for church, and surely she didn't attend his father's funeral in a housedress and slippers. But he couldn't see it. All remembered images of her were as she was now, in a housedress flipping potato cakes.

The hot oil sputtered and spat, the pop of it punctuating the quiet. Neither mother nor son was able to say much to each other. They had things to say; in fact, Mrs. Wosileski had a lot on her mind. She had some problems. Big problems, which she would have to discuss with John, but because she didn't yet know where to begin, she said only, "You want two cakes or three?"

"My *bubba,*" Judy Weinstein said, "could you believe, had five children, five." She held up a hand with her fingers splayed. "Five on the kitchen table."

"They all did then," said Edith. "What did they know from hospitals? They were ignorant."

Judy, Sunny, and Edith had settled themselves into chairs, like a trio of exotic birds all in a row, in the maternity-ward waiting room. The chairs were covered in orange vinyl. Magazines, worn and torn and out-of-date, were strewn across a glass coffee table. Two expectant fathers sat in chairs across from The Girls. One of the expectant fathers was obviously seasoned; he read a magazine, *Time,* and occasionally glanced at the clock. The other, it had to have been his first, what with the way he kept springing out of his seat like a jack-in-the box wound too tight. He paced and ate at his fingernails as if they were his dinner.

"Sweetheart." Sunny Shapiro rose up and took the man's hand from his mouth. "Calm down. Every day millions of women have millions of babies with no problems. Mother Nature knows the routine."

Judy Weinstein and Edith Zuckerman nodded sagely, and the man wondered who the hell were these three old bats.

"Now go get yourself something real to eat," Sunny told him.

~

John enjoyed the food, sliced ham and potato cakes, but his mother's company, her very presence, her long-suffering face, left him queasy, as if he, the very fact that he was born, were somehow to blame for her wretchedness.

~

Valentine's face was scrunched up rather hideously at the onset of another contraction. Miriam kept a cold compress pressed to her daughter's brow, although she couldn't say what good it did. But she kept it there nonetheless and whispered, "Okay, baby. It's going to be all okay. Shhhhhh," and cooed at her daughter, her own baby girl. "Shhh," she said, but Valentine let go with a wail which pierced Miriam's eardrums as well as her skin, in the way that it cut right through her, like light through glass. She gave Valentine her hand to squeeze, *hard, harder,* and for the first time in years Miriam believed in God, or at least believed enough to pray that He watch over them on this night because no matter that this hospital was state-of-the-art, giving birth was no walk in the park.

~

Mrs. Wosileski cleared away the dishes and poured the coffee and cut John a slice of cinnamon crumb cake. Then she sat back down and said, "I have to talk to you about something. It's not good."

It's not good. His mother was ill. That had to be it. Cancer. She was going to tell him that she has cancer, and John realized he'd been expecting it for years now, that every time he saw her he expected to be told that she had cancer, cancer that had spread, cancer that was eating her up alive, that she had only months, maybe weeks, left to live.

But his mother did not have cancer. What she also did not have was money. "I have no money, John," his mother told him. "Your father's insurance policy covered the funeral expenses, but there wasn't much left over." There was a small savings account. Very small, and already it was close to depleted. "I don't know what I'm going to do." Mrs. Wosileski put her hands over her throat, as if to protect herself, as if she thought her son might throttle her. Which was ridiculous. John Wosileski would never have throttled his mother, no matter how much he hated her.

"I can get by for another month or two. But that's it."

After dinner—Romanian skirt steak and roasted potatoes and peas and carrots from a can—Beth Sandler went to her bedroom. Sitting on the floor, which was covered with baby-blue shag carpeting, she took in hand her Princess phone, also baby blue, and she dialed the number with the 203 area code. The area code for Connecticut. New Haven. It rang twice, and when Joey Rappaport said, "Hello," Beth hung up. She wanted only to hear his voice.

Valentine, bathed in sweat, her hair matted from perspiration, let go with a bellow, a roar that sounded primal. Who knew she had such a set of lungs on her? The doctor took another look and said, "Relax, there's plenty of time yet." *Relax?*

~

Cheese sandwiches with margarine on white bread, that was their dinner; a dinner the likes of which Sunny Shapiro wouldn't have fed to a dog, but what can you expect from a vending machine in a hospital. Then The Girls recruited the nervous Nellie expectant father as a fourth for a friendly game of hearts. Edith Zuckerman never left the house without a deck of cards in her purse because you never know when you'll need them. A deck of cards can be a lifesaver. The other expectant father had already gone home. It was his fourth child and his wife's delivery was no more arduous than blowing her nose.

~

A teacher's salary can support one household, but barely. There was no way John Wosileski could pay the rent for two apartments, never mind gas, electric, and phone. Thus he was faced with two choices: he could give up teaching and find a job which paid more, or he could give up his apartment and move in with his mother. Either way, it was too much to ask, and Mrs. Wosileski did not want to do this, to ask her son to make sacrifices for her. He was a good boy, her John. She wanted more for him, better, but what could she do?

Seated on opposite ends of the couch, Mrs. Wosileski and John watched *Wheel of Fortune* on television. "You can win a lot of money on that show," Mrs. Wosileski said. The host of that show, Pat Sajak, was Polish.

~

For what might have been the first time in her life ever, Miriam Kessler gave no thought to dinner.

~

When the nervous Nellie expectant father was down forty-five cents, a doctor came to tell him, "A boy," the doctor said. "You have a son."

"Mazel tov," The Girls cried in unison.

The man's broad grin faded slowly, as if he didn't quite understand when the doctor said, "We need to talk."

~

During the commercial break, John Wosileski got up from the couch and headed toward the bathroom. He was halfway there when his mother called out to him, "Don't forget to jiggle the handle on the toilet. Otherwise it runs."

~

After dinner—reheated tuna casserole from the night before—Joanne Clarke sat at the kitchen table grading the pop quiz she'd given that day. "Clear off your desks," she had announced, and there was a collective groan from the students. They knew that *clear off your desks* meant a pop quiz, an exam for which they had no opportunity to study. "That's not fair," one of them, one of the pretty girls, had complained.

"That's right," Miss Clarke said. "It's not fair. Life is not fair. Get used to it.".

While Miss Clarke went along putting big red Xs next to incorrect answers, The Captain and Tennille began to sing. Sing as she'd never heard them sing before, chirping and warbling melodious trills and tweets. She got up from her chair and draped the cloth cover over their cage.

~

Screaming, howling, swearing, as if curses were javelins, Valentine hurled maledictions at God and at her mother and at the nurses, the doctor, and the world at large. *Fuck. Fuuuuuuuk. Fuck you all.* It would seem that the Demerol had little effect on Valentine's pain. Miriam was not horrified at her daughter's language the way she would have been had Valentine used the F-word in other circumstances. Miriam knew, as all women know, that giving birth induces a kind of temporary Tourette's syndrome.

~

Like dominoes, in the orange vinyl chairs, The Girls dropped off to sleep, each of their heads turned to the right. Sunny Shapiro snored loud enough to wake the dead, but Edith and Judy slept through it.

There must have been something off with Sunny's septum because, on top of the snoring, she snorted when she laughed. And still, she had a husband and children who loved her.

~

John Wosileski got up from the couch and stretched. "I ought to be getting home," he said to his mother.

Mrs. Wosileski extended her neck, proffering her sallow cheek for a good-night peck, and her son recoiled. Just a flinch, but she saw it. John could not kiss his mother good night, not even a quick peck on the cheek. Mrs. Wosileski wanted to ask her son, *What happened? What went so wrong for us?* but she could not because, although curious, what would she do with such knowledge? Or rather, what would such knowledge do to her? It was a wise decision, not to ask, because had she asked, John would have said, *We got born. That's what went wrong for us. We got born.* Instead Mrs. Wosileski said to her son, "Good night, John. Safe home."

"Push," Miriam told her daughter.

"Bear down," the nurse instructed.

"Fuck you," Valentine said.

At the second stage of labor, Dr. Hammlisch administered a local anesthetic, but Miriam couldn't see that it was doing much good either. "She needs something else," Miriam, distraught at the suffering of her child, snapped at the doctor.

Despite a slightly chaotic ambience, everything was *status quo*. As it should have been. Nothing out of the ordinary was happening. Every day babies were born in Brooklyn by the dozens.

"Fuuuuck. Ah, fuck," Valentine cried out, and Dr. Hammlisch went for the nitrous oxide, and then he went in with the forceps, which looked like the sugar tongs at one of Alice's tea parties. In those days, the forceps were an obstetrician's friend. Who needed all that yelling and carrying on when a little nitrous oxide and the forceps could, barring complications, extract a baby as easily as a rotten tooth.

In the middle of the night, Joanne Clarke woke up as if struck by a bolt from the blue. Her heart was beating fast. In the dark, her fingers fumbled for the chain on her bedside lamp. Her eyes adjusted to the light, and nothing seemed awry. *I must have had a nightmare,* she reasoned with herself. She looked at the clock, which read two fifty-six. As long as she was awake, she might as well go pee.

~

Sometime around three in the morning, Miriam came into the waiting room. Miriam shook Sunny Shapiro awake first, and then Judy and Edith.

~

On her way back from the bathroom, Joanne stopped to check on the birds. She lifted the cover and, sensing something was wrong, she turned on the overhead light to discover The Captain's head on the floor of the cage near to, but not attached to, his body. Tennille, Joanne surmised, had pecked off The Captain's head. Now Tennille sat on the perch alone, gazing off in the direction of the window as if expecting someone.

~

"A girl," Miriam told them. "A beautiful baby girl." And The Girls fell over one another, hugging and laughing and crying. As if the infant belonged to them all, they were joyous over the birth of the child. A girl.

~

A girl?

The light of dawn blanketed the bed, swathing across Valentine, across the baby in Valentine's arms. Miriam dozed in a chair in the far corner of the room, which was still dark. At the foot of the bed, a nurse fingered the small gold cross she wore around her neck.

Valentine gazed at her baby as if the infant were a star in the sky, something far away, something she saw perfectly well, but could not fathom. Then the baby urinated, and Valentine passed her off to the nurse, saying, "She peed."

John Wosileski emerged from his bedroom, sleep crusted in his eyes. Worries and miseries should have kept him tossing and turning, but apparently Morpheus took pity on him, granting him a good night's rest. But fat lot of good it did him. Now he was awake and had to face the day. Wearing nothing but his Jockey shorts and a T-shirt, John opened his door and tiptoed across the hallway to

Mr. Schaefer's doorway, where he snatched the New York *Daily News.* John wasn't stealing his neighbor's paper. He would return it after perusing the help-wanted section.

~

It would be untrue to assert that Joanne Clarke wasn't unnerved by, that she wasn't moved by, the death, and the apparent cause of death, of The Captain. But, aside from being a biology teacher who had to dissect frogs and fetal pigs in college, Joanne had grown adept at concealing her sensitivities. She wrapped them up in five layers of who-cares encased in a steel box of sublimation so that no one, not even Joanne herself, could recognize them for what they were.

With the edge of a magazine Joanne swept the decapitated bird into a body bag made of newspaper. That she put into a brown paper bag, which she left in the hallway right outside the door with the intent of putting it in the garbage bin on her way to work. Not much of a funeral, but for crying out loud, it was only a bird.

~

A candy striper—she of thick legs and thick-lensed eyeglasses and no older than Valentine, who volunteered to work in the hospital before and after school two days a week in preparation for her calling—set up the breakfast tray alongside Valentine's bed. With a flourish, she lifted the metal cover from the dish as if to reveal a four star meal or the result of a magic trick, as if there would be something remarkable on the plate. But instead of a pair of white doves or the queen of hearts, there was a soft-boiled egg and an orange cut into halves and halved again. A demented still life.

A cup of coffee with milk, no sugar, and two slices of cinnamon toast for breakfast, and Joanne Clarke went to her bedroom to get dressed. Only after she'd put on her panties and panty hose did Joanne pull her nightgown up over her head and off. Not even when she was all alone in the world did Joanne Clarke feel comfortable being naked. Given her stellar shape, you'd think she'd have liked looking at her body, but Joanne was always quick to cover up, thus denying herself what beauty she had.

Rifling through her closet, Joanne took out the gray wool jumper with the decorative red buttons. She hadn't worn that in ages, and she couldn't think why not. It wasn't that she'd forgotten the day the students in her classes went wild with laughter; it's that she made no connection between their hilarity and the jumper she was wearing.

Accountant, Must Have 5 Years' Experience. Housepainter, Must Be Experienced and Bonded. Experienced Keypunch Operator Wanted. Telephone Sales. Watch Repair. John read the help-wanted section from beginning to end. It didn't look at all promising, which, in the final analysis, was something of a relief. If a potential position had revealed itself, he would have had to apply for it. And then what? Either would have faced rejection or else he would be hired, in which case he'd have to leave Canarsie High School. He didn't want to leave Canarsie High School.

Joanne Clarke turned the key to lock the door and bent down to pick up the bag containing The Captain's remains, but the bag was gone. Someone, a thieving neighbor, must have taken it, perhaps expecting to find something of value in it, because it didn't just up and fly away. *Well, won't whoever be in for a little surprise*, Joanne let go with a "heh," which was as close to a laugh as she could get.

~

As spontaneously as if something inside her head had combusted, Beth Sandler went left instead of right, which was the way to Canarsie High. She'd never done this—cut school—before. Hardly a model student, still Beth Sandler had a respect for institutional authority which could have been considered unhealthy, depending on who was doing the considering. Like most people who follow the leader, it was the fear of getting caught breaking the rules which motivated her obedience. So this—cutting school—should have been a big deal. But it didn't seem like a big deal. There was no adventure to the spirit of this reckless behavior, no sense of the madcap, no adrenaline rush, no pulse quickening. Rather, as if it were Sunday and not Thursday, she blithely turned left instead of right and, like a homing pigeon, one who'd been temporarily off course but now righted its compass, Beth Sandler found herself at the Ice Palace.

Yet, some part of her was genuinely surprised, not to find herself at the Ice Palace, but surprised to find the Ice Palace there where it had always been. That somehow she thought if she no longer skated there, it must have vanished or been turned into a Vic Tanney's exercise studio.

The Ice Palace didn't open until eleven, although why they opened at all before school let out was a good question. Monday through Friday the rink was deserted until figure-skating lessons started at three-thirty in the afternoon, when a half-dozen or so prepubescent girls in flippy skirts would skate onto the ice, forming a semicircle around Miss Denise, who was the resident coach. It was Miss Denise who first saw talent in Beth Sandler; it was Miss Denise who had said to Beth, "You know, you could be the next Sonja Henie."

It was just after nine when Beth entered the coffee shop across the street, where she sat at the counter and ordered a toasted bagel with butter and jelly. She would wait it out because, on that day, Beth was determined to skate on ice.

~

Five students were at the blackboard when John Wosileski heard a commotion in the hall. Poking his head out the door, he was nearly decapitated by Joanne Clarke, whipping past him as she raced down the hall.

Shutting the door, John turned his attention to the five geometry problems on the blackboard.

~

Joanne Clarke locked herself in a stall in the bathroom. They were laughing at her. That much was clear. But why? What about her was so damn comical?

Nothing about Joanne Clarke was comical. Nothing.

~

Rejuvenated after what amounted to no more than a catnap, The Girls, filled with the spirit of a mission, descended upon the Kings County Mall. No frankincense and myrrh for this infant; this baby would be showered in precious outfits, which were, for these women, one of the gold standards.

Holding up a dress, red velvet, that seemed better suited to a Madame Alexander doll than to a person, Judy Weinstein said, "Is this adorable? I ask you? Is this adorable or is this adorable?"

"It's adorable." Edith Zuckerman displayed a pair of shoes, dangling them from her fingers; shoes an inch long, of white patent leather. "Tell me the truth. Are these the cutest things you ever saw or what?"

"Girls." Sunny Shapiro held out a pale pink sweater that fit in the palm of her hand. "Look at this. Will you look at this? Look at the little itty-bitty buttons. Could you die?"

~

Having composed herself, Joanne Clarke stepped from the bathroom stall and over to the sink where she splashed cold water on her face to ease the sting caused by the laughter of those pimple-faced morons. Pimple-faced? It is safe to assume that the maxim about people in glass houses etc. had no place in Joanne Clarke's code of rules to live by.

With paper towels that had more in common with sandpaper than terrycloth, Joanne patted her face dry, and it was then, at the mirror, that she discovered head-on the source of the hilarity. There, in the mirror, looking back at her, were two of the red buttons, erect and perfectly aligned with her nipples. She might as well have been wearing tassels there for all the dignity these strategically placed buttons had stripped from her.

Shame and anger are often related by rage. Fury can cause the adrenaline to pump, which can result in an abnormal show of strength, the way it's said that a mother can lift an automobile if her child is trapped beneath its wheels. With her bare hands, Joanne Clarke tore the red buttons from her dress.

After two buttered bagels with jelly and a cup of hot chocolate, Beth Sandler, yet again, checked her watch, a Bulova, her Sweet Sixteen present from her maternal grandparents. It was seven minutes before eleven. For her Sweet Sixteen, her other set of grandparents, her father's parents, gave her a United States savings bond, which thrilled her not at all.

Having stepped out to get them something nourishing to eat, because who could eat hospital mush, Miriam returned carrying two shopping bags laden with dried fruit—apricots and figs and prunes for purposes of regularity—and a jar of cashews and a box of crackers and a package of Swiss cheese and two quarts of fresh orange juice and a bottle of milk.

Miriam was unpacking the groceries—she put the perishables out on the windowsill to keep them cold—when The Girls arrived bearing gifts. They sat Miriam down and arranged their chairs in a semicircle around her. As if it were Miriam's Sweet Sixteen party, they ceremoniously bestowed upon her gaily wrapped packages. Miriam received the first box; she untied the ribbon, she parted the tissue paper, and lifted out the lavender-colored angora sweater big enough to fit a kitten. "This is too cute," she said. "It's killing me, how cute this is."

"Wait," Sunny Shapiro said, and from the same box she took out the matching cap. "Now it's too cute."

The Girls presented Miriam with a cornucopia of cuteness—

pink leather booties, *feel that leather; it's like butter,* a bunny-rabbit print smock for day wear as opposed to the red velvet dress with satin collar and cuffs, *for an occasion,* six pairs of socks adorned with itty-bitty bows, white leggings of the softest Egyptian cotton, a plaid jumper with buttons shaped like flowers, and a sweatshirt with DISCO BABY emblazoned across the front in silver glitter.

With boxes and paper and ribbons at her feet, Miriam broke open the jar of cashews and a package of dried apricots.

At some point during the festivities, Valentine got up from the bed and, wearing hot-pink fuzzy slippers and a green hospital-issued gown over her nightshirt, she shuffled down the hall to the nursery where the babies were kept, where she looked through the plate glass as if she were window-shopping, and then, as if not finding anything to her taste, she moved on to where the vending machines were located and got herself a can of Diet Pepsi.

~

Because she didn't have her skates with her, Beth Sandler was reduced to renting a pair, size seven, and she sure hoped there was no crud or athlete's foot or gangrene or funk lingering.

The rented skates did not fit her like gloves. The heel chafed, and when she skated onto the ice, her knees and ankles wobbled, which she should have expected. She was long out of practice. She could not even recall when she last skated, but whenever it was, Valentine was there watching, which meant it was another lifetime ago.

No one bothered to turn on the sound system just for Beth. There was no music to skate to. Beth's thoughts were her own then as she cut across the expanse of pristine ice; actually the rink was nearer in size to a bathtub than an expanse, but Beth was thinking of it as *an expanse* because to have the rink all to herself was both glorious and surreal, as if it were a daydream stepped outside of itself.

Around and around she skated, cutting smaller and smaller circles, until she found herself in the center of the rink, where she arched onto her toes, or rather onto the points of the blades of the skates, and spun and spun like cotton candy.

Perhaps she'd spun herself dizzy, spun herself right out of her frigging mind, because there on the ice she saw another girl, maybe ten or eleven years old, wearing a baby-blue skating costume that Beth recognized as identical to the one she'd worn those years ago. Beth watched this girl, this echo of her former self, this ghost of the skater past, do figure eights. It was not lost on Beth that she was watching this girl the way Valentine always watched Beth do her figure eights. Valentine was a good friend. Beth knew this now, but she knew it then and always. It was she, Beth, who behaved badly. Now this phantom skater did a flawless pirouette, just as Beth's own pirouettes were once flawless. One time, after such a pirouette, Valentine had said to her, "I expected you to spin into an angel."

Valentine. *She had to go and get weird on me,* Beth thought, *the way she got quiet was so queer. It was like I had to do the talking for both of us,* and then, like smack on the head, it hit Beth that maybe Valentine got so quiet because Beth was talking enough for two; maybe Valentine got quiet because Beth never shut up, all day and night with *Joey this* and *Joey that.* Maybe Valentine was quiet because she was listening.

Beth could have redressed her bad behavior over these last few months. She could have gone back to Valentine, apologized, spent every afternoon at the Kessler house, being there for Valentine the way Valentine had always been there for her. She could have. But she didn't because Beth rallied to her own defense. *If that was it, that Valentine was such a good listener, well, isn't there something queer about that?* Couldn't it be considered extremely peculiar to hang on every frigging inane word that Beth Sandler uttered?

And as her pirouette wound down, when she came to a full stop, Beth Sandler said, to no one at all, "I was almost a champion."

~

Visiting hours were over for the afternoon. The Girls went home. Miriam was watching *General Hospital* on the television mounted on the wall across from the bed where Valentine was sitting up reading the newest issue of *Seventeen* when a nurse came into the room with a sheaf of papers and a pen. "You'll need to fill these out," she said to Valentine. "And you'll have to cosign," she told Miriam. "It's for the birth certificate. You need to give the baby a name. Do you have one picked out?" the nurse asked.

A name. It was only then that it struck Miriam how odd that she and Valentine had not heretofore discussed a name for the baby. Everything else, but not a name. How very strange that she had given no thought at all to a name. Miriam then made the assumption that Valentine would want to name the baby in memory of her grandfather Sy, may he rest in peace. A name beginning with an S. *Susan. Susanna. Suzette. Sally. Sonia. Sandy. Suzette. Yes, Suzette. Suzette Kessler. That is a name!*

"Ronda," Valentine said. As that name is traditionally spelled *Rhonda,* Valentine clarified, "No *h.* R-O-N-D-A. Ronda. In memory of my father."

Cardboard cutouts of Santa Claus and elves and giant candy canes were taped to store windows framed with garland. The streets bustled. Blinking lights in red and green and blue wrapped like ivy around posts and gates and railings and the trim of houses, and little white lights laced through the branches of trees. The world was ablaze with the decorations celebrating the Christmas season, and as if the glitter brought warmth, neighbors greeted one another with *ho-ho-hos* and *happy holidays*.

John Wosileski, however, was impervious to the good cheer and prevailing jolly mood as he carried the last of the cardboard cartons up the stairs. Cardboard cartons filled with his worldly goods, which didn't amount to much. He'd left behind his furniture; it wasn't worth the cost of moving it, and where would he have put it? So he arrived and returned whence he came, all in one trip, with his clothes, a few books, a miniature silver Christmas tree in a pot, a puny diamond ring in a velveteen box, his skis, and his television set. Two television sets in one small apartment was excessive, but perhaps some night he'd want to watch a ball game while his mother's game shows were on. John put his TV in his bedroom, on top of the chest of drawers.

~

Miriam had been up half the night with feedings and diaper changes, just as she'd been up half of every night since the baby was born. A baby is exhausting under any circumstances, but Miriam was no spring chicken and it wasn't like she had any help either. Whether Valentine would have been any real help is moot. Miriam insisted that Valentine get back to the business of being a teenager; business which had nothing to do with the care of a baby. "When you fall off a horse, you get right back on," Miriam said, and never you mind that the analogy was strained. "You know exactly what I mean. I want you to start living your life. You'll start the new school in a few weeks. Go to the mall, and buy a new outfit."

And so Miriam took on all responsibility for Ronda and never once complained. She did, however, take advantage of every and any chance to nap, to sleep like one of the dead.

~

Tennille was dead, although unlike The Captain, whose cause of death was readily apparent, Joanne had no idea how this bird died. It was just there, dead in the cage, on its back, stiff, its bird legs sticking straight up in the air. Two dead birds in a matter of what—five weeks? This was no reason to rejoice.

~

While her mother and her daughter slept, Valentine was on her hands and knees rooting around under her bed.

~

In the top drawer, John Wosileski put his socks and underwear, and he tucked the red velveteen box with the puny diamond ring in the back corner behind a balled-up handkerchief which might, or might not, have been used. His shirts went in the second drawer. His pants he hung in the closet. And that was it. He was back in that place where he did little but dream of a day when he could be free of it. There should have been something significant to mark this occasion of utter defeat; something other than John shelving a few tattered paperback books, science fiction mostly. Shouldn't such an event, at the very least, have been heralded by a bugle-blowing clown?

~

She was not exactly glad that they were dead, but Joanne did experience a kind of relief. It had been a mistake to get those birds. They were demanding creatures, what with feeding them, cleaning the cage, giving them fresh water. Joanne Clarke had enough on her plate, thank you very much, without all that too. So really, it was for the best that they'd passed away.

For the best, but, Joanne could not help but think, strange. The circumstances were odd. Suspicious, even. It would not have been unreasonable to consider that after she'd pecked her mate to death, guilt ate away at the bird Tennille until she could bear it no longer. Perhaps guilt killed her. But such a cause of death was not a possibility that Joanne Clarke could willingly entertain. Nor could

Joanne consider that while yes, Tennille did kill The Captain, she nonetheless might not have been able to, nor wanted to, live without him. It hardly would have been the first time that love had gone awry in such a sorrowful fashion. Still, how could Joanne Clarke face up to the bird's decision that it was better to die than to live alone in a cage, tended to by a woman who would feed you and clean up your mess but would never love you as you needed to be loved.

~

Some years before, Mrs. Wosileski, John's mother, had read an article in a woman's magazine, *Redbook*, maybe, one that had been left behind in the Laundromat. The article was titled "Ten Surefire Ways to Put Zing in Your Marriage." Not that Mrs. Wosileski had any itch whatsoever to put zing in her marriage, but she read the article anyway, and number seven on the list struck her powerfully. It, number seven, prescribed cutting comic strips from newspapers and *putting them in his lunch box or on his pillow or taping them to the bathroom mirror*. From that day forward, Mrs. Wosileski began cutting comics from her husband's discarded newspaper, although she never did leave one on his pillow or anyplace else where he'd be likely to find it. Rather, she hoarded them, and on days when she felt particularly sad, she would, with her eyes closed, chose one and slip it into the pocket of her housedress. Then, when the sadness seemed unbearable, she would take it out, as if she'd found it there, as if it had been put there by someone other than herself, someone who loved her. She would unfold it and read it and feel better, especially if it was a *Peanuts*.

On the afternoon that her son returned to live with her, she went looking for those cutout comic strips. She was fairly certain they were in a shoebox under the bed.

~

Rather than dwell on the cause of Tennille's death, Joanne stewed over the injustice of it. She'd paid good money for those birds, birds which were clearly defective. She'd been sold damaged goods. And not for the first time either, Joanne Clarke had been cheated. Life was always cheating her out of something or other.

~

The homemade pierogi were a considerable improvement over the peanut butter spread on saltines that John Wosileski usually had for lunch on Saturday afternoons. Still, John felt cheated. Deceived somehow. And then there was the bit of weirdness with the cartoon. A *Peanuts* cartoon, Charlie Brown and Snoopy in the doghouse together, cut out from the newspaper, an old newspaper from the looks of it—yellow and brittle—and placed beneath his glass of milk like a coaster. What was that about?

~

One advantage to silk as a fabric is how compactly it folds. The two silk shawls fit easily into Valentine's pocketbook; not her new pocketbook, which was a Day-Glo pink satin disco bag big enough to hold keys, a lipstick, a mint, and nothing else. The snappy and useless disco bag had been one of this year's Hanukkah gifts from Miriam. Hanukkah had come early this year. Already, it seemed something of the distant past.

Next, Valentine turned to her bookshelf, where she scanned

the titles. Between *Goodnight Moon* and *The Catcher in the Rye* was *Jonathan Livingston Seagull.* Turning the pages she extracted, not treacly and trite sagaciousness courtesy of a bird, but money. From between pages five and six, she claimed a fifty-dollar bill. Two twenties were plucked like daisies from between pages nine and ten, and a crisp one-hundred-dollar bill from the last pages. What she did not take—one ten-dollar bill, another twenty, and a prayer card—was sheathed between pages sixteen and seventeen. She simply might have forgotten they were there. That happens often; we squirrel away our things of value, and then forget where the gems are buried. Sometimes we even forget that we had gems in the first place. Then we happen upon them by accident and try to remember the circumstances of them.

~

Just because life cheats you on a more or less regular basis doesn't mean you have to take it. It doesn't mean that *they* should be allowed to get away with practically murder, and so Joanne Clarke called Pet World to lodge a complaint.

As soon as she got the manager on the phone, she told him, "You sold me defective birds. One canary pecked the other's head off and then it died from I don't know what. Mange, maybe. Cooties or something."

For the benefit of the employees who stood around him, the manager made small concentric circles with his index finger pointed just above his ear, thus indicating that he had a Looney Tune on the phone. "Ma'am," he said, in that tone always used on the mentally ill, "we don't sell canaries here."

"Right," she said. "Not canaries. Yellow parakeets."

"And one yellow parakeet murdered the other one, you say? Did he do it for the insurance money?"

Joanne wasn't going to get anywhere with this manager; another condition—not getting anywhere—with which she was familiar. Also, Joanne recognized the tone of voice he used, and it both frightened and shamed her that such a voice would be used when speaking to her. She knew too that it was pointless to say, *I am not crazy*. The minute those words, *I am not crazy,* are uttered, you're pegged a headcase for sure.

Joanne hung up without saying good-bye, which was all the satisfaction she was going to get from this transaction.

~

On a piece of her best stationery, which featured Snoopy at his typewriter on the doghouse roof, Valentine left her mother a note—*Dear Ma, I don't know when I'll be back. Take good care of Ronda. I love you. Valentine*—the *i* on Valentine dotted with a little heart that she colored in with a purple crayon.

~

Ronda's cry, brought on by the distressed state of a soiled diaper, woke Miriam. There is much to be said for experience, and changing a diaper is like riding a bicycle. No matter how much time has elapsed between rides, you can always hop on and go. Miriam cleaned the baby and got a fresh diaper on her lickety-split.

The miracle of genetics is something at which to marvel. Ronda was a cookie-cutter copy of Valentine as a baby. So cute, you could have eaten her with a spoon and a cherry on top.

Déjà vu is also something, and for one second there, when Miriam lifted the baby to her shoulder, she nearly sang, as she did when Valentine was a baby, *Clap hands, clap hands, 'til Daddy comes home, 'til Daddy comes home.*

But Daddy never did come home, and now Miriam carried the baby to the kitchen, where she would get dinner started and give Ronda a bottle. There she found the note from Valentine.

Most words, if not all of them, are open to interpretation. Miriam took Valentine's words—*I don't know when I'll be back*—to mean that she went to the mall after all and might not come home in time for dinner. *These kids think pizza is a meal,* Miriam thought, but who was she kidding? The very idea of Valentine eating pizza and shopping at the mall satisfied her deeply.

~

The air was cold and crisp like an apple, and the streets were swarming with the holiday weary on their way home, burdened with packages and, at this point in the day, short on holiday merriment. Feet aching, heads aching, and aching backs bent from the weight of their shopping bags, *frigging Christmas,* no one noticed Valentine Kessler as she walked among them. Perhaps if it had been earlier in the day when the sun was high, she might have been seen by the sidewalk Santa, a scrawny man in a red costume that hung on him like a chicken's neck, standing beside the Salvation Army kettle. But the teenage girl passing by, her head covered, didn't register as he rang his bell and called, *Ho-ho-ho. Merry Christmas,* trying to get these *cheap fucks to part with a few pennies.* Also, the lavender dusk, the absence of bright light, altered the colors of her shawls. The fact that one was a very specific shade of blue would've been lost on him, and in the December twilight, white can look more like mauve.

~

Ronda burped and Miriam cooed at her, talking baby-talk nonsense. Then Miriam nuzzled her nose against Ronda's belly and reveled in baby smell. There's nothing that smells so good as a baby, and like the nose on Rudolph the reindeer, the very same Rudolph who led the team on the Sabatinis' roof, Miriam glowed so bright. She understood that this baby, this baby who came with no man, no man to break Miriam's heart, this baby was a gift from God.

~

The thought of rubbing shoulders with all those happy revelers, with their chortling and good tidings and jingle bells, shopping for gifts for their friends and family, depressed and repulsed her. Joanne Clarke didn't have so much as one, not one, Christmas present to buy. Not for anyone. Oh, she could've bought something for her father—new pajamas or slippers—but why waste the money? It's not as if he'd know what new slippers were or what to do with them. She could have bought a little something for Vivienne, the nurse who bathed her father and changed his diapers, but such a gesture never occurred to Joanne. What did occur to her was that she was hungry for dinner and the cupboards were bare.

~

Under the fluorescent lighting of Enzio's Pizzeria, the colors of Valentine's shawls were revealed in all their splendor. It was a quiet time in Enzio's, the hour's lull in the pizza business. Too late for lunch, a little too early for dinner. Enzio was behind the counter looking over the spread for Sunday's games. Enzio liked to bet a little something on football. He heard the door open, but his mind was on the Jets. He didn't look up until she said, "Two slices plain and a Diet Pepsi, please."

~

Valentine took her two slices of pizza and Diet Pepsi to a corner table and Enzio tiptoed, as if fearful of disturbing something, into the kitchen in the back of the pizzeria where his cousin Paulie was kneading dough. "Paulie," he whispered. "Paulie. Come here. You got to see this." Then Enzio said, "Wait. Clean yourself up first."

Paulie wiped his hands on his undershirt and smoothed his hair and followed Enzio to the counter. There he saw, alone at a table, the Blessed Virgin Mary eating a slice of pizza. His pizza.

"You see what I see?" Enzio asked, because he wasn't sure if he was seeing things or not.

Paulie nodded his head yes because he did not dare to speak, as if he feared locusts or frogs would emerge from his mouth instead of words. Guilt and sin; for all of his thirty-seven years on this earth thus far, Paulie lived with his mother, who was always on his case for not going to mass with her. He should've gone to mass with his mother.

There are psychiatrists and academics who interpret such things, things such as visions of the Blessed Virgin, in a traditionally Freudian way; that is, when a boy or a man thinks he sees the Virgin Mary, it really is nothing more than the manifestation of a repressed sexual desire for his mother.

But fuck that. She was here, eating pizza. The Blessed Virgin was eating pizza that Paulie made with his own two hands.

Enzio pulled Paulie back into the kitchen and asked, "The camera. Where's the camera?"

"You're going to take her picture?" Paulie was incredulous, as if to take her picture were the same as defiling her.

"And you think anyone is going to believe us if I don't take her picture?" Enzio had a point. Without evidence, there'd be jokes up the wazoo about the two of them going soft in the head.

The cousins kept a Polaroid camera on the premises from that time when the health inspector came looking for a handout. Enzio wanted evidence then too, on-the-spot proof that in his pizzeria, you could eat off the floor, it was so clean, and let that money-grubbing *scifoso* try and claim otherwise.

While Paulie reached for the camera, which was on the shelf behind an industrial-size can of tomato paste, Enzio went for the telephone.

"What are you doing?" Paulie asked, and Enzio, covering the mouthpiece with his hand, said, "I'm making us rich, Paulie. Rich." Enzio planted his lips on Paulie's forehead. "Now get out there and take the frigging picture."

Having decided to order in a pizza rather than go out shopping for food, Joanne Clarke called Enzio's and got a busy signal, which she took as a personal affront. As if Enzio knew she was going to call and took the phone off the hook, which would have been a crazy notion even if Enzio knew who the hell she was, which he didn't.

She had come to this: Joanne Clarke would have rather gone hungry than give Enzio's Pizzeria the satisfaction of calling for a second time. Lucky for her, there were other pizzerias in Canarsie who delivered, and Dominick's answered on the first ring.

There was only one shot left on the roll of film and one flashbulb to go with it, so it figures that Paulie put his thumb down on the wet print before it fully developed, which schmushed her face a little, but still, you could tell it was her. There was a halo around her head, a white glow like an aura, and maybe that was the result of the flash but maybe not.

By the time Enzio got off the phone and came out front, Valentine was gone. "Where is she?" he asked his cousin, and Paulie shrugged. "How would I know?"

Enzio went to the garbage can and extracted an oily paper plate, a couple of used napkins, a paper cup, and a straw. The same articles of debris that Valentine Kessler had, moments before, put in the trash. Enzio arranged them neatly on the table. He took the picture from Paulie, shook his head over what a *stugatz* his cousin was, schmushing it like that, and he propped up the photograph of Mary, Mother of God, against the red-pepper shaker. Outside, the Channel 11 News van pulled up to the curb.

The Sandlers were having a few friends in for a buffet. Nothing fancy. Deli. Pastrami and corned beef and a rye bread, and as Mrs. Sandler transferred the food onto plates and platters, she was struck with the fear that she didn't have enough. There was nothing worse—*nothing worse, I tell you*—than putting out a chintzy spread. "Bethie," her mother had called to her. "Do me a favor and run to Murray's and pick up a pound of potato salad and a pound of coleslaw."

At Murray's Appetizing Store, Beth took a number, eleven it was, and last in line, she stood three inches taller than her God-given five-foot-one. The extra height was due to the platform shoes she wore, forest green with a perfectly squared toe, and uglier shoes you could not find if you combed the annals of fashion history for all of eternity. When Murray called, "Six," Beth felt a chill at her back, the wind rushing in as the door opened and in walked, *be still my heart,* Joey Rappaport, looking so handsome but, Beth noted, also a teensy bit queer wearing a toggle coat and gray flannel slacks from J. Press—what did Beth know from J. Press—and Earth Shoes. He had brown suede Earth Shoes on his feet. Earth Shoes were yet one more sartorial blunder of the decade, a decade of fashion which was remembered by the fashion mavens as a time best forgotten because it was all, from head to toe, ill-conceived, ill-made, and just plain offensive to the eye.

"Well, will wonders never cease," Joey Rappaport said, and stepping into line behind Beth Sandler, he took number twelve.

Old habits don't die easily, if at all. Despite the fact that she was rarely hungry at that hour, Mrs. Wosileski served dinner at five-thirty sharp. Even with her husband dead and buried, she served dinner at the time he demanded it.

At six o'clock, John Wosileski loosened his belt and went to the couch to watch the news, leaving his mother to clean up after dinner. She was drying a pot when John called out to her, "Ma! Ma, come here. Look at this."

The babe reporter held a microphone for Enzio after some other babe had powdered his nose. "So you looked up and she was just there? You didn't hear her come in?"

"I didn't hear nothing." Double negatives be damned, Enzio was lying. He did hear the door open, but no one would want to think that she walked in through the door, the same as anybody else would. "Out of nowhere, she appeared and asked for two slices and a Diet Pepsi, which she ate at that table there." The camera zoomed in on the table, the oily plates, napkins, and the photograph as proof positive, and then the camera was turned back on the babe reporter, who said, "This is Margaret Giffin reporting live from the Holy Miracle at Enzio's Pizzeria on East One Hundred and Third Street, Brooklyn."

~

Angela Sabatini watched the television and made the sign of the cross.

~

Miriam Kessler had the television on, but tuned in to Channel 2. Not that she was paying much attention to it regardless. She was seated on a chair, the baby in her arms, and all of Miriam's attention was fixed on the child.

By the dozens, maybe the hundreds, maybe more, they came. Enzio's Pizzeria was transformed into a shrine to the Holy Mother. Prayer cards were taped to the walls, votive candles crowded the tables, and on the sidewalk out in front, the pilgrims left more candles and flowers and wreaths, some of which were even real, although most were of the plastic variety. Plastic *was* better because it could withstand the elements. Among the candles and the resinoid foliage there were some personal effects—an orthopedic shoe, a photograph of a child, a Barbie doll in the bridal costume, a ceramic Siamese cat—*ex-voto* offerings, requests for prayers to be answered. And all these people who came, or at least most of them, ordered two slices plain and a Diet Pepsi as if two slices plain and a Diet Pepsi might be the new Eucharist.

Joanne Clarke turned on the television before getting into bed. It was her habit to fall asleep to Johnny Carson, who wouldn't come on for another few minutes. A few minutes during which Joanne caught the tail end of the news. The human interest story, some preposterousness about the Virgin Mary showing up at a pizza parlor.

~

Margaret Giffin, perky-babe reporter, was over-the-top, euphoric. This story, her story, the story she scooped, was proving to be the biggest Christmas story since that one with Jimmy Stewart. "This story," she told the cameraman, "is bigger than Santa Claus."

Indeed, it was big, and to maximize its effect, for the late-night report, it was given an additional two minutes of airtime, an extra cameraman, and a writer, who was now, as the camera came in for Margaret's close-up, holding the cue cards for her to read. "As Albert Einstein once said"—Margaret Giffin, consummate professional, spoke her lines as if she were not scratching her pretty head over what the hell some Jew scientist had to do with the appearance of the Blessed Virgin—" 'There are only two ways to look at life. One is as though nothing is a miracle. The other is as if everything is.' "

The camera pulled back and panned the flock who believed.

~

How pathetic can you get? Joanne Clarke wondered, and then sat up and squinted at the television screen. She couldn't be sure, but she thought she saw John Wosileski's face among the faithful.

~

By midnight, having already called everyone whom she thought of as Valentine's friends—none of them had seen her anywhere—Miriam Kessler moved on from *worried* to *worried sick*. At a loss as to what to do next, she then called Judy Weinstein who called Sunny Shapiro who called Edith Zuckerman.

With The Girls by her side, Miriam called the police. "My daughter is missing," she said, and then Miriam went to pieces.

Two policemen arrived at the house, along with Angela Sabatini, who saw the squad car pull up. Angela came to check on Miriam, who was in no kind of shape. Judy Weinstein took over. "She left a note," Judy said. "Sometime this afternoon."

"Show them the note," Sunny prodded, and Judy produced the sheet of Snoopy stationery for the policemen to read, while Edith tried to get Miriam to drink some sherry.

"Who is Ronda?" the young cop asked. A baby himself, this cop.

"The baby. Valentine's baby," Judy explained, and the cops exchanged a look.

"The kid who's missing has a baby? And she left a note saying she doesn't know when she'll be back? Has anybody here considered that she's run away?" They, the policemen, had, for their purposes, solved the mystery of Valentine's disappearance; it was one more case of a runaway teen, some kid off in search of a jazzier life, no doubt tempted by the lights across the bridge, and all too often coming to the same kind of end as the moth tempted by the flame.

"You're wrong," Judy said. "She's not that kind of kid. She's a good kid, this one."

The policemen, they'd heard it all before.

By midnight, Enzio and Paulie had more money than they could count, and really this bonanza could've gone on all night, but the cousins had to get some sleep. "Tomorrow. Come back tomorrow." Enzio herded the pilgrims out the door.

Enzio and Paulie walked home, and along the way, when they paused at one house, where a six-foot-tall polystyrene snowman stood guard over a molded plastic Nativity scene, Paulie sang softly, "Silent night, holy night, all is calm, all is bright."

~

First thing in the morning, before her husband and children woke, before she had so much as a cup of coffee, Angela Sabatini—she of such a good heart—made her way to Enzio's Pizzeria, which was closed, but out front she lit a candle and prayed to the Virgin to please see to the safe return of Valentine Kessler. *As a mother yourself, you understand what Miriam is going through.* Angela spoke to the Blessed Virgin as if they were neighbors on good terms, as if she were borrowing a cup of sugar instead of asking for what might well be a miracle. *And as long as I'm here, watch over my Frankie, would you? I worry with him and drugs.*

~

That ludicrous story about the Virgin Mary making an appearance at a local pizzeria showed up on the morning news show too. Not that she believed it, not any of it, but Joanne Clarke did own up to a degree of curiosity. *Who or what had they seen, and then so grossly mistaken for a miracle?*

~

Decisions had been made. Lots drawn. Judy got care of Ronda, Sunny got care of Miriam, and Edith would take care of everything else, which entailed working the phone and feeding everyone.

Coffee was ready and Edith took six chocolate-covered donuts from the box and put them on a cake plate. Judy Weinstein came into the kitchen, jiggling the baby over her shoulder. "I forgot what it's like," Judy said. "The three A.M. feeding. The diapers. I'm dead on my feet."

Sunny, bleary-eyed and looking worse for the wear, joined Judy and Edith at the table. Nodding in the direction of upstairs, meaning Miriam, Sunny said, "She hasn't stopped crying. My heart is breaking for her. I don't know how she's going to survive this. That one person could have such bad luck . . ." Sunny trailed off, and reached for a donut. "Freihofer's?" she asked. Freihofer's made the best donuts.

They were swarming like maggots in front of his pizza parlor. Enzio had to push his way through a motley crew like you never saw before in your life. The lame, the blind, the ugly. Two—*two!*—hunchbacks. An old lady with a phlegmatic cough that sounded as if it rose up from the bowels of the inferno. An albino boy with his mother. Some broad with great legs but with pimples on her face that were like boils. A Vietnam veteran who'd lost an arm along with half his mind. The devout. The devoted. The disciples. The sorrowful. The righteous. The good. The lonely hearts. All the meek who shall inherit the earth had come for their piece of the pie.

Judy Weinstein accomplished the impossible: She persuaded Dr. Rosenzweig, who lived next door to her cousin Didi so it was a personal favor, to pay a house call to sedate Miriam.

With Miriam resting quietly, Edith was able to resume her calls to the area hospitals. You never know. Maybe Valentine got hit on the head and now had amnesia or, God forbid, she got run over by a car and was in a coma.

After Edith struck out at each and every Brooklyn hospital, but before trying those in the city, Sunny reached out and put her hand across Edith's wrist. "We're going to have to start calling the morgues. You know that, don't you?"

Pushing up from the table, Edith went to Miriam's bedroom. She stood over her friend, who was sleeping, but not peacefully. Miriam whimpered, and Edith took her stole, her precious white mink, and draped it over Miriam's bosom.

~

Mrs. Wosileski, having finished her housework, dressed with care. She put on fresh-from-the-package nylons, something she didn't don even for her husband's funeral. But for this occasion, there was no holding her back. Today, like a bride, she would wear all her finery. She was going to go to the Blessed Pizzeria, to the place where Mary, Mother of God, the Holy Mother, revealed herself.

Saving the best for last, Mrs. Wosileski put on her hat. Her one good hat, and so what if it was two decades old. It was a snappy black felt toque with a half veil, netting that stopped at the tip of her nose. In her oversized handbag, along with her wallet and change purse, she put two candles, three prayer cards, and a framed photograph of Jesus in a meadow surrounded by little children.

Perhaps it was the fault of the veil or maybe it was simply one of those blind spots, but Mrs. Wosileski did not see it coming, the car that hit her, the car that tossed her in the air as if she were a Frisbee. Crumpled and broken, she lay on the pavement, her eyes open, her hat gone, one shoe missing.

Judy Weinstein was upstairs, trying to get Miriam to eat some soup. She, Miriam, was like an invalid, getting up only to go to the bathroom. Downstairs, in the living room, Sunny Shapiro played tickle-poo with baby Ronda. She had to admit it: she was head over heels for this baby, this poor little baby who was something of an orphan. "Don't you worry, little Ronnie," Sunny cooed. "You have four *bubbas* who will watch over you."

And although it was most certainly the result of gas, the baby smiled.

In the middle of the day, John Wosileski left school because of a family emergency. At the hospital John met with the attending physician. Clutching a file, the doctor said, "She's lucky to be alive."

Lucky to be alive. *That,* John thought, *was debatable.* Not for the first time, John considered how it might have been better if she'd never been born. And if she hadn't been born, then John wouldn't have been born, and even though to contemplate such an idea defies logic, as it is your own consciousness deliberating the world without yourself in it, John pondered it nonetheless.

"Her hip has been shattered." The doctor took an X ray from the folder and held it up for John to see, as if looking at an X ray made it more official somehow. "And that's about the nastiest break there is. She's going to be in a lot of pain. She's going to be bedridden for a long time. She's going to need physical therapy, and even then, she might not ever walk right again. Do you have any questions?"

John had been thinking about money, about how much all this was going to cost, and how was he going to pay for it, but he didn't know how to ask that, so instead he asked, "Will she be home for Christmas?"

"No way," the doctor said. "Not a chance."

~

In and around Canarsie High School, the fact that Valentine Kessler had run away from home was news, but it was not big news. Perhaps it would have been more exciting at another time of year, but not now, not with Christmas upon them, and the ten-day vacation that went with it.

~

Joanne Clarke figured the little slut must've run off with her boyfriend, who was probably a sailor.

~

For John Wosileski, Valentine's disappearance changed nothing; for him she remained there and not there, as always.

~

Beth Sandler was unable to concentrate on whatever it was Miss Ryan was babbling on about, something to do with comma splices. Staring out a window which offered a view of nothing but a patch of frozen ground, Beth did not have a good feeling about things.

Ever since she'd heard that Valentine went missing, Beth felt uneasy. As if she were somehow to blame, which was ridiculous. Beth hadn't done anything. *Nothing at all.*

At the end of the school day, under the rubric of It-Couldn't-Hurt, Beth Sandler journeyed to Enzio's Pizzeria, where she could not believe her eyes. It was like a mob scene at Dracula's castle or like the *Phantom of the Opera* with all those candles and the dripping wax and the portraits of the saints or popes or whoever they were.

Beyond the crowd and the first impressions, Beth honed in on some of the personal effects left: one of those copper MIA bracelets that were all the rage a few years before when Vietnam was still something of an issue, a pair of baby shoes designed for a kid with a clubfoot, a color photo of an old man with poofy hair holding a small dog with even poofier hair, a teddy bear, a bottle of wine, a drawing done in crayons of a Christmas tree.

Beth took off her red mittens and put them in the pocket of her bunny-fur jacket and from her wallet she took out a picture of Valentine and Leah Skolnik and herself; a picture taken one afternoon three summers ago at Coney Island, in front of the Steeplechase. Each of the girls is holding an ice-cream cone.

Down on her knees, suppliant before a row of candles, as if she were going to pray the way the Catholics do, Beth Sandler fed the picture of the three girls to the flame and, the way memory does, it more melted than burned.

Twenty-six

With one shopping day until Christmas remaining, the stores were bedlam; a melee of pushing, shoving, grabbing, snapping, poking, yanking, bitching all to the tune of "(I'm dreaming of a) White Christmas." At this late date, perfume was a bestseller, as were handkerchiefs, because really, *who gives a shit?*

The line at the Italian pork store tacked left, right, out the door, and around the block.

Pies were baking, gravy was simmering, and countless women said, "Oh, what the hell, it's Christmas" as they popped yet another sugar cookie into their mouths.

At office parties the world over some doofus wearing a red hat with a white pom-pom was blocking the path of whatever woman happened by: *Hey, let's do the bump.*

"One small thing to be grateful for," Judy Weinstein said, "is at least we don't have the Christmas thing to deal with now too. On top of all this, could you imagine?"

While Judy and Sunny were imagining such a scenario, there was a knock at the Kesslers' door. Edith got up to answer it, to find Angela Sabatini there holding out a baking tray the size of Staten Island. "I made a little extra manicotti. I figured you could use it here."

Edith took the tray. "You're a doll," she said. "Come on in. We're sitting down for coffee."

"I can't," Angela declined. "Between now and tomorrow, I haven't got a minute to myself."

Presenting the manicotti to Judy and Sunny, Edith said, "From that Angela Sabatini next door. Is she a saint or is she a saint? I ask you? What a good heart that one has."

~

On Christmas Eve, on his way to visit his mother at the hospital, John Wosileski remembered that he'd forgotten to buy her a Christmas gift. Luckily, he passed Walgreen's drugstore, which was still open, and there he bought his mother a bottle of perfume. Some brand called Charlie.

In the hospital room that Mrs. Wosileski shared with two other women, neither of whom was conscious, on the television mounted on the wall, John and his mother watched the Yule log burn until visiting hours were over.

At home, John made himself a salami sandwich, and sometime around ten-thirty, he went to get ready for midnight mass. As he rooted around in his dresser drawer for a fresh pair of socks, John's hand brushed against the velveteen box he'd hidden there. At first, he pulled back as if the texture of it had burned him, but then he returned to it, took it out, and opened it. The very tiny diamond twinkled.

John Wosileski, it would seem, was incapable of retaining lessons learned. As if all pain were like the pain of childbirth, forgotten in a moment and worth it regardless. Then again, it was Christmas Eve, and if one couldn't have hope on that night, of all nights, well then, there was no hope to be had.

With the ring in the box warming in his pocket, John took in the cold air, the black sky, and the hush which was a quiet all its own. A holy quiet, *all is calm, all is bright*. And, at least then, at that moment, he believed, he believed in it all, the poor dumb fuck.

John rang the bell that read CLARKE, and again his memory skipped a crucial line, having deleted recollections of how, just weeks ago, he was repulsed by the thought of kissing her. Rather, now his selective memory latched onto the time when he wasn't alone, exaggerating its goodness because, really, the hours spent with Joanne Clarke weren't anything to write home about.

Even through the static of the intercom, Joanne Clarke managed to sound crotchety. "Who is it?"

"United Parcel delivery." John was delighted by his clever deception, which apparently worked because Joanne buzzed him in.

Apartment 5C was at the end of the hall, and Joanne stood in the open doorway, wearing a pair of black slacks and a white sweater. She was barefoot. "You," she said to John. "What do you want?" It did not appear that she was pleased to see him.

John took the red velveteen box from his pocket and snapped open the lid. He held it out to her as if it were a piece of chewing gum he were offering her, and as if it were a piece of chewing gum, she snatched it from him. "I've come to ask you to marry me," John Wosileski said.

Joanne peered at the ring and then looked at John much the way her birds used to look at her, head cocked and quizzical. "You're asking me to marry you?" she said, and when John responded in the affirmative, Joanne started to laugh. And laugh. And laugh. She laughed so hard that from the sides of her eyes, big tears rolled out like a matched set of red carpets. She laughed so hard that her stomach cramped, and when she stopped laughing she said, "Me? Marry you? You think *I* would stoop so low? You think I'm as desperate as all that? Me? Marry some wormy little schoolteacher? Some pathetic excuse for a man? Everyone laughs at you behind your back," she said, and with that, she closed the door on him.

John wondered if she realized that she still had the ring, that she hadn't returned it to him. He wondered if he should knock on the door and ask for it back, but why? For what? It's not as if he'd have use for the ring. And he really didn't want to face her again either, so he let it go.

Here is a curious footnote to this incident: She wore it. Joanne wore the puny diamond engagement ring. On Christmas morning, she put the ring on her finger and never took it off.

~

The sky on Christmas morning was overcast, and it was cold enough for snow, although a white Christmas wasn't in the forecast. Little Christian children were tearing into their gifts, their mothers were in the kitchen preparing the big meal, which they started on at the crack of dawn, and Judy Weinstein went to the Kessler house to relieve Sunny Shapiro, who had spent the night. Both the baby and Miriam needed round-the-clock care, so what choice did they have? If nothing else went right for her, Miriam Kessler was blessed with extraordinary friends. Like sisters, they were. Better than sisters.

"I don't know how much more of this I can take." Sunny took the bottle of formula heating in a pot of water on the stove and shook a drop onto her forearm, testing the temperature. "You know, I didn't even get to the beauty parlor this week."

"You don't have to tell me. I'm ready to drop." Judy took the bottle from Sunny and lifted baby Ronda from the bassinet. Ronda sucked hungrily on the nipple, and Judy said, "But what can we do? She needs us."

The two women sat on the couch, the baby cradled in Judy's arms. A ray of sunlight broke through the clouds and in through the window, and if you looked directly at the way it refracted off the diamond pendant Judy was wearing—a two-carat Hanukkah gift from her husband—it could have maybe caused you to go blind.

"So I guess it's not going to snow," Sunny said. "That's too bad. It would've been nice for them, *the goyim*, if it snowed."

Judy agreed, and then both women watched as the baby sucked on the bottle. They were adoring her, this precious baby, when their attention turned to the stairs, which, despite the pile carpet two inches thick, were creaking and groaning under Miriam's weight. Miriam looked dreadful, but what could you expect what with no bathing or even running a comb though her hair in all this time. There were dark circles under her eyes, and frankly, she smelled. But she was up and out of bed, and that was something to be grateful for, at least Judy and Sunny hoped it would prove to be something for which to be grateful.

With bated breath, Judy and Sunny waited to see what would happen next, and Miriam held out her arms, as if she were about to receive firewood or else had just discovered that her palms were bleeding. Her two friends exchanged an anxious glance, and then Judy stood up and carefully and gingerly passed the baby to Miriam.

The Christmas music traveled from the Sabatinis' rooftop—*the angels did say*—to the Kesslers' living room, and the love, the love that emanated from Miriam to the infant as she gazed down at Ronda, waves of love—invisible to the eye but invincible, like sound waves or an electromagnetic current—flowed between them as if gliding along a Möbius strip, seamlessly and without end.

There were sightings.

John Wosileski thought he saw her in a Kentucky Fried Chicken on Flatbush Avenue, but he wouldn't have sworn to it.

Vincent Caputo, however, did swear that he saw her in a Times Square peep show.

Lucille Fiacco was sure that was her doing the high kick, the third Rockette from the left at Radio City Music Hall, where Lucille and her fiancé took his daughter for the Springtime Spectacular. Her fiancé! Love at first sight when a Parents Without Partners group met at the library.

Weighted down with two sacks of food, which included four pounds of her homemade ravioli and two loaves of sausage bread, Angela Sabatini made her way along Bedford Avenue with great trepidation because this was not exactly what you'd call a nice area. In fact, it was a *frigging slum*, but miracles do not come without a price, and a miracle was what Angela Sabatini was after.

At the corner of St. John's Avenue, the monastery of Our Lady of Mount Carmel was set in a block-long garden. No doubt it was once imposing; Italianate and three stories high, with a steeple and bell tower and a stained-glass dome, which was now cracked. The outer wall, made of stone, was covered with graffiti—none of it spiritual.

Angela Sabatini was buzzed in through the gate, then buzzed into a vestibule before being buzzed into a small sitting room, where she was face-to-face with what looked like a huge barrel cut vertically down the middle and set into a brick wall. Above was a handwritten sign which read: IN THE HOUSE OF GOD, TALK OF HIM OR DO NOT TALK OF ANYTHING.

Our Lady of Mount Carmel was a Carmelite nunnery. The sisters were cloistered; they never went out. No one saw them. No one even knew how many of them were in there. They'd shut themselves in, off from the world, and devoted their lives to prayer. Because they asked for nothing, they'd have starved to death if not for the faithful who brought them food; food left in the half barrel along with notes asking the nuns to pray for this one or that one. *Pray for my mother in heaven. Pray for the soul of the baby I aborted. Pray that my uncle Joe recovers from being brain-dead. Pray for me to get married. Pray for me to hit the trifecta. Pray for me. Pray for me. Pray for me.*

Along with the ravioli and the sausage bread and a broccoli and three pounds of oranges and a package of dried figs and six cans of tuna fish—all white meat—and a jar of olives and another jar of marinated artichoke hearts, Angela Sabitini left her note: *Please pray that this lump in my breast is nothing. Please don't let God give me cancer.*

The half barrel was really a medieval contraption called a turn, named because that's what it did. It turned. Like the revolving bookcase in drawing-room mysteries.

Instead of leaving the food and the note and then departing immediately thereafter, Angela Sabatini waited as if she were expecting confirmation or a receipt or an answer. And when the barrel turned, she glimpsed a sliver of space and light on the other side, and Angela Sabatini could've sworn that she saw her there, on the other side of the turn. She was wearing the heavy brown wool habit of the Carmelites.

Angela Sabatini took this as a sign, but of what?

~

Here is the proof, *ecce signum*, all this happened, *nostra aetate,* in our time.

SUMMIT FREE PUBLIC LIBRARY